DREAM
WITCHES THREE

DREAMS OF THE WITCHES THREE

Eric Linke

My sincerest thanks to my mother for using her years of experience as an editor to help me make this book the best it can be.

I would also like to thank my father for his invaluable feedback on my story.

Thank you Alyssa, for all of your love and support.

This book would not exist without you.

Table of Contents

Part I: The Fated Meet
Chapter 1   3
Chapter 2   9
Chapter 3   20
Chapter 4   29
Chapter 5   42
Chapter 6   53
Chapter 7   68
Chapter 8   81
Chapter 9   85

Part 2: Wulfgeld
Chapter 10   99
Chapter 11   117
Chapter 12   142
Chapter 13   155
Chapter 14   162
Chapter 15   169
Chapter 16   176

Part 3: The Howling Nightmare
Chapter 17   193
Chapter 18   205
Chapter 19   210
Chapter 20   219
Chapter 21   225
Chapter 22   237
Chapter 23   243
Chapter 24   253
Chapter 25   263
Epilogue   276

Part I:
<u>The Fated Meet</u>

<u>Chapter 1</u>

Dawn crept out over the distant horizon, casting golden light that illuminated the clouds and painted the treetops below. A wolf's howl echoed against the distant snow-capped mountains, the singing of birds floated excitedly through the air, and searing pain tore down the arm of a wounded man. This man had watched many such sunrises and sunsets without the interruption of sleep for some time now. The impact of their beauty was losing its majesty for him.

At the forest's edge this wanderer rode his beloved horse. The horse's brown fur was rippled with the muscles he had built through years of hard service to his master and friend. The horse's mane was as black as the eyes of a wolf, and his amber eyes searched the tree line for any sign of danger. Once the horse was sure it was safe he stamped his foot impatiently; eager to enter the forest and begin the search. He loved his master very dearly; and he felt the urgency with which the man wished to continue their long venture.

His master's appearance was far from plain and often elicited frightened responses from those that saw him on the roads he traveled. He wore a gleaming mail hauberk that covered him from his shoulder to his elbow and from his neck to knee. His helmet shone brightly in the morning sun, and the mail aventail that hung from it covered his entire face except his eyes; which were guarded by an iron goggle welded to his helmet. His sword rested in the scabbard at his hip, hidden under the black cloak he had draped himself in. His ax and short bow were mounted on his saddle. In his right hand he held his spear and in his left he held the reins. With no hands free to carry it, he had slung his round, center-gripped shield across his back. Unlike its wooden counterparts wielded by other men, this heavy shield was made of hardened steel. Only he had the strength to wield such a weapon and it was impervious to attack from mortal enemies. The front edge was also sharpened to visit doom upon any foe who thought it would be safer to face his shield than his sword. At one time the shield's face had been painted with the likeness of a knot work dragon whose color matched the golden autumn that stretched out before him, laid against a background as green as the grass they trod upon. However, years of use had scratched the image until it was almost unrecognizable.

The man underneath the armor was tall and broad shouldered. His eyes were a deep brown and his hair matched. While it remained hidden under his helmet, his face bore the beard of a man who had once been able to keep it well trimmed and groomed, but hadn't been afforded the opportunity for some time. He had instead settled for scraping it to length with an old knife he had carried since his travels began. Given the amount of time he spent outdoors his skin should have had a more olive color than it did, but too much time in armor had lightened his complexion.

The warrior let out a weary sigh and patted his horse before entering the forest. When the rider reached down to pat his horse's neck, he let out a sharp gasp as pain ripped through his chest and sword arm. His last fight had been brutal. He had had the misfortune to encounter an old and powerful vampire. The bloodthirsty monster had landed several hard blows on him before he had been able to outwit it and end the fight. He was sure he had at least one bruised rib, but that wasn't the worst. He had also been bitten on his sword shoulder. While he would not turn into a vampire himself, the wound refused to heal, and his armor grated painfully against the open gash in his arm.

The wanderer guided his horse along a narrow dirt path that led through the trees. His eyes darted among the ancient trunks, looking for any sign of danger. As he did so, his fingers began unconsciously tracing the outline of a peculiar ring he had on his shield hand. His most beloved possession, the ring was small, tight fitting, and engraved in silver with green images of horses carved around its band. A spell was woven into the ring when it was forged so that horses close by could understand his every word. This had allowed him to form a bond with his horse unlike any other. In addition to the ring's practical uses, there was another reason it was important to the rider...it had been a gift from his long lost mother.

Deeper and deeper into the forest the horse and rider drove. Wherever they trod, the birds around them fearfully ceased their singing until the rider passed. They went like this for a great length of time, and as they went the horseman noticed that the trees began to grow older. The oldest and wisest trees groaned and creaked as he approached, seeking to escape from his presence. The diffused sunlight made it difficult for the traveler and his loyal mount to keep to the trail. The rider frequently found himself backtracking to find the path again, or to avoid some ominous omen from the shadowed areas of the forest where all light was swallowed. After what seemed like an eternity, he encountered a wizened old hermit at the side of the path. The hermit was dressed in rags and leaned upon a walking stick that appeared to be as old as the man whom depended upon its strength. He too was bearded, though his beard appeared to have never been well kept and was as long as the man was tall. He stared at the ground as though lost in a world unseen and undreamed of by his fellow men. As the traveler drew closer, the vagabond's vacant eyes snapped to focus on the armored rider with sudden awareness; and he began to speak to him…

4

"Be gone wanderer! This road is not for you!"

The horse stopped, and the armored warrior replied.

"I seek the pool of healing, old man. My name is—"

"I know your name!" The aged man interrupted. "You are Radnor, son of Magnus, the King of Amaranthar! You ride your trusted horse and only friend. I know his name as well...Darestr. Because I know who you are I *must* bar you access to the pool!"

Radnor blinked in surprise, it had been many years since anyone had called him by his true name, let alone known Darestr's name. He chose to ignore the comment about his "father", and studied the old man anew. Under his gaze, the aged man seemed to grow taller, and a sharp breeze whipped through Radnor's eye slots and stung his eyes. Radnor then was sure of to whom he spoke.

"I have need of its power, you should know this. Your duty is to allow all those in need access to the pool, Great Keeper."

The Keeper grimaced to himself, for it was necessity, not malice that forced him to bar Radnor from the deliverance he sought.

"The pool cannot help you. One touch of your flesh to its waters, and its countenance would turn foul forever. I see you are well armed...none of your weapons will help you find the pool, nor will they allow you to gain it by force."

Radnor closed his eyes and let out a frustrated sigh.

Why does everyone always assume I'm looking to kill people? He thought bitterly.

However, Radnor knew that the Keeper's words were always truth, and that he truly could not use the pool. He would need to go elsewhere for the help he sought. Radnor opened his eyes again and spoke once more to the Keeper.

"If I cannot make use of the pool's healing waters, then I must ask you: is there anything that can help me with this wound so that I may resume my journey?"

Radnor winced as he moved his armor and tunic aside, and revealed the holes in his shoulder. Blood and pus slowly oozed and dripped from the wound. The Keeper stood in silence for a moment and seemed to lose himself in his own private contemplation. Just as Radnor was about to demand an answer, the Keeper made his reply...

"It would take a powerful sorcerer to provide what you seek, and there are none near here. I have only words to offer you, though you may not be willing to hear them now."

Radnor spoke sharply, already disliking the man for the disappointment he brought and for wasting his time.

"Out with it, I do not wish to drag from you all that you are willing to offer piece by piece."

The Keeper nodded and resumed his speech.

"Know that blind vengeance will only serve one purpose: to speed you on your way to meet the cold embrace of death. If you ever wish to find what you seek, you must set aside who you have decided you *have* to be, and embrace who you *wish* to be."

Radnor's blood boiled at this statement. How dare this man tell him not to seek his just vengeance? How dare this man whom had not walked the roads he had walked, had not seen the things he had seen, and had not lost what he had lost, tell him of who he had to be?

Radnor felt cold, hard, blood rage fill him. In his mind's eye he could see nothing but his hand going to his sword and cutting the Keeper down where he stood. But at the thought of his sword, Radnor called up what his old master, Halbjorn, had taught him. Remembering his teacher's words, Radnor searched his heart and found his place; the center of his soul. He forced himself to breathe slowly and found the calm he needed to ride away.

While pulling on the reins, Radnor lightly tapped Darestr with his heels to get back on the road and start forward again. As they passed the Keeper, Darestr snorted with contempt which matched the anger Radnor had just shown.

The Keeper spoke one more time.

"May you find better tidings elsewhere. Your father and I knew each other. In fact, if the circumstances had been better, I would like to think he counted me among his friends all those years ago."

Bitterness overtook Radnor in that moment and he felt the need to correct the Keeper.

"I suppose it makes no difference now, but I know Magnus was not my real father; neither by blood, nor love."

As Radnor turned once again to follow the path, the Keeper sighed with great sorrow at Radnor's words.

"That wasn't the plan," the Keeper muttered, thinking Radnor would hear nothing.

Radnor turned to ask what the Keeper had said, but could only watch as the old man's motionless form faded into the depths of the forest.

Radnor slowly traced a path out of the forest. Now that he was alone, the shield of calm he had raised came crashing down. He was bitter, angry, and wished only for relief from his torment. His thoughts turned to the vengeance he sought. He wanted to end it all, starting with those he needed to kill, ending with himself. But before he could die, there was a reckoning to be had.

As he rode and the minutes passed by, the anger gradually washed away from him; and he began to feel normal again. The desire for death fell away from his thoughts, though the pain in his arm tempted him to cut it off. As his feelings subsided, Radnor turned the Keeper's words over in his mind like a man turns a coin in his hand. Before Radnor could really start to think about them he was at the edge of the forest, where a large black bear blocked his path.

The great beast was massive, and it saw him too. Radnor did not want to have to kill it; so he dismounted from his horse and placed his weapon and shield on the ground. The bear stood and snarled, baring a set of fangs that would induce fear in the strongest of lions. In the hopes of calming it, Radnor started to undo the chinstrap on his helmet so that it might look upon him and see the man underneath the armor, and not the monster it believed him to be. But the beast had already begun to charge.

Radnor leaped out of its path and the bear bowled past him in its attack. Radnor spun to face it, but it had already turned back to him, fangs bared. It swiped a massive paw at Radnor, and before he could react it smashed into his chest. Man and armor went sailing into an ancient tree that creaked in its own discomfort from the impact. Radnor landed hard on the ground, and pain washed over him for a moment. His wounds ripped at his senses and he could not breathe. Gasping, Radnor clambered to his feet, momentarily dazed. He shook off the dizziness and looked at the bear; which had begun roaring at him. Pain washed over him again and fed a rage that overtook him. His anger gave him the strength to ignore the pain, but he caught himself as he started to blindly rush the bear. Some part of himself remembered his training, and he found his place again. Radnor's blood flamed to life, and then the true battle lust took him. Everything became as calm and serene as a garden in the moonlight. But this was not the calm of a man who had read poetry in that garden. This was the calm of a man whose day to day life trained him so that killing came as naturally as breathing. The autumn leaves seemed to fall more slowly, and each blade of grass had its own story to tell.

The bear came again, but this time Radnor was ready. He sidestepped its charge and drove his hand into its side as it went by. The poor animal stumbled and roared in pain. It turned to face him and went up on its hind legs with the intent to drop its heavy weight on him. Radnor saw an opportunity, and stepped into the monstrous animal. He struck it dead center in the chest, and felt the familiar sensation of ribs snapping under the force of the blow. It howled in agony, and fell backwards to land in a heavy heap on the dirt. The bear rolled over and tried to stand up.

Radnor was too fast for it. He moved to its side, and brought his elbow down on its head, crushing its skull and killing the poor beast. Radnor looked at it with pity for a moment and considered its plight with the remorse and aggravation he usually felt after these sorts of encounters. Most animals fled from him, but a few would stand and fight what they perceived as a threat. It always ended the same way, and Radnor had grown weary of killing defenseless animals. Radnor turned to find his horse.

"Darestr!" he shouted.

Darestr came galloping towards him, and Radnor swiftly mounted him. Once astride, he secured his weapons and re-fastened his helmet. The sorrowful warrior then continued to follow the path that led out of the forest, casting one final glance at the poor, helpless animal that now lay dead.

Chapter 2

At the southern edge of the greatest forest on the continent, known to Radnor's kin as "Gammelskog" and by the locals as "Grountra", was a village of around one hundred people. The wooden thatch roofed buildings lined a single stone-paved road which led from the forest to this village and beyond. The houses had been built by the settlers thirty years ago, but no one knew who had built the road. A creek ran just next to the small village which supplied drinking and bathing water to the pig farmers who lived there. The town was surrounded by a palisade made of pointed posts lashed together and dug into the ground to check the vicious appetites of wolves. At one end of this wall sat a small gate that would be little more than a mild obstacle to an armed band. Near the center of this town was a single tavern whose occupants were engaged in conversation.

"Hey, Halmda!" yelled the Innkeeper.

"Yeah, what do you want Bron?" replied Halmda.

"Your house finished yet?"

The two men sat at opposite ends of the dusty tavern, drinking their ale in the midday. Today had already been a good day. The hunting party had left well prepared in the early morning, the harvest was going well, and it was one day closer to the date he was to marry Elena, the prettiest girl in the village.

"After the wedding," Halmda replied.

Halmda was about twenty-nine, and a bit rough. His intellect was not above average for the area, but Elena's was, which sometimes got her into trouble. Bron could have been Halmda's brother, sandy haired and blue eyed. He was not the wisest man, but not an uncouth brute either. That he left to Halmda. Bron's actual brother, Klane, sat at the table with Halmda. The pair had been discussing the wedding with him earlier. Klane had also gotten a head start to the evening's revelries, his fourth drink now in hand.

"Where is the lucky lady anyway?" Klane asked.

"Probably skulking about, the way she does now," answered Bron.

"I know. She didn't used to do that. Ever since my father made the arrangements, she's been…odd," Halmda said, while wearing a most discouraging scowl.

"Yeah, I hear you mate. She should be happy she's goin' to be married at all!" slurred Klane in his drunken manner. "With her father gone and all her silver spent feedin' herself, I would say you're doin' her a favor!"

Halmda snorted in agreement, and began to gripe again.

"Not even a mother of the bride to help with the planning. It all rests on my shoulders. And, she goes off on this stuff, see? Like how I never talk to her right. I treat her as good as she earns. Can I help it she doesn't earn?"

The friends were interrupted by the return of the hunting party. Three men returned with a large wooden cart. To the astonishment of everyone who saw it, the cart was overflowing with the remains of a hulking black bear.

"What have you there, my lord?" Bron demanded.

The lead hunter, a powerful man named Leif, replied as he bent to lift the carcass from the cart.

"A black bear, enough meat in this thing to last us a week with nothing else to eat."

"Who got it?" asked Halmda, through a large drought of his ale.

"Only great Caelum could know," replied Leif.

"I keep telling you, I saw it!" came a young voice from behind the wagon.

Leif turned angrily.

"I told you to stop telling lies!" he yelled.

A sandy haired boy about the age of twelve came out from behind the wagon.

"Ay, you brought Rolf with you?" Klane asked.

Leif glared into Klane's eyes for a moment before answering.

"His father's on a trading run to Wollendan…won't be back for days still. Figured that was as good a chance as any to bring him along and show him how it's done. I also had him pegged as a good spotter."

"And of course you don't believe me! Tell me how that makes *any* sense!" Rolf yelled indignantly.

"Silence!" Leif yelled. "I have had enough of this!"

The small boy shrunk back behind a wheel of the wagon.

"Do as he says, boy," Halmda said with a cruel grin. "Or else I might have to show ya why horses don't like our sticks very much. And like a horse, you'll learn *to do as you're told*!"

Rolf shrunk back even more, until he was nearly swallowed by the wagon's wheels.

"What's he keep going on about anyway?" Bron asked

Leif rolled his eyes.

"He keeps going on about someone in the forest. He says he saw someone kill this thing...alone."

"Alone?" questioned Halmda. He looked at Rolf. "My...don't we tell mighty big tales now?"

Rolf tried to make himself look smaller, an impossible feat at this point.

"And what's more," Leif continued. "He says the man did it with his bare hands."

He held out his hands and gestured with them like he was hitting the bear.

"No man could've done this here bear in by himself," Klane said, staring at the crushed skull on the beast as it lay in the cart.

"I know," Leif said. "Must have been another bear. Halmda, let Elena know Rolf's been lying. Tell her to handle it."

Halmda was disappointed. He believed Elena would be too lenient, but he also knew better than to question Leif's authority. Halmda left to fetch Elena, and found her sitting in her room in what had been her father's house. Since her father's passing, Halmda noticed that even though she had found that the empty halls had little appeal to her now, she would still rather sit here than be with him.

Elena was sitting in her chair backwards, bent forward over the back. She was watching a tiny insect on her windowsill and pondering how much happier it was than she. When he entered the room, Halmda just stood and marveled at her beauty for a moment. He watched the way her ebony hair flowed down her back. Her skin was a soft white, but his eyes fixed themselves on the gentle motion of her breasts as she breathed. Soon they would be married, and he would get to see what was under that worn yellow dress she was wearing. Despite its aged appearance, it enhanced a radiance from her that stirred even Halmda's dull heart.

"Elena. I have a task for you."

"Yes?" Elena asked sullenly, not looking away from her new pet.

"Rolf has been telling lies, you need to beat him."

"Why don't you do it?" she spat.

"Because he hasn't learned his lesson from last time."

Now, she looked at him, and her blue eyes turned to ice.

"Last time *you* were the liar Halmda, I know it was you who stole that ale from Paruig."

Halmda's hand came upon her so quickly; she didn't even have time to blink. His blow sent her crashing to the floor in a heap. Silently, Elena cursed herself. This was not the first time Halmda had hit her, and again, she was not prepared for how fast his hands were. Halmda came to stand over her with a self-satisfied smirk on his face which infuriated her even more.

"You ever say that again, and it will be one short marriage my love."

Without a trace of irony, Halmda offered her a hand to help her up. Before Elena could slap his hand away, cries were heard from the gate, and Halmda spun to look out the open door.

"Beat the boy, now, I'll see to this alarm," he ordered.

With that, the man stalked out of the house, and Elena began to search for Rolf.

"Man at the gates!" yelled the watchman.

Two men with bows leaped to the top of the watch tower, and took aim. Leif and several of the other townsmen stood ready, armed with axes and knives.

"Has he given any indication of his intentions?" Leif yelled.

"Not yet," called the man in the tower. "But he is not within calling range yet. All we can see is that he is on a horse, and heading this way."

"Alone?" Leif asked

"Yes."

Leif pondered this for a moment, then gave his order.

"One man cannot attack us all and come out alive. Open the gate."

The strongest men of the town moved forward, and gradually pulled open the oak doors that were the only entrance into the small village. A few moments later, a towering man atop a war horse rode inside. Leif took a step back and began to rethink his words at the sight of the titan he had let enter his village. The man was armored from head to toe, and carried as many weapons by himself as four of Leif's men wielded. Leif felt himself shudder as he was reminded of the stories and songs of Veigarand, the vengeful phantom from a kingdom now ashes. The mounted warrior swiveled his head to Leif like an animated statue, and spoke in a voice that commanded authority.

"I thank you for your trust my lord. I would hope to spend the night here, only one though, for I am traveling far and need to move with much haste."

Leif sighed with relief at the brevity of this man's desired stay, and replied.

"You are most welcome, noble warrior. There is an inn down the road. What, may I ask, is your name?"

Radnor looked down the line of men and began sizing them up. He judged the group of men and the threat they posed by age, size, the way they carried themselves, and their weapons. Within a few moments Radnor had a plan to kill every man that stood before him, just in case. They all stood in awe; few had seen a warrior armed like Radnor was. He had hidden his shield under his cloak; as he didn't want anyone to have even a small chance of recognizing the remaining scratches of the coat of arms emblazoned upon it. As Radnor surveyed the men before him, he paid special attention to the man who led the group. He was a tall man, with sinewy muscle that seemed to stretch in unnaturally long fibers across his body. This man, whom Radnor was to learn was Leif, wore his long gray hair tied back, and his beard long enough to be fashionable, but not so long as to be easily pulled in a fight. Radnor saw a caution in Leif mixed with a stance that marked him as an experienced fighter. Radnor guessed Leif had seen a few battles more than the people standing next to him.

This was a moment Radnor needed to choose carefully. No one had known him by his born name in many years, and the name given to him by the barbarians who lived along the northern rivers of Aquis and Avosn was well known enough it would cause panic among these people. Fear would not serve Radnor's purpose, so he chose to use his real name.

"I am Radnor, my lord."

"I am Leif Edricson...ealdorman of this village."

Radnor smiled lightly to himself. Based on Leif's stance and bearing, it now seemed obvious that he would be the leader of any men called to arms by the earl, and by extension the village's leader.

"Would you allow me to pass, my lord ealdorman? I am quite weary, and would much like to reach the inn," Radnor said.

Radnor chose his next words carefully. He did not trust these people, and felt it best to add a lie that might make anyone there think twice before trying to rob or otherwise harm him.

"I have friends who are meeting me up the road at midday tomorrow. I shall make my stay as uneventful as possible."

Leif stood aside and gestured for Radnor to pass.

"The inn here is maintained by the earl for the purpose of entertaining guests such as yourself. I hope you will find it most pleasing."

Radnor nodded vigorously, but the gesture looked subtle when hidden under his helmet. Realizing this, Radnor politely thanked Leif for the information and went on his way.

Leif watched as the ironclad colossus rode past him...and could not suppress a shudder. Again, he found the stories of Veigarand entering his mind, and also found himself reminded of that ugly business in Halden a month back. If the story was to be believed, the town was left burned to ashes, and not a single living soul could be found among the dead. Leif tried to push the thought from his mind, but he couldn't help but fear what he had just allowed to enter his town.

As Radnor started his ride towards the inn, a young woman who looked to be the same age as he caught his attention. She was chasing and apologizing to a young boy who seemed to be named "Rolf". Rolf had a few red marks showing across his face, but it looked like the majority of his pain was emotional rather than physical. Radnor couldn't help but notice the woman's enchanting beauty. Hers matched the beauty of the women told of in songs from Radnor's homeland. The boy came running from his home, and had just reached the road when he stopped and stared at Radnor.

"It's...him. It's him!" the boy screamed. "It's the man from the forest!"

Radnor looked at him, and chose to keep silent. He wanted to avoid attracting any attention if at all possible, and addressing the boy's claims would not further that goal. So Radnor kept riding, and winced as he heard the commotion and yells of the boy being beaten once again for his lies.

The inn was a quiet building with two floors, with community stables just behind the back. Many horses were kept there to save maintenance expenses for everyone in the town. Radnor made sure Darestr was comfortable in these stables, giving him a final pat on the snout before heading inside. Once inside, Radnor found that the bottom floor was a drinking hall, with many tables and a bar at one end of the room. The staircase leading to the upstairs bedrooms was set at the back of the building. The place was much larger than Radnor thought needed for an out-of-the-way town such as this. The innkeeper, who introduced himself as "Bron", was all too eager to tell Radnor the history of the inn, and how it was planned to transform their town into a trading city with roads to the kingdoms that rested to the north. The first part of that plan was to make the inn an inviting place where people would be happy to stay. Departing the conversation took some doing, but Radnor was finally able to make his excuses, and trudge up the stairs.

Now that he was finally inside his room, Radnor roughly dropped his belongings on the wood floor. He then set to removing his armor and underclothes. Each piece was unceremoniously dropped to the floor as he sought to free himself from his metallic tomb. Once down to his underclothes, he gently unwound the blood-soaked bandage, and examined his arm with a frown...the vampire had certainly left his mark. The deep bite still burned with pain, and the wound still refused to close. The best course of action would be to clean it, and the best place to do that would be in the creek just outside the palisade.

14

He wrapped the makeshift bandage around his arm again, hoping it wouldn't attract too much attention. He threw his tunic back on, took a scrap of torn fabric he kept with him to use as a washcloth, and headed outside.

As he stepped outside, Radnor took a moment to enjoy the cool breeze which tenderly brushed his face. The sweet aroma and the joyous light of the burning braziers which were now being lit along the street helped distract Radnor from his brooding. He enjoyed being near other people again.

As he stood, Radnor took a moment to survey his surroundings. Several wooden buildings dotted the open ground within the walls. There were a few dozen houses, each with enclosures for pigs and sheep. There wasn't anything Radnor could identify as a market or trade building, which told him the villagers must regularly send out small caravans out elsewhere. The most impressive feature of the village was the temple to the god Caelum. While all of the other buildings were made of wood, this one was made of stone. It was far taller than the other buildings, and looked almost like it had originally been built as a fortress. Radnor could even see the rough work that had been done to add windows to the walls on the bottom floor, and the doors looked to be heavy and strong. He also had to admire the artistry involved in carving the icon of Caelum above the door. A sun, painted yellow with its red rays spreading in all directions. The sun was overlapped slightly by a second circle that was the moon. It was painted clean white. Once Radnor had surveyed the town, he continued on his way.

Past the temple, he was able to clearly look out and watch as the sunset was at its most beautiful. The sky was colored the same as the fires which now invitingly lit the solitary road of the village. Radnor found himself feeling wistful, wondering if it was possible to live like this every day. Could he be someone else? How would that someone else look? How would they think? Would they have a family? He shook his head at himself, flinging the thoughts from his mind. Radnor finished his trudge to the babbling creek that shared its waters with the world.

Radnor took off his tunic and stripped the bandage from his arm again. Sitting down at the creek's edge, he soaked the washcloth in fresh water, and began to work the cleansing water into the wound. He tried to generally wash himself as well as he could. It had been a few days since his last opportunity, and his tolerance for his own smell was diminishing. As he continued to bathe and care for his arm, he heard the shuffling of small feet behind him. Radnor abruptly turned and saw the beautiful dark haired woman he had seen earlier that evening. A nervous tension arose in him. For the first time in a long time, he was unsure of what to say or do.

She was wearing a simple yellow dress which when looked upon from Radnor's seated position, blended into the setting sun so well it seemed she had just stepped down from it.

"My lord?" she started. "I do not mean to disturb you. But I must ask: are you the warrior whom took a room in the inn?"

Radnor started at her blankly for a moment, unable to speak. After longer than he would have liked, Radnor finally found his words.

"I have taken a room, yes. Who told you I'm a warrior?"

Elena laughed in surprise that he would make such a jest.

"I saw you ride into town, and I heard Leif talking to some of the other men. You scared them half to death when you rode through that gate."

Radnor sighed with mild frustration.

"I'm sorry. I can have that effect on people. I only have one set of saddle bags, so the best way to carry my armor is to wear it."

Elena found herself laughing again, but then stopped when she saw how confused he was by her response.

"Oh, I do not mean to make a jest at your expense. Many of the men, especially those like Halmda and Leif, can be overly sure of themselves. It is nice to see them quaking in their boots from time to time. I think Leif even spoke aloud that you might be the dreaded Veigarand, the ghost of the north, come to destroy us for sins unknown. By the look of you, I think it's nonsense. Halmda rejected the idea, and has you pegged in his mind as a mercenary between jobs."

Radnor's blood ran cold when she spoke the name "Veigarand". It was a name that haunted him frequently, and he wanted to change the subject as fast as possible.

"My lady, if you don't mind, I need to continue washing. This water is getting colder by the minute, and I would very much like to finish before I must freeze myself to death to get a bath."

Elena was slightly taken aback by Radnor's sudden brusqueness. She found herself a little hurt, but this feeling dissipated quickly when she spied the bleeding gash in Radnor's arm.

"My goodness, what happened to you?" she said, disregarding Radnor's last statement.

She stepped to him and practically pulled him to his feet as she took his arm to look at it. If her purpose had been to be helpful, she failed as Radnor stifled a cry of pain. He almost wrenched the arm away from her, but decided against it. Despite the pain, it felt good to have someone touch him who *wasn't* trying to hurt him. Elena looked up at him, and spoke again.

"Well, are you not going to answer me?"

16

Radnor finally found himself again, but he stammered a little with his lie.

"It was…it was a wolf attack. My fire went out during the night, and this was how they woke me up."

"You poor thing," Elena replied, now unsure what to do. She found herself in a conundrum. Here she was, standing at the riverside with a strange, shirtless man, and holding his arm! She abruptly dropped the arm and took a step back. "I'm sorry to have bothered you, but I must also take a bath as well. Tonight is a reception in honor of my engagement to Halmda. I must be properly dressed for such an event."

It was Radnor's turn to be taken aback by the sudden shift in demeanor, but he tried to take it in stride. It wasn't until this moment he noticed there was a bruise forming over her eye. Radnor thought better of asking how she acquired it. He quickly wrapped the fresh bandage he'd brought around his arm, and threw his tunic back on. As he started to walk back to the village, he saw her start to undo her dress, and Radnor was surprised at how difficult it was for him not to take a peek. He straightened his head and kept his eyes locked on the path ahead of him. He heard her speak out to him again from the water.

"Stranger? I never did learn your name."

"It's Radnor," He replied. "I never did catch yours either."

"I'm Elena!" she shouted back. There was a moment's pause, and just as Radnor started to continue walking again, she yelled out to him again. "If you like, you should come down to the tavern tonight. That's where the reception is being held, and we all might enjoy seeing a fresh face."

Radnor's heart skipped a little at that. He had dearly missed the company of other people, and he desperately wanted to go. But, his mind didn't let him hold onto his moment of joy for long, as he remembered that he was here to rest, and nothing more.

"Thank you my lady, I will consider your offer," he replied, trying not to be rude.

Radnor continued down the road to his quarters, scolding himself along the way. He was letting his weakness take hold of him. He knew there was no way he could live among these people, or any people. Once the night was done, he must move on. Nothing was a more painful reminder of this fact than the song he now heard issuing from a window in one of the houses on his way. Radnor listened to the lyrics, and felt the sting of the remorseful tune.

> *Children come, and listen here.*
> *Attend, children, oh, most dear,*

For you must listen,
A lesson you must learn,
For if you do not,
You shall surely burn.

Wicked things do stalk the woods,
Wolves, ghouls, and dark brotherhoods,
But none can compare,
To the vilest deed,
Done by this monster,
A wraith with no creed.

From the north snow lands he came,
Good, bad, it is all the same,
His wrath is fearsome,
His sword thirsts for blood,
For all men he meets,
His blade drinks red flood.

Who is this man we must fear?
When will his visage appear?
His name, Veigarand,
Wayfaring death they say.
Spy the ghost of ashes,
You will meet sorrow that day.

Radnor picked up his pace. This was a song he had not heard before, but it painted the same picture as all the others. He was a figure of fear and death, and Radnor knew this to be true. Even though men did not know the true name or the face to go with his wrath, the violence which Radnor had wrought across the north was well known. It brought anguish to his heart, knowing that the songs only told the stories of the slain. If any would listen, the slayer would sing a very different tune. His was a tale of revenge, and of how he had destroyed those wicked dark brotherhoods that the awful song said were not as wicked as he. No, the only songs that were heard were requiems for his foes. It was a fact that Radnor resented, and he futilely hoped to never hear the name "Veigarand" again. It was given to him by the barbarians of Aquis when he killed every warrior and priest he could find and threw down their temple to the evil god Adramelach. But there was one thing the song got right: the name did indeed mean "wayfaring death". It was a name Radnor found hard to ignore, for as much as he hated it, the description fit.

Radnor reached the inn, and saw great casks of mead and beer being arranged around the drinking hall. Candles were being lit, and musicians began setting up in a corner of the room. The party would begin soon.

Chapter 3

Hours passed by as Radnor sat uneasily in the plain wooden chair which his room had been furnished with. A general sense of restlessness overtook him, and he felt the unavoidable pull of his desire for human companionship. Its nagging tug became even greater as he heard the noise of the reception start downstairs.

At first, Radnor tried to ignore the jubilant sounds of laughter and music; but his thoughts still turned to the celebration; and how dearly he missed being able to speak to other men and women. He denied himself this impulse at first by reminding himself that he didn't really belong there. But still his loneliness clutched at his heart, and its grip tore him from his seat. Radnor changed into a fresh red tunic and black pants. He took his goblet and walked downstairs to the tavern below to fetch some ale.

"Just to say hello to Elena....just to be polite." was what he told himself as he descended the stairs.

Upon entering the tavern he discovered a truly raucous celebration as Halmda kissed Elena. He felt a twinge of jealousy run through him. She was truly beautiful, and love was something that had been denied to Radnor by the path he must walk. This jealousy turned to anger as Radnor couldn't help but notice the bruise that had finished forming around her eye, nor did he fail to notice the resentful way Elena looked and acted towards Halmda.

The room was brightly lit with a candle on each table and many more hanging from the ceiling on small iron chandeliers. There was a roaring fire at each end of the room, and the smell of cooking meats filled the air. Radnor spied the sewn together head of the bear he had killed on display over the mantelpiece of one fireplace. Light glinted off of the eyes in the head of a great stag which rested over the other. The men moved about the room, singing and dancing with the ladies of the town. Few men did not have a drink in their hand and a woman on their arm, though none of the women were any match for Elena in beauty. They more closely resembled the female equivalents of their husbands and brothers. Shadows danced gaily against the brightly lit walls as people took to the open spaces of the room to forget their troubles in each other's arms.

Radnor took a seat, and within moments a very drunk man plopped down next to him. Radnor turned to him and in an effort to be social, asked the man his name. The disheveled man was only able to answer Radnor through sporadic bursts of hiccuping.

"My name's *hic* Klane. You're *hic* Ragdor, right?"

"Radnor."

"Sure thing Rafgor."

Radnor shook his head to himself, and filled his goblet with ale from the cask that rested on the table.

"I'm not intruding, am I?" Radnor asked.

Klane started to open his mouth, but before he could speak, a voice sounded.

"No, not at all," came Leif's voice. Radnor turned, and saw that Leif stood directly behind him. The ealdorman gave him a reassuring smile, and spoke again. "We follow great Caelum's laws of hospitality here. As long as strangers start no trouble, they shall receive none."

Radnor hesitated as he caught himself before he could make his scathing remark about the worship of such a useless god. Radnor instead chose to change the subject.

"My lord ealdorman…" Radnor started.

"Call me 'Leif'," Leif interjected.

"Very well…Leif. I have never been this far south. To whom does this village owe its allegiance?"

"We are loyal to the Earl of Wulfgeld," Leif replied.

"Is that not far south...in the foothills of the Morakors Mountains?" Radnor asked.

"Aye, it is. We were sent to build a long range trading outpost. I'm sure Bron already told you this, as he tells all strangers here."

"He told me this town was a trading post, but not for whom," Radnor replied.

"Ah. I see. He was so excited to tell you about the inn, that he skipped over those details?" Leif responded.

"I'm afraid so. Is Godric still the Earl of Wulfgeld?"

Surprise flashed across Leif's face.

"The earl now is Lord Sigaberht, son of Godric the Fierce. Earl Godric fell in battle when Duke Piarin sent his army from Drakomar and tried to take Godric's throne at Wulfgeld. Sigaberht proved himself to be a skilled warrior that day."

Leif began to reminisce, and people gathered around and eagerly awaited the tale of Sigaberht the Brave.

"This was five winters back, before I was ealdorman here. The gate was broken, burned and battered by the enemy's siege engines. The lines of battle were still drawn outside the gate house. All of our men atop the wall had been slain by arrows from the enemy. It was just our shield wall between them and our riches and women. Piarin's champion stood at the front of the line, and ordered the first of many charges which shook our resolve to the core. Back they drove us, further and further. Each time they hit us, I watched as brave men around me fell."

Leif choked up for a moment as he spoke, and stopped to wash his throat with ale before continuing.

"Sigurd, my brother by blood was knocked to his back and slain before I could help him. Grief overtook me then. Sorrow weighed heavy upon my shoulders as I saw more and more of the men of great Wulfgeld slain by the vicious southern dogs. After the last charge...I saw...to my horror...that Earl Godric had fallen, his throat cut by a terrible blow. I felt only despair in that moment, and a desire to throw down my arms and weep. But before you judge me…you must understand…our lord was dead! There was to be no victory! Only sorrow!"

Leif took another gulp from his cup, and paused to look upon the faces of those listening to his tale. They all knew it well, and they eagerly awaited its conclusion. Time seemed to stand still, and even Radnor found himself swept up in the fervor with which Leif told his story.

"The day was lost, and all that was left was to remove our lord's body, and bury him in the manner that he deserved. But those thoughts were soon banished from my mind when I saw Sigaberht, clad in sunbright armor, spear in hand, leap over the lines, and attack the enemy before their shield wall could reform. Behind him leaped his two brothers, Cynaric and Eadwulf. Never have I seen a man fight as Sigaberht fought in that moment. Before the enemy knew they were engaged again, Sigabehrt had already slain two. With his brothers behind him, Cynaric with his spear, and Eadwulf with his shield, Sigaberht began to drive the Southern Whoresons from our gates. As they tried to reform the shield wall, Sigaberht battered them down, hewing both shield and man in his rage.

"Piarin's champion and his guards strode to the fore and did battle with the brothers. None of the other cowards could stand before the fiery wrath of Sigaberht. Together our Earl and his brothers slew over a dozen men in the brawl. The rest of us reformed the shield wall behind them. We feared that if we tried to help, we might distract one of our lords and cause his death. In the heat of battle, Sigaberht was forced to aim a thrust wild of his intended target so that he could protect Cynaric from a blow which would have smote him to the dirt. But in that moment of protection, Sigaberht opened himself to attack from Piarin's champion."

Leif again choked up as tears sprung from his eyes. A look of anguish swept over the crowd, for they knew what came next.

"As the champion struck, Sigaberht made peace with Caelum and prepared to join Earl Godric in the Hall of Kings. But it was not to be. Eadwulf in haste threw himself before the blow, and died to save his

22

brother. It was then that Sigaberht spun and struck Piarin's champion with such force that he cleaved through mail and man from collar bone to hip. Seeing our lord smite his enemy so thoroughly inspired our commander to give the order to charge. 'Our lord is dead!' he shouted. 'Vengeance!' we cried, and into the enemy we charged. Again and again we smashed them down, beating and screaming like demons. And there was Sigaberht at the front, hewing and slaying like a man possessed by the wrath of Caelum himself. We drove the enemy back that day. We killed so many that Piarin decided to withdraw from our walls. What was once a sure defeat became victory, all due to Sigaberht's bravery in battle."

Leif raised his glass for a toast. "To Sigaberht!" he shouted.

"To Sigaberht!" shouted the crowd in unison, joining in Leif's toast.

Radnor joined their toast, always appreciative of a tale of battle such as this. Leif turned to face Radnor and grinned sheepishly. "I do apologize, I hope I answered your question satisfactorily at least."

Radnor nodded enthusiastically.

"It was an answer worthy of your Hall of Kings! I am sure that if Godric heard it, he would be most proud."

Leif blinked in surprise.

"'Our' Hall of Kings? You say that as though it does not belong to us all? Where are you from stranger? Everyone in these lands knows the truth of Caelum, god of light and all that is good!"

Radnor started to think of a way out of this social gaffe on his part. He did not want to talk about his homeland at all, let alone its religion. Before Leif could press him further, Elena caught sight of him and waved him over to where she and Halmda were standing. Radnor excused himself, and walked over to their side of the room. Radnor again saw the way Elena looked at Halmda, and knew it was he whom had put that bruise on her. Radnor felt his blood boil, but refused to allow his anger to show. Not here, not now. As Elena started to speak to Radnor, Halmda cut her off…

"Hullo stranger, would you like to play a game?"

Leif came over to join them, wary of what Halmda had in mind.

"I hope there is no problem," Leif said to Halmda.

Halmda wheeled to face Leif with an impish grin.

"I just want to play a game with him, that is all."

Radnor shot a glance over at Leif, who nodded to him, so Radnor replied to Halmda.

"Sure, I will gladly play a game with you."

Halmda led him over to a table encircled by the men of the town. Sitting at the table were two men who took turns striking each other's hands. Halmda gestured to the two men playing this game and began to explain it to Radnor.

"It's called 'Iron Hand'. The rules are simple. Keep both hands on the table. When it is your turn, you may remove one hand to strike either hand of the other man. Then, you must immediately place your hand back down on the table. The defender may then attempt to strike your hand as it comes back. If he succeeds, you lose use of that hand for the rest of the game, and it can no longer be held on the table. If both hands are eventually struck on the way back, or the pain becomes too great and you remove both hands from the table; you lose. When you lose you take a drink, and you continue in this manner until one man empties his cup."

Radnor watched as the two men played this game. Eventually, one man hit both of the other man's hands. Radnor's wounded arm ached as he watched, and he started to think this game would be more trouble than it was worth. But when he saw that mark on Elena's face...Radnor could not help but seek an opportunity to hit Halmda. As the two men finished striking each other's hands, the loser took a drink; and they started again. Halmda led Radnor to a seat at the next table, and was about to sit down across from Radnor when Leif took his place. When Halmda started to object, Leif stared him dead in the eyes.

"I would play the man first Halmda, I want to be sure he understands the rules before playing one of your wager games."

Halmda took a step back.

"Of course, my lord ealdorman. That seems like it is best."

A crowd gathered around to see the stranger play against Leif. Bets were made, with Halmda setting the odds.

The other men snickered at the hopelessness of Radnor's predicament. Leif was by far the best at "Iron Hand".

"Normally, we would decide who goes first by the toss of a coin. But since you are the newcomer, you go first," Leif said.

Radnor lifted his left hand and brought it down upon Leif's hand, sturdily, but not trying to cause undue pain. Leif yelped and looked at Radnor, shocked not only from the force of the blow, but also its speed. Leif hadn't even seen Radnor twitch.

The ealdorman gathered himself for his turn, and then fiercely struck Radnor's hand. Before Leif could even start to retrieve his hand, Radnor struck it with his own. Leif looked stunned, and placed his hand at his side. Radnor dramatically wound up for the next blow, hoping Leif would take the hint. Leif removed his other hand from the table rather than get hit again. He yielded the rest of the rounds to Radnor, and drank his tankard all in one gulp. The room went up in a roar of yells. It was not often that Leif lost at iron hand, and never had he been defeated so decisively! Halmda had a sour look on his face; he had just lost some pretty coin on that match up. Radnor looked up at Halmda,

"So, I believe you wanted to play a game with me?" he said, waiting for the response he knew was coming.

Halmda seemed to almost visibly squirm inside his clothes, desperately searching for a way out, until he finally replied.

"I am sorry to disappoint, but I no longer have the coin on hand to place a bet with. Therefore, I shall not play you this evening."

Radnor chuckled a little, and made Halmda an offer. Radnor really wanted a chance to hit this man.

"Do not worry. If you win, I will give you thirty pieces of silver. If I win, you lose nothing. Before you object, think of this as…" Radnor paused to look at Elena for a moment. "…a wedding present."

Greed filled Halmda's eyes, this was a chance to not only make back what he lost, but also make a little extra tonight, and at no risk! Halmda turned to face the silent crowd.

"I will face the stranger!" he bellowed, whipping the crowd into cheers. But over the cheering, Halmda heard Elena's voice above the crowd.

"Don't do it," she said. "I don't see you doing anything but getting slapped silly."

"Can you see this?" Halmda snapped as his hand started to wind back. Halmda then remembered where he was and stopped before his hand could continue on its path. Radnor sat at the table and pondered his predicament. Only now was he realizing that his temper had gotten him into trouble again. Halmda wasn't going to give up easily, and Elena's taunting was not going to help that. But every time Radnor looked at that bruise around her eye, his rage grew fiercer and quickly blinded him to anything but the image of hurting Halmda. Radnor stared icily at the slimy man, and nodded. Halmda then sat himself at the table.

"I'll go first!" Halmda yelled.

He then struck a blow on Radnor's hand. It hurt, but for Radnor pain was an old acquaintance. His memories of training with the sword were filled with many blows far more painful than this.

Radnor didn't even flinch. In fact, Radnor smirked at him, and let Halmda's hand return unharmed. Radnor wanted to maximize how much pain he could cause. Lazily leaning back in his chair, the muscular warrior took a moment to drink in the varied expressions running across Halmda's face. The main one was confusion. Then Radnor struck a fierce blow with far less compassion than he had shown Leif. Halmda screamed, and both of his hands left the table. The first round was Radnor's!

After a moment, Halmda regained his composure and took a drink from his glass. Then, he drove the glass straight down towards Radnor's hand on the table. The glass slammed down hard against nothing but wood, and Halmda barely had time to see that Radnor's hand had moved before Radnor's reply swept across Halmda's face. Radnor struck the man with a simple open handed slap across the cheek. It was the kind of blow one would use to discipline a child doing something stupid and dangerous in Radnor's homeland, but the force was much greater, intended to punish rather than instruct. Halmda toppled out of his chair from the strength of the blow. A few people came to help Halmda back up. Most took a step back from Radnor. The only one in the room who did not move at all was Elena. She stood her ground to drink in the sight of Halmda having been knocked senseless, just as she had said he would be. Radnor looked at Halmda coldly, like a wolf stalking his prey. Unable to let things stand as they were without making one final statement, Radnor spoke to Halmda in the formal manner of the royal court of his homeland.

"Your betrothed must know you well, for she knew you would do something to provoke a fitting punishment for your childish treachery."

At that taunt Halmda wrestled out of the arms of his friends and reached for the knife on his belt. Halmda's temper overtook all of his better judgment, and he now intended to kill the impetuous stranger before him.

Blinded by rage, the only thing Halmda could see before him was his own hand driving the knife into Radnor's stomach, and beginning to rip upwards through his whole body until the arrogant ass was split in half.

Radnor felt himself start to fall into an uncontrolled battle rage driven not by his training, but only his temper. Struggling, he was able to force it down, hoping this could end without more violence. The pain in Radnor's arm fueled the fire though, making it difficult for him not to kill Halmda where he stood. Forcing himself to be controlled instead, Radnor stepped back from the table and let Halmda draw his weapon, hoping someone would intervene.

"That is not wise," Radnor said.

"I'm going to make you feel pain like you've never imagined!" Halmda bellowed.

Halmda took two steps towards Radnor with his knife, but Radnor was already on him. The next thing Halmda knew was that his arm was broken, his knife was on the floor, and he was being held down on one knee while Radnor held him in a choke hold. Radnor leaned into him and whispered in his ear.

"Pain? What do you know of pain? Have you ever felt the teeth of a Soldar demon buried into your flesh? The flame of a dragon as it burns the home you grew up in? Been cursed as I have? I think not."

Radnor was just about to let the man go when one of Halmda's friends came up behind him with his own knife. Radnor's already bubbling anger slid effortlessly into the empty violence of his battle lust, but the calm did not come. In that moment, Radnor released his grip on Halmda and turned to face the new threat. Some part of Radnor recognized the face of Bron the Innkeeper for just a moment as he smashed the knife out of Bron's hands and wrapped his fingers around the man's neck. Radnor had lost all control in the moment when his life had been threatened. The candlelight which had painted the tavern with such joyous light before, now served to illuminate the horror in Bron's glassy eyes as he lay on the floor, his neck twisted until his head had nearly been torn off. The shadows which flickered across the room almost seemed to dance with obscene joy at the violence Radnor had wrought, and the people knew him then.

Silence fell over the room for a moment, followed by the panic stricken screams of the villagers. Radnor regained control of himself and realized what he'd done. Shame washed over him at his lack of control; he had failed again just as he had against the bear.

Radnor looked down at the corpse under him and then looked up at Elena. She stood rooted where she had been before. There was no longer a look of satisfaction on her face. This had been replaced by an expression only possible for someone who had just experienced true terror for the first time.

Leif stepped forward from the crowd with several men with him. All of them were armed with clubs and sharpened weapons that they hoped could help them bring Radnor down. Leif tried his best to sound as though he was in control, but his words came out shaky and hoarse.

"Radnor, I hereby place you under arrest for the murder of one of my people. You will come with us now and await your sentencing for your crime."

Radnor looked about him and saw more than twenty men armed with knives and makeshift clubs in the room with him. He quickly considered his options for escape. He could not allow himself to be captured, but he was without his weapons.

Radnor ran forward and smashed his first foe to the ground. As he ran over the man, a stout blow came at his head. Radnor ducked from the knees and let the swing go by. But, in his moment's pause to evade the blow, Leif got behind him and struck him with a thick club. Radnor heard what sounded like a woman's scream, maybe Elena's, and he went down.

Chapter 4

Radnor swam in a dream world, his mind poring over the night's terrible events. There were times he thought he might awaken, but it was not to be. Instead, he was haunted by hazy dreams and nightmares. A beautiful woman at first, but then covered in bruises and beaten so sorely she was unrecognizable. There was a brightly lit party, then death. A man talking to Halmda…it was Bron. At the thought of Bron, the man's distant, staring eyes came screaming back to Radnor's mind. He wished for them to go away, to leave him in peace! Instead, many, many more pairs of equally vacant eyes burned into his soul. Faces started to come into his mind. Some he knew instantly, others he didn't know he remembered. How long had it been since he killed that one? Or this other one? Radnor did not know anymore. He did not know how long he had been running, running from…

Radnor awoke with a start to the impact of something hitting him in the face. Unsure of where he was, he clawed at the object, and soon realized it was dirt. He was lying on his back, and once he brushed the dirt aside, Radnor saw that he was in a shallow grave. Above him stood a man frozen in fear; a man who had just realized that Radnor was awake.

"Alban, why the ever loving fuck did you stop digging? The quicker we put that bastard in the ground, the better!"

Radnor did not recognize the voice, so it didn't belong to Leif, or Halmda. Radnor was unsure what threat lay above him, but whoever it was, he would not sit idly by and let himself be buried!

With catlike speed and agility, Radnor leapt up to his feet and snatched the shovel away from Alban before the poor man could react. Stunned, Alban fell backwards in fear. As soon as Radnor saw the man wasn't a threat, he turned his attention to the direction from which the other voice had come. No time to get out of the hole! Radnor turned, and he was barely able to duck a blow aimed for his head by another man with a shovel. The sharpened blade of his foe's shovel came around again…but this time Radnor had a chance to use the haft of his shovel to turn the other's blow aside. The man stumbled from the force of the deflection. With Radnor's foe knocked off balance, it was easy for him to grab him by the ankle and pull him to the ground. Radnor then aimed a fierce blow of his own at the man's chest. The shovel made a resounding gong which was quickly drowned out by a yell of agony as the flat of it drove into the man's stomach. Radnor cursed his luck. He had meant to cut his foe in half with the sharp edge.

With his enemy defeated, Radnor took the opportunity to scramble out of the shallow grave before Alban could get his wits again. Radnor hurried to the man he had downed, and kicked the other shovel away from his struggling grip. Alban finally recovered his wits enough to draw his knife, shouting for his friend.

"Klane!" he yelled. "Klane, I'm coming!"

Radnor responded to the shouting by pulling Klane's knife from its sheath and holding the blade to Klane's throat.

"One more step, and he dies!" Radnor yelled. Alban stopped in his tracks, unsure what to do. "Drop the knife!" Radnor commanded of the terrified farmer.

"How do I know you won't just kill us both!" Alban yelled back.

"I'm not promising you shit until you drop the fucking knife!" Radnor yelled back. "You people have tried to kill me three times now! In my mind, the fact your head is still attached to your shoulders is quite a gift. So if you don't want me to change my mind, drop…the…fucking… knife!"

Alban finally did as Radnor commanded, and backed away from his blade.

"Please lord, let him go," Alban pleaded.

Radnor released Klane from his grasp, but stood over him, ready to kill him at a moment's notice.

"All right," Radnor said. "Why were you trying to bury me?"

"We thought you would never wake up," Alban said. "It was decided that we would bury Bron first. There's a berry, Aleas, that if mixed with other herbs and water, will make someone stay asleep. Some wanted to kill you, but Leif was worried about incurring the wrath of the friends you said you were going to meet. So, we kept you asleep until it was decided your friends weren't coming. You were to stand trial for the murder when you awoke, but someone gave you too much of the potion, and we thought you dead. It was decided that if you didn't wake up before we had buried Bron, you would be buried in a shallow grave, and your possessions given to the Temple of Caelum as payment for giving Bron his burial prayers...and for overlooking yours."

Radnor felt his anger begin to rise again, threatening to boil over. But his rage was tempered by a horrible thought. Panicked, Radnor asked another question.

"Wait, how long have I been unconscious?" Alban began to stammer, fearful of Radnor's change in demeanor. "Out with it you fool, answer quickly!" Radnor yelled.

Without warning, a bolt of lightning crashed across the sky and into the heart of the village beyond the tree line. Thunder shook the earth beneath their feet, and Radnor turned pale.

"Six...days," Alban stuttered out. "Today...marks the...seventh day."

Radnor turned to face the village, his face full of despair and sorrow. Darkness overtook the sky, and the sun now illuminated the countryside with an eerie light unlike anything Alban had ever seen before. He watched with fear and curiosity as Radnor's face changed from sadness to that of grim resolve.

Radnor spun back to face the Alban again, startling the poor young man.

"You, Alban, carry Klane back to the village! If we hurry, we may still save some of your people!"

Alban stood dumbstruck for a moment, unsure of what had just happened.

"Do it man, I need to keep my hands free for fighting. If we are to have any chance of escape, we must take the people now, and flee!" Radnor scooped Klane up into his arms, and draped him over Alban's shoulder as easily and gently as if he was draping a shawl around a woman's neck.

"Come on!" Radnor yelled as he dove headlong into the trees. Alban did the only thing he could think of, and followed the madman back to the village.

Twice Radnor had to backtrack and help Alban carry Klane. It had been so long since Radnor had worked alongside normal people, he had forgotten how to take their lesser strength into account. Alban was a small, skinny young man who clearly had yet to see a battle. It was a pity, since Radnor would not wish anyone's first fight to be the one that lay before them. Hot rain began pouring down from the sky, and Radnor knew the time was close. He needed to move fast if they were going to make it back to the walls in time. As the two got within sight of the walls, Radnor swore to himself. They were on the wrong side of the village, and would have to take the time to walk around to the other side to get to the gate. Just as Radnor was about to offer to take Klane's weight to finish the last sprint, the worst happened. A howling shriek pierced the air for miles with its terrible cry, and a wave of energy knocked even Radnor from his feet. When he stood again, the walls had been blown to splinters. Radnor helped Alban regain his feet, and spoke for the first time since they had begun their mad dash.

"Stay here with Klane, and stay out of sight! I will come back for you as soon as I can!" he said.

Before Alban could reply, Radnor tore off into the village, leaping over broken fragments of the wall and into the shadows of the buildings. Alban did what he was told, Radnor's urgency convincing him to follow orders.

Radnor darted from building to building along the street, keeping a close eye out for the monsters he knew would be lurking somewhere nearby. It did not take him long to find them. Already, houses were starting to burn as distantly seen horrors danced wickedly among the flames. People scrambled out of their homes, looking to escape the fire and smoke. Instead of safety, they met only the teeth and claws of Adramelach's demon servants.

Through the billowing smoke Radnor saw the shapes of men headed towards the houses. Radnor recognized Leif leading his warriors in a shield wall that advanced bravely towards the monsters that slaughtered their kin. Radnor looked at the shovel in his hand, and knew what he had to do. It did not matter that his only armor was the dirt stained clothes he had worn at the party, and that his only weapon was a shovel. These people needed to be protected from what he had brought here. He could not save them all, but he would certainly try.

Radnor moved forward through the smoke filled street as silently as possible. The demons had massed in response to Leif's shield wall, and would begin a slaughter if Radnor did not get behind them in time. Their backs were to him, and he had the element of surprise. Just as Radnor was coming upon the demon line, he saw that the struggle had already begun. Leif's men fought bravely to protect their wives and children, but the demons were simply too much for the lightly armed men. Their monstrous claws tore through wooden shields in a single blow, and their mouths were so broad they could bite a man's head clean off.

Four men had already fallen by the time Radnor picked his first target. There stood before him a monster of great stature. It looked almost like a reptile with its sickly yellow scales; but its mouth was more akin to that of a lamprey. Its hands were long and spindly with fingers that looked to be nothing but razor sharp claws. It turned just in time to focus its black, empty eyes on him. With a yell, Radnor drove the sharpened edge of his shovel into the demon's face, and blood poured forth from the wound. Other demons turned to face Radnor, but he paid them little heed. He struck the same demon again and again, until its head was in too many pieces to count.

A deadly claw drove towards Radnor's head, but he was able to turn it aside with the steel blade of the shovel. Another monster lunged for Radnor's chest, its fangs seeking his flesh. Radnor jammed the haft of the shovel in its mouth, and held it back for a moment. The monster stood back up to its full height, taking the shovel with it. With a quick tightening of its jaw, the monster snapped the shovel in half. Radnor was too enraged to care that his weapon was shattered, and he hurled himself upon the reptilian beast.

The demon did not expect such aggression. It was struck with the full force of Radnor's assault, and toppled to the ground with him on top of it. Radnor drove his fists into the monster's skull, again and again. Once he was sure it was dead, he stood to face the rest of them. The remaining demons faced him, and hesitated. Radnor started toward his next foe, his only intent to kill every monster that stood before him. Leif saw his opportunity, and drove the blade of his sword into the neck of one of the demons while its back was turned. The creature fell, choking on its own blood.

Following Leif's example, the other men of the village leaped forward. Taking advantage of the demon's confusion at Radnor's assault, the men began to wound and slay them. In spite of Radnor's distraction, it was not a one sided fight, for it took three men to bring down a single demon. By the time the bloody struggle ended, ten demons lay dead, and over twenty men had been killed in the brawl.

His blood lust sated for the moment, Radnor stood up to see the survivors staring blankly at him. One man stared in disbelief at the corpse of the demon Radnor had beaten to death. Leif was now facing Radnor, the point of his sword aimed for Radnor's heart.

"You are a murderer. What you have done here does not change that."

Radnor scoffed at the man who was so overtaken with a desire for revenge he was blind to what was happening around him.

"Do you not know what is happening?" Radnor spat at him. "A portal to Narakim has opened. These demons we killed here were just scouts. If your people are to survive this, you must gather them all, arm every warrior, and flee from this place."

Leif gestured to the men still standing with him.

"These men are all that are left. The rest either died in the fight or died when their houses were set ablaze. I assume you killed Klane and Alban?"

Radnor shook his head.

"Klane is wounded, but Alban is unharmed. They wait for us outside the village. Quickly, there is no time for talk, we must gather the survivors!"

Leif and his men ran to the houses not yet burning, and began gathering their terrified occupants. All were given orders from Leif to get to the temple, and two men were sent to begin boarding up the windows and all but one door in case there was a siege. Radnor followed them, and through the doorway, he saw the torn and bloody remains of the priest of Caelum. Once through the door of the temple, Radnor found himself inside a large hall with many seats for those wishing to worship the god of light. It had been a long time since Radnor had set foot in such a place. He did not like it. As the two other men went to work, Radnor headed to the back of the hall where he found the priest's personal quarters. Inside was everything Radnor hoped to find. His weapons, his armor, his ring, and the rest of his possessions were neatly stashed in that room. Within moments Radnor was fully armed and armored, and ready for the brutal fight to come.

Wincing as he threw his saddlebags over his shoulders, Radnor stepped out of the back room to find the scene in the temple was very different. There were close to fifty people huddled in the center of the room. They were praying to Caelum, not knowing their god was long dead.

Leif's surviving warriors were hard at work barricading the windows and doors to the temple. There appeared to be about a dozen of them remaining. Radnor was searching the crowd for Elena and Halmda, but could not find either one. His blood ran cold at the thought of her body lying in the pouring rain outside. Radnor's thoughts were interrupted by Leif, who glared fiercely at him.

"I see now that my suspicions were correct!" Leif shouted as he stepped towards Radnor in rage. "If you were not who you are, I would have my men kill you where you stand…Veigarand!"

Leif spat the name with venomous malice. Radnor stared into Leif's eyes with his icy gaze, his hand ready to draw his sword if required.

"Then why don't you, lord ealdorman?" Radnor replied. There was a brief pause before he continued.

"Kill me! Leave my body for the demons to feast upon! I'm sure they would appreciate your gift most fully!"

Leif took a step back, and gestured to the men around him.

"Because if the stories and songs are even half true, my men and I would be nothing but more victims in another tale of woe."

"If it makes you feel any better…" Radnor started. "I would take no pleasure in killing you. You would be yet more screaming faces that haunt my dreams."

Leif belted a sardonic laugh.

"Something makes me doubt that. But right now, I have no choice but to work with you. I have had my men secure the temple as you ordered. Now, what is your plan of escape?"

Radnor eased his sword hand slightly. It seemed that for the moment, these people were not a threat.

"Where is my horse?" Radnor asked.

"We left him at the stables by the inn. There was nowhere else to put him, and he was given to Bron's family as restitution."

Radnor nodded his acknowledgment, and spoke again.

"You and your men must stay here and protect the survivors. I will head to the stables and gather as many horses as possible. I will bring them back to you, and we will all ride out of here together."

Radnor waited for Leif's reply, but none came for a long time. Finally, Leif looked up from his thoughts and agreed to the plan, reluctantly citing Radnor's clear expertise on these demons. Radnor started to leave, but turned to Leif to ask a question.

"Are the survivors here all that are left? Is there any chance there will be more?"

Leif sighed sadly.

"I don't know. Everything has happened so fast, I'm not sure of anything right now," he answered.

Radnor turned and raced back out into the pouring rain. He ran at a breakneck pace and found the stables, suppressing pain as the saddlebags bounced against his wounded shoulder. As Radnor approached the stables, a demon materialized from the air before him and struck at him with its deadly claws. Radnor turned the blow aside with his shield, its steel proving strong enough to survive a blow from the beast undamaged. Radnor shoved back against the beast, and sent it stumbling away. The monster's empty, black eyes focused on Radnor, and it bared its needle like teeth at him. The howl that the scaly monster let out rattled the windows in the buildings around them. It stepped towards him, claws drawn. Radnor threw his spear at the demon with immense strength and drew his sword in one motion. The demon swatted his spear out of the air as though it were a common stick thrown by a boy. With its other claw it attempted to tear through Radnor's helmet and into his face. Radnor dropped beneath the raking claw, and severed the monster's leg at the calf. The demon fell to the ground howling in agony, and Radnor silenced it by severing its head from its body.

Retrieving his spear as he moved inside the stables, Radnor discovered two more of the same monsters crouched feasting on the flesh of a white mare. Before the first one could stand, Radnor stabbed it in the back with his spear, passing through its body and out its chest; splashing its blood onto the mare's coat. Its partner stood and swung at Radnor. He blocked with the sharpened edge of his shield, and let the demon cut its hand in two upon its edge. The monster screamed in agony and clutched at its mangled hand. Radnor then withdrew his spear from the body of the first one, and thrust through the head of the remaining demon. Darestr stood calmly, waiting for him at the back of the stable.

Radnor called to him, and Darestr joined his master.

"We cannot leave this place yet, Darestr," Radnor whispered as he fastened the saddle bags to his loyal horse.

"There is good here--we must save it, and I must ask a favor of you."

Darestr snorted gently, indicating he was listening to his master's commands.

"I need you to lead the other horses here to the building I'm pointing at. I must search for someone right now. People there will take these horses, and ride away from this place. I will meet you at the building, hopefully with a friend."

Radnor patted Darestr on the shoulder, and took off for the houses. He needed to find Elena, even if all he found was her corpse. Radnor darted from building to building, and found that more and more demons were materializing from the invisible gateway that had formed here. Many were the same as the ones he had seen before, scouts and trackers; but a few were warriors, armored not only with scales, but with the bones of their brethren that they had killed. In place of hands they had weapons -- bony claws, spikes, or other blades -- integrated directly into their limbs. Their wrists were articulated with multiple joints so they could use these weapons with the same dexterity as a human, but with little chance of being disarmed.

Radnor watched as they stalked from house to house, smashing down doors and hunting for meat. At one house in particular, Radnor watched as a demon summoned a ball of fire into its bony hand, and hurled it through the doorway. A scream told Radnor the fire had struck its mark. Radnor charged the beast from behind, his spear set for a deadly thrust.

As the demon turned to face its new attacker, Radnor drove his spear point deep into its armored chest, cracking bone and tearing flesh aside. The beast toppled over onto its back, writhing in pain. Before it could stand back up, Radnor withdrew the blade, and stabbed it in the neck. Radnor made sure it was dead by twisting the blade of his spear, tearing the demon's head from its body. Without wasting time, Radnor stormed into the house to look for survivors. He almost tripped over the charred corpse of a man with a short ax near the door. Radnor's thoughts turned for a moment to honor the man for trying to fight.

"Hello!" Radnor shouted. "Is there anyone here?"

"I'm over here!" came a boy's voice.

36

"Come to me, it's safe now!" Radnor yelled through the burning house.

Rolf burst out of the bedroom, but stopped short when he saw Radnor's armored form.

"I'm not going to hurt you boy, I'm going to take you out of here. Where are your parents?"

Rolf gulped in a breath of air before answering.

"My father is in Wollendan, and my mother lies in the earth next to her mother."

There was another pause.

"Where are you going to take me?" Rolf asked.

"To the temple, from there we will flee this place."

"Is Elena there? I won't leave without her!" Rolf said.

"No, she isn't," Radnor replied. "Do you know where she might be?"

"She might be at her house, taking care of Halmda, but that is just a guess," Rolf said.

Radnor asked Rolf where her home was, and Rolf was surprisingly cogent in his explanation despite the horror which unfolded before them.

Carrying Rolf under his arm, Radnor went tearing through the streets in search of Elena's home. It seemed the demons had almost finished their murdering among the houses, and were stalking in the direction of the outlying woods, looking for survivors. Radnor felt some guilt for his feelings of relief. This development meant that he met no resistance on his way to Elena's house. When Radnor finally arrived, he found Halmda's head torn from his body, resting in the muddy road a short distance from their destination. There was no sign of the rest of him. Radnor had to suppress the urge to smile, as he felt that the bastard had met a fitting end.

After finding a hiding spot for Rolf among the wreckage of an overturned carriage on the street, Radnor came to the door of the house which rested on the edge of the town, and smashed it down. He had to duck when he entered the house as a candlestick went rushing past his head. Radnor turned to face Elena as she wound up for another swing. Radnor knocked the makeshift weapon from her hand, and spoke to her like he was a prince giving an order to one of his subjects.

"Come with me, we're leaving."

"Like hell we are!" Elena replied, not caring what he had to say. "There's no way in hell I'm coming with you after what you did!"

"I thought you would feel that way, but the boy said he wouldn't leave without you!" Radnor snarled back at her.

"What boy? Do you mean Rolf?" she asked.

Radnor nodded. He wasn't sure if he was right, but he hoped that agreeing would get her to leave with him.

"Then let's go!" she shouted.

Elena went rushing out the door before Radnor could have a chance to check if any demons had come to investigate the shouting. Thankfully, none had yet found them. At the sight of Elena, Rolf broke from his hiding place and ran to Elena's embrace. Suddenly, a bony spike smashed against the ground at Rolf's feet, fired from an unseen monster. Radnor stepped to place himself between the direction of the shot and Rolf. A second spike pinged off of Radnor's shield, forcing him to duck behind the weapon.

"Run for the temple!" he yelled.

Radnor did not have time to check if they were all right, as the demon had honed in on him as the target and did not lighten up its assault. Spike after spike pinged off of Radnor's shield, keeping him blind as he held it up to protect himself. Radnor ran for the cover of the nearest building on the temple side of the street, and eventually was able to check his surroundings. Demons gathered in the street, and Radnor saw that Elena and Rolf made it through the temple door just in time to escape a demon that had begun chasing them. The horrific monster slammed against the iron bound door, clawing and scratching. Thankfully, the heavy oaken door did not budge. To Radnor's relief, a spear came stabbing out from a nearby window, and gouged the creature's eye out. The monster writhed in the mud in agony, and was soon dragged away from the door by two other demons. Within seconds, a host of a dozen monsters began tearing at the front window and wall of the building, smashing and cutting the building apart piece by piece.

Radnor decided to take a chance, and he made a break around the back side the building he was using for cover, and then ran for the back window of the temple, trying to keep a building between him and the demons for as long as possible. Once at the back of the temple, he spotted Darestr and the other horses waiting at a safe distance. Radnor breathed a sigh of relief; Darestr was a wise horse indeed.

An inhuman snarl broke Radnor's thoughts as he spun to face the new threat. One of the demonic warriors had spotted him and drove its bony mace-head hand at him with all its might. Radnor barely placed the shield in the way but was lifted off of his feet and launched through the back window of the building. Screams were heard over the crash of shattering glass as Radnor toppled inside, followed closely by the angry demon. Radnor quickly threw himself to his feet and drew his sword. The monster swung at him again, and Radnor sidestepped the downward blow of the demon's weapon.

38

A bony blade suddenly appeared in the demon's other hand, and stabbed upward towards Radnor's throat! This blow was stopped by a counter cut from Radnor's sword as he reversed the direction of his step, carrying himself past the demon's shoulder. Radnor lashed out with his shield, striking it in the face with the edge. The warrior's bony armor cracked and broke against the force of the blow, but the demon underneath remained unharmed. Stunned for the moment, the demon tried to recover its balance, but Radnor did not give it the chance. A well-aimed blow from his sword caught the demon in the unarmored neck, neatly severing its head from its body.

Several of Leif's men came to help Radnor, only to discover the fight was over. Radnor turned to face Leif, whom was shouting angrily and stabbing his spear through an opening in another boarded up window. Radnor shouted for him.

"Leif, it's time to go! The horses are ready!"

Leif did not notice Radnor's words as he desperately stabbed the monsters outside. Radnor ran towards him and pulled him away from the window. Finally understanding, Leif began to lead his people out of the back window. Radnor took a quick glance to make sure Rolf and Elena were among them, and took up a position to block the door to the temple.

"Leif!" Radnor shouted. "I will hold them off here, but someone needs to get Alban and Klane! They are hiding in the woods just south of where the walls stood!"

"I will get them, Veigarand, do not worry!" Leif replied.

Radnor felt a touch on his shoulder, and turned to see Elena standing there.

"Aren't you coming with us?" she asked.

"Elena, you and the boy ride on Darestr, my horse. He is the swiftest and most cunning horse I know of. He will guide you safely out of here. I will be right behind you."

"How will I know which horse he is?" Elena asked.

Radnor hesitated for a moment, and slipped his ring off his finger. With a tense look, he then handed Elena the ring.

"Put this on. It will allow him to understand you. Call his name and tell him I'm asking him to take care of you two."

"Which name shall I use for you? Radnor...or Veigarand?" Elena asked.

"He knows both," Radnor said.

Elena slipped the ring onto her finger. She was about to thank him when a loud crash interrupted her thoughts. The wall of the building started to crack and break, the demons were finally starting to force their way inside.

Radnor drew his sword, and stared down at the demon that started to crawl its way through the new hole in the wall. Elena ran to join the others, and the fight began anew. As vicious as the demons were, they were wholly unintelligent without a leader to guide them. None of the leaders had yet joined this stage of the invasion, so at first Radnor was simply able to kill them as they tried to squeeze through the same small hole. Easily half a dozen of them were killed by violent thrusts from his spear.

There was a pause in the assault. Radnor had a moment to grab one of the candles lighting the room and began to set the tapestries in the sanctuary ablaze. He intended to retreat through the back window using the smoke and fire for cover, but his plan was interrupted when a massive demon managed to break down the reinforced door to the temple. The creature stood easily a foot taller than Radnor, and was the most manlike of the demons that had so far appeared. It was covered in armor made from the bones of other demons it had killed. The beast carried an ax in one hand, and a shield in the other.

Radnor swiftly engaged in his bloody profession. He immediately stepped towards the monster and positioned himself so that it had to respond to the threat his movement posed. Predictably, for a demon, the monster swung its ax at his head. Radnor ducked the fearsome blow, and reversed direction to step under the monster's arm. Throwing a tight, close range blow, Radnor drove his blade into the monster's armor; but the bones were thick and the sword merely cut a groove in them. Radnor followed up his sword blow with a strike from his shield to the same spot. Cracks streaked across the demon's armor, but it still did not break. The demon turned to face Radnor again, and brought its shield to bear, striking at Radnor's sword shoulder. Radnor twisted away from the blow, but the shield still grazed his arm. Ordinarily, the pain would not have slowed Radnor down at all, but with the open wound on his shoulder, the pain was so severe Radnor dropped his sword.

Confidence filled the demon's heart, and it swung another heavy blow down at the annoying human. Radnor was able to turn his center grip shield in his hand, and keep the face of it between him and the demon's ax. The blow slid along the face of the shield and away from Radnor's body. Radnor backed away from the demon, and waited for a follow up blow. None came. Radnor peered out from behind the shield to find the monster was waiting for him to come back for his sword, which it now guarded. Radnor saw more demons start to come through the door, but the big one waved them back. It wanted this kill for itself. Radnor saw only one weapon he could get to, as his spear lay on the floor at the other end of the hall. Radnor stepped towards the demon, but did not make a move towards his sword. The overconfident monster swung a blow straight down at Radnor, intending to split him from head to groin.

Radnor timed the blow perfectly. He simultaneously stepped aside and deflected the blow with his shield. Off balance, the demon took a split second too long to realize what was happening. Radnor smashed his shield into the exposed elbow joint of the demon's arm. The monster howled in pain, and its grip on the ax loosened enough for Radnor to pry the weapon from its hands. He rolled the ax into an arcing slash and drove it into the beast's exposed elbow, slicing the arm to the bone. The demon let out an agonized howl and frantically swiped at Radnor with its shield. Radnor stepped around the incoming shield, and found himself behind the demon. Radnor drove the ax blade as hard as he could into the unarmored back of its leg, and the beast crumpled in a heap on the floor. Dropping the ax, Radnor scooped his sword back up, and finished the crippled monster with a thrust through its eye while it still lay on the ground.

Not waiting for the other demons to attack, Radnor ran through the burning building, smoke stinging his eyes. As he approached the back window, he sheathed his sword and snatched up his spear. Leaping through the window, Radnor found himself face to face with another scout demon. Radnor kicked it in its lamprey mouth as he landed, sending it stumbling backwards. A quick thrust to the face finished the monster off. Radnor then spied another monster headed away from him, presumably chasing the fleeing people. He hurled his spear with all his might, and watched as it stuck in the back of the demon. The monster fell to the ground in pain, and struggled to get back to its feet. Radnor stopped and twisted the spear as he tore it from the creature's back. As the warrior continued past the beast, he was careful to stomp on the monster's head to trample it into the mud. Radnor then spied what at first he thought was a stray horse, until he realized Darestr had somehow convinced it to wait for him. The horse was agreeable to being ridden, and Radnor rode on, away from the burning village, and away from the new hell that his presence had created...just like before.

Chapter 5

It was several hours before Radnor finally caught up with Darestr. Body aching from the fierce battle, Radnor came upon a clearing in the woods next to a river and found the people he had saved. The survivors from the village were gathered around several freshly dug fire pits. Radnor examined the crowd, and was pleased that as many people made it out as did, given the circumstances. There were probably close to fifty survivors, plus ten of the fighting men Leif still had at his disposal.

Leif and his men were gathering wood to keep the fires burning, and Alban knelt beside a now conscious Klane. Klane sat upright, leaned against the rotting stump of a fallen tree. Alban held a cup to Klane's lips, and Klane tried to sip from it, wincing as he did.

Radnor dismounted from his horse and walked it into the clearing. Several people screamed in terror as he came out of the brush, and several of Leif's men stood with axes at the ready. Radnor stopped in his tracks, but chose not to draw his sword. Leif soon stood before him, sword drawn, and malice shined in his eyes. Despite the outward aggression from Leif, Radnor saw that the ealdorman was truly exhausted. Leif's weight sagged in his armor, his eyes drooped, and his step was slightly unbalanced. The ealdorman's armor was soaked in a mix of the blood of the demons, and the blood of his comrades whom now lay dead miles away.

"I mean you no harm, lord ealdorman," Radnor said.

Before he could continue, Leif began shouting at him.

"You mean us no harm? How much harm was meant for us when you brought those monsters to our home? Is this what you do Veigarand? The stories said you bring death wherever you go, but none ever intimated that you brought friends with you as well!"

Radnor felt his hand go to his sword hilt at the mention of the demons being his "friends". He caught himself before escalating the situation, and dropped his hand back to his sides.

"My lord ealdorman, I am deeply sorry for what has happened today. Yours is not the first home the demons have destroyed. It is my aim to make it the last," Radnor said.

Leif turned to face his people, who were still standing ready to attack on his order.

"Do you hear what he calls me?" Leif shouted. "He calls me 'ealdorman'! I must ask you, ealdorman of what? My home is burned to the ground, more than half of the people I was responsible for are dead!"

"Kill him Leif!" called Klane's gasping voice. "Kill him, and avenge our people!"

At this urging, Leif started towards Radnor, sword raised high. Radnor drew his sword to defend himself just in time to parry Leif's blow. As he did, Radnor took hold of Leif's sword arm and tossed the man onto the ground. While Leif groaned in pain, Radnor stooped low and picked up Leif's sword. The rest of Leif's men started forward, but Radnor held the ealdorman down at sword point. Seeing their lord's life threatened, the villagers held back.

"I know it is difficult now!" Radnor said, looking down at Leif. "But you must not think of those who have died, but instead think of the living. You have people you are still responsible for. How will you fulfill your duty by making me kill you? Think man! You still have a lord to return to. Tell him what has transpired! Have him send men to hunt me to the end of the Earth if you desire it! But, for the sake of all you believe in, do not give up!"

Radnor sheathed his sword and lifted Leif to his feet.

"Do you have your oath ring?" Radnor asked.

Leif instinctively felt around his person, until coming to the realization that his oath ring, the tool of the power his position held, was still resting among the ashes of his home.

"By Caelum, in my hurry to save my people, I have forgotten the one thing that makes me lord of these people. But it does not matter...I don't think a white oath would hold you to your word. I'm sure the oath breaker's mark would blend in with the other scars which must already pit your body."

Radnor knew what he had to do. He knew in his heart that in a way, he was responsible for what happened. He knew what his curse was, and he came to the town anyway. He had gambled with the lives of everyone there, and they had lost. Radnor dropped to one knee before Leif.

"I would have offered a black oath," Radnor said.

Leif found himself astonished. It was forbidden by the laws of Caelum for men to swear such oaths. To break a black oath meant a fiery, torturous death that even the god of light felt was too cruel a punishment. Radnor continued.

"But for now, you must take only my word. I swear to protect your people with my sword and my life. If further harm should seek your people, I will be sure to hurl myself in its path."

With those words, Radnor offered Leif his sword back. Leif hesitated, took a few deep breaths, and finally accepted the blade. Leif then gave the order for his men to stand down, and they allowed Radnor to move past them and towards Darestr.

Darestr had chosen a spot near where the river bulged out into something resembling a small pond to set down his riders. Darestr stood watch over them, as he knew that neither Rolf nor Elena could move quickly enough to escape from an attack without help. Radnor's new horse was exhausted, so he unsaddled it and walked it to where Elena and Rolf sat.

All was quiet. Even the birds did not chirp, though whether that was from the sorrow of the moment or because of Radnor's presence was unknown. Radnor approached the trio quietly, and Elena looked up at him with tears in her eyes. She looked down at Rolf, who had cried himself to sleep with his face buried deep in her shoulder. Radnor looked at them with a mournful gaze, and sat down. After what seemed like an eternity, Elena spoke first.

"I heard the commotion. Did you kill my ealdorman?"

Radnor took his helmet off, shaking his hair loose as he did. It was calming to feel the cool evening air glide across his face once more. After a moment, he answered the question.

"No. I was able to make him see reason, for now at least."

Radnor then turned to face her more directly.

"Have you been told of Halmda's fate?"

Elena nodded, thinking on the fates of all those people still in Wulfgeld. It felt wrong to her that she felt no particular sorrow for her fiance's death, but at the same time felt justified in her malice towards the dead man. She thought back to their party. She had wanted him hurt the way he had hurt her. She had wanted to embarrass him, but death was not what she intended. The more she thought about it, the greater her own feelings of guilt became when she realized she had pushed the situation the way she did.

Elena sighed, shut her eyes, and let out a slow cry. Radnor wished to comfort her, but he restrained himself, feeling it was not his place. After a few moments Elena stopped and recomposed herself.

Radnor took note of the boy in her arms.

"Is he your son?"

Elena glared up at him.

"No! With his mother...gone, and his father often away trading with Wollendan and Ranrike, I became a big sister to him."

Elena's words made Radnor think longingly of his brothers, Ulfr and Kjeltil. He started to say something, but saw that Rolf was awakening. Rolf turned his head, and began to cry. These were not the controlled tears that Elena had shed; these were the sobs of a boy who had lost almost all those he loved. Radnor looked from Rolf to Elena, and stood up.

"Tend to his tears. They won't be his last," Radnor said.

Radnor turned away to go to Darestr, but Elena stopped him.

"Here," she said, holding his ring out to him.

Radnor took it, slipped it on his finger, and continued wordlessly on his way. He retrieved his short bow and the few arrows that were tied to Darestr's saddle.

"And what about you? What are you going to do?" Elena asked.

Radnor turned slightly, and responded.

"My tears were shed long ago, and I have no time for more. We need food, if I am to get that before dark, I need to start immediately."

He ran off into the woods, bow in hand.

Elena sat there by the pond, and stared as Radnor vanished into the forest. His movements were graceful, even when wearing full armor. And his horse…there was never a horse so mindful and loving of its master as his horse. It followed his commands without question. How could a man who commanded such love from his horse be the cause of such destruction? How could he have let this happen? Elena wrestled with anger, sorrow, and confusion in her own feelings. Rolf let out another stream of tears, and Elena's thought process was broken. She stroked Rolf's hair, and stared out over the shimmering water.

Radnor walked for over an hour before he found the tracks of a deer. He followed them to an open clearing in which he saw a whole herd moving about. He hid and waited for the herd to become complacent. As he waited, Radnor became lost in thought. He found himself in a bind. These people needed protection, at least until he was sure they were clear of any demons that might try to follow. But to them he was Veigarand, a hated monster from legend, and any one of the villagers would gladly slit his throat in his sleep given the chance.

Well, best not to sleep, then. He thought.

Then there was the question of Elena. He pondered whether or not she would be among those eager to kill him. Despite that possibility, Radnor felt she was somehow different. He felt a strong need to protect Elena, that much he knew, but Radnor also found himself perplexed about *why* he felt such a strong need to protect her. He understood that his general desire to protect the others grew from his sense of guilt over their tragedy. But his protectiveness of Elena began the moment he laid eyes on her. Because he didn't know where this desire came from, nor why it was so overpowering, it left him feeling powerless and uncontrolled...and this terrified him.

There were other problems to consider as well. Her being in his presence was dangerous enough as it was, let alone traveling with him. Monsters had a habit of finding him, and there was another problem Radnor faced: these people would slow him down. The task of protecting them was yet another obstacle on his path to revenge. For almost a decade, killing the demon god Adramelach had been all he lived for, and he resolved to himself that this would not change. However, Radnor could not leave these people here. He owed them everything now, no matter the cost to himself. He would just have to watch his back, and hope no more trouble found them until they reached wherever Leif had decided to lead them.

After a while the deer herd began to move. None of them stayed except a fawn. It stumbled forward on its thin legs, and tried to catch up. A doe came back to help it, but was having no luck. Radnor came out of the trees slightly, and drew back the stiff bowstring. As he prepared to loose the arrow, he recited an ancient saying from his homeland.

"Compassion is the weakness of the strong, but it is the strength of the weak."

With that, he let the arrow fly.

The sun was setting; its golden rays had turned to a crimson fire that scattered across the sky. The lush, green leaves of the trees had taken on a slight orange hue, and the river reflected these rays out onto the horses and onto the fair face of Elena. She sat before a fire and prepared a meal of freshly caught fish while she waited for Radnor's return. Just as she was starting to heat the fish in a pan she had found in Radnor's saddle bags, Elena finally saw Radnor's hulking frame enter the firelight. To her amazement, she saw that he not only carried a doe, but there were also three other deer slung across his back. Elena felt the urge to help him, but wasn't sure if she would get in his way or not. After a moment's thought, she chose to leave him alone, and waited for Radnor to finish his approach.

Elena also felt confused at herself for wanting to help him. This man killed Bron, whom she had known all her life, and brought a horde of demons that burned her home and killed even more of her friends. If anything, she felt that she should be plotting to kill Radnor. But...she could not bring herself to think that way.

Lost in her thoughts, Elena did not see that Leif had also spotted Radnor's approach, and had moved to the shadows closer to her so he could keep an eye on Radnor.

Radnor checked the outline of the trees and made sure that Darestr was still in sight. There were several small fires burning now, with groups of people huddled around each. As he approached, Radnor saw Elena sitting by the fire with his skillet in her hand. Rolf was sitting by it, staring at the hot pan with a mix of anticipation and sadness. As Radnor drew closer, he recognized the smell of cooking food. Elena looked up at him for a moment, then quickly drove her eyes back to the skillet.

"There are fish in the river," She remarked.

Radnor smiled a little to himself. Perhaps these people would be less of a hindrance than he thought. He glided along in the grass, and gently placed the deer on the ground next to the fire. He would bring the deer to Leif…later. Radnor looked at the sad pair, and then at the sun.

"Rolf…" Radnor started, struck by the sorrow on the boy's face. "Can you help me cut the meat from this fawn, and start smoking it? The fish we can eat tonight, but I would like to preserve the deer meat for our journey."

Rolf looked up at him, his mouth still drawn tight from his grief and pain, but he did as Radnor asked.

Elena glared up at him from her seat by the fire, then finally spoke to him.

"What journey are you referring to? Where are you taking us?" she demanded.

Radnor looked up from his work impatiently.

"It is obvious we cannot stay here. I am assuming Leif has a place he will want to take you. I would urge him to take you past Drakomar, as far away from here as possible."

"The Southworld," said Elena. "Why would we want to go there?"

Radnor looked up again from his work.

"Because of the presence of seven fortresses like the one at Drakomar that hold possession of all of the passes through the mountains. Once the demons finally make their move and destroy the rest of the Northworld, those fortresses will make it much harder for them to break into the South."

"Are you so unaware of the world that you do not know that my people have been at war with Drakomar for nearly a decade?" Elena asked. While she felt somewhat conflicted about Radnor, her anger could no longer be restrained.

"For that matter, what gives you the right to tell us where we must go? You…you monster! Leif knows what is best for us! He will lead us where we need to go! You came to our village and brought with you murder and a plague of monsters! It is because of you that our homes are burned, our families gone, and the only reason we have to trust you is that—"

"I'm all you've got," Radnor sternly interrupted. "Do you really think that these people can survive what is to come? You might last three days. You have no idea what you are up against! Those monsters will not stop. They hunger for murder and slaughter in a way that no man ever could. If they find you they will cut you down like they did those who weren't so lucky to escape. They were created for one thing…war."

Radnor stopped there, a thought striking him mid speech:

Just like me.

Elena looked ready to throw the skillet at Radnor, but she restrained herself and only glared.

"Fine," She snarled. "But you still haven't answered my first question yet."

"The answer to that is simple. It doesn't need to be Drakomar, but I don't want to take you anywhere but the Southworld because nowhere in the North will be safe. The nightmare you witnessed today was just a taste of what Adramelach has planned for the entire world. If he has his way, all of the cities north of the Morakors Mountains will be nothing but ashes in the next year. The Southworld is the only place that stands a chance of being able to survive for a time. That is why I must take you to its threshold."

It was Rolf's turn to join the conversation now. He stammered a little when he spoke, still almost too upset for words. Despite this, his curiosity was able to overtake his anguish.

"Who is Adramelach?" Rolf asked.

Radnor leaned down slightly to look at Rolf.

"He is the king of all Krigari, though you might call them "war gods". All demons bow before him. It is only a matter of time before he has assembled a large enough army in our world to incinerate all of the kingdoms in the Northworld. The people of my homeland fought him for a long time. They fought him until the end."

Elena suddenly looked up at Radnor, focused her eyes on his face, and had a sudden realization.

"You're an Amarantheon, aren't you?"

There was silence in the air as Radnor resettled himself.

"Yes. I am from the realm of Amaranthar."

A look of pure hatred overtook Elena's face as she made another connection. Before she could voice it, Leif came up from where he had been eavesdropping, and spoke.

"The ashen ghost. The stories are all true then. You do bring death wherever you go. So tell me something *Veigarand*, what makes a man like you bring death to innocent lives?"

"The fact that I'm not a man," Radnor growled.

Radnor paused and stared into the dirt with shame for a moment before looking back up at Elena. He wasn't sure why he was about to tell them this. He had never told a living soul of his true nature. After what felt like an eternity, he decided these people deserved to know the truth.

"This is the reason your village was destroyed."

"I don't understand," Elena said.

"I am not a man, I am a weapon...bred for one purpose: to destroy Adramelach. The king and queen were warned of the coming invasion. I don't know all the details, but I know a sorcerer they trusted told them that Adramelach was going to discover how to break through the barrier that protects our world from them."

There was a pause as Radnor chose his next words carefully. Given how firmly these people believed in the power of Caelum, telling them that their patron god had died in a war with the Krigari was not going to go well. Radnor chose to leave this information out.

"How did he know this?" Leif inquired.

"My mother told me he had a unique gift that allowed him to look into their world from ours. He saw what our enemy was planning, and decided to act. There are cults that seek to aid Adramelach, and with their help, his success was nearly certain. At the sorcerer's urging, the king and queen made a choice, and infiltrated one of the cults that worshiped the Krigari. With help from the cult, and this same sorcerer, they opened the door slightly ajar themselves, and tricked Adramelach into impregnating my mother. I am the result of that sickening union. From the moment of my birth, I was trained by the best sword masters of the Eight Kingdoms, and learned to defeat them all. I was forged into a most excellent weapon for the King of Amaranthar. But, something went wrong, horribly, horribly wrong. Shortly after I was recognized as an adult by my people...I was at our capital city of Arendale, when a portal opened to their world. It seemed like the invasion had begun. Demons like the ones you saw today poured through. At first our warriors could hold them off, but then the demons grew ever more powerful. It was an onrushing tidal wave of destruction."

Radnor took a deep breath as memories of fire and death flashed before his eyes.

"It wasn't long before we were knee deep in the dead. The king called for the armies from all of the corners our kingdom to fight this invasion. My mother went mad, and spoke of the joyous days ahead under Krigari rule. The king sent me away, as he needed to be sure there was an heir to reclaim the throne when the war ended."

"Wait...an heir?" Elena asked.

Radnor sighed to himself. He had said too much to suddenly stop talking now.

"Yes, my mother was the queen of Amaranthar. The king had to keep my true parentage a secret, so publicly I was the oldest surviving son. I am a prince and the heir to the throne of Amaranthar."

Silence overtook the four weary people for a brief moment. Despite her anger, Elena couldn't help but feel some compassion for the warrior seated before her. Leif however, did not share her feelings. His face grew colder and angrier. Radnor's story only furthered his opinion that Veigarand needed to be killed once this crisis had passed.

Radnor began again.

"The war took over a year. For that long, they were inside our walls and it took almost a year to overcome our armies of thousands with their armies of millions. The same day that the first portal was created, I became stronger than any man, stronger than most of the demons. My skill in battle more than tripled. My coordination doubled, and my tactics became more cunning. At first I thought that it was the newfound practice in battle. I convinced myself that it was my own learning and conditioning that caused this sudden increase in power."

"Your strength, it's…?" Elena started.

"Directly related to my heritage. When I became an adult, my full power was realized. The portals are caused by me. My presence in an area for more than six days causes a portal to form. Once the sun hits its zenith on the seventh day, the portal opens. I am the cause of the doorways to Narakim, the home of the Krigari."

"How do you know this?" Leif asked.

"As I said, the King begged me to flee. He told me a dead weapon was a worthless weapon. My mother wanted me to stay and bask in the joy of the new age. She had gone mad, so I followed the King's command. I rode for the nearest fortress of our kingdom, and tried to prepare what was left of our armies there to launch a counter-attack. On the seventh day, a gate opened, and all of the forces I gathered were slaughtered. Again, I ran. I rode to another city, and the same thing happened. After that, I went into exile. I would not know what has become of the rest of my people except for the whispers that have reached me. They are all gone. It seems that until now, so were the Krigari. I doubt very much that will stay this way for long. For the past ten years I have been wandering the Northworld, searching for a way to kill them all. There is none to be found. I've been delayed time and time again. Recently, I had the unfortunate luck to meet a particularly old and powerful vampire. That's why I came to your village. I just…"

Radnor paused, trying to recompose himself after telling his tale of woe. After a brief moment, he spoke again.

"I needed a place to rest for a day."

Elena bit her lip; her anger had faded as she had listened to his story of sorrow. She started to see him more as a man, and not just a monster. Rolf began to sob, as he only saw before him the cause of all of his misery and pain.

Radnor spoke to them all.

"I am truly sorry for what happened. I did not plan for any of this. I thought that I could just stay one night, as I had done in other small villages where I stayed peacefully, and left in the morning. No attack ever harmed those villages."

"Oh, you mean like in Halden?" Leif exclaimed. "Or do you mean to tell me that the dead there were not also done by your hand?"

Radnor let out a sound somewhere between a sigh and a growl.

"That's where I met the vampire. The people there worshiped the damned thing, provided him with *meals*, and in exchange, he made some of them into lesser vampires. I would have been another *meal* as well, if I hadn't done what I did. And since I'm a man who can take on a vampire and his followers, *and* live to tell about it, I think you should feel glad I'm on your side."

Elena tried to force herself to give Radnor a disarming smile, but couldn't. She knew Radnor was right; he was their best chance for survival. She also knew that the only way to get along was to try to accept his apology, and make the best of a bad situation.

"Radnor, I know it isn't your fault. If I hadn't dragged you into my fight with Halmda we wouldn't be in this situation."

"Like hell it isn't!" Leif said. "He knew he was being hunted, and he brought the monsters to our homes! When we reach Wulfgeld, Sigaberht will have your head on a spike!"

Leif abruptly turned, and stormed off.

Rolf stared at Radnor with confusion in his eyes. He hated Radnor for bringing this destruction on his life; but this same man was offering to help him.

Radnor stared into his eyes, and spoke to him.

"I will not blame you for hating me. I am responsible for the deaths of those you love."

Rolf averted his gaze, and looked down at the grass. Radnor went over to Darestr and retrieved his blankets. He gave one to each of his new charges.

"I never did learn the name of your village. What did you call it?" Radnor asked.

"Neugeld," Elena responded.

Silence fell between them, and Radnor got the sense that he was not wanted there any longer.

"I need to bring the deer to Leif, and try to convince him Drakomar is a better destination than Wulfgeld." The warrior stood, and went to find Leif in the crowd.

The sun finished its slow descent under the horizon. Its rays were now hidden. The only light that remained was the soft glow from the embers of the fire. After a brief time, that glow gave way to darkness as well. The refugees slept, and Radnor stood watch over them, a sentinel in the night.

Chapter 6

Dawn broke over the tree tops. Radnor sat unmoved by this change in the sky. The conversation with Leif had not gone well. While the ealdorman had expressed reluctant gratitude for the food Radnor brought, he was not interested in Radnor's advice about where to go. Leif intended to bring his people to Wulfgeld. Only there could he get help from Earl Sigaberht and get justice against Radnor. Elena and Rolf slowly shifted awake. As the sun rose to join the clouds and the bright blue sky, so did Rolf and Elena.

"Good morning," Radnor said gruffly, his eyes locked on the forest's edge.

"Good morning," Elena replied.

Rolf said nothing.

"Why do you not look at us?" Elena asked.

"There is someone beyond those trees."

"Is that a problem?" Elena asked.

"Almost certainly," Radnor growled. "Drink some water, eat some of this."

He handed each of them pieces of bread.

"I'd cook some deer meat, but whoever is out there may not be willing to hang back much longer."

The party downed the bread pieces, drank some water, and stood up. Radnor donned his helmet, and handed Elena his ax.

"You two need to join the rest of the group. Be ready to defend Rolf. I do not know how many there are, or if I can defend you both by myself."

He looked at Rolf, and tossed him a knife.

"Did your parents teach you how to hunt at all?"

"Yes."

"Good. Use that skill. Sneak," Radnor said. "Attack only when the enemy has his back turned, and make it quick. Stab and get out, leave the knife in the enemy if you have to. Survive first, then kill."

Radnor then went to Darestr and the new horse.

"Darestr, I want you to take Elena and Rolf out of the fight again. They're fighting only if you can't find a way out."

Radnor turned to the horse he had ridden the day before.

"You, once more I must ask you to be brave. Together we shall ride into battle."

The other horse snorted its assent.

"Thank you," Radnor replied.

Elena tugged on the short sleeve of Radnor's mail to get his attention.

"What makes you think they want a fight?" she asked.

"Their eyes glowed by night," Radnor replied.

With a sharp tug, Radnor tightened the chinstrap on his helmet and readied his sword and shield. Elena and Rolf seated themselves upon Darestr. The pair rode over to Leif's position, and told him of what Radnor had seen. At Elena's insistence, Leif got the party of survivors to gather up their things and his men readied for an attack. As they gathered their weapons, Leif ran over to Radnor's position, the tall man leaping from foot to foot in his haste.

"What do you see Veigarand?" he yelled as he approached.

Radnor peered into the tree line as best he could, his inhuman eyes piercing the forest deeper than mortal eyes could.

"Ghouls," he said.

"Ghouls? I've heard of them, but never actually faced them. Have you seen them before?" Leif asked.

"Not around here, but I've run into them on a few occasions further north."

"How many did you face there?" Leif asked.

"Lone packs, six to seven members only."

"And how many do you reckon are here?"

"I'm not sure; it seems like a larger pack than usual. I've seen three distinct pairs of eyes so far. From my experience that could mean anywhere up to a dozen…about twice the size of a usual pack."

"Do packs typically work together?" Leif asked.

"No, from what I read years ago, if a pack gets any bigger than six or seven members, they start to fight among themselves," Radnor replied.

"What would cause so many of them to gather in one place?"

"They are probably on their way to your village. With the dead women and children added into the mix, that place will be even more enticing to them than a battlefield with three times as many corpses."

Radnor turned back to see Leif's steady glare.

"I'm sorry," Radnor said. "It has been many years since I traveled in the company of people. I am out of practice at tact."

A shout from one of Leif's men interrupted his angry reply. The men were ready for a fight, though Alban was needed to hold Klane onto their horse. Leif had the fighting men surround the women and children. He turned to Radnor.

"It sounds like you've fought them before. What would you recommend?" Leif grudgingly asked.

"We need to move quickly. The ghouls aren't sure if we are worthwhile prey yet. If we stand still, they will wait for individuals to separate, and pick us off one at a time. If we move now, and as a group, we may convince them we aren't worth the effort, and they will continue on their way."

"And if they attack anyway?" Leif asked.

"Then we kill them all."

Once Leif's people were ready, Radnor gave the signal to move into the tree line away from where the ghouls had stood. They held their formation tightly, and Radnor kept his head on a swivel. All of the people were very nervous, each man looking as though they were ready to break under the strain. None did. With great caution, the group entered the trees, and it was then that all hell broke loose.

In a move Radnor had never seen before, the ghouls had set up a trap for them that was sprung when one of the horses got caught in a snare. Panicked, the animal reared back and threw its riders: a woman and child. Grey shapes darted from under the cover of piled leaves and seized them both, dragging them further into the woods. Their struggles were still audible as they tried to grab a hold of anything they could in the underbrush. Two of Leif's men went tearing after them, looking for an opening to kill the monsters without hurting their own people. Horses panicked in turn as more ghouls appeared in the trees, their spindly gray bodies and limbs scrambling up and down the trunks like insects. Their number was in the dozens as they came pouring from every imaginable place.

Radnor turned to Darestr and yelled "Ride!" Darestr did not hesitate, and broke through the ghouls as fast as he could, trampling one in the process. Rolf and Elena almost fell off from the suddenness of Darestr's charge, but barely managed to hold on. Radnor then turned to the monsters in front of him, sword drawn, ready to fight.

An arrow pierced the side of the horse he rode, and something leapt from the trees and landed on Radnor. The ironclad warrior toppled to the ground and rolled with his attacker. Disorientation struck him as he rolled, but not enough to stop him from seizing the neck of the ghoul and breaking it like a twig in his hands. His roll finally stopped, and Radnor was able to stand up.

Blinking to refocus his eyes, Radnor picked up his fallen sword, and spun, looking for the origin of the arrow. One of the evil darts hit him square in the back, but it bounced harmlessly off of his armor. As he turned to face his attacker, the ghoul threw its bow to the ground in anger and leaped at him. It was a small, gnarled thing with sharp teeth and claws, but its primary weapon was a small knife meant for the carving of rotten meat and the slitting of throats. Radnor ducked and slashed his blade through the creature's belly as the over eager ghoul flew over his head.

As the ghoul landed with a sickening thud, Radnor had a chance to get a better look at it. It was a sickly, gray looking thing with hollow eyes and sharp teeth. It was generally humanoid, but only stood about half as high as Radnor did. Like most ghouls, its childlike size belied a sinewy strength that allowed it to present a greater threat than most people expected.

Before Radnor could continue his assessment, several more of the savage creatures leapt out of the trees, shrieking as they charged him. One of the vicious monsters rushed ahead of the others as it felt an unholy drive to kill the steel titan.

Radnor stepped to the side, sword arcing through the air. His blade connected with the back of the ghoul's head, sending blood spattering across the ground. Yet another unseen foe leapt atop his back, and started trying to rip Radnor's helmet off. Radnor swiped at it with his shield, and sent it careening into a tree with a gut wrenching crunch. There were three more ghouls left facing him. They held back and observed him, now more wary of their prey. Radnor could hear the sound of Leif shouting commands in the distance, but he could not break off to find the scattered villagers.

Still more ghouls crawled from their hiding places to join the fight. Radnor slowly moved to the side, keeping each of them in his sight. He took a second to count his foes, and made five. This didn't make any sense. There were far too many ghouls here. Radnor began scanning over the ghoul's bodies, looking for markings of any kind that would link them as a pack. There were signs of ritualistic scars and even a tattoo among them, but nothing he could see that linked them together. It was like every pack for over a hundred miles had smelled the blood of the village. His thoughts were interrupted when one of the ghouls finally decided to rush him, and another dance of death began.

Radnor's first blow took the arm off one of the assailants. The creature let out a shriek of pain, and fell to the ground, clutching its stump. The other creatures turned to run from Radnor, but the warrior took one more deft swing, and decapitated the ghoul that was slowest to turn. Radnor started to run after the final two creatures, but remembered his job was to protect, not slaughter, so he instead veered off towards Elena and Rolf.

He paused only a moment to look at his fallen horse where it lay dead from the arrow that had pierced its heart, and offered his thanks.

56

Now that the ghouls knew Radnor was dangerous, they would shift their attention to easier prey. Radnor had to hope that Leif had the sense to regroup his people and get out of there.

Rolf felt the world spinning around him. He was unsure of where it all went wrong. First, they were moving into the woods as a group, then a scream sounded. Then Veigarand's demon horse flew like the howling wind. Rolf had barely managed to hang onto Elena with that sudden rush, and now was just praying for it all to end.

Unfortunately, it did end. A line of cord suddenly came up in Darestr's path, and there was no way for the horse to evade it. Darestr tripped over the strong rope, and toppled. Rolf and Elena both fell hard, with Elena being knocked unconscious. Rolf was stunned, his vision now blurred from the fall. Once his eyes adjusted, he could see Elena's unconscious body sprawled out in the fallen leaves. Darestr groaned in pain, struggling to regain his feet. Several ghouls began stalking out of the trees, preparing to make their kills. Rolf struggled to get up, but he was still too disoriented, and fell back to the ground, helpless. Despair overtook Rolf then, as he tried to crawl over to Elena's seemingly unconscious form. As he got closer, he realized she was actually wide awake, and knowing they were trapped, was just waiting for a ghoul to get close enough for her ax to find its mark.

Elena looked up at the ghouls, their hideous faces shining with delight at the new morsels they had caught. One of the ghouls reached her body, and raised its spear for the killing blow. Elena slashed out with her drawn blade, hoping to cut one throat. Her aim was true, and she felt grim satisfaction as the horrible beast fell gurgling to the ground. But it didn't matter. More ghouls dropped from the trees, and now knew she was awake. They surrounded her, and blades raised, prepared to make the kill.

Rolf could only watch helplessly, still too dizzy to stand. Just as he started to scream, an armored figure dove through his vision.

Blinking rapidly, Rolf finally believed what he saw as Radnor's armored form danced and leaped among the ghouls. It seemed like the whole forest had come alive with the devils as they poured from the branches of every tree, but their numbers did not matter. Rolf watched in amazement as Radnor's sword arced around through the air. Every time the demigod moved, another ghoul fell dead at his feet.

At first, Radnor's ferocity only drove the ghouls to be more aggressive. They came at him three or four at a time, but their numbers did not stop the whirlwind of death. One ghoul tried to get inside the reach of Radnor's sword, but instead was killed by a blow from Radnor's shield that crushed its skull. After a few short moments, the ground was littered with the corpses of the ghouls, and soon their assault began to waver. Rolf watched as they became more focused on carrying away their wounded and less on trying to kill the legendary Veigarand. The ghouls had never seen fury to match that which Radnor inflicted on them. Soon the ghouls abandoned their wounded and fled, scattering in terror before their slayer. The battle was over.

Radnor leaned over and offered his hand to Elena.

"Are you alright?" he asked.

"Never mind me, where's Rolf?" Elena asked.

She took Radnor's hand, stood up, and immediately started looking for her friend. Rolf finally found the strength to stand, as did Darestr. Elena came over to her would-be brother, and began checking him for injuries.

"Did you hit your head? Do you feel dizzy at all?" Elena asked worriedly.

"I'm scraped up, but I'm fine," Rolf replied.

"Thank Caelum!" Elena said, giving Rolf a firm hug.

The pair turned and fixed their eyes on Radnor. He had been checking Darestr for injuries. Thankfully, Darestr was no more hurt than Rolf.

Elena came over to Radnor, and looked into his eyes. She placed a hand on his shoulder, not caring that it was covered in ghoul blood.

"Are you alright?" Elena asked.

Radnor felt touched by her concern. He was about to make his reply when a fierce cry in the distance drew his attention away from Elena. He gestured to Darestr, and spoke.

"We should get moving before more ghouls arrive. You and Rolf should ride Darestr. Don't worry, I will be right beside you."

Once Rolf and Elena were astride Radnor's horse, the group made their escape.

It was hours before Radnor, Rolf, and Elena were able to meet back up with Leif and the others. The sun was well past its zenith, and had just begun to fall behind the horizon. Streaks of red and orange hues cast themselves upon the clouds, and a strong wind whipped through the trees. Radnor only found Leif because of the signal fire the ealdorman had taken the risk to light. The ealdorman had hoped it could guide other lost refugees to the camp. His hope was not misplaced, and several other lost refugees had found their way back to safety because of the smoke.

It had been a harrowing trip back. Every rustle of leaves in the wind could have been another pack of ghouls, hungrily awaiting another chance to strike. Thankfully, the party made their way to Leif's new encampment unmolested.

Once they arrived, the group found a grim scene. Given the circumstances, Radnor thought Leif had done an excellent job of holding his warriors together. All of them still breathed. There was a signal fire in the middle of the group, with several of Leif's warriors using their bloody tunics to capture and release puffs of smoke. Walking alongside Darestr, Radnor scanned the crowd of refugees for Leif. It did not take long to find him.

Leif was standing with the rest of his people over freshly dug graves. In the absence of a living priest to give funeral rites, the responsibility fell upon the ealdorman. The wearied man felt the heavy weight of his words as he prayed for the souls of those they had lost today. One of his men tapped him on the shoulder, and gestured towards Radnor. Leif turned, and saw him walking alongside Rolf and Elena. Anger took hold of the ealdorman mid-sentence. He forgot the rites, and found himself yet again storming towards Radnor.

"'No more than a dozen,' you said! You said we could make our way out unharmed!"

Two of Leif's men rushed forward and restrained him from approaching Radnor, fearful of Veigarand's wrath.

"Instead, you led us directly into their ambush! We walked straight into a trap!" Leif shouted, still wrestling for the freedom to rush the monster that stood before him.

Radnor stared in silence for a moment, unsure of how to proceed. Leif was right, he had gotten people killed. Had they formed a shield wall and stood their ground, they could have avoided the ghouls' trap…waited them out until the dreadful creatures got bored and left. At the very least, they could have made the creatures impatient and tempted them to make a suicidal rush against their shield wall. But instead, he had tried to blow through the bastards, and people died because of it. After what seemed like an eternity, Radnor found words to reply.

"I am so very sorry. But I promise you, I have never seen ghouls act like that. They are scavengers. A pack of ghouls will sometimes attack a stray traveler, believe me, I know. But… they don't gather in numbers like what we saw today."

Leif scoffed at Radnor's words.

"Well, they sure as fuck do now! Do you know how many I lost today? Look at them Veigarand!"

Leif angrily pointed at the freshly dug graves as he spoke.

"Three more children are dead! I still have nine more people lost in the forest somewhere!"

Tears streamed down Leif's face as he continued to speak.

"One of them died in my arms. His name was Algred. One of the ghouls had ripped him from his mother's arms and dragged him up a tree. The damn thing didn't even wait until he was dead to start eating him!"

Radnor found himself rooted to the earth where he stood. He knew he was on trial for the death of this child, and he wasn't sure it was unjustified. Leif stammered as he continued.

"I killed that sickening fiend and got the boy down…but…but it was too late. I held him in my arms…listened as his cries stopped…and the light left his eyes. Do you…do you know how old he was? Barely two years!"

The whole area was eerily silent as Leif continued in his rage. Not a soul made a sound, be it man or beast. The leaves themselves seemed to stop their restless rustling in the breeze.

"You see that woman, kneeling at the grave? That's his mother, Brida. Her husband was killed yesterday…murdered by one of the monsters you summoned. But that wasn't enough for you was it? You needed more death! Now you have taken her only child from her! I've had enough of you for one day. Get out of my sight!"

Having finished his torrential rant, Leif turned on his heel and went back to completing the funeral rites.

Radnor stood in place for a long time, still drenched in the blood of the ghouls he had killed. His muscles ached, and the pain in his shoulder tore at him unlike any other time before, but out of respect he stood still as Leif spoke a prayer for the dead.

"Oh, Caelum, who lights our way by the sun, the moon, and the stars, please fight for the souls of those who died this day, just as you have fought the wicked monsters that destroyed our home. We beseech you, find a home for them in your halls, and grant them plenty. These poor souls were kind, gentle folk, who deserved a better end than this. Please, care for their souls as they move on to a better world."

There was a long pause, and Leif finally broke his posture, signaling the end of the final prayer. Only when this was complete did anyone else in the camp move.

Radnor turned away and found where Darestr had stopped. Upon finally reaching his horse, Radnor found he barely had the energy to tear the helmet from his head and toss it to the ground before he fell to his knees. Darestr turned and nudged him, making sure Radnor was all right. After a few moments, Radnor patted Darestr gently, and assured him he was unharmed. Darestr snorted in protest, knowing full well of Radnor's injuries. Radnor bent over to check Darestr's legs. There was some bruising from where he fell, but by the mercy of the god Hymmur, there didn't seem to be any damage to the bone.

Now that he had a moment to breathe, Radnor shed his armor for the first time in two days, tore off his blood soaked tunic and prepared a clean shirt. He took a moment to inspect his wound. The wound in his shoulder was completely open again, and Radnor had to tear the least blood covered section of his old tunic apart, and wrap it around his arm as a new bandage.

Radnor noticed how no one seemed to take notice of his work, not even Elena. He then marveled at himself for a moment. Why should he care if Elena noticed his pain or not? Again, he shook the thought from his mind. With a certain bitter reluctance, Radnor donned his mail shirt yet again, and buckled his sword to his side. He had just finished preparing himself to take first watch, when word came they were not going to camp here. Leif wanted to continue on until it was too dark to move. He wanted to be as far away from this place as possible.

Radnor decided it was best not to challenge Leif on this. It seemed that despite his hatred, Leif had reluctantly accepted that Radnor was a part of their group until they reached Wulfgeld. Arguing with him now would jeopardize that acceptance, and it was clear these people needed Radnor's protection. As Leif organized everyone to return to their march, Radnor patted Darestr gently.

"I think you need a night off. I'll walk tonight."

Darestr gave a slight whinny, thanking Radnor for the chance to not carry the extra weight. They then joined the others, and continued their trek through the forest. Radnor decided to hang at the back of the group, afraid his presence among them would stir up tempers best left alone. He slipped into a distant state of brooding over the recent events. This was not to last, as he soon found himself joined by Rolf and Elena. The three walked in silence for a time, no one sure of what to say. Finally, Elena spoke.

"We wanted to thank you for saving our lives earlier today. We both saw what you did, the way you threw yourself at those things. If you hadn't done that…we'd both be dead right now."

"I gave my oath," Radnor replied. "I swore to protect the people here. I will do that, no matter the risk to myself."

There was such a weight to the way he said it, Elena felt the need to convey her appreciation. Despite how Leif regarded Radnor, she couldn't help but see the man beneath the blood and steel. No matter what else had happened before, she knew he was doing everything he could to make up for what happened. Elena couldn't help also feeling a little responsible; the way she had goaded Halmda. She had *wanted* Radnor to hurt him for her. If she had kept her mouth shut, maybe the two of them wouldn't have played that awful game, and none of this would have happened. Radnor would have come and gone, and have been nothing but a happy memory of fantasized retribution for her to think on.

Unthinkingly, she placed her hand on his shoulder, and jumped as he yelped in pain. She could hardly believe the way he sounded. But then she remembered the wound on his shoulder, and felt truly awful.

"I'm sorry!" she exclaimed. "I forgot about that wolf bite!"

Radnor rolled his shoulder a few times, fighting the pain down.

"It's all right. Unfortunately, to tell you the truth, it wasn't wolves. Remember that vampire I said I ran into? This is my souvenir from him. The damn thing won't heal."

Elena's hand went up to her mouth in shock, knowing full well what this meant. Rolf however, brought the issue out into the open.

"If that's a vampire bite, then why aren't you dead?"

Radnor smiled gently to himself.

"I think it's because I'm half Krigari. It seems that whatever dark magic infests my wound isn't quite strong enough to kill me, but it won't leave me in peace either."

"Is there anything we can do?" Elena asked.

"Well, for starters, please don't touch that shoulder again."

"I guess this is good for us though," said Rolf.

Radnor and Elena both turned to Rolf with confused looks on their faces.

"Because if you ever get too mean, we can just smack you on that spot, and you'll stop. It'll be like swatting a bad dog on the nose!"

Radnor and Elena were surprised by their laughter at Rolf's joke. Despite all of this, somehow the boy had found a way to pull himself out of the gloom of the situation. Rolf then continued his questioning.

"Did you kill it?" he asked.

"Oh, the vampire? No, it was a sort of draw," Radnor replied. "I'm not sure there is a way to kill a vampire like that one. He was old, very old. He claimed to be the first one, the first soldier in a forgotten war between gods long dead. I left him trapped for eternity, and made my escape. But that's a story for another time."

The trio talked of other things for a time. Rolf spoke at length of his father. His father always returned from his trips with gifts for him, and always made sure to spend time with him when he was at home. Rolf also spoke of how much he missed his father. He told Radnor about a time when he was very little, and the two of them were seeing who could run the fastest, but his father was running while kneeling the whole time. Tears formed in Rolf's eyes as he spoke.

"What's wrong? It's a beautiful story," Radnor said.

This question broke Rolf, and tears streamed down his face as they rode.

"He was in Wollendan during the attack. What if he comes home and finds it burned down? What if the monsters are still there and they kill him? What if he goes looking for me...and the ghouls get him? What if he decides I'm dead and goes away forever?"

Elena held him close in her arms as his tears overwhelmed his speech.

Radnor struggled to find words for a moment, but finally found them.

"What's your father's name?" he asked.

"Leofric," Elena said.

Radnor shook his head.

"I want Rolf to say it."

Rolf pulled his head up from his tears, and spoke again.

"My father's name is Leofric Cellestan."

"And do you tell me that Leofric Cellestan would assume his son to be dead without proof?"

"No!" Rolf exclaimed.

"And do you tell me that Leofric Cellestan, the trade master of Neugeld, a man who has made many dangerous trips across bandit infested roads would allow himself to become the victim of creatures like ghouls?"

"No!" Rolf sternly said again.

"And of the demons I say this…they will have left that area by the time your father gets there. If history is any indicator, now that I'm gone, they will go back to their world."

These words seemed to cheer Rolf up some, and his tears began to ease.

"So…" Radnor continued. "What do you think your father will do when he finds Neugeld destroyed?"

Rolf's eyes lit up.

"He'll look for me, and when he can't find me, he'll do what we're doing and go to Wulfgeld."

"Exactly," Radnor said. "Hopefully, it'll be a short wait for us until he arrives."

Time passed, and night was beginning to descend upon the travelers. Leif called everyone to stop, and people began making fires and setting up camp. Radnor sent Darestr to keep warm by one of the fires, and started to keep track of the activity in the camp. By the time camp was made, the sun had completed its arc in the sky, with only the barest traces of its illuminating rays painting subtle lines in the now moonlit sky.

Leif had arranged the pits to form a large circle, with all of the people resting on the inside of that circle. Extra fire wood was gathered, so that if attacked, they could throw more fuel on the fires and create an obstacle about which their foes would have to think twice.

At first, Radnor assisted in this endeavor where he could, but found his help mostly unwanted. Instead, the weary warrior relegated himself to keeping watch while the others worked. As the work concluded, Radnor was just about to find Darestr when Alban came to him with a mug of water.

"Here, drink this. I assume you need water like the rest of us."

Radnor looked down at the cup, and shook his head.

"I can't take from people who need it more than me. I can go for much longer without food or water than you."

Alban smiled lightly and shook his head in return.

"You swore an oath. How are you to protect us if you are not at your full strength?" he asked, shoving the glass into Radnor's hand.

Radnor finally assented, and took a long drink from its contents. The water tasted so sweet, and it was just too refreshing to stop. Once he had finished the mug, Radnor handed it back to Alban, with his thanks.

"Where did you get this?" Radnor asked.

Alban turned slightly, pointing to the south.

"There's a creek just past those trees. That's part of why Leif wanted to stop here."

Alban turned back to Radnor, feeling his legs ache from the day's walking.

"Do you mind if I sit with you awhile?"

Radnor gestured to the grassy earth, and the two sat and talked. Alban told Radnor of Leif's current plans. The ambush had thrown everyone's sense of direction into disarray. No one was exactly sure where they were. But Leif knew they had one principal direction to go in… and that was south, towards Wulfgeld. The river Argirn snaked its way along the entire route between here and Sigaberht's throne. Leif was counting on finding that river, and hoping this creek connected to it. Once Leif had found the Argirn, he, having traveled this route the most, would know where they were and the best direction to go until they hit Wulfgeld. Until then, they were to head straight south. Radnor agreed with the plan, as it was the best bet they had for the time being. Alban then asked Radnor an unexpected question.

"I heard people talking, and I have to ask…what was it like… growing up a prince?"

Radnor shook his head and laughed.

"The prince's life was only a show for the people. For most of my life, all I had to do in public was stand in court and stay quiet; that is until I got older. But, from the moment I was born, I was prepared for war. I do not remember a time I was not being instructed on how to wield every weapon made by man. Sword masters from all corners of the continent were brought to teach me all of their crafts."

Radnor paused to stretch his legs. He saw that Alban was genuinely interested in the story, and continued.

"Early on, some of the masters were not so good. I'm sorry…that's unfair. They were all skilled swordsmen in their own way, but their understanding was limited. They had each mastered some element of the sword well enough that they could use it to great effect against lesser men. But, against other masters, it was a coin toss as to who would best whom. After learning from enough of them, I learned a fundamental truth: the sword isn't my weapon, I am the weapon. Once I understood that, none but the very best sword masters had anything to teach me. I also had a temper, a violent rage that many found difficult to tame. I used it to great effect for much of my childhood. It was a motivator that allowed me to push myself beyond my limits. Combined with the skills that I had been taught by my teachers, I was a deadly adversary. But, do you want to know something funny?"

"What?" Alban replied.

Radnor leaned back on his elbows, taking a moment to enjoy reminiscing about his youth.

"The king saw something in me. He saw that I was a finely sharpened sword, with the physical skills to overcome most masters. But, a sword needs to be balanced. At my core I was still nothing but raw violence driven by rage. He knew a rage fueled weapon could not be controlled, and was afraid that I might turn against him. So, he found a man who was easily the best swordsman who ever lived, and commissioned him as my teacher. Halbjorn the Ghost.

"The ghost?" Alban asked.

"Yes, that is what they called him," Radnor chuckled.

"You see, fighting him was like trying to fight a ghost. You would go to strike him, and he did not block or parry. He did not directly meet your attack in any way. I tried to strike him, and he simply wasn't there anymore. Then he was back again, hitting me. Naturally, this fanned the fires of my rage. Again and again I attacked him in our sparring matches, and again and again I was driven to the dirt. The harder I went, the harder I got hit. Over time, he taught me to control my anger, to not let it drive my actions. Anger was blinding me the same way fear blinds others. The king only wanted a more controllable weapon, but Halbjorn did far more than that. He made me into a better person."

"It sounds like you have a lot of respect for him," Alban said. "Did you ever best him?"

"Not truly," Radnor replied. "There were times I was able to land a strike, but every time I did, something in him would change. He would increase the difficulty of the challenge he laid before me. It was always obvious in the aftermath that the blow I landed wasn't really victory over him, just over the goal he had set for me...a victory over a previous version of myself that I had grown from. You know Alban...the swordsman you see before you is the result of over a decade of failures against Halbjorn. I do miss him dearly."

"What happened to him?" Alban asked.

"He had an unusual death for a swordsman. Eventually, old age took him from this world."

"I'm sorry to hear that," Alban said. "He sounds like a man I would have liked to meet."

"It's a pity you didn't. You know, there were three times other masters came to our court to challenge Halbjorn for his position. The fee for teaching me was immense, and some duelists thought it worth risking their lives against another master for the fortune that awaited success."

"What happened to those masters?"

Radnor chuckled as the memories came back to his mind.

"Halbjorn died of old age. They didn't."

Radnor smiled to himself, now lost in musings and memories. Alban took note of this, and left to rejoin the others.

Night fell, and most of the people found themselves too exhausted to avoid sleep no matter how much their sorrows troubled them. Leif had posted several of his men to guard in shifts, but Radnor stood alone. He stood with his back to the fire and stared into the depths of the dark forest. The warmth felt good against his back, and Radnor was almost comfortable enough to bring himself to sit down again, when he heard the rustling of fallen leaves behind him. Radnor spun abruptly, and found himself face to face with Klane. Radnor felt something jam into his stomach. It hurt, but the mail stopped the blade from meeting flesh.

"For Bron," Klane hissed as he started to thrust again, this time aiming for Radnor's throat.

66

Radnor's training took over, and Klane's knife was now his in an instant. Radnor held the knife in one hand, and Klane's throat in the other. Having been thinking of Halbjorn helped him stay his temper. Unlike in the tavern, Radnor did not kill the man before him.

"Do it!" Klane demanded. "Send me to join my brother in the Hall of Kings!"

Radnor held the knife in his hand, still ready to strike, but instead of indulging his anger, he let go of Klane's neck.

"Who was Bron?" Radnor asked, not remembering that was the name of man he had killed.

Klane brought his hand to his throat, and rubbed it gingerly.

"He was my brother," Klane said.

"I'm sorry," Radnor said, still not recognizing the name.

Klane saw this in Radnor's eyes, and spat at the armored warrior.

"He was the innkeeper. My brother was the man you murdered with your own hands!"

Klane looked like he was about to lunge at Radnor, but never did.

Confronted with the grieving brother of the man he had killed, Radnor found himself unable to say a word. In the rush of everything that had happened, Radnor had forgotten Bron's name, but the innkeeper's terrified face was something that would be burned into Radnor's mind forever. He wished to express his deepest sorrow for Klane, but there was nothing he could say that would make it right. Klane spoke again, interrupting Radnor's thoughts.

"Oh, so you remember now, do you? I would tell you that he had a wife, and a daughter. But, they're both dead now too. You murdered a man in his own home, and you didn't even know his name."

Having said his piece, and no longer having any means of killing his enemy, Klane stalked away to rejoin the others, leaving Radnor holding the dagger in the darkness.

Chapter 7

It was another cold, sleepless night for Radnor. He watched as the shifts of Leif's guards changed periodically, with Leif himself taking a post, sword in hand. The autumn wind blew through the encampment, whispering of the cold winter lying in wait. Sleeping people huddled and crowded by the fire for warmth, seeking respite from the icy murmurs which brushed their skin.

As always, animals were eerily quiet around the demigod, as not even a cricket dared make a sound. Radnor spent most of the time caught in his own feelings of guilt about the situation. His brooding did not go unnoticed. Leif spent his shift at the watch studying the ghost of the north.

Even from a distance, Leif could see the lines running across Radnor's troubled brow. He also saw a regular pattern of movement in Radnor's sword shoulder. The wound in his arm clearly troubled him, something Leif found some unsettling satisfaction in seeing. He knew there was nothing he could do to Veigarand that wouldn't also put his people in danger. The brute's oath to protect them seemed sincere for the moment, though Leif didn't believe he could do anything about it if that changed. Violence wasn't an option if Leif wanted justice done. He would have to wait until he could bring him before Earl Sigaberht. So for now, Leif decided to leave Veigarand to his guilt, and let death wait for the right moment.

Leif found his thoughts drifting back to his home. He found himself wondering what Sigaberht would do to him after this was over. He was still an ealdorman, but now he was *the* ealdorman who had allowed his people to be slaughtered, and had fled in such a hurry that his oath ring rested not on his person, but instead lay among the ashes of his home.

He thought back to the day Sigaberht had presented him that oath ring, and he was officially recognized as a landed noble in the eyes of his lord. Years of hard service to the earl had been richly rewarded, only now that reward had been squandered. He had sworn on Sigaberht's oath ring, and had been given his own. Leif had been so proud that day. Knights of the south are given jeweled swords when they take their oaths of fealty. Leif scoffed at the idea. Any man can swing a sword, and any rich man can have gems set in its hilt. In the north, enchanted rings of iron were given to any man who had proved he had the strength to lead other men, and the courage to hold true to the men that swore to him. Any who dared break an oath sworn on such a ring would find themselves faced with a swift vengeance. Leif had checked his body several times, looking for the oath breaker's mark that should have seared his body, should great

Caelum, the overseer of all oaths, see his failure as a transgression against his lord. He was quite relieved to have not found any marks so far, save for the scars of a lifetime of struggle and humility.

Elena could not sleep. She had never seen Halmda's body; so her imagination haunted her with gruesome visions of his mangled corpse that refused to leave her mind. As much as she had despised the man, she hadn't really wanted him dead. Sitting up, she found her body ached from lying on the uncomfortable, lumpy ground. Scanning the encampment, she caught sight of Alban. He was still awake and taking his shift at the watch. Radnor also caught her sight. She could barely make him out, but there was no mistaking the faint glint of his armor where fire dared to illuminate the shadows where he stood guard. Deciding Alban would be the better conversationalist for the night, Elena walked over to him, and noticed as she approached that he held a strange black disk in his hand. She couldn't quite make it out in the darkness, but she noticed Alban seemed to stare so intently at it.

"What is that you have there?" Elena asked inquisitively.

Alban jumped at her words, and spun wildly.

"By Caelum's grace! You startled me! You walk as silently as a stalking lion!"

"I'm sorry Alban, I could not sleep, and I saw you staring at something in your hand. I grew curious."

Alban laughed to himself, still nervously keeping one eye on the tree line.

"It's all right. After what happened today, I'm still quite jumpy."

The two stood in silence for a moment, until Elena restated her question.

"So, what is that you hold in your hand?"

Alban looked back down at the small round disk still clutched in his hand.

"Oh this?" he said. "It's a good luck charm, sold to me by a merchant from Wollendan this past summer. I wasn't sure I believed him, but it caught my eye, and I had to have it. Perhaps it was fate that brought it to my hands."

"What makes you say that?" Elena asked.

"Because, I hadn't carried it on me much since I bought it. Then, a funny feeling overtook me. When I went out to bury Veigarand, I had this sudden urge to bring it with me. Well, you know how that went, so I think maybe there is some luck in this trinket after all."

"May I see it?" Elena asked.

"Sure."

Extending and opening his hand, Alban revealed the charm in full. It was a strange thing, seeming to have been carved from a single piece of basalt rock. It was formed in a perfect circle, and there was an odd symbol carved into its face, one that Elena could not quite describe. It looked almost like the lines of a written word or name, but not in a language that she could recognize. Something about it was unsettling, so she decided to simply thank Alban for showing it to her, and took her leave of him. She briefly considered going to talk to Radnor, but decided he would not want to see her right now. It was impossible to judge his mood under that armor, especially with his face covered by his mail draped helmet. Instead, Elena chose to try to find a warm spot at the fire, and make another vain attempt at sleep. Sadly, she found only more visions of death, but now with Alban's good luck charm woven into the chaotic images that flooded her mind.

The night passed fitfully for all who had sought shelter by the fire. Only the red sunrise provided respite from brooding, as it signaled the continuation of their journey. This night was the first of several spent this way. The group traveled south for several hellish days. Food was scarce, as was warmth. While it was still early autumn, the refugees had little clothing meant for the cooling weather with them. It was decided that the children would be allowed to take turns sharing Radnor's cloak, a gesture of kindness which did not go unnoticed by some of the parents, nor by Leif. As Klane recovered from his wound, Leif began putting him to work, intelligently placing Klane as far away from Radnor as possible. Food was foraged on every occasion it could be found.

Leif found himself reluctantly having to acknowledge Radnor's aid during his nightly musings on the matter. As much as he hated Veigarand, Leif found himself unable to maintain his hostile pose, and acted in a basically polite manner whenever the demigod did something charitable for his people. In Leif's more emotionally vulnerable moments, he found himself feeling grateful for Veigarand's help finding food. Radnor had lived like this for a long time, and knew not only where to find food, but which of the enticing fruits were edible, and which spelled death. There was never quite enough food, but some was better than none.

However, the journey was not all horrible for Radnor. Rolf and Elena were often by his side as they walked. It was during their talks that Radnor finally learned more about the founding of Neugeld.

It was a colony established by the city of Wulfgeld. Sigaberht had convinced his father to set up the village as a great trading town with the northern kingdoms. Radnor was also inundated with stories about Leif's stellar leadership since he became the ealdorman two years prior. Under the previous ealdorman, the people of Neugeld had been plagued by recurring famine for years. The grain they had been trying to farm just simply did not take to the soil there, and took far too much care to get even a small amount to grow. It was Leif who convinced Sigaberht to send pigs. Once the transition to pig farming was done, the people of Neugeld had plenty of food again. Alongside regular hunting parties which helped keep the town in supply of meat, they had begun to be able to save the pigs for trade, and sell them for the money needed to buy bread and other supplies. Based on Elena's testimony, it was Leif who had finally begun to realize Sigaberht's goal. And…Radnor's arrival had brought it all crashing down.

Alban frequently joined the trio when the party stopped to rest. It was from Alban that Radnor learned about Sigaberht's precarious position in Wulfgeld. Duke Piarin, the lord of the mountain, fortress city Drakomar, had made more than one attempt to take Sigaberht's throne. According to Alban, Leif's tale of battle alongside Sigaberht was no exaggeration. The young Earl had fought with the ferocity of a lion every time Duke Piarin sent his men to seize the land.

Drakomar was a city built into one of the great passes in the Morakors Mountains. However, Drakomar was chiefly a fortress– one of the mightiest ever built. Sigaberht was then faced with an enemy that could strike at will with no fear of reprisal from his victims. The earl simply did not have the manpower to besiege it. His only hope of forcing Piarin on the back foot was to make allies in the north. Trade was one of the fastest ways to make allies, and that's why their village was so far from the rest of Sigaberht's lands. His father had originally sent men and had founded the town on land that none of their northern neighbors cared to claim, and it was Sigaberht's goal to see to it that alliances with those neighbors were forged.

Radnor took great pleasure in his conversations with these three. For the first time in a long time, the demigod felt like he had friends.

Finally, during this period, a day came when the somber mood of the party was transformed to elation. They had finally found the river they sought! Cries of happiness were heard as the people rejoiced in the fact that they now knew where they were, and the way to safety behind the walls of Wulfgeld was clear. Radnor quickly joined Leif at the front of the group to see what the next step was. He found the ealdorman staring into the flowing water, watching the waves and ripples that ran across the surface.

"The question is…" Leif said, turning to Radnor as he mused aloud, "whether or not it's shallow enough to cross here."

"Should we not simply travel along the river in the direction of Wulfgeld until we find a bridge? Or a known crossing?"

Leif shook his head, and gestured back to the resting refugees.

"We are in the depths of autumn. You can see even now the leaves change color, and with it, each night gets colder. Despite our best efforts on foraging, we are short on food, and despite your... generosity with your blankets and cloak, we have nothing but camp fires to ward off the cold. The horses haven't been properly fed, and are even more exhausted than the people. If we don't cross now, we may not have the strength left to cross later."

Leif returned his gaze to the river, contemplating how best to work out a crossing. The solution seemed obvious to Radnor's aggressive way of thinking.

"Can I trust you?" he asked of the contemplative leader.

Taken aback by the question, Leif hesitated to answer, until he saw Radnor start to strip off his armor. Understanding the man's purpose, Leif finally replied.

"As long as your actions work to help my people, you can trust me."

Radnor then looked hard at the ealdorman, and handed him his ring.

"Give this to Elena. I want her on my horse, and this is the best way to get him to cooperate. Don't lose it," Radnor said.

Leif nodded even though he was annoyed at being given orders. He had to restrain the impulse to throw the ring into the river out of spite.

Having stripped now to his underclothes, Radnor began to wade into the muddy water. The channel was wide, which he hoped would mean the water would be shallower here than in other parts of the river. The water was very cold, and he knew that no matter what, this would be an unpleasant crossing. As he went, he felt the current gently, but firmly, try to move him further downstream.

As he neared the center of the channel, he found that the depth increased gradually and evenly as he went. The rushing water was now at the level of his neck, and taking a deep breath, Radnor continued on until he was totally submerged. Leif almost called out to him, until he saw arms sticking out above the surface, allowing him to see Radnor was still trying to measure out the depth. The river was at its deepest in the middle, where the water came up to Radnor's wrists. There was a sudden tumult at the surface as Radnor came up for air.

Others had gathered at the river's edge, and Leif was working to get them all on horseback. It was clear that wading on foot was not an option. As Radnor continued his crossing, the river gradually became shallower again, and Leif was relieved to see the drenched warrior striding along the opposite bank of the river. Radnor waved his arms to be sure he had Leif's attention, and called out.

"The current isn't too strong, but it is enough to be wary of. Otherwise, we're in luck!"

Leif sighed a heavy sigh, thankful to Caelum for this respite from danger.

"Wading on foot is out of the question, we need to send people over on horseback!" Radnor said, unaware that Leif had already guessed as much.

"Also, I would appreciate it if you would put my armor in my saddlebags before you send Darestr over!"

Leif snatched up Radnor's armor and stomped over to Darestr. He was surprised to find that Rolf and Elena were already astride Radnor's great horse. Leif gave the pair an inquisitive look as he approached Darestr's enormous frame, to which Rolf only shrugged. Elena felt more of a need to explain herself.

"Darestr seems to prefer us if it's not Radnor he carries," Elena said.

Leif felt himself stiffen in anger, and threw the ring at her.

"So it's 'Radnor' now? I may be accepting his help, but I will not forget who he is. He is Veigarand. Need I remind you that he attacked your fiancé at your own party, who still lies unburied in the burning remains of your home?"

If looks could kill, the glare Elena gave Leif would have slain demons. Defiantly, she slipped the ring on her finger before speaking to Leif again.

"You know as well as I do that there was never any love between Halmda and I, or do I need to remind you of the black eye that blessed my face until only a few nights ago?"

Leif laughed to her face then, a nasty, spiteful laugh that caught even him by surprise. That surprise didn't stop him from saying what he would say next.

"So that's it, isn't it? Do you expect to find love from the ghost of the north? Or do you just wish for a man to keep you warm on these cold nights?"

Darestr had heard enough. Before Elena could reply, Darestr stomped towards the river, with the intent to join the line of horses which were now prepared to begin crossing.

The crossing was slow; as the exhausted horses found difficulty in resisting the current. There were also times it took some coaxing to even get a horse to begin to cross, as the great beasts were simply too tired to have any desire to add more trouble in the day. It wasn't until Darestr, strong and proud, crossed that the other horses became willing to carry their burdens without further prodding. Darestr's example had been set. As Radnor and Leif were leaders among men, Darestr was a lord of horses.

The crossing was abruptly interrupted when one of the horses, having gone past the limit of its endurance, collapsed off its feet and crumpled into the water. The rider tried to dive away, but got caught in the reins as the horse went down, dragging him to the bottom. The rider was Klane. Other horses began to panic, and started in random directions away from their dead comrade. Alban found himself thrown from his panicking mount, but was able to quickly swim to the surface, a look of panic striking his youthful face.

Radnor reacted to the panic faster than anyone. In a flash, he was in the water, swimming rapidly to get to Klane. Only a man of Radnor's strength would have been able to reach Klane in the time Radnor did, as he swam through the water as fast as a man can run on land. Radnor found Klane was unconscious, having hit his head against the rocks on the bottom. Radnor quickly went to work, desperately tearing at the leather reins with his hands until they came apart, allowing Radnor to grab Klane by the midsection, and push to the surface. When Radnor's head finally breached the surface, he found a hellish scene laid out before him

Small black arrows whistled out from the trees where they had been camped. Several panicked horses had been struck in their flanks. Blood flowed freely in the water, and Radnor caught only a glimpse of Leif and his men forming a shield wall, trying to protect the rest of the refugees as they completed their crossing. People were in disarray, with most of the refugees trying to make their way to the far shore. Ironically, the attack worked in their favor in regards to the horses. Panicked or not, the fearful beasts recognized the danger on the near shore, and worked to make it across the river, whether their rider had any say in the matter or not. Alban was the exception. The terrified man was repeatedly diving under the water for an unknown purpose. Thinking Alban was searching for Klane, Radnor shouted to him the next time the youth surfaced for air, but the frenzied man seemed not to hear Radnor's bellows.

Radnor then did the only thing he could do, and finished dragging Klane to the shore where others awaited. As Radnor climbed out of the water, he was met by Elena and Rolf, who took Klane off his hands and began to work to get the water out of Klane's lungs.

"What the hell is happening?" Radnor yelled.

"I don't know," Elena said.

"Someone, I suppose bandits, have attacked us from the trees with bows, but no one has shown themselves yet."

Radnor growled in anger, and immediately turned and dove back into the river. Bandits were not something he needed to add to his day. He was without his weapons or armor, and Elena found herself surprised by how much she feared for his safety above all others.

Despite appearances, Radnor was not yet totally consumed by his anger this time. He had enough sense to swim wide of Leif's shield wall, and use the fact that the enemy focused on harassing Leif's people to his advantage. As Radnor came onshore, he moved as stealthily as possible into the shadows of the trees, hoping to catch the enemy unaware. The whistling of arrows filled the air around him, and Radnor thought he heard strange chittering, as though it was an inhuman language spoken by inhuman tongues.

Finally, Radnor caught sight of two of the attackers huddled by a tree overgrown with bushes. Their small, pale forms were unmistakable. Ghouls! There was no time to ponder why the monsters had followed them, now was only the time to kill. The little devils never knew he was there, as each of Radnor's hands grasped them by the throat, and suddenly squeezed until there was nothing left of their necks but blood and bone. Moving quickly, Radnor seized the bow dropped by one of the monsters, and let fly with a hail of arrows into the trees. He couldn't see exactly where other devils were, and no cries of pain spoke of a successful hit. But he didn't need to hit the little bastards; he just needed to make them keep their heads down long enough to allow Leif and his people to escape.

After he had exhausted his arrows, Radnor turned to the river to see that Leif had made the right choice. He and his men were now swimming across the river, though Radnor spied that one of Leif's men now lay still among the rock and sand of the shore. Radnor picked up the daggers that the ghouls had carried, and began watching for movement among the brush.

It did not take long for him to spy several ghouls cautiously working their way through the overgrown plants, hunting him. One of them stepped out into the open, greedily looking to the river to see if it could get a taste of the dead warrior. Radnor seized his moment, and, feeling the weight of the dagger in his hand, whipped it end over end at the ghoul. Radnor cursed as his throw was misaligned, and the dagger hit handle first. The ghoul toppled to the ground, senseless for the moment, but otherwise unharmed. Now knowing his position, the others rushed him. There were fewer of them than Radnor had thought, each carrying their daggers or short spears. The leader of the pack came at him with the most ferocity, and was the first to feel one of Radnor's daggers slip past its ribs and into its heart. As Radnor tried to pull the dagger out of the carcass, the primitive blade got stuck in the ribs, the final insult the hellion could muster.

Radnor was forced to let go of the weapon and hurriedly sidestepped a spear thrust aimed for his heart. Turning on his feet, Radnor found himself dancing amid the blade strokes meant for him. Remembering his master's teaching, Radnor found the calm place he needed to be in, living in the moment, and only in the moment. Their wild blows were easy for him to track as they went, but hard to predict before they started. The ghouls lacked the tactical discipline of a swordsman, and their attacks resembled the wild flailing of angry children.

Finally, Radnor found his opening! His fist brutally smashed into the head of the one of the spearmen, and he was able to snatch up its weapon as his opponent fell. Now armed again, Radnor was able to regain the offensive. The crude weapon was light, with a spearhead made from stone instead of iron. But, it didn't matter to Radnor. It still killed all who opposed him. Two more of the monsters fell, and the ghouls seemed to fall back slightly. Mistaking this for a retreat, Radnor started to consider making his own retreat to rejoin the others. Only a sudden rustling in the leaves above his head provided him any warning of what was coming.

Radnor spun to face the ghoul that now leaped for his back, dagger driving down to his neck. Radnor tried to evade the blow, but only partially succeeded. He heard himself scream in agony as the blade dug deep into the already existing wound on his shoulder. Pain lanced through his whole being, and he collapsed with the monster on top of him. Blinded by pain, Radnor seized on the first thing his hands could find. Fortunately for him, it was the ghoul that sat astride his chest, aiming its dagger for Radnor's heart! In a flurry of violence, the monster was torn limb from limb as Radnor's hands ripped and tore at anything they could reach. Acting on blind instinct, Radnor was able to smash and crush the ghouls who tried to jump on him while he was down. Scrambling to his feet, Radnor finally regained enough composure to watch the remaining ghouls flee before him. Blood dripped from all across his body, and Radnor spat to try to rid the acrid taste of it from his mouth. No success. He checked his shoulder and saw that it bled freely again. Shocking pain ran through his arm if he even thought about moving it. There was a new cut that ran perpendicular to the vampire bite, making the wound even more ghastly. Radnor found himself cursing Hymmur, the god of his homeland, for leaving him in this predicament.

As Radnor trudged to the shoreline, he was pleased to find that Darestr awaited him on the other shore. He was less pleased to see that the others were still there as well. In fact, Radnor saw that Leif and his men, now fully armed, were riding their horses back across the river towards him. Radnor's mind raced. They were coming for him while he was unarmed and wounded. In his current state, Radnor knew this was a fight he could not win, nor escape from. They would exact revenge on him while they had the chance. Well, if that was their plan, he intended to make the river run with blood before he fell. Radnor stood defiantly, hands open and relaxed, ready to face his foes head on. No matter what else happened, he would be sure that Leif would be the first one he killed.

"Veigarand, are you all right?" Leif asked as he and his men came ashore. Radnor did not reply, but instead watched for them to try to encircle him. To his surprise, they did not.

"Are you deaf man? I asked if you were all right!" Leif scolded impatiently.

Radnor finally came to the realization that they were not here to kill him.

"More or less," he said, still regaining the frame of mind needed to talk to the man he had just planned to kill.

Leif stared grimly at Radnor's blood covered form, and noticed the blood trickling from where Radnor now clutched his shoulder.

"Looks to me like less. Come on, we need to keep moving."

The ealdorman abruptly broke off the conversation and with his men, headed for the trees where the ghouls lay.

"That's all right," Radnor muttered to himself sarcastically. "I wouldn't like any rest. I think I'd rather take a bath right now anyway."

Mechanically, Radnor trudged to the water's edge and slowly swam across the river. Fire lanced through his arm at every stroke, but he simply gritted his teeth and kept going. The cold water felt good soaking into the wound, and helped to wash the acrid taste and smell of ghoul's blood from his mouth and nose.

As he painfully trudged up the opposite shore, Radnor smelled smoke and fire. Turning, he saw that Leif and his men had set fire to the trees in the area, hoping to prevent the ghouls from following them for a time. Several ghouls had been flushed out of hiding, and Leif's men took great joy in butchering the monsters as they fled.

As Radnor came out of the water, he found himself totally drained of energy. He hadn't eaten or slept for several days, and this fight had taken more out of him than usual. Once on shore, he dropped to his knees, and found himself slumping over in exhaustion. A frightened yell from the people around him reached his ears, but he could pay them no heed as he just focused on breathing for the moment. Rolf, Elena, and Alban came running to him and helped him to sit back up. Alban, like before, had a cup of water ready at Radnor's lips. Radnor turned his head away from the drink.

"Alban, don't you think I've had enough water for one day?"

The four of them couldn't help but laugh a little, as they all helped Radnor back to his feet, and led him back over to where Darestr had stood, patiently but worriedly, waiting for his master. As Radnor's friends walked him to where he could sit and have his wounds attended to, Radnor turned to Alban and asked a question.

"What in the devil were you doing in the river? Right after you were thrown, I saw you keep diving down, but you never made any move to swim out of the water."

Alban found himself laughing at Radnor's question, as though it were a strange jest. There was a gleam in his eye that suggested the stress of the events had not quite worn off, despite his calm demeanor.

"Oh, curse my foolishness! It seems I went mad when the fight broke out. I had lost my good luck charm in my fall, and in the heat of the moment, I placed so much faith in that trinket that I lost all sense!"

Radnor sympathized with Alban. If he had lost his ring in that river, it would have taken Adramelach himself to tear him away from searching for it.

"Did you find it?" Elena asked.

"Thank Caelum, I did!" Alban exclaimed.

"Good," Rolf replied. "Now maybe you'd like to share some of that luck with the rest of us?"

Elena tore a section of her skirt away, and began trying to wrap it around Radnor's shoulder. It was messy work, as he was still bleeding. As she tightened the knot on the bandage, Radnor yelped in pain, and his hand went to grab hers. Their fingers met, and Radnor stopped. The two shared a look, but it was broken by Leif's return.

"All right!" Leif yelled

"I know you're all tired, and if you're anything like me, you're so tired you want to just lie down right here and sleep until it's spring again. We do not have that kind of time. Our enemy has just proven his relentlessness, and we need to stay one step ahead of him. Fill every container we have with water, and get ready to ride. We will not stop at sunset. We must ride now, and not stop until Wulfgeld!"

As people began gathering their things, Leif turned to Radnor, who was still sitting. The others had gone to collect their things or help collect water, leaving Leif and Radnor alone.

"What made you wait for me?" Radnor asked.

But Leif did not answer. Instead, Leif grabbed Radnor by his wounded shoulder, and squeezed, resulting in a gasping cry of surprise and pain from him. Leif leaned in close to Radnor's face, his eyes alight with anger.

"I lost another man today. His name was Heston. The forest now lies as his funeral pyre. If ghouls are just scavengers, do you want to explain to me why they're following us? Or is it that they're following *you*?"

Leif squeezed tighter now. Pain lashed through Radnor's body with such strength his vision began to narrow, and he struggled to breathe. No amount of training could have prepared him for the agony he was in. Exhaustion and pain took him, and Radnor felt himself start to black out. Leif felt a strange sort of pity when he saw Radnor's defenseless state, and let go of his arm. Radnor let out a gasp as the pain stopped, and his vision started to clear again. Leif's face came into focus, and anger swelled in Radnor's heart. Radnor's eyes locked onto Leif's neck. The enraged demigod was about to leap upon the ealdorman with the last of his strength when he remembered his oath to protect Leif and his people, and chose instead to answer his question.

"I don't know. I've never seen ghouls act this way. I've never been hunted by them, and I've only run into them myself on two occasions in ten years. Both times were small packs of five or six, and both times were as I was camped near the sites of the battles where I earned the name you love to use so much. They were scavenging from the dead, or trying to ambush a lone man in his sleep. Never have I seen them band together and become active hunters."

Rolf came over to investigate the noise, but only found the two conversing.

"Is everything all right?" Rolf asked.

"Yes," Radnor said, through gritted teeth. "Leif tried to help me up, and I yelped in pain."

"Yes," added Leif hastily. "I accidentally took him by the wounded arm. I wasn't thinking."

Rolf took their words at face value, and went back to his work.

Leif then stared down at Radnor.

"You confuse me, Veigarand. That's the only reason you're still alive."

Radnor glared back up at Leif, angry at his treatment, but not enough to repeat his mistake when he killed Bron.

"If you want me to go, I'll go. If the ghouls really are only hunting me, as you say they are, then they'll follow me and leave you alone."

"I've considered that already," Leif said. "I considered many things as I rode up on you on the far shore, all covered in blood. You have brought ruin upon my people, but in the wake of that ruin, you have brought salvation. Even here, I drive my hands into your wounds, bringing you searing pain, and you choose not to lift a finger against me. But when Bron tried to defend his friend, you struck him down without any hesitation. Like I said, you confuse me. And that's why I will have you fulfill your oath, and help escort us to Wulfgeld. You see, if I'm wrong, and the ghouls are hunting all of us, sending you away will only condemn my people to certain death. That's a chance I cannot take. I need your ability to kill working for me."

As Leif started to walk away, he turned to look back at Radnor.

"And to answer your question, I stayed because there was too much protest to leaving you behind. It seems that some have already forgotten what put us on the road to begin with."

"Who was it?" Radnor asked. "Elena? Alban? Rolf?"

"Yes to all three," Leif said. "But Klane was possibly the most vehement that we not leave you behind. He said he had unfinished business with you that he needed to attend to himself."

Leif then left Radnor to puzzle over Klane's involvement. Rolf then returned to see if Radnor needed anything, and to find out more of what had just happened between Radnor and Leif. Radnor explained things to Rolf, but left out the part where Leif had briefly tortured him. The rational part of his mind told him that the last thing these people needed was to be divided about Leif's leadership, and he had a hard time blaming Leif for his anger. The less rational part of Radnor's mind could only picture his hands around Leif's throat. Upon hearing the situation, and seeing that the ride was about to resume, Rolf felt the need to make a witty remark.

"It could be worse. It could be raining!"

Chapter 8

It rained…two endless nights of cold, unending rain, with a third well on the way. No one ate, and what little sleep anyone got was done in the saddle. Radnor did find some relief on the night of the second day.

Alban snuck off unnoticed at one point, and returned with the juices of a berry that he had spotted growing in abundance around them. A berry that Radnor had noticed no one was choosing to ease their hunger with. The berry was called "aleas", and was a powerful pain killer and sedative. Taken in small amounts, it was enough to act as an effective pain reliever. Take a little more, and it would put you to sleep. Eating enough of the berries to satisfy one's hunger was enough to kill. By Alban's explanation it was used to make the potion they had used to keep Radnor asleep all those days ago back in Neugeld. How long had it been…a week? A month? Radnor could not remember. It was probably only a week or two since they fled that place, but it was hard to keep track. Radnor had been thankful for the aid, as his arm tore at him more and more each day. A few drops of the tasteless juice added to his water each day helped to ease his pain a great deal.

Elena also found time to check on Radnor, and Radnor was often glad of her company. They talked of their childhoods, and found ironic comfort in their mutual hardship. This is how Radnor learned that Elena was an orphan who had been found and adopted by a man named Tryggr.

No one in Neugeld knew where she had come from, and no worried parents had ever arrived to claim her. Even the traders from the kingdoms of Wollendan and Ranrike were unable to explain Elena's origin. Her raven hair was a giveaway that she was not from the north, as the northern peoples had hair in various shades of red, blonde or brown. Black hair was only found on people from the Southworld, and none of them had the same pale skin tone that the northerners did.

Despite being well cared for by Tryggr, Elena always found herself somewhat of an outsider among the people of Neugeld. She had considered running away on several occasions, but her love for her adoptive father had kept her there. Tryggr was an old man even when he took her in. His own wife had passed on to the Eladden Fields, where peace loving folk loyal to Caelum were free to roam and rejoice. Tryggr had never had any children, and was well past the age of sowing his own. He had truly loved Elena as his own daughter, and she did not wish to abandon him. Radnor learned that the marriage to Halmda had been arranged by Tryggr on his death bed as an attempt on his part to make sure that Elena was cared for after he was gone. It was during this conversation that Klane rode to join them, and timidly asked to speak to Radnor alone.

Elena nervously took her leave, unsure of where this was going, and joined Rolf and Alban in their vigorous conversation about how nice it would be to have hot rain right about now.

Klane pulled up alongside Radnor, but did not look at him. Radnor may not have looked anything but tired, but behind the baggy eyes a killer still lay in wait, ready for any attempt Klane might make to kill him. Klane had a score to settle still.

"Veigarand, it has taken me two days to work up the courage to speak to you thus. It was but days ago that I tried to put a blade through your heart."

"Tried?" Radnor said. "Were it not for my armor, you would have succeeded!"

Klane winced at the reminder.

"I also tried to kill you at the grave. I must also confess to you, there was a third time I tried to kill you. We kept you asleep for several days. I...saw my chance, snuck into the cell where you were being kept... and gave you an overdose. I thought I had killed you...your heart was so still," Klane stammered. "I needed to confess this to you now, and, ask for your forgiveness."

There was an awkward silence between the two of them, as Radnor tried to process what he had just heard, and Klane nervously awaited his reply.

"What made you decide to do this?" Radnor asked.

"The events at the river, and some words from Elena, have made me see some things differently. I don't know if I can ever forgive you for killing my brother, not really. But, Elena told me you were the one who dove in and saved my life, despite my attempts to kill you."

Klane paused for a moment, whether it was to draw breath or to gather his thoughts, Radnor did not know.

"In fact, you were the only one who tried to save me. No one else even lifted a finger. I know that the ghoul attack happened quickly after I fell, so maybe I can't judge too harshly...but...you were the only one. When I learned that, and after seeing you come staggering out of the river, bleeding, out of breath...all because of your efforts to save us. You could have abandoned us, but instead you have endured punishment from not only those monsters, but also from the people you seek to protect."

"Given that I'm still riding among you, not too much punishment, thankfully," Radnor said.

Klane almost cracked a smile, and resumed his speech.

"I saw what Leif did to you, and I was surprised to find that I wanted to stop him. I didn't know what to do, and I am ashamed to say...I did nothing. I haven't known what to do for the last two days. While I may never be able to call you my friend, I think I am able to call you my ally."

There was silence between them, for a time. Radnor finally issued his reply.

"I don't know if it helps, but I know what it is like to lose a brother. I lost my older brother when I was a child."

Klane found himself taken aback for a moment. Veigarand, the ghost from the kingdom now ashes, had had a brother.

"We were training in combat from horseback. I was maybe ten years old at the time. He was fourteen years old, and would be a man in three years' time. The prince-ling would become the prince. My sword master Halbjorn was also watching, as well as the king. It was a long, tiring day. Most of the time the two of us were doing drills regarding controlling our horses to out maneuver an opponent. We were both well versed in controlling our mounts in general, but against an opponent, that was new. Imagine the most visceral game of chess imaginable, as each move would spell victory or death in a real fight. Well, my brother, Ulfr, made a move that spelled death. There was a collision, and both of our horses tumbled to the ground. I was able to roll away from the falling bodies. Ulfr wasn't. Both horses came down on top of him. By the time we got the horses off of him, it was too late. He died in my arms. I miss him dearly. He was a kind soul. He had a strong sense of duty, and his mind was set on becoming a good and proper king, one who would lead his people to prosperity."

Radnor trailed off, as memories of his brother's death haunted him. There were details of the collision that Radnor did not tell Klane in that moment, details even Radnor was unsure of.

"Did you have any other siblings?" Klane asked.

"Yes," Radnor replied. "I had a younger brother, Kjeltil. He died when my people were attacked by the Krigari."

More questions burned in Klane's mind.

"People have been talking, and your words I think prove it true. You were the heir to the Amarantheon throne?"

"Yes, officially I was. Though, if you heard that from the others, then I'm sure you've heard of my blood and what I truly am. How can I be the heir if I wasn't actually from the blood of the king? Well, the union between my mother and Adramelach was a secret, but my existence was not. To the public and to the court, I was a legitimate son of King Magnus. I was the heir as soon as Ulfr died. This fact chafed Magnus to no end, but it had to be done to prevent suspicion. If the truth got out, then the cults that worship the Krigari would know and the element of surprise would be lost to us. I would be a useless weapon."

"So, what did you do?" Klane asked.

"I did what I was told. By day, I was educated to be the new heir to the throne. I was given lessons in geography, history, politics, and economics to name a few subjects. And believe me, there was a lot of catching up to do. These studies had been neglected for much of my life, as I had instead been taught almost exclusively how to fight. Up to that point, my academic studies had been just enough to pass for the child of nobility. After Ulfr died, every waking moment that I wasn't training with Halbjorn was spent reading and writing."

"I wish I could read," Klane said. "I never had a teacher. All I've ever known is swineherding. I can tell you everything you could ever want to know about planting seeds, or working with pigs and other animals. But I would never be able to write it down."

"Well, since our blood feud is at an end, perhaps you will allow me to teach you someday!" Radnor exclaimed.

Klane's eyes lit up at the thought. But first, they had more riding ahead of them.

Chapter 9

The rain finally stopped at noon on the fourth day. However, the weather provided no relief. Behind the rain arrived a new wave of cold wind, whipping the water still clinging to the trees into the eyes and faces of the weary travelers. Much to the relief of most of the refugees, Leif finally called their party to a stop. This change made Radnor worry more, and he hastily moved from the back of the line to the front.

Radnor was not surprised to see that Leif did not share the happiness of the crowd, but was instead staring at a river with a troubled look in his eye. The Argirn River zigzagged around and was blocking their path again. Radnor focused on the terrain in front of him, and he understood the problem. The torrential water rushed along at a rapid pace, a pace which would carry a man from his feet if the river was even shallow enough to wade. And from the look of things, that in itself was also doubtful. The river was perhaps only twenty feet wide, but that distance might have well been a mile the way the water rushed and crashed against the rocks of the shore. To make matters worse, the bridge that stretched across this part of the river had lost several supports, and the rotted wood of those that remained looked unable to hold the weight of even a single man. Leif spoke first.

"Fuck."

"Fuck indeed," Radnor replied. "Is there a better place to perform a crossing?"

Leif cursed some more before replying properly.

"There are, further upstream, back where we came from, and I'm not sure we'll survive more than a few more nights out here like this. Fucking rain! You see those supports there?"

Leif pointed angrily at the space where pillars that should have connected the bridge to the riverbed were now damaged or missing.

"The river here is overflowing from all of the extra rain this past week, and I would eat my own beard if the added strength in the river didn't carry those supports away."

"Then, I guess our only choice is to move along the river to somewhere we can wade across, like last time," Radnor suggested.

Leif shook his head in disgust at the situation.

"It's getting colder by the day, and the food we've found is simply not enough. The people are starving, and at some point we will need to take food from the children if we are to save their parents."

"Well, there should be fish in the river, correct?" Radnor asked.

"Not around here. It's spawning season for the fish that live in this river, so they all headed south, to Wulfgeld. The fishermen there are having their best days of the year right now."

Radnor now found himself cursing with Leif; luck had yet again turned against them in every conceivable manner. It wasn't until Elena came forward to join them that the two men were brought from their not so silent profanity.

"People are asking about what we are to do next. A few have seen how harsh the river is, and people are too afraid to attempt a crossing. I happen to agree with them."

"Tell them we are trying to think of something," Leif said gruffly.

Elena took a moment to look at the river herself, saw the broken supports, and had an idea.

"Leif, what were the missing supports made from, wood?"

"Yes, what of it? People are starving and freezing. We have to cross now, or not at all."

Elena sighed in frustration.

"And what are we currently surrounded by?"

It was at this moment that excitement gleamed in Leif's eye. Radnor was still at a loss.

"You are a brilliant woman! In my exhaustion, the simplest solution escaped me!" Leif exclaimed. "All we need to do is fix the damned bridge...and we're in the clear!"

"In the clear?" Radnor said.

"Yes, the main trade road that leads to Wulfgeld is not far from the other side of this river. Once we can get across, it will not take long for us to find some inn or other homestead where we can find shelter! Come on! We have no time to lose!"

Leif wasted no time in setting his men to work felling trees and gathering the materials needed to tie the timber together. Progress was slow, as nearly half their number were dead, wounded, or otherwise incapable of helping because of the ghoul attacks or illness from the weather. Radnor proved most helpful; as he was able to fell and split the logs from two trees by himself in the time it took groups to fell a single great oak. Women and children were set to the task of taking every strap they had off of saddles, bags, and clothing. The plan was to patch up the damage done by the river by tying pieces of wood into place to reinforce the areas missing supports, and to simply cross one at a time to minimize the strain of the weight on the bridge.

While this work went on, a few pairs of men were sent out with weapons to find kindling to use for camp fires. It was clear that that bridge was not going to be finished before the next morning. Once the trees were felled, next came the splitting of logs into usable pieces. The work was hard and slow, as the few axes they had were dulled in the recent combat, or by the felling of the trees in the first place. But, piece by piece, they were able to make slow but satisfactory progress.

Radnor, with his superior strength, found himself given the task of tying the crude wood planks into place with whatever scrap material they could find. Leif grew impatient with Radnor's work here. The Amarantheon noble had been very cautious in his work. He spent time soaking everything he was given to tie into knots, as anything tied dry would stretch and loosen once the river water had a chance to thoroughly soak through the fabric and leather. It took a considerable effort, and a sizable dose of the aleas juice to dull the pain in his arm, but the job was nearing completion by the time the sun had finished setting.

When Radnor came ashore from his work, having hit a point where even the light of a torch held aloft by Elena hadn't been able to provide enough light for him to work by, he found a tense scene. Leif was ordering men to be armed, and for a defensive line to be formed from the remaining pieces of log and firewood. Radnor came running to Leif, and hurriedly asked to know what was going on.

"Alban and Klane haven't returned from their last trip to find fire wood. I fear that means ghouls."

Radnor felt a pit form at the bottom of his stomach. He had to find Alban as quickly as possible. Whatever it took, he was not going to leave the young man out in the woods alone.

Dashing back to Darestr, Radnor threw on his armor in a blinding flurry of action, seizing his sword and shield as he went. Once done, Radnor turned to enter the forest and begin his search for the two men. However, Radnor did not need to leave the encampment, as Alban's frantic screaming was heard but a moment before he came dashing from the tree line and into the mob of worried people. His breathing was ragged, and the poor young man's clothes and face were splashed in blood. His panicked shouts were totally incoherent until Leif was able to shake him back to sanity.

"Klane! They got Klane!" Alban yelled.

"Ghouls?" Leif demanded, already knowing the answer.

Alban nodded intensely, and stuttering, he began again.

"They came pouring from the trees, more than we've ever faced before, it's like they knew we would be here. It's like they knew we would be..."

"Trapped—" Radnor finished.

Radnor turned to face Leif.

"I think you'll have to eat your beard Leif, it wasn't the water that tore those supports down. The ghouls somehow got ahead of us and they wrecked the bridge. Then they only needed to wait for the cover of night to steal upon us."

Radnor turned back to Alban.

"Was there any hope for Klane?"

Alban could only shake his head.

It was Klane's blood that was smeared across Alban's clothes and face. Leif grabbed Alban by the shoulders, and hoisted him back on his feet.

"You listen here!" Leif barked. "I need you to go get a weapon, make everyone grab a weapon! If the ghouls are here for us, then we'll need anyone capable of holding a sword or tree branch to be swinging one!"

Alban took a deep breath, swallowed his fear, and ran to join the others. Orders erupted from Leif's mouth, as the spare wood was now set ablaze, both to provide illumination for the men to fight by, but also to force the enemy to worry about avoiding the fires as they fought.

All was still. Even the wind seemed to wait in anticipation of the battle that was to come. Firelight danced wickedly against the grass and trees, taunting the defenders with shadows of death. But, no attack came. Leif's men held their formation, and Radnor grew impatient. He would not let the monsters wait them out and wear them down. He would not sit among the flames, exhausting himself in nervousness while the damned creatures sat lazily in the shadows. Radnor stepped forward, and with a few great strides had fully separated himself from the others. It was at this moment, that all hell broke loose.

Over a hundred pairs of glowing eyes suddenly made their presence known in the shadows, and started a frenzied rush to bring down the steel titan. Leaping backwards as he slashed, Radnor found himself among a horde of his enemies, all of them clawing and slashing at him with a crazed ferocity unknown to any man. The distance back to Leif's men was short and bloody, as Radnor hewed and slaughtered his way through more than a dozen of the little monsters until he was able to rejoin the shield wall. Despite their losses, the ghouls kept up their assault. The tidal wave of sharp toothed monsters slammed into their line, unable to flank them due to the fire pits between which Leif had done well to place his line. Snarling, clawing things ripped and tore at men's shields, crazily trying to overwhelm the warriors with sheer force of numbers. At first, the strength of the men held, and they beat back the suicidal assault the ghouls mounted. However, in the dim, fire lit night; one man found that two ghouls he tread upon and thought were dead were anything but. The little monsters slashed and stabbed his legs with their primitive stone daggers. The man came toppling to the ground, screaming in agony as the ghouls started to cut him to ribbons.

Leif started to throw an avenging stroke with his ax, but there was no time! More ghouls flooded through the hole in the line that was left by the dead man. Ducking the leap of an attacker, Leif screamed for help from the rear. And help came. Elena and several of the other women came rushing to the fore. While not as well armed as the others, the sudden ferocity of their attack came as a surprise to the ghouls, and the women successfully stopped the ghouls from overrunning the shield wall. It was also much to Radnor's pleasure to see that Alban had recovered his senses enough to join the fight. Out of the corner of his eye, he saw Alban's ax connect with a ghoul's head, and saw as Alban grimly tore the blade from the monster's skull, ready to swing again. Upon seeing the element of surprise was lost, the ghouls ended their frantic assault, and faded back into the shadows. While they may have retreated for the moment, the glow of their yellow eyes never faded from the night. They would try again before the night was over, but first, both sides needed to lick their wounds.

Leif had the body of the fallen man removed from the blood soaked battlefield. Two of the brave women whom had joined the fight had also fallen. With no armor to protect them, the ghoul blades had torn their brave souls from their bodies. Both of them had children they had died to protect, and more orphans were made that night. Children cautiously came forward with cups of water for their fathers and mothers to quickly drain before the fighting could begin anew. Alban withdrew to the horses, and seemed to be looking for something. Radnor was about to call out to him, when Leif approached him.

"What do you think? Is the bridge ready for us to attempt a crossing?"

Radnor shook his head.

"Not yet, especially if we had to cross all in one go. I like your thinking though. The bridge could be used as a bottle neck, or we could fire it and keep the ghouls on this side of the river."

Leif laughed sardonically at this.

"Keep them trapped on this side? My dear Veigarand, the damn things seem to be able to outpace us at every turn! They managed to not only follow us across the Argirn, but to overtake us without us knowing, wreck the bridge here, and lie in wait for us whilst we rode day and night to get here! There is as much chance of us escaping these vermin as there is of you escaping the curse that hangs over your head!"

Radnor fell silent. Leif had a point. The monsters had inexplicably been able to keep up with them at every turn. Any time they were vulnerable, the damn creatures were there, ready to pounce. Nothing made any sense to this. During Radnor's conversation with Leif, Alban returned with a glass of water which he offered to Radnor.

"This has become a tradition now, hasn't it?" Radnor said as he took the cup.

Alban laughed as yet again, he found himself being the one to bring Radnor water after a hard fight. Alban hoped it would be the last time.

An angry growl from the shadows sounded almost as soon as Radnor finished his drink. The fight was about to begin again. The shouts of men echoed around the trees as the snarls of monsters shuddered through the air. The shield wall was set, and not a moment too soon. Again, the ghouls came leaping like things gone mad against the defensive line set before them. The men were more cautious this time. They were careful not to let any of the creatures get a chance to rush in close to their legs, where the men's shields blocked their vision. This caution also meant killing the beasts was slower work. Men grew tired and breathless. Days with poor sleep and poor eating were taking their toll, and their movements became more and more sluggish.

Even Radnor found his strength waning. He felt out of place, as though he were no longer inhabiting his own skin, and despite the adrenaline rushing through his body, he felt the inevitable pull of sleep tugging more and more at him, dragging his arms down. The painful jab of a ghoul's blade into his armored abdomen brought him back to reality long enough to drive his sharpened shield through the creature's brain, but that was it. For reasons he could not explain, his vision blurred, and he realized that it was not exhaustion that now made him lose all feeling in his limbs, but something else…

There was a scream as he collapsed in a heap on the ground. Ghouls broke off their attack on the others, and tried to swarm him. Leif reacted quickly, and his men were able to kill the first wave of monsters that tried to reach Radnor. The ghouls seemed even more visibly angry at this setback, and resumed their assault on Leif's men. Panting, Radnor tried to bring himself to his feet, but could do no better than kneel. Radnor dropped his weapons, and struggled to remove his helmet, which now felt like it was smothering him. As he finally sat back up from dumping his helmet in the dirt, a ghoul blade arced to his head. Instinctively, Radnor caught the monster by the wrist, and answered with a punch that sent the creature dead into the dirt. However, a second blade went soaring for his neck, and Radnor could not turn in time. In desperation, Radnor tried to spin his body away from the attack, but found he couldn't get his body to cooperate in time. Only a well-placed block by Leif's shield saved Radnor from certain death. Radnor felt the ealdorman start to drag him away from the fight, when an enraged shout echoed above all of the violence and clash of weapons.

"*No*! Let him suffer his fate!"

Radnor thought the voice sounded familiar, but couldn't think well enough to place it.

"*Stop*!" The voice commanded, and stop they did.

Every single ghoul stopped its bloody assault, and took a step back. Radnor slowly looked up from the dirt, and saw a pile of the dead. Mostly ghouls, but two more of Leif's men had fallen, and Radnor also saw that a boy of around Rolf's age had joined the fight, only to be cut down in the melee. As Radnor raised his head, he finally saw the owner of the domineering voice. Alban stood above him, ax raised, with only Leif between him and Radnor.

"Alban? What are you doing?" Leif demanded, eyes darting anxiously between the ghouls and the sight before him.

"What you should have done long ago!" Alban cried.

"You would take revenge upon him right now of all times? Have you gone mad?" Leif bellowed.

"No, my mind has never been clearer. I finally found a way to make it work!"

Alban then withdrew the strange trinket Elena had asked about, his "good luck charm", from his pouch.

Radnor could barely make it out in the dim light, but the now burning sigil showed the mark of the Krigari god Ashrahan, the power giver.

"What the fuck are you talking about?" Leif demanded.

Stammering, Radnor tried to explain.

"He…he worships them."

Alban, soaked in blood and framed against the fire lit sky, laughed the laugh of a mad man.

"You stupid fool! I don't worship them! I never heard of these damn monsters until after you arrived! When you left me alone to fend for myself after you set fire to my home, they came to me. The demons found me, but did not kill me. Instead, their leader, a black-eyed man gave me this amulet, and told me that if I did not take my revenge, that he would never stop hunting us until we all were dead. With this, he told me, I could command the ghouls, and I would be able to take my revenge upon you! Ghouls from every corner have been converging on us since we left Neugeld. These ghouls didn't catch up to us…these came in from across the river!"

Radnor tried to process what Alban was saying. If a black-eyed man gave him that amulet, it could only mean that one of the Krigari themselves came through the portal with this tool.

Leif stood up in front of Alban, in shock, and enraged by what he heard.

"So, you sent these monsters to kill us all, just so you could have your revenge?"

Alban took a step back, and looked genuinely hurt by Leif's accusation.

"No...no...it's not like that! The amulet...is difficult. It takes more than rage and intent to make it work. The ghouls attacked on my command, but they attacked indiscriminately. I dropped it when we first crossed the Argirn, and my control was lost. But now I have finally mastered the amulet's power!"

"You call this mastering its power?" Leif cried, waving his arms over the bodies of the fallen.

"They died protecting a murderer. They died because they were helping Veigarand! They forgot who they were, and betrayed all of us when they gave him help!"

Radnor's head still swam, but he still fought to regain control of his muscles. Alban had poisoned him with the water he had offered, overdosed him with that damn berry juice. He wasn't sure, but Radnor thought he heard Elena's voice ring out over the crowd.

"If you wanted him dead so badly, why did you demand Leif wait when we were attacked the other day? Why did you try so hard to help him time and again?"

"Because, you stupid bitch, I had to make sure he died! I need to be able to tell the black-eyed man I accomplished my task, or he will kill us all! I thought I had succeeded back at the river crossing! When the bastard came stumbling out of the trees still breathing, it was too late to do anything but play the game I'd been playing the whole time."

Alban furiously returned his gaze to Leif.

"And *you*! You had him at your mercy when we first crossed! If you had had the guts to kill him then, we would be free of all of this already!"

In his frantic madness, Alban turned back to Elena.

"I needed him to trust me, so I could get close enough, and maybe take revenge without needing the ghouls. But, the fucker never takes his armor off! Slipping a knife between his ribs was out of the question. Klane proved that one already."

Radnor finally was able to bring himself back up onto his knees. If he could get to the knife in his boot, and aim a throw...

"What really happened to Klane?" Radnor asked. "Was he in on your plan? Is he about to reveal himself from behind the trees?"

Alban sneered down at Radnor.

"No, the pathetic fool really did have a change of heart. I tried to break away from him so I could summon the ghouls, but he caught me in the act. I had no choice. I'm not an experienced fighter, and there was no way I was going to overpower him without help. At least the ghouls made it quick."

Radnor finally felt his fingers reach the hilt of his boot knife, now he needed to draw it without Alban noticing. His strength was already returning; his body having grown accustomed to the drug in his system through his use of it as a pain killer for his arm. The effects were wearing off faster than Alban had predicted.

"Now, my lord ealdorman…" Alban started "If you would kindly move from my path, I will avenge our fallen brothers and sisters, and we can be gone from this place!"

"And what of the ghouls?" Leif asked.

"Were you not listening?" Alban exclaimed. "I command them with this!" he shouted, waving the amulet in Leif's face. "Once Veigarand is killed, I will send them away to their little holes where they came from!"

Leif turned to look at the ghouls that now surrounded them. Their glowing eyes and salivating mouths told a different story from the one Alban believed.

"Send them back now, Alban, and I'll move from your path," Leif said.

Radnor cursed inside his own mind. He only had time for one throw, and Alban needed to be the one to go down. But as soon as he killed Alban, Leif would cut him down anyway. Radnor heard Alban's voice ring with cold malice as he ordered the ghouls to retreat. There was a moment's pause, then the ghouls did as he commanded. One by one, the glowing eyes faded further and further back into the trees. Even though they had retreated, their shining eyes could still be seen against the oppressive darkness.

Seemingly satisfied by the ghouls' retreat back into the trees, Leif stepped aside, leaving nothing but open air between Alban and his prey.

The vengeance crazed man stepped forward, his eyes revealed nothing but malice as firelight danced within them. Radnor needed to wait for his moment, right when Alban was committed to his swing before Radnor could be sure his hazily aimed throw would strike true.

Alban smiled with satisfaction at having finally achieved his goal. He drew his ax back for the stroke that would slay the ghost of the north, the wayfaring death. But, his blow was not to be. Screaming in pain, Alban found that he stood transfixed in place. His right hand dropped his ax, as his left hand found the blade of Leif's ax buried deep in his side. Alban gasped for air, but instead only choked on blood. Radnor then saw his own sword pierce through Alban's body from behind, and only then did he see Elena's form step away from the man she had just stabbed. As Alban collapsed to the ground, more of Leif's men attacked him, taking their vengeance upon the man who had caused them to be hounded and killed. Radnor sat in place, stunned by what he saw before him. However, the time for such things was not now. With angry howls, the ghouls came pouring from their hiding places, ready to finish the slaughter.

While Radnor's condition had improved, he found that he only had time for one knife throw before the things would be on top of them, tearing and slashing and biting. Dead or not, Alban had doomed them all. Radnor let his knife fly and watched with some satisfaction as his final blow found its mark in the throat of one of the hideous monsters. Leif gave orders to his men, and they reformed their shield wall, facing death with bravery that matched that of the most seasoned warrior of Amaranthar. The men braced themselves for the impact of the charge, but it never came.

Much to their amazement, the ghouls stopped in their tracks. Stunned, Leif spun to his left and right to find the cause of this sudden change. It was not until he turned all the way around that he saw what was happening. Elena stood, hands still coated in Alban's blood, with the amulet clutched between her fingers. Silently…wordlessly…she commanded the ghouls to stop. Frozen in place, the monsters found themselves in her thrall. When Alban had commanded them, it was only a suggestion, they felt a desire to obey, but in the end, their hunger would overtake any control he had. This was not so against Elena's command. Her unspoken order to stop had thundered through the minds of every ghoul there. They had no choice but to obey. Leif saw his opportunity, and set his example by hewing the head from the shoulders of every ghoul that stood before him. His men followed suit, and soon every single person capable of bearing arms took to killing the helpless ghouls, frozen by Elena's will, unable to defend themselves against the mighty wrath of those they had planned to devour. The slaughter was over in a matter of minutes, and by the end, every single ghoul that had dared come to satisfy its monstrous hunger lay dead upon the field. Breathing heavily, Leif surveyed the carnage before him.

The field they camped in was now marked not by forest, but instead by fire, steel, and blood. Leif came over to Radnor, and helped him up by Radnor's unwounded arm. Staring unwaveringly into Radnor's eyes with a look of bitterness, Leif spoke.

"I think I begin to understand you, Veigarand. Perhaps they will have a name for me soon."

Leif left Radnor standing alone in the field of death, and began to put out the fires started for the battle. Radnor stood alone among the remains of the carnage; until he saw Rolf and Elena come to where he mourned. Elena met him in a close embrace, caring not for the blood and filth which covered Radnor's body. Radnor was surprised to find that even Rolf joined in the embrace. The three stood like this for what seemed like an eternity, until Radnor finally had to break from them to begin the painful process of washing the blood from his body, and redressing the wound in his shoulder, which had opened yet again.

Part 2:
<u>Wulfgeld</u>

Chapter 10

Two days had passed since Alban died. In those two days, Elena had not heard Radnor speak a single word. She found herself growing worried for him, as it seemed that Alban's betrayal had hurt him far more than any of the physical injuries Radnor endured during the fighting. Leif had ordered the dead to be buried the morning after Alban's death. The ealdorman had excluded Alban's body from the funeral rites, and were it not for Radnor's intervention, Alban's body would still be lying in the open, waiting to be picked clean by scavengers. While Leif had performed the ritual of Caelum for the others, Radnor carried Alban's body deep into the woods around them.

Unbeknownst to him, Elena had secretly followed. She kept her distance, barely keeping sight of him. If Radnor ever noticed her, he gave no sign as they picked their way through the dimly lit trees. The sunlight was partially blocked by the overhead canopy, and cast mournful looking shadows over the foliage. After what seemed like an eternity of walking, Radnor stopped at a clearing, and gently laid Alban's body on the ground. Elena saw Radnor rolling his wounded shoulder, stretching it out from the pain caused by resting Alban's body on the fearsome vampire bite. After a moment, Radnor began digging. He did not have a shovel, so he dug by hand, breaking the dirt into chunks with his sword before pulling the pieces away with his fingers. Elena wished to go and help him, but she felt like he needed to do this alone. As Radnor worked, he hummed a sorrowful tune from his homeland. It was a sad melody that looped over and over as he dug.

Finally, the grave was deep enough to house Alban's body. Radnor laid Alban in his final resting place, and began covering him, packing the dirt down tightly. Once his work was done, Radnor marked the grave with a collection of stones found nearby, forming a circle around where Alban's head lay. Then, Radnor sang a song with words from a language Elena did not recognize. Some ancient Amarantheon dialect maybe? After the song was over, Radnor wept over the grave for a time. Once it was over, Radnor stood, and made his way back to where the others had been. Elena made sure to follow until they were both back with the group. Leif inquired about where she had been, and she told him that she had needed to be alone. He accepted that answer, though she doubted he believed her. With the burials over, it was time they were on their way.

Thankfully, crossing the newly repaired bridge was trouble free. The refugees were still tired, cold, and hungry. However, the overall mood among the group had lifted a little, as the threat of ghoul attack was no longer hanging over their heads. Elena made sure to spend as much time near Radnor as possible as they marched. She couldn't bear to see him in his current state. At night he kept up his vigilant watch over them, and Elena found herself wondering how long it had been since Radnor slept. Sometimes she saw him checking the vampire bite on his arm. She noticed it subtly at first, the way he would roll his shoulder to readjust how his armor rested on it, and the way he would wince when he moved, though he never made a sound. Finally, on the third day, Elena did something she hadn't wanted to do, but she felt there was no other way to break Radnor from his silent mourning. She withdrew the unholy amulet from the pouch at her belt, and asked Radnor what it was. Finally, he made eye contact with her and answered.

"It's a gaulderen. It helps sorcerers cast spells. The use of magic requires energy from a person's soul in order to work. Most people don't have the right kind of energy bound to them, and so never develop the ability to use magic. Gods or powerful sorcerers can cast a spell and store its effects inside an object like this amulet. Sorcerers who have the strength to do this are rare, but I suspect you can see the powerful application this ability can have."

Elena took a moment to ponder the implications of what Radnor had just told her, and made her guess...

"A sorcerer can cast powerful spells that would exhaust him and store them here. Then when he needs them he just uses the...gaulderen... and can use magic without wearing himself out, like in a fight."

"Exactly," Radnor said. "With a lot of preparation, a sorcerer can have a whole host of the most destructive spells imaginable at his disposal, and can unleash them all in a matter of moments. Usually, the gaulderen is broken when the spell is used, and cannot be used again."

"Can you tell who made this one?" Elena asked.

"Not usually, but with this one...you see that main rune in the center?"

Radnor pointed at the center of the circular amulet. At the tip of his finger lay a precisely carved symbol...it looked like someone had taken a circle, cut it into pieces, and had tried to put them back together in a pattern that seemed somehow integral to the power of the whole thing.

"Yes. What does it mean?"

"That is the mark of Ashrahan. He is one of the Krigari gods, the power giver. He's made an art of making gaulderen. It was he who taught the first men how to make them, and he still holds more secrets about them than anyone else...mortal or not."

100

"That doesn't sound good," Elena said. She paused to think for a moment, then continued.

"You've talked about killing Adramelach, but are you sure it isn't Ashrahan you should kill?"

Radnor laughed for the first time in days. While it was better than nothing, it was a cold, sinister laugh that Elena didn't like. Seeing her perplexed expression, Radnor tried to explain.

"I focus on Adramelach because he is their king. But don't worry...I'm going to kill them all."

Elena was startled to hear Rolf's voice chime in from behind them.

"So I see you've got him talking again."

Radnor turned quizzically to see the boy coming up on them from behind.

"What?" Rolf shrugged. "You think Elena's the only one who's been keeping an eye on you?"

It was Elena's turn to laugh as Rolf came up alongside them.

"I was listening in on your conversation. How come we've never heard of these "gaulderen" before?"

"Oh, but you have," Radnor replied. "The oath rings you use are a different kind of gaulderen, specially made with powerful spells meant to inflict punishment on an oath breaker. Unlike other gaulderens, they take their power from the soul of the owner, and thus can be reused almost indefinitely. There is a sort of magical bond between the oath ring and its owner. And this…"

Radnor pointed to his ring.

"This is also a gaulderen."

"But wait a minute," Rolf started. "You said Ashrahan invented gaulderen, but Caelum is the god who fulfills the promise of the oath. Aren't the oath rings his?"

Radnor shrugged.

"Maybe Caelum came up with the oath ring, and Ashrahan found a way to make other spells work. It's also possible that I'm wrong, and Caelum taught Ashrahan the process."

Radnor pondered the idea for a moment. *He could have taught Ashrahan how to make them, and then Ashrahan would have beaten him to death with one.*

Elena saw Radnor was starting to fall into his own thoughts again, and turned the topic to merrier subjects. Radnor seemed to warm to this, and the three of them continued their conversation throughout the day.

Night fell. Cold darkness once again enveloped the band of refugees. It was a crisp cold that gave a hint of the winter that would soon be arriving. Wind chilled everyone to the bone, and many people huddled close as they walked. Despite their discomfort, the refugees felt elated. They were now all standing just outside an inn that was positioned beside the road. It had taken some effort to prevent everyone from rushing inside, but Leif knew that the innkeeper would be less willing to help a disorderly mess of people than an orderly group. Leif knew this inn, The Dancing Bear. He had never stayed there before, but he had passed it many times when going to and from Wulfgeld. They were only half a day's journey from the city, and even more importantly, they were ten feet from warm food and warm beds.

The building was two stories high, and made from finely cut stone bricks. There looked to be enough rooms that if some people were willing to sleep in the lobby area, there would be enough space for everyone.

Leif had to be stern with his people, who wanted to rush the door to get inside. The ealdorman decided that he would go in, accompanied by Radnor, and two sets of mothers and their children. Leif hoped that he could press upon the innkeeper the importance of providing shelter to his people. He wanted the mothers and their children with him so that their plight would be known. The tired ealdorman hoped that sympathy could win the day. Leif planned to promise payment to the owner in the name of Earl Sigaberht. His status as ealdorman gave him the authority to invoke Sigaberht's name when making promises in certain emergencies. This, he felt, was one of those emergencies. Leif also wanted Veigarand beside him when meeting the innkeeper. As much as Leif hoped the owner would take pity on the mothers and their children, he couldn't rule out the possibility he'd have to take what they needed by force. He hoped that Veigarand's mere presence would prevent any resistance from the innkeeper to the idea of waiting for payment.

The ealdorman was still conflicted in his feelings toward the demigod. Leif hated Veigarand for all of the deaths he had caused. But at the same time, Veigarand had done all he could to protect them, and when Leif had an opportunity to let someone else rid him of the man he hated so much...Leif killed Alban instead. The fatigued leader had spent the last several days pondering over *why* he had chosen what he did. Despite all of his hatred, he had begun to feel sympathy for the monster that had joined his company...*by Caelum!* Leif had realized that he had even grown to respect him in a strange way.

Word had also filtered to him of Klane's attempt to poison Veigarand, and that maybe if Klane hadn't done that, they wouldn't be in the mess they were in now. He needed time to think, and figure out how he felt. But, of course, there was no time. Leif sighed to himself as he saw

Veigarand approach the entrance to the inn still wearing his armor, sword at his side, and shield slung across his back.

Radnor was ready to provide the help they needed. The weary warrior was a little bitter about being used as an unspoken threat, especially since he knew that if it came to it, *he* was going to be the one to get his hands dirty. But despite his bitterness, he knew he owed Leif.

Leif stopped him at the threshold, and spoke for a moment.

"I don't want anyone to get hurt, and I especially don't want anyone to die tonight."

Leif couldn't see it behind the armor, but Radnor smiled to himself before making his reply.

"But, you'll do what you have to do."

Leif turned inward for a moment, and found his hand resting on the dagger he had at his belt.

"Yes, I suppose I will."

Opening the door for the selected families, Leif had them file in first, with Radnor and himself bringing up the rear. The warmth of the nearby fire proved too enticing for the children, and the mothers found themselves struggling to keep up as their sons and daughters dashed for seats by the fireplace. Leif and Radnor chose to ignore this and continued over to the bar, where the innkeeper stood awaiting their introductions. As they walked, Radnor surveyed his surroundings. There were no windows, and only one door that stood shut at the back of the inn. Radnor stepped to take a closer look to see if it was another exit from the building. The stairs leading to the second floor were near the back door, providing a bottleneck if Radnor needed to defend against attackers using the stairs. Radnor then turned his attention back to the main room he was standing in. There was a bar on the right, with what looked to be a door leading to the kitchen behind it. The left side of the room was filled to the brim with tables that could be used for cover. A cough from Leif brought Radnor's attention away from planning for a fight, and back to the innkeeper.

The innkeeper was a small, portly man. By the silver speckled hair and worn features, Radnor suspected the man was in his mid-forties. The innkeeper stood casually behind the bar, gently scrubbing out the dirt from an old clay mug with an even older looking towel. Radnor stayed behind and stood in the shadows at a corner of the room. His goal was to look intimidating enough to give Leif a better chance of getting the help he needed. It also gave Radnor a chance to continue his assessment of his surroundings. Taking a closer look at the dining area, he saw it wasn't actually that large a space, offering only one fireplace and maybe five or six tables for people to eat from. The walls were adorned with simple carvings…images of bears and lions locked in battle with each other. But most importantly, the door at the back side of the tavern looked like it did go to the outside, as Radnor had hoped.

A man and a woman sitting at a table caught Radnor's attention. Their flirtatious gossip with each other had abruptly ceased when Leif and Radnor had entered the room. The woman's lavender perfume filled Radnor's nostrils, and if it hadn't been so overwhelming, Radnor might have thought her the man's wife. At another table, there was a cloaked figure seated alongside one other gentleman. The two also spoke in hushed whispers, and Radnor was sure he saw the nervous exchange of gold from one man to the other. Keeping one eye on the suspicious pair, Radnor turned the rest of his attention to Leif as he now spoke to the innkeeper.

"Greetings, my dear landlord! I hope great Caelum smiles upon you this evening! I come into your wonderful inn with a number of my people. We are in desperate need of food and shelter. Those two mothers and their children you just saw run in are only a few of many families I have waiting outside. All I ask is that you provide food and lodging for my people tonight."

The innkeeper continued nonchalantly cleaning dishes, as he switched to wiping clean a different mug. He replied to Leif in a gruff, uncaring voice.

"Aye, food and lodging I have a plenty, for it is my business. But, what, may I ask, do you plan on using to pay for my services? I must beg your pardon, but if I do not receive payment, then how will I feed myself if your company eats me out of my stores tonight? How am I to wash bedding without gold to replace the soap and water I use?"

Leif paused to contain himself for a moment. Angered at how indifferent the innkeeper was to their plight, Leif had almost sicced Veigarand on the poor man in front of him. Instead, Leif implored the innkeeper again.

"Ah! In my urgent need, I forgot myself! I am Leif Edricson, ealdorman of Neugeld. Our town was destroyed in a horrific attack that killed most of those living there. Those I bring with me are the only survivors of the attack, and we have been hounded by not only the cold and hunger, but also by ghouls in vast numbers. By the mercy of Caelum, I must beg of you to aid us. If you were to provide for us tonight, you would not only be reimbursed by Earl Sigaberht, but you would be greatly rewarded on top of that."

The innkeeper continued scrubbing his dishes, and looked up at Leif's face. The vendor rolled the thought through his mind, like running a coin through his fingers...but the coin stuck in his palm.

104

"If you truly are the ealdorman of Neugeld, then where is your oath ring? I see it not upon your arm."

Leif again found himself caught off guard by the innkeeper's reply, and found himself caught in feelings of shame from having left it behind. Before Leif could muster a reply, he heard Veigarand's icy voice pierce the air behind him.

"When it came to the safety of his people, the lord ealdorman chose them over a trinket. He commands their love and respect...because he does not carry his oath ring on his arm, but in his heart."

The innkeeper's face fell when he heard the threatening voice come from the warrior standing in shadow. It was only now that the heavyset man had *truly* noticed the dangerous figure which stood in his lobby. He couldn't see Radnor well in the dim light, but what he could see was the glitter of firelight that danced off armor, and the burning in the eyes inside Radnor's helmet. Despite his fears, the innkeeper wanted to know more before relenting to the invaders in his lobby.

"Do you travel with them, oh shadowed figure?" the innkeeper said, in a tone less courageous than he had hoped.

Radnor took his moment to step into the light, revealing his full, imposing form. He joined Leif at the bar.

"I do. *I* say this man is the ealdorman of Neugeld, and *I* say his tale is true."

The innkeeper finally stopped scrubbing dishes, and looked in terror at the steel behemoth that stood before him. There were whispers in the room. Everyone wanted to leave, but no one was willing to move quite yet. Radnor continued to speak as he reached for his belt.

"But, I understand your position, my friend. So I offer you this."

Instead of his sword, Radnor withdrew a coin pouch he had taken from his saddle bags. In it were silver coins minted in Arendale. They bore the face of Magnus, the king of Amaranthar.

Radnor poured over a dozen valuable coins onto the bar, and looked into the innkeeper's now relieved face.

"I know we are close to the mountains, but I hope you value northern silver more than southern gold."

The innkeeper nodded, and had just moved to take the coins into his fist when Radnor leaned in close to whisper to him in a low voice that no one, not even Leif, could hear.

"I want you to remember this. I could have taken everything you have by force if I wanted to. I still can. I expect my silver to have bought the best food and accommodations you have at your disposal. If they don't, I will feed these people with every ounce of food you have, and I will warm them with a fire that will burn this place to ashes. Do you understand me?"

The innkeeper's face grew pale, and he nodded.

"Thank you, my friend," Radnor said.

Radnor turned to Leif.

"My lord ealdorman, I do believe our lodgings for the night are paid for."

Leif found himself grinning in spite of himself, and slapped Radnor on the shoulder as he went back outside to bring the others in. Leif did not notice Radnor grit his teeth as Leif had just accidentally struck his wounded shoulder. The innkeeper called to his wife, and the two of them began earnestly cooking food for their starving guests.

Several hours passed. Radnor had observed from afar, and was pleased as the innkeeper provided the best for Leif's people. There was barely enough bed space to go around, but they managed it. People were warm and fed. Even the horses were well cared for. Radnor had stood in a dark corner of the lobby as people were given the food he had paid for. Radnor did not join them, but instead found himself studying the carvings of the fighting bears and lions which circled the walls around him. He found them unsatisfying, as the two great beasts were locked in a struggle that went on for eternity. Each image of combat flowed into the next in a great circle, and there was no final end, no victor. Radnor found that upsetting at some level, but he shook it off as the evening wore on.

Now all of the guests were asleep, and dreamed soundly...except Radnor. He chose instead to walk in a patrol around the perimeter of the inn. His job was not complete until they were all in Wulfgeld. Thankfully for him, the wind had finally stilled, and he was left only with the crisp night air. There was a fire pit in the grass behind the inn, and Radnor had set a fire in it so he could stop from time to time to warm himself. Darestr stood by the flames and kept Radnor company during his moments of rest. On one of Radnor's passes by the fire, he was surprised to see Rolf and Elena had seated themselves on one of the benches that surrounded the pit.

"What are you two doing still awake?" Radnor asked.

"Rolf couldn't sleep," Elena replied.

"Something in the food upset my stomach," Rolf said. "How did your stomach handle it?"

"I didn't have any problem with it," Radnor lied. He hadn't eaten any of it.

"Oh," Rolf said. There was silence for a time.

Radnor began tending to his fire. As he was working, Rolf walked up next to him.

"Radnor?"

"Yes?"

"Teach me to fight."

Radnor stopped working on the fire for a moment, startled by Rolf's serious tone.

"And why would I do that?" Radnor asked.

Rolf did not hesitate in his reply.

"I've watched too many friends die."

"I know that feeling," Radnor said. He resumed his care of the fire, speaking as he worked.

"But why not seek training from Leif? Or any of the fighting men in Wulfgeld?"

Rolf gave Radnor an irritated look.

"Stop playing dumb. It's obvious you're the best swordsman in the world."

Radnor chuckled at that.

"I'm flattered that you think so, but I'm sure there are others better than I."

"Have you met any of them?" Rolf challenged.

"I don't know yet," Came Radnor's reply. "And I won't know until the better swordsman beats me."

"You don't know how good a man is until he beats you?" Rolf asked.

"Or I beat him. If I think I know how good someone is before the fight ends, there's a chance he's better than I think, and can catch me by surprise."

"So what do you do?" Rolf asked, starting to catch onto the word play Radnor had led him through.

"When I'm being smart, I assume my opponent is better than me, and knows not only everything I know, but that he also knows something more than I do. It's that 'something more' that will kill me if I'm not careful."

"So...don't underestimate your opponent?" Rolf asked.

"Simply put, yes. There's more to it than that, but your first lesson is not the time to get into it. Are you ready to learn physical skills?"

"Yes!" Rolf started impatiently.

"Good. Pick up my shield."

Rolf went over to pick up his shield, and struggled to lift it. He could carry it, but it was cumbersome. Rolf was simply not strong enough to use Radnor's steel shield effectively.

"Now, block," Radnor said.

Rolf found himself stumbling backwards under the force of several, sharp impacts of Radnor's hands against the face of the shield. After the third blow, the shield came out of Rolf's hands, and he hit the dirt.

Radnor stood over him, and lifted the shield easily.

"That was the first lesson. Do you understand it?"

Rolf glared at Radnor and shook his head violently. Radnor understood why and ignored the boy's obvious frustration.

"Almost all of the enemies you will fight right now are much stronger than you are, and more experienced in the ways of war. I have an advantage over them. I am not only experienced in fighting, but I am also far stronger than any man I have ever met. You don't have those advantages, so you need to replace them with skill and cunning. Do you understand?"

Rolf nodded, calming down as he understood the lesson.

"Very well," Radnor said. "Now walk."

"What?" Rolf asked.

"Walk," Radnor replied. "If you are to learn to fight, the first thing you must do is walk."

Rolf began to walk across the ground. Radnor continued giving instructions.

"Now, when I say 'stop', stop moving in the exact position you are in when I say it."

Rolf nodded again as he walked, listening as intently as possible.

Radnor waited a few moments, and then gave his command.

"Stop!"

Rolf almost fell over in his effort to stop mid-step. He regained his balance, and looked at Radnor quizzically.

Radnor walked over to him, and asked him a question.

"Why did you finish your step? I told you to stop moving."

"Because you caught me when my foot was in the air. I had to finish my step."

"Why did you have to finish the step?"

"Because it was the direction I was moving. Once I started, I couldn't stop."

"Exactly!" Radnor exclaimed. "The untrained man falls from foot to foot as he walks. That is what you just did. You stuck your foot out and fell onto it. Because that is the way you walk you could not stop yourself when you wanted to."

"So?" Rolf asked.

"So if we were fighting each other, you would be dead in that moment. As you closed with me I would have moved to your side, away from your sword side."

Radnor stepped to Rolf's side to illustrate.

"In that moment you were not able to adjust. It means that you are not in control of the distance between us and the timing of the fight. From here, I would simply kill you with a single blow and it would be much more difficult for you to defend yourself."

"How many fights have you actually won like this?" Rolf asked.

Radnor looked at his hand, and began mock-counting on his fingers before grinning at Rolf.

"Enough that I'm still breathing."

Rolf looked at him, feeling mildly annoyed. This felt more like tricks than training.

"I have done these two things to you to show you what I will teach you. Your movement and balance are flawed, as are those of all new warriors. Now, I am going to teach you the fundamentals required to fix this movement error."

Elena watched as Radnor worked with Rolf, and felt some joy. Rolf was learning from this man, and was slowly taking to it. *Hell, Rolf seems to be enjoying it!* She thought. Even Radnor seemed to take some pleasure from the distraction of working with the boy and thinking of something other than Alban. Watching him here, she again felt as though Radnor was more than a dark, protective shadow. When Rolf had asked to be taught, it let Radnor open up and interact with him. The only thing Elena wondered now was how long it would last once they reached Wulfgeld.

An hour later; Rolf lay down on ground, exhausted. They had spent all of that time on movement, and Rolf found it even more exhausting than herding pigs.

The fire still burned brightly and hotly. Rolf moved over to Elena, who sat by the fire under a blanket they brought out, and he rested his head on her shoulder. She rested her head on his, and sat contentedly as Radnor added more wood to the flames. He sat across it from them. At first he simply stared into the flames. Elena couldn't tell what he was looking at exactly, but she thought it might be some brief moment of happiness which had been called up from his past. Then Radnor did something highly unexpected. He stood up and went to start digging in the saddle bags that rested beside Darestr.

When he came back, he held a curiously shaped piece of wood. As Elena examined it more closely, she saw it bore ornately carved, endless knotwork dragons. After a moment, Elena finally recognized the instrument was a lyre. After getting comfortable, Radnor sat down, and began to play, delicately plucking the strings. The melody of this warrior's lyre hovered in the air and rang out against the silence of the birds. The song was simple, but it progressed so elegantly it was truly marvelous to listen to. It danced through the leaves, and for a moment the trees of the ancient woods ceased their creaking as the music soothed their old, aching branches. After the music was finished Radnor set his lyre down and walked around the flames. Elena started to move and say something, but Radnor put his finger to his lips. Elena looked down and saw that Rolf was sound asleep, still leaning on her shoulder. Then Radnor gently lifted Rolf, and carried him over to a spot near the warm fire. Radnor laid the sleeping boy down as gently as possible. He then moved back to his own spot, and sat down across from Elena once more.

"That was a beautiful song," Elena said. "What is it called?"

"It is called Drumon's Lullaby."

"What's a Drumon?" Elena asked.

Radnor picked up the lyre, and played a few quiet notes.

"Drumon was an ancient warrior of Amaranthar. He was in a fortress that was besieged by an enemy nation in the North. They were vicious men called the Fiendein. The forces Drumon was with were hopelessly outnumbered, and there was no escape from the ruthless enemy. The Fiendein had burned several of the outlying villages, and the survivors had fled to the fortress for protection. Children were trapped in that fortress."

"It's strange…" Elena started. "I have heard of your people, so far north, but I have never heard of the Fiendein."

A vengeful smile cracked itself across Radnor's lips.

"There's a reason for that."

Radnor then continued to play, the tempo and rhythm becoming slightly more energetic.

"During one of the nights, the enemy attacked with siege weapons, trying to knock down the walls. The noise was deafening, as rock smashed against rock."

As Radnor continued to play, the tempo quickened, and the notes were slightly shriller.

"As the walls were slowly torn away from the city, Drumon went to the children. They were terrified, but some of them wanted to fight. Drumon knew that the final attack would not come until daylight. He also knew that no one in those walls would be shown mercy."

110

The lyre he was playing almost seemed to writhe in agony as Radnor rushed the melody of his story.

"So, in an effort to calm them, he played this lullaby on a lyre very similar to mine."

Radnor then replayed part of the lullaby from earlier.

"When daylight came, the enemy stormed the fortress, and began to slaughter all who dwelt within. What few warriors that remained made a final stand in the feast hall, and all of the children were handed weapons to fight. It was that, or they would all die slow deaths as slaves or simply for the sadistic pleasure of the Fiendein."

The lyre switched to a haunting melody that drifted through the clearing.

"During the final stand Drumon played the lullaby one more time, and the children were inspired to the calm they needed to fight with skill and bravery. Many Fiendein fell to their biting blades before the hall was taken."

Radnor then finished his melody with the lullaby, but it was different: the music was somber and mournful instead of calm. After this, Radnor put the lyre down.

"What happened to the children?" Elena asked.

Radnor stared through the flames.

"Five of the children were returned to us, their thumbs cut off. Without your thumb, you cannot hold a weapon and become a warrior. This is a grave insult to a people such as mine. But, these children were able to help us learn this melody, and thus it was written down for generations of my people to remember."

"And what happened to your enemy, the Fiendein?"

Radnor smiled slightly at this question.

"Their footprints haven't blackened the Earth for many generations now."

With that, Radnor got up again.

"We should get some rest, for tomorrow will be a long day for us all."

Radnor then sat up on a boulder, gazed at the moon in the sky, and watched how the clouds moved to hide it from his gaze. Elena lay down in her blankets, and was awake for some time. That is until she heard a familiar sound, but before her drowsing mind recognized the lullaby, she fell asleep.

Radnor sat staring past the firelight for a long time. His eyes searched through the trees, making sure nothing was coming up on them. He heard Rolf rustling in his sleep, and when Radnor came to check on him, saw that the boy had kicked his blanket off and was shivering. As Radnor was replacing the blanket, a man's voice called to him.

"Hello."

Radnor spun in the direction from which the voice came, and saw a dark haired man standing at the edge of the firelight. He was tall… almost as tall as Radnor. While Radnor was heavily built, the stranger was thin and wispy; his frail appearance masked the wiry strength he possessed. The man wore a black cloak which revealed very little of his other features. His face was pale, and his long, dark hair was slicked back over his head elegantly. He carried no weapon which Radnor could see, but Radnor was still wary.

"Who are you?" Radnor asked.

"I am a weary traveler whose journey takes him to this inn," answered the strange man.

"It seems we are not so different," Radnor replied.

"No truer words were spoken," said the tall man. "I had hoped to stay at the inn, but if you're sleeping out here, it must be full. I have no fire of my own, do you mind if we sit by yours and chat for a while? I have been alone for a long time, and would enjoy some company."

Radnor weighed the risks in his mind, and decided that any threat this man posed would be minimal. He motioned for the strange man to sit beside him on a bench near the fire pit. The strange traveler stretched himself out as he sat on the bench, and looked over at Radnor.

"I thank you for your hospitality my friend. It is not often I meet someone so accommodating with his fire."

"I'm happy to oblige you good sir, as long as you hold no ill intent for me or my companions," Radnor said, a hint of malice in his tone.

The stranger chuckled at Radnor's remark.

"Ah, but I would not dream of such a thing! I would never willingly do anything to endanger the peaceful slumber of your wonderful companions! They must be supremely special to you. Are they your wife and son?"

"No," Radnor replied.

There was a brief pause as Radnor noticed that an unnaturally chill breeze was stirring.

"But I do care for them," he added.

The stranger stared at Radnor for a moment, with a hard, focused gaze that one usually reserves for prey.

"Splendid!" the man cheered. "It is so rare to find men with such heart who are willing to care for others so openly! I like that about you my friend!"

Radnor was starting to feel more uneasy as the conversation wore on. It became time to learn what was really happening.

"Compliments flow from your tongue very freely. It makes me begin to suspect that you want something from me."

The man smiled with a wide grin that seemed filled with too many teeth.

"You are clever, aren't you? Yes, there is something I want from you."

Radnor felt his temper rising as this stranger played games with him.

"Out with it man! What is it you want?"

"Oh, I want the same thing you want my dear friend." said the pale man, as a sinister gleam illuminated his eyes. "I want to kill Adramelach."

Radnor leaped to his feet and glared at the stranger.

"Who are you?"

The stranger began to laugh. The laugh echoed eerily off the trees, and they seemed to recoil in terror at the sound. He then leaned forward to reveal his black eyes that now shined in the firelight. Radnor instinctively took a step backward at the sight, and the stranger spoke again.

"How silly of me! I forgot to introduce myself. I am Ashrahan."

Radnor drew his sword and wound up for the fiercest blow he had ever struck.

Ashrahan put his finger to his lips.

"Shhh! We mustn't disturb the sleep of your wonderful companions! Besides, unless that weapon was forged by a god, it cannot harm me."

Radnor aimed his blow straight to the crown of the Krigari god's head, swinging to split him in two. The blade passed through Ashrahan like he was air. Instead, the blow split the bench in two and drove deeply into the dirt below.

"Bra-vo!" jeered the god. "If I were actually here I might have been worried! Now, if you would kindly stop trying to kill me, I would very much like to get back to the task at hand."

Radnor glared impotently at the mocking god who sat lazily before him.

"How am I seeing you if you're not here?" Radnor asked.

"Oh, we can project our forms into your world at any time we wish. We just rarely wish to. While we cannot boldly stride across the threshold between our world and yours, we can still take a peek."

"Why are you only now appearing to me?" Radnor demanded.

"Because I couldn't find you!" Ashrahan giggled.

"For years I reached out with my mind, but you were nowhere to be seen! I almost got you when there was that business with the river people years ago, and again recently with the vampire."

Ashrahan laughed to himself at some jest which was hidden to Radnor's understanding.

"I have to tell you…it took us all by surprise when you first showed up, I can assure you of that! No one knew of Adramelach's little misadventure that brought you into the world. At least, not until the cat got out of the bag and he had to explain why there was suddenly a half-breed son of his wandering around in your world! Oh, was *that* a fun conversation to have!"

Ashrahan lapsed into reminiscences of fond memories for a moment before getting back on track. Shaking his head to himself, the smirking god continued.

"But, this most recent incident in that village a few weeks ago gave me the opportunity I needed. When the portal opened, I made sure Adramelach sent my amulet through. From what I heard, he chose to do it personally."

Radnor realized that Ashrahan was talking about the gaulderen Alban used to summon the ghouls, and that Adramelach was the black-eyed man Alban had raved about.

"How does sending a gaulderen meant to help someone *kill* me let you *find* me? And if Adramelach came through himself to deliver it, why does he not seek me out, or send his armies and begin his conquest?" Radnor demanded.

Ashrahan smirked.

"To answer your first question, I must ask you...did you see my mark emblazoned upon the amulet? That has been letting me track you since it was left with your friend. My king wants you dead, so I couldn't just send a friendly letter through, now could I?"

Ashrahan took a moment to stretch out his legs and let out a contented sigh before continuing.

"As for your second question, the answer is simple: Adramelach is cautious to a fault. The portals opened by men can only hold him here for a short time. Your portals are unique. They stay open as long as you're in the area, but they close if you leave for more than a few days. If *your* portals close, anything left on this side is stranded. If he invades and you escape, the portals collapse and he is stranded. If he invades, and he kills you, the portals collapse and he's still stuck here. Trying to invade and fight you directly before he has a way of getting back to Narakim is a bad idea. So, when he has the opportunity, he will try to kill you at a distance, like through the actions of deranged mortals summoning ghouls."

There was a pause as Radnor processed what he had just been told. It explained why the Krigari had not yet invaded beyond the borders of Amaranthar. When Radnor went into exile, the invading demons were stranded with no hope of reinforcements.

"Does that satisfy your curiosity?" Ashrahan asked.

"For the moment. Why are you so interested in finding me?" Radnor demanded.

Ashrahan sighed in exasperation.

"Were you not listening? We seek the same thing. We both...want to kill...Adramelach!"

"You're a god, why not do it yourself?" Radnor snarled.

"My, my, do you always use that tone with your friends? That might explain why you don't have any."

Seeing that Radnor looked angry enough to make another fruitless attempt on his life, Ashrahan proceeded to the point.

"But to answer your question, I can't. I am sworn by an unbreakable oath to never take up arms against Adramelach, and to follow all of his commands to the letter. No matter how much I want to, I cannot lift a finger against him. But that doesn't mean I can't lift a finger to help you, as long as he doesn't know we're meeting like this. You won't tell him will you?"

Ashrahan smirked at Radnor, waiting for his reply.

"What do you mean 'meeting like this?' If you think this is going to happen again, believe me, you are sadly mistaken." Radnor barked. Ashrahan found his own irritation growing.

"Oh, are you *really* so bullheaded? Do you think you have a choice in this? How are you going to stop me from coming to see you? I'm *asking* you for your help to be *polite*, not because you actually have a choice. You will help me kill Adramelach. There is no reason to refuse me. You already want to kill him, and you must have figured out by now that you cannot do it alone."

Ashrahan stood up from his comfortable seat, leaving the sword beneath him.

"I will visit you again soon. Think on this...you will see that helping each other will make this a lot easier for both of us."

Radnor still glared into Ashrahan's eyes.

"Why do you want to kill him?"

Ashrahan laughed again.

"There are too many reasons to count. We might discuss some of them next time."

Ashrahan then faded into the darkness where he stood, laughing until he was gone from sight.

Radnor removed the sword from where it had become buried in the soil, and sat down. He found himself shivering, his eyes scanning the tree line even more furtively than before. This would be a long night.

Chapter 11

Dawn came swiftly to Elena's eyes. As she awoke, she smelled cooking meat which Radnor had begun preparing for them. As she sat up, Elena realized that she had never seen Radnor sleep. Every night for the better part of two weeks, he was always awake and in his armor by the time she woke up. She stood quickly and walked over to Radnor. She looked at his face, and it showed the expression of a man who had definitely not slept the entire time that she had traveled with him.

"Is there something I can help you with?" Radnor said.

"How long has it been since you slept?" Elena asked.

"Not too long yet."

"What does that mean?"

"It means that I can manage."

"Oh no you can't. Look at you…those bags under your eyes…in fact your eyes show nothing but weariness."

Radnor looked up from his cooking to shoot her a quick glare and then back down to his task.

"All right then, nothing but weariness…and stubbornness," Elena remarked.

"I cannot endanger you by sleeping when we are so exposed," Radnor argued.

"But you need sleep; you're torturing yourself for no reason."

"I don't like sleep. It leaves me and anyone around me exposed to attack," Radnor retorted.

And if you dreamed the things I dream... he thought to himself.

"And who is going to attack us?" Elena asked.

Radnor's thoughts turned to Alban when she said that, but before he could say anything, Elena continued.

"You know what, when we get to Wulfgeld, we are going to stay at a nice inn, with good beds, you are going to sleep, and I will keep watch if I have to!"

Radnor looked at her once more, and finally relented when he realized that he did not have the energy to argue with her anymore.

Rolf slowly awoke, and smelled the food.

"Food, just what I need."

He then trudged over to the fire, plopped himself down next to the licking flames, and waited eagerly for his morning meal.

"Someone's in a good mood this morning," Elena commented.

"Well, we're almost there. And once I'm there, all I have to do is wait, and my father will find me."

Radnor took some of the meat, and put it in a bowl for Rolf to eat. Rolf devoured it.

"This is delicious."

Radnor grunted slightly.

"What's wrong with him?" Rolf asked.

"He's just a bit of a grump this morning," Elena quipped.

Elena shot a wry smile at Radnor as he handed her a plate of food. Radnor took his own helping, and found himself wolfing it down like a starving animal. After they were finished, Radnor packed their utensils up. When he was finished with that, he took off his armor, and put on a simple, unadorned tunic.

"You know what else you need Radnor?"

"Hmm?" he grunted.

"A bath. We haven't been near a place where you could really take a bath in days."

Radnor looked at her again, partially annoyed, partially amused.

"Neither have you, so isn't this sort of hypocritical on your part?"

"I never said that I didn't need a bath. Look at my hair, it doesn't feel exactly like the hair of the Queen of Ranrike."

Radnor laughed slightly at that, thinking of the queen and her legendarily long, silky hair.

"What was so funny about that?" Elena asked.

"I have met the Queen of Ranrike. Her natural hair fell out when she was twenty due to a failed attempt to poison her. She's worn a wig ever since."

Rolf giggled to himself envisioning someone as important as a Queen having to resort to a wig, but quickly stopped when Elena glared over at him for laughing at something so sad.

Their conversation was interrupted when Leif came into view and beckoned to Radnor, who hurried to talk to him.

"Walk with me, Veigarand," Leif quietly commanded.

Radnor pulled up just behind Leif's left shoulder. If the ealdorman meant to attack him, the right handed man would have to reach across his own body to strike him. After the two separated from the rest, Leif snorted in annoyance when he noticed how Radnor had positioned himself.

"Do you think me stupid, Veigarand? I already know how a fight between us would turn out, and I would not leave my people leaderless. Or are you so stupid that you don't know this?"

Radnor grimaced at the insult.

"I know. But I've *known* things before. I also *knew* that Alban was my friend."

Leif lost himself in thought for a moment. He had been feeling gratitude to Veigarand for his help the night before. But that was then, when the journey ahead was still long and grueling. They were nearing the end of their road together, and Leif knew he had to make a decision about Veigarand's fate. Leif turned that thought over in his mind. No, the decision had already been made. He had to deliver Veigarand to Earl Sigaberht, and bring him to justice for the pain and suffering he had brought down on them. Once that was finally settled in his mind, Leif spoke again.

"I didn't want to talk to you of that. We need to talk about what happens next, what happens after—"

"You bring me before your lord," Radnor interrupted.

There was a deafening moment of silence between the two men.

"Yes. Once we arrive at Wulfgeld, you know I have to bring you to him. After that, his judgment is his, and out of my control."

Radnor did not need time to think of his reply.

"I will stand before Sigaberht, and I will hear his judgment."

"Very well then," Leif said, and he started to turn back to the tavern, when Radnor caught him gently by the shoulder.

"Before we leave, you need to know why I will allow myself to become your prisoner once we reach Wulfgeld," Radnor said. "I know I am responsible for the deaths of…so many of your people. Even though I tried to prevent them, everyone who was killed on the road, even Alban's madness was my doing. And it's not just your people either. You clearly know all the stories. You use my *other* name so often."

"You hope that by hearing judgment on your actions, that redemption is in your grasp," Leif said.

"In a way…I want to see if it is possible for me to ever be accepted among my own kind again." Radnor replied.

Leif felt the anger rising in him.

"Perhaps you never will be, because there is one thing you forgot: it's not about you! It's about those people who lie unburied in their burned homes! It's about *them* not *you*!"

The angry ealdorman stormed off, leaving Radnor to contemplate his place among them once more.

It wasn't long before the refugees were underway on the final leg of the trip to Wulfgeld. They continued in much the same formation as they usually did, but with one exception. Radnor moved ahead of the group, acting as a forward scout. Or at least that's what he told Leif, and himself. In reality, he wanted to be alone, and felt himself not wanting to say goodbye to anyone. He was certain that Sigaberht would condemn him to death, and that his own escape would be necessary. Radnor promised to face Sigaberht's judgment, but he did not promise to see that it was carried out…at least not until his own purpose was carried out first.

As the sun continued its arc over the everlasting sky, Elena began to feel like she should say something to Radnor. This would probably be her last chance to talk to him, as he would leave their company as soon as his promise was fulfilled. Elena knew Radnor may face Sigaberht's judgment, but she had no doubt in her mind that Radnor would never submit to it. His revenge was too important to him. So, Elena took the plunge and came over to him to speak with him. Rolf started to join her, but Elena gently waved him off, a signal he took in good stride and returned to his spot in the caravan.

As Elena came over to him, Radnor wasn't sure what to make of the look on her face. She seemed…determined? Like she was steeling herself for something? Considering how comfortable they had become with each other, he was surprised to see this look on her face. Radnor slowed his pace to let her more easily catch up with him. She came alongside him, and just…stared for a moment. She looked like she wanted to say something, but no words were spoken. Unsure of what to do, Radnor continued to walk beside her. His heart raced, feeling desires he neither understood nor wanted. Every fiber of his being told him to take her into his arms; but everything about whom he was told him not to. So the two of them walked in silence, neither sure of what to say. Their pace slowed, and eventually they had fallen back into the middle of the caravan. Radnor's mind was jumbled and unclear, wandering from half formed thoughts to half formed words. It was Elena who made the first move, as she reached out to take his hand in hers. Just as her fingertips started to brush his, Radnor abruptly turned away and broke off at a run. Elena had to suppress a yelp as his sudden movement startled her, and she could only continue her silent walk.

Radnor's mind raced as he ran to find Leif. The demigod had noticed that there was something wrong with the horses. It was the frightened way their eyes darted about, and the nervous breaths they took. They were more skittish than normal. Darestr seemed especially cautious. All of the horses smelled something in the air that Radnor couldn't. Could it be more ghouls? No matter the threat, Leif needed to know.

The few surviving warriors in their company started to fan out from the sides of the column, weapons at the ready. They were moving like they were searching for something. Radnor found Leif hurrying to the back to the convoy.

"Veigarand!" he exclaimed.

"Something's wrong. The horses—" the ealdorman started

"They're afraid of something," Radnor finished.

"You noticed it too, eh?" Leif said.

"Yes, I was just coming to warn you."

"Good. My men are checking the surrounding woods, just to be sure. I want the column to keep moving, and I need you to anchor our rear."

"Where will you be?" Radnor asked.

Leif took a moment to scan the trees before answering.

"I'll be at the front. We need to keep up our pace and get ahead of whatever is out there. I want you and my men to act as a defensive screen in the event that they do find somethi—"

Leif's instructions were interrupted by the shout of one his scouts as the man came dashing out of the brush.

"Wolves!" the man exclaimed. "There's a pack of wolves nearby that look to have healthy appetites...and they're keeping pace with us."

"How many?" Leif asked.

"I'm not sure. I counted six and left before they noticed me."

Leif became lost in thought, weighing his options.

"I don't think it should be a problem," Radnor said. "Wolves don't attack humans in large numbers. If we keep moving and stay together, they'll break off."

Leif scoffed at Radnor's advice.

"Veigarand, the last time you told me monsters in the shadows would leave us alone if we just 'stick together and keep moving', I lost good people. I'm inclined not to trust that guidance. I want those wolves off our backs. Do whatever it takes, but I want them gone!"

Leif turned to his scout.

"Signal the others to come back; I don't want anyone getting singled out by the wolves."

Leif's man nodded and dashed back into the underbrush. Leif turned to Radnor, and gave him a curt nod before returning to the front of the group. Radnor ran back to Darestr, looking to retrieve his helmet and shield from his saddlebags. Elena was still there, but before she could speak, Radnor answered her unspoken question.

"There's possible trouble. Leif is leading you all on ahead."

"And what are you going to do?" Elena asked.

Radnor finished buckling his helmet on, and spoke.

"I'll take care of the trouble."

He started walking back behind the column, and once a bit of distance was between him and the others, Radnor planted his feet, and waited.

He did not have to wait long before the first wolf came stalking out of the trees and onto the path. A second wolf came shortly after, and a third after that. Soon there were nine wolves on the road. The lead wolf snarled hungrily. The pack slowly advanced on Radnor, moving to encircle him. *Perhaps Leif was right.* Radnor thought to himself. Wolves normally wanted nothing to do with him. Bears saw him as a threat to be eliminated, but wolves usually saw him as a threat to be avoided. But not these, they rose to his challenge, ready for a fight.

One of the wolves suddenly rushed him. The lead wolf barked after it, but it ignored the Alpha's command. Radnor drew his sword and caught the animal with an arcing slash as it tried to leap upon him. A second wolf hurled itself into the fray, and it met its own swift end as Radnor drove the sharpened edge of his shield into its skull. The other wolves hesitated, and the Alpha barked again. The rest of the pack faded into the trees while the Alpha glared at Radnor with intelligent, rage filled eyes. Radnor took a step towards it, and the wolf fled back into the forest. Satisfied his work was done, but unnerved by the willingness of wolves to attack him, Radnor returned to the convoy.

Radnor paused briefly to speak with Elena. She was worried from the onset of his departure, but grew even more worried as she saw the blood spattered across his armor. Before she or Rolf could ask, Radnor told them he was all right, but that he needed to speak with Leif. Rolf threw a rag at him as Radnor started to leave. Radnor took it and used it to help clean the blood off his sword and armor, thanked Rolf, and continued on to make his report.

Despite the wolves retreating, Leif was very much on his guard, and told Radnor to act as a perimeter scout. Radnor understood Leif's fear, and choked down his anger over the fact that this meant he couldn't spend any more time with Elena or Rolf. He didn't like it, but he resigned himself to the fact that his time with them was over.

As the party walked, they found the road leading into the city. This road was paved with brickwork that belonged to that long lost empire whose architecture dotted the landscape with ever growing frequency as they approached the Morakors Mountains. Wulfgeld was nestled into the foothills of those mountains, with farmland stretching up to the north and west. This was the land that Sigaberht's family had paid with their own blood to protect. The main gate of Wulfgeld rested on the north side, facing away from the invading forces habitually sent by Duke Piarin, whose fortress lay southward within Drakomar pass in the mountains. A water gate shrouded a canal that ran through the south side of the city. This canal took water from a distributary of a river that ran from the mountains and later became a tributary to the Argirn, the river that Radnor's company had had to cross earlier on their journey. In the mid-afternoon, the company was overjoyed when Radnor returned from his scouting trip and brought the news that he had seen the gates of the city. Jubilant cries overtook the crowd as they realized their perilous journey was almost over.

As the refugees approached, they saw several trade caravans enter and exit the large gates of Wulfgeld's fortified walls. Leif took the lead and brought them all to the gate. The group was met by a trio of guardsmen, all of whom looked very concerned. Radnor kept his eyes scanning the battlements of the stone walls, looking for signs of treachery out of sheer habit. It was irrational, he knew, but he couldn't stop himself from checking his surroundings. He saw that he himself had garnered some attention from some of the soldiers manning the walls, but no one raised any sort of alarm. Leif was in the process of explaining the situation to the guards, when their captain came to the gate, having been summoned when this unusual crowd arrived.

He was a short man, but built like an anvil. The mail armor he wore looked heavy as it draped his stocky frame. His deeply tan face was pockmarked and chiseled by age and experience; and his black beard was speckled with flecks of gray. His high cut brow and smallish nose created a sense of bred nobility about him. Radnor guessed that he was probably the lesser son of a rich landowner from the Southworld. Once the captain saw Leif's haggard appearance and torn clothes, he gasped in shock at seeing the ealdorman in such a state The captain quickly ordered his men to open the gate at once. The guards scrambled to open the gates as quickly as possible, and the mysterious captain nearly jumped from the battlements to get to Leif. Once the gates were open, the captain ran through and clasped hands with Leif as Leif yelled.

"Talkos!"

The two men embraced, and Leif spoke again.

"Talkos, thank Caelum you came down! I was afraid I'd be here arguing with your underlings all day. I don't recognize them, are they new?"

"Aye, they are," Talkos responded.

Talkos' accent confirmed Radnor's suspicions, as it showed Talkos was indeed from the Southworld, probably the kingdom of Castellus. The company was ushered through the gate, which housed a portcullis as well as several murder-holes through which men standing on top of the gate could rain death on any unwanted visitors trying to force their way inside. Once they were all past the gate, the refugees were offered food and water, which they gratefully accepted. Talkos and Leif continued their conversation, and Leif began to tell him their story. Before Leif could get into too much detail, Talkos cut him off.

"You need to see Sigaberht right away," he said.

Leif turned and pointed in Radnor's direction.

"Make sure he comes with me...at spear point if you have to!"

Talkos gestured to his men, and one of them reached for Radnor's sword as the other two moved to seize his arms. Radnor reflexively took the man reaching for his sword by the wrist and almost broke the man's arm before stopping himself. The other two reached for their weapons, but before they could finish being drawn, Elena leaped in the way.

"Stop!" She yelled.

The guards froze, unsure of what to do. Elena turned to Leif and Talkos.

"Radnor swore an oath that he would go before Sigaberht when we arrived. Radnor is a man who keeps his word."

Elena then turned to Radnor

"Isn't that right? You'll keep your word?"

Radnor nodded. Elena touched his arm, and looked him in the eye.

"Then let the poor man go. You don't need to hurt him."

Radnor released his grip on the wincing guard, and once that was done the steel titan withdrew his word from its scabbard, and handed it to the guardsman.

"I guess I am to see the earl," he said to Leif.

Radnor marched with Leif, Talkos, and their escort, leaving behind the rest of the refugees; who were now being given blankets against the cool autumn air that was settling in as evening approached. Radnor was led uphill along winding streets that eventually culminated in a great hall at the highest point in the city. The hall had been built upon the ruins of an ancient stone building, which like the road, was originally built by that long lost empire. It had taken much work to restore it to working order, and the structure was a hybrid of ancient stone and new lumber.

Once inside the doors of the hall, Radnor was stripped of his armor and left to stand in only his pants and blood stained tunic. Talkos announced their presence to the steward, and informed the officious man that an emergency meeting with the earl was needed. The steward went away in a hurry, clearly uncomfortable with Leif and Radnor's unkempt appearances. It did not take long before the party was granted entrance. Leif was uneasy, as he had a lot on his mind that needed to be said.

The doors of the throne room were opened to them, and the group entered the long room. Inside were many tables, arranged for large gatherings of warriors to meet and feast. The walls were lined with great banners, bearing the wolf's head sigil which Sigaberht's family used as its coat of arms. There were also majestic tapestries set upon the walls. They all told of the deeds of Sigaberht's ancestors, going all the way back to the founding of the city. Great battles were depicted on some, while others showed pastoral scenes of farming and construction during times of prosperity.

At the far end of the long hall was a dais, and on that dais were five thrones. The thrones at each end were empty, and draped in black fabric that marked the mourning for lost family members. Based on this, Radnor guessed the empty thrones must have been formerly used by Sigaberht's brothers, Eadwulf and Cynaric. Radnor remembered Leif's story of how Eadwulf had died in battle saving Sigaberht's life. But how had Cynaric died? Radnor decided it was best not to ask.

The center thrones were occupied by the rulers of Wulfgeld. On the left sat Erelda, the wife and consort of Earl Sigaberht. Touches of gray were somewhat masked by the shine of her bright blonde hair. It was braided into a single braid that ran along her back. She had the poise of a woman who has seen and done many things over her lifetime, and expected to weather still more hardships down the road. On the right sat Sigaberht's son, Ashveldt, barely old enough to be called a man. His short cropped blonde hair was cut very cleanly and precisely, close to the head. He was lean, but strong. Sigaberht's heir stared at Radnor with intense concern. He wasn't sure what to make of the group yet, but he knew enough to understand that their arrival in this manner was not a good omen.

In the middle sat Sigaberht himself. He too was blonde, with his hair also kept cleanly cut close to his head. Atop his head sat a golden crown that signified to all that he was the earl. Upon his arm he wore his silver oath ring upon which all of his vassals swore their loyalty. He was a tall man, and like his son, he was well muscled. While Ashveldt's eyes showed concern and worry, Sigaberht's eyes were filled with a variety of emotions. He leaned forward on his throne, and even across the long hall, Sigaberht could see how exhausted and underfed Leif was. He was concerned for his ealdorman, both as his vassal and as his friend. When Sigaberht turned his gaze to Radnor, his eyes focused in cold appraisal.

He had no knowledge of who stood before him, but would learn all he could in the coming moments. Despite Radnor's imposing size, Sigaberht instantly recognized the high level of training in the way Radnor moved. This was no brute that stood before him. There was a grace to Radnor's movements that Sigaberht had only seen in the best sword masters. Sigaberht looked directly into Radnor's eyes, and was disturbed by his own need to look away. There was something unsettling about looking into the stranger's eyes. Sigaberht began to wonder what sort of foul thing Leif had brought before him.

Sigaberht stood and greeted Leif as an old friend, embracing him despite Leif's dirt covered clothes.

"My dear Leif! What has happened to you? Why do you come to me in such a sorry state?"

Leif held his head in shame before his lord.

"Your grace, I have failed you. Neugeld has been destroyed."

There were gasps from Erelda and Ashveldt, and all eyes turned to Sigaberht. He did not gasp, but instead chose to be silent for a moment, considering this shocking news carefully. His plans for the area had been thrown upside down, and he needed to think hard on how to proceed. Even as he burned to know more, Sigaberht chose to appear calm, and spoke again.

"How? Who has attacked us?"

Leif took a deep breath, working to keep himself calm as he knew he had to in order to get through his story.

"It is a long tale my lord, a tale of death and sorrow."

Sigaberht gave Leif a reassuring squeeze on the shoulder, hoping such a gesture would allow Leif to be more at ease and tell him every detail he needed to know. Sigaberht spoke again.

"Please, my lord ealdorman tell it."

Leif nodded.

"Before I begin, my people are still at the gates. They need food, shelter, and medicine."

Sigaberht nodded, and motioned to one of his retainers, an aging bald man who had served their family well for a long time.

"Make sure that our newly arrived citizens are well cared for. I want rooms for them at Wecta's inn; since he probably has the space needed. I want food supplied to them, and notify the Hexverat that we have people in need of their healing powers."

Radnor nearly gasped at the name "Hexverat". They were a triumvirate of powerful witches whose reputation had spread across the continent as being among the best healers in the world. They traveled across the continent, healing wounds and helping to end plagues wherever they went. For the Hexverat to be here was a welcome surprise.

Radnor's focus snapped back to the moment at hand as Leif told the story of what happened in Neugeld: from Elena's engagement party, to the attack by the demons, to the battles against the ghouls, to their arrival in Wulfgeld. There were frequent gasps from those listening, be they from the guards or Ashveldt and Erelda themselves. Sigaberht remained focused. The only reaction he gave was an ever growing look of worry mixed with calculated thought that only those that knew him best could discern. Food was brought in for Leif, and the sun had long set before Leif had finished answering all of Sigaberht's questions. Radnor noticed that Leif had carefully avoided using either of his names, choosing not to acknowledge him as "Veigarand". After a moment of eerie silence, Sigaberht spoke again.

"From what you have told me, my beloved friend, this man is the one responsible for both the destruction of Neugeld, and for the salvation of the survivors? How many ghouls did you say he killed? How many of these demons did he kill? There's something you're not telling me…" Sigaberht said, the anger in his voice involuntarily rising. He caught himself, and brought his temper back down.

"Why have you not told me this man's name?" Sigaberht asked, gesturing to Radnor.

Leif gulped, and answered.

"I am afraid you would not believe me. For this…this man is the subject of many songs and legends. Many a tale of terror has been whispered in the shadows about this man. He is the ghost of the north, he is…Veigarand."

When there had been gasps before, there was laughter in the room now. People chuckled at such a silly notion that a monster from song was here in the flesh. Some in the room were starting to think that Leif's mind had snapped under the pressure of the attack. Only Sigaberht's now booming voice ended the jeers.

"Cease this inane mockery!" he yelled to those laughing. "Leif is one of my most trusted men. He has sworn directly to me on this oath ring!" he said, as he gestured to the ring bound on his arm.

The room became silent, and people started to return to their normal, more dignified behavior. Sigaberht surveyed the room. The others might not believe this was Veigarand, but in Sigaberht's mind, the pieces were starting to fit together. Not only in Leif's story, but the things Sigaberht had noticed as he had observed Radnor, whom had been silently standing the entire time. He might believe Leif, but if the others didn't, word would spread, and he couldn't have people doubting him now. There was an opportunity here, but Sigaberht knew if he wanted to make the best of it, he had to act now.

"Now that things are settled again, I must admit I am skeptical of your statement Leif. I do not doubt that you believe this man to be Veigarand, but can this be proven?"

Before Leif could answer, Radnor spoke.

"Your grace, I may be able to supply the proof you need, but I need to ask first…do you have any special love for this table that I stand next to?" Radnor patted one of the heavy wooden tables.

Sigaberht leaned back in his chair, anticipating Radnor's next move.

"No, you may do as you will to that table."

Radnor nodded, and struck the table with a single, heavy blow. Wood cracked and splintered under the force, and Radnor's hand easily smashed through. Using his other hand, Radnor grabbed the new hole he had just made, and lifted the table above his head. Without breaking eye contact with Sigaberht, he tore the table in half, and threw the pieces against the wall of hall, shattering and splintering them.

There was not a sound in the room as the guards looked to Sigaberht, unsure of what to do. There was absolute silence as the shock of what they all saw sank in. Sigaberht was the first to break the silence with applause.

"Bravo!" he shouted, even as his mind raced in both fear and anticipation. A new plan was already forming in his mind.

"I expected nothing less from the ghost of the north!"

Sigaberht turned to his steward, and gestured to the guards.

"I want this room emptied. Leave us," he ordered.

"But…your grace…" stammered the steward.

"I said leave us!" Sigaberht barked.

There was a flurry of activity as people bustled from the room, leaving only the royal family, Leif, and Radnor in the hall. Once the final door was closed, Sigaberht spoke to Leif.

"My dear ealdorman…you say this man here is responsible for the destruction of your home, but also is the savior of the survivors? You have brought him before me, presumably for judgment. I know him not, but you do. What judgment do you render unto him Leif?"

Leif hesitated, unsure of how to answer. He found it difficult to condemn Veigarand fully when he had done so much to help him. As much as he hated the man, there was a sense of honor Leif felt that kept him from speaking from his heart.

"I do not rightly know, your grace, I…"

128

Did you not tell me this man is the one responsible for the destruction of Neugeld? Your home? The homes of the people you called yours? I noticed you are not wearing your oath ring. Where is your oath ring, Leif?"

Leif started to answer, but was cut off again.

"How many of your friends lie dead now? How many, Leif, how many are dead?"

Radnor could see what was happening. Sigaberht was working Leif into a frenzy, tapping into his rage and conflicted emotions. It was working.

"I don't know!" Leif yelled. "It all happened so fast, and we lost so…so many good people! I buried children on that road, *children*!" Leif shouted, his grief taking hold.

"Then what judgment do you render upon him!" Sigaberht yelled.

"*Death*!" Leif screamed.

"*Death*! *Death*! *Death*!"

Tears began streaming down Leif's face as he made his declaration.

Radnor felt his blood run cold as Sigaberht's gaze fell fully upon him. There was power in that gaze that Radnor hadn't fully understood until now.

Without looking away from Radnor, Sigaberht spoke to Leif.

"I am sorry I had to push you like that," Sigaberht said. "I needed to know your true heart on the matter, and now I know how you really feel. Thank you for sharing it with me."

Leif dropped to his knees, sobbing, all pretense of leadership gone from him. In this moment, Sigaberht had broken all of Leif's composure, and pierced him through his sorrowful heart. The thought frightened Radnor.

"My dear, dear friend, I must ask your forgiveness. I cannot grant you your wish just yet. You must be patient a while longer."

Leif looked up from his tears.

"Why?"

Sigaberht stepped from his throne, and lifted Leif back to his feet.

"Because, if we are to beat back Piarin's wretched soldiers, and stop them from ever assailing our gates again, we need Veigarand's help. He will do penance, and he will pay for what he did. But not yet. I need you to be strong, strong for me, strong for our people!"

Leif regained some of his composure, and started to resume his role as ealdorman.

"What would you have me do, my lord?"

Sigaberht smiled at Leif.

"Thank you my friend. As always, your loyalty is without measure. I need your people to understand that when they tell their story, it was not demons nor monsters that destroyed your home. It was an attack by Duke Piarin's men. They came and burned your home to the ground in the dead of night. They did this."

Leif looked shocked.

"But, my lord, do you not believe me? I thought you..."

"No, I do believe you!" Sigaberht said reassuringly. "I believe every word of it. That's not what's most important now. What's important is rallying support in our cause against Piarin. Word of Neugeld's destruction will reach the trading partners that you strove to build such good friendships with...and if it was Piarin that destroyed Neugeld, then those trading partners will become our allies on the field of battle. So tell your people that no one is to speak of monsters or demons. It was men from Drakomar that destroyed your village. If you do this for me, your people will not have died in vain."

Leif nodded, but did not speak. Lying like this didn't sit well with him, but Sigaberht's wisdom was sound, and Leif wanted to end the wars with Piarin as badly as he wanted revenge against Radnor.

Sigaberht scribbled onto a piece of parchment, stamped it with his seal, and spoke again.

"In my haste, I forgot to send a letter with my retainer. Leif, you must be exhausted. Go...be with your people. I have written this note. Take it to Master Wecta at his inn. He will provide you and your people with lodgings and food, at my expense. Eat, drink, be with others who love you. I will deal with Veigarand."

Leif bowed before his beloved lord, took the letter, and exited the throne room, leaving Radnor alone with the earl and his family.

Sigaberht stood from his seat, and approached Radnor. As he did so, he began loosening the oath ring from his arm.

"Veigarand, you have said very little today. What have you to say in this matter?"

Radnor let out a slight laugh.

"I suspect you care little of what I have to say. You expect me to bend to your will like Leif did."

It was Sigaberht's turn to laugh now.

"No, I don't suppose you will. Perhaps I should just have you killed. But it would be such a waste of an opportunity. That, and we both know that if I gave such an order, none of us would leave this room alive. If even half the stories are true, having you fighting by my side could turn the tide of my struggle against Piarin. The rumors alone would cause half his men to desert! But no, you will not submit to me because *I* will it. You will submit to me because *you* will it."

"I beg your pardon?" Radnor asked.

"Oh, drop the act Veigarand," Sigaberht said. "We both know the only reason you're still here is because you chose to be. Something is keeping you here. If it were up to you, you'd have me believe it was some sense of duty or honor that made you allow yourself to be taken prisoner. That may be part of it, or just what you tell yourself. But, based on the story Leif told...it's someone that's become special to you over these past weeks that's really kept you with them all the way to the gates. This is why you will be motivated to submit to me."

Radnor was shocked at how accurate Sigaberht's appraisal was, and felt his temper start to rise at the implied threat to Elena.

"If you harm her in any way..."

Ah! It is a "her"! Sigaberht thought, glad his bluff had paid off. Sigaberht spoke quickly to assuage Radnor's temper.

"No, no. I have no need to harm her to motivate you. All that would do is motivate you to kill me, which certainly runs contrary to my hopes, wouldn't you agree? No, but she is here. And here she shall remain, kept safe within these walls, available to you at any time you wish."

Radnor was offended at the implication of this last comment.

"It's not like that—" he started.

"Oh, I'm sorry!" Sigaberht interrupted. "I did not mean to imply that I was offering her to you so you could just have your way with her like she was a common whore!"

Radnor shrugged his shoulders, physically shrugging off the realization that Sigaberht was already in his head. How long before he kowtowed as easily as Leif did? Trying to regain his composure, Radnor tried to take back control of the conversation.

"So, you're offering me a deal, is that it?"

Sigaberht smiled.

"In a manner of speaking. You will serve me as one of the warriors in my household. Do not worry about your six day limit, the work I have planned for you will keep you traveling...with occasional visits back here of course. But to be sure you stay loyal and don't lose interest in her; you will swear your obedience to me on this oath ring."

Sigaberht unfastened the ring from his arm and gestured for Radnor to take hold of it.

"But I also need insurance that you won't just kill my family and me in my sleep. I doubt an oath breaker's brand would bother you that much. So here's what we are going to do…you will take an oath of obedience to me that will last for one year from today. One year, and you are released from bondage. However, you must take a black oath, so that if you break it, you will die."

There was a gasp, followed by an outcry from Ashveldt…

"This is against Caelum's law! No moral oath can be taken as a black oath!"

Sigaberht turned to face his son.

"I admire your dedication to what you think is right, but this is the price of leadership. I do the unthinkable so that our family may survive. One day, you will be faced with the same hard choice, and I hope this example inspires you to take the right one."

Radnor found himself confused by the idea that Sigaberht was the one making a hard choice, when it was Radnor being forced to take an oath that could get him killed.

Radnor spoke again.

"And if I refuse to take your oath? I have gods to kill."

Sigaberht's face became very grim as he held out the oath ring for Radnor to take hold of.

"Then none of us will leave this room alive."

Radnor looked into Sigaberht's gaze, and saw that Sigaberht meant it. The earl must be more desperate than Radnor realized. He really was gambling it all right here and now. Maybe this was the hard choice he had been referring to?

Now it was Radnor's turn to choose. What was he to do? He weighed the possibility of escape in his mind. He might be able to take Sigaberht hostage, and use him as leverage to escape. But with so many men and castle walls to overcome, the odds of success were low. All it would take was an arrow to the back, and he would be killed. As skilled as Radnor was, he could only fight a few armed men at a time before he would be overwhelmed. It is hard to kill gods when you're dead. And then there was Elena. Radnor was drawn to her in a way he had never experienced before. It was more than just sexual or romantic desire. The thought of leaving her tore at him in a way that surprised him…and he had to know why. His choice made, Radnor reached to take the oath ring in his hand. Sigaberht stopped him, and clarified something.

"For an oath such as this, the ring requires your blood as well as your hand."

Radnor nodded grimly, and lifted his tunic so that he could better access the vampire bite on his shoulder, still oozing blood. Sigaberht had to hide his shock in the way Radnor did not break eye contact as he placed his hand on the very painful looking wound. Once Radnor's hand was soaked in blood, he took hold of the oath ring.

Each man held the oath ring in their hand, its cold steel burning into Radnor's palm. Relief stole across Sigaberht's face for a moment before he focused on what was to come next.

"Do you, Veigarand, swear to fight for me, to protect my family, and to obey my every command, for a period of one year?"

Radnor drew breath, it was now or never.

"I, Radnor Magnusson, do swear upon this oath ring that I will fight for you, protect your family, and obey your every command for a period of one year."

Sigaberht winced upon hearing Radnor's real name, knowing what was meant by the gesture.

The deep, icy, cold Radnor felt in the ring slowly gave way to a gradually increasing heat.

"Upon this ring, you have sworn to uphold these oaths. The penance for oath breaking is death."

The heat in the ring intensified, growing uncomfortable for both Radnor and Sigaberht. But, Sigaberht steeled his will, and continued.

"Do you accept the terms of your oath?"

The heat grew ever more intense, and Radnor grew afraid of what would happen if it continued. But he too carried on.

"I accept the terms of this oath. I am sworn to you, Earl Sigaberht!"

Fire lanced up the arms of both men. Erelda screamed in fear for her husband, but neither of the men paid any notice. Ashveldt leaped from his throne and rushed for his father, hoping to separate the two men.

"Stay away!" Sigaberht yelled, terrified his son would become included in this death pact. Ashveldt did as he was told, but he did not retreat back to his seat.

The pain in Radnor's arm became too much to bear as fire consumed his flesh. His screams echoed across the entire hall, and were matched only by Sigaberht's own cries of pain. Onward, the flame burned, creeping further and further up their arms. Neither man could let go of the oath ring, their fingers fused to the burning silver. The fire began charring the flesh in Radnor's arm all the way up to his shoulder, and suddenly he felt an even more intense burning erupt in his chest. Radnor could only close his eyes and scream in agony, until suddenly, it all ceased. The fire was gone, and all that was left was the sound of his and Sigaberht's yells. Radnor collapsed to the floor, his will and power all sapped by the ordeal.

After he opened his eyes, Radnor saw that Sigaberht had collapsed into his son's arms, and his son was now carrying Sigaberht back to his throne as Erelda offered her husband water. Dazed, Radnor finally dared to look at his arm, and found that he was actually uninjured. Sigaberht gave Radnor a grim smile.

"So, Veigarand, you are now bound to me by a pact that the followers of Caelum consider to be unholy. If you can keep a secret, so can I."

Radnor was amazed at how quickly Sigaberht regained his sense of self. If the earl was shaken at all by the experience, he hid it well.

"Now, you should go visit Leif. You will need to retrieve your things. I have lodgings in the hall that you can use during your time here."

Radnor shook his head.

"Your wish is my command my lord, but if I may, I would prefer to stay with the people of Neugeld for the time being."

Sigaberht laughed.

"Of course, you may sleep where you wish! Just be sure to stay in Wulfgeld. I know you will want to rest for a few days, but when you are ready, we have much to discuss."

Radnor returned to the gatehouse to find that the citizens of Neugeld were still there. Tired as they were, their spirits were still bright. They were gathered around numerous fires and had ample blankets and food to keep them happy. They conversed with the guards, and the wounded were being cared for by the Hexverat. It was for this reason they had not yet departed for their new lodgings. The Hexverat were witches who specialized in all kinds of magic meant for healing, and were capable of treating grievous wounds and diseases. Death was the only thing they could not cure. They had traveled the world for decades giving people the aid they needed, with their only payment being in food, clothing, and a place to work and sleep. They had dedicated themselves to their craft in a manner which few witches or sorcerers did.

Despite their many years, they were still as beautiful as they were when they started practicing magic. They had clearly mastered their craft, as neither of the two sisters present looked a day over thirty. The two sisters were easily distinguished at a distance, as one sister's long, flowing hair was golden blonde while the other's hair was raven colored. Both of them moved with a grace Radnor usually only saw in trained swordsmen.

Radnor also lost himself in the way the freckles on the blonde sister's face complemented her eyes, and in the calming, reassuring smile of the raven haired sister. He had to shake his head to break from whatever trance their aura pulled him into. Radnor was wondering if this aura was a spell the witches cast to help calm their patients, when suddenly the raven haired witch looked straight into Radnor's eyes and darted towards him.

"You're wounded," she said matter-of-factly.

Radnor stared dumbly for a moment, caught by surprise that she knew this already.

"It's your shoulder, isn't it?" she asked, pointing at the shoulder where Radnor had been bitten by the vampire.

"Yes, it is," he said.

She looked at him flatly.

"If I'm going to help you, I need you to let me examine it."

Radnor lifted his tunic to expose his shoulder to her. A look of utter shock and disgust crossed the witch's face when she saw the wound.

"How long has it been like this?" she asked him.

Radnor had to think for a moment to be sure.

"Over two months. This isn't an ordinary wound."

"I can see that!" she muttered as she continued to examine it. "What in Caelum's name did this to you?"

Radnor grimaced as she shifted his arm to get a different angle to look at the wound.

"I got in a fight with a vampire. This is the souvenir he left me."

A look of concern flashed across the Hexverat's face, then a moment of realization.

"Have you had any aversion to sunlight since this happened?"

Radnor laughed a little in spite of himself.

"No, not in the least. I have shown no sign of turning into one of his servants so far. The wound just won't close."

The raven haired witch turned to face her sister.

"Hilda! I need your help!"

After collecting herself, the blonde witch came over to see what was wrong. Her sister, whom Radnor learned was "Bruna", explained the situation. Hilda looked thoughtfully at the wound for a moment, and then returned her gaze to Radnor.

"Can you live with it for one more night? We have what we need to help you, but the potion needs to be mixed, and it won't be ready until tomorrow evening."

Radnor nodded, relief washing over him. He had found the healers he needed! He could finally be rid of this damned wound!

"Thank you, where shall we meet?" Radnor replied.

"We're staying at a cottage just outside the earl's hall. Come there as the sun sets, and we will have something for you that should leave you right as rain when we're finished," Bruna said.

"Thank you," Radnor repeated.

He was unsure of what to say after that. He had never expected he would ever recover from the damned vampire bite! The healers quickly returned to treating the other refugees. As they did this, Elena and Rolf came from the shadows, leading Darestr over to where Radnor stood. Radnor hastily put on his tunic as Elena came closer.

"I see you're still here," she said.

"Yep," Radnor agreed.

"So we're stuck with you awhile longer?" Rolf asked playfully.

Radnor gave the boy a gentle swat on the shoulder.

"It looks like. My penance for the damage I caused is to help Sigaberht fight against Piarin."

Elena got a worried look on her face. Without knowing it, Radnor had spat Sigaberht's name when he said it. Elena tried to say something to help, but didn't come up with much, so she went with the first question on her mind.

"But what about your plans?"

Radnor's gaze lingered on Elena for a moment before he responded.

"My plans have changed slightly. Don't you worry; I'll still have the head of every Krigari that stands in my way."

"And what will you do after that?" Rolf asked.

"After? There is no *after*," Radnor said, allowing his anger at his current situation to show.

An awkward silence fell over the trio after Radnor said that. Something in what he said hit Rolf, hard, as the boy began to look visibly upset.

"Are you all right?" Elena asked.

"Is there an 'after' for me now? Do you think my father will find me?" Rolf replied.

Tears started welling up in his eyes. Even as it sank in that he was safe again, new fears about his future began unfolding in his mind. Elena embraced the boy, holding him tight.

"If he can, he will," she said reassuringly.

There was nothing Radnor could do to offer his support in the moment. Elena and Rolf were like brother and sister, and he was an outsider. The moment was interrupted by a boisterous announcement from Leif.

"Attention, people of Neugeld! We have been given rooms at Wecta's inn for the time we are here, to be paid for by his grace Sigaberht!"

Cheers and praise for Sigaberht interrupted Leif's announcement as the excited folk began to pick up their few possessions. Once the noise died down, Leif continued.

"The Hexverat, whom have been so kind as to help us with our wounds and our sick, have finished their work."

There were more cheers as the two witches bashfully made small curtsies for the applause they were receiving. Despite many years of such work, they had never quite gotten used to the praise that was heaped upon them.

Leif rolled his eyes, exasperated at the interruptions.

"Please now! If you would all follow me, I will lead you to the inn where we shall receive food, warm clothing, and shelter for the night!"

As they left, one of the guardsmen tipped his helmet to the group, and said

"May your days be ever as merry as they may be, and may your slumber be as restful as can be!"

"Thank you," replied Rolf and Radnor simultaneously. The two looked at each other and laughed at their shared moment before starting on their way.

The company of refugees was led along wide, paved streets that moved in linear patterns throughout the city. There were quaint shops, and even a blacksmith that caught Rolf's interest as the group walked happily to the inn. He had always wanted a chance to see Wulfgeld, and he was finally here. His father had often told him stories of the lights and crowds, and they did not disappoint. Torches set up along the sides of the streets lit the way, while the moon also provided its own faint illumination for the throngs of people going about their business. A cold wind whipped down the road, whistling as it went, causing many to shield their faces under their cloaks. This breeze didn't faze Rolf. He stood up in the stirrups to get a better view, and looked on with excitement at the city of endless possibilities.

"What a lovely atmosphere," Elena commented, trying to lighten Radnor's mood.

Radnor looked around him, and shrugged.

"Still a grumple-monster, are you?" Elena teased, looking at Rolf while she did it.

Rolf smiled a little as Radnor grunted almost inaudibly. Elena laughed a little at her own merriment, and Darestr stopped for a moment, and snorted.

"Oh, come now, you know it's only a bit of fun," Elena said to the mildly annoyed horse.

After another block, they reached the inn. Radnor and Darestr walked to the entrance, and Darestr lowered himself to let Elena and Rolf dismount.

"I'll be back in a few minutes," Radnor said to the pair.

With that, the two people entered the inn, leaving Radnor to lead Darestr to the stables that were in back of the inn. Once Radnor had found a comfortable stall for Darestr, he took a moment to pat his loyal friend on the head, which Darestr repaid with a nuzzle from his snout. Radnor smiled a moment before he unfastened the saddlebags and threw them over his shoulder. In them he carried the last of his clothes. He then snorted at himself in annoyance as he awkwardly tried to put his helmet on with the saddle bags on his shoulder. It occurred to him that he was more tired than he had realized. After a few more moments, his armor was on, his weapons were all buckled to him in some way, and his saddlebags were back on his shoulder. It was a strange sight to behold, but he didn't want to take multiple trips carrying his baggage into the inn. It occurred to him as he walked through the door that he had more possessions than anyone else in the group.

Once he joined the others inside, he found Leif handing over the letter to Wecta, the innkeeper. Wecta gave it a skeptical glance at first, but after examining the crowd assembled before him; the aging man relented, and happily accepted the customers. It took him a moment at first, and then it suddenly occurred to him that everything was being paid for by the earl, and as such, he could force as much food on the starving people as he wanted and make a great deal of money this night. This is exactly what he did, and the people of Neugeld were all too happy to indulge him.

The lower floor of the inn was a big open space filled with tables and chairs, with a bar on one side of the room. There was a kitchen in the back, with cooks rushing to fill the new orders of food from the hungry survivors. Bread shared by the guards did not appease hungry stomachs the same way a fully cooked meal would. Elena spotted Radnor and waved him over to where they were in line for food. Radnor gave a nod in their direction, and worked his way through the crowd. Rolf and Elena ordered their food in the kitchen, but when Elena turned to see what Radnor wanted to eat, she found that he had disappeared in all of the commotion. While they were busy, Radnor had gone to the innkeeper, collected a key to a room upstairs, and had departed for that room. The two started to look for him, but Rolf pointed out that if Radnor wanted to be social, he would be found. It was hard to miss a man like Radnor, even in a crowd like this.

Radnor opened the door to his room, dropped his saddle bags to the floor, and tore his armor off. He threw his ragged, blood soaked tunic and pants on the floor, leaving himself totally naked for the first time in a long time. He just took a moment to stand, free of clothes torn and ruined by his bloody work, and looked to his own body. Of course, he could not shed the skin that was also damaged during his fights. Frustration built up within him, the inescapable nature of what he was began closing in around him, and it wasn't until he remembered Halbjorn's training that he started to regain his sense of self. Slowly, Radnor was able to calm himself again, and soon he felt comfortable in his own skin.

There was a wash basin and a mirror in one corner of the room. Radnor took a moment to look at his reflection, and noticed how scraggly his hair and beard had gotten. He decided that he would take advantage of a barber's services if he got the chance. He washed his face in the water from the basin, and tried to clean himself as best he could. Once this was done, he changed into his last fresh tunic and pants. The pants were dark brown, and his tunic was long, dark blue, and draped down to his knees. After belting the tunic down, Radnor went to his saddlebags for his mug, only to find it missing. He had been drinking from borrowed cups since that night in Neugeld. He had forgotten that his mug was probably still sitting on the floor of the inn back there. Radnor sighed, and looked at his door. It wasn't until after what felt like an eternity of thought that Radnor opened the door and headed back downstairs for some food and company.

The ground floor of the inn was full of conversation, and even the beginnings of genuine merriment. But when Radnor came down the stairs, there was a sudden stop to the chatter. All eyes turned to him to see what he would do. Some of the people gathered there strained to get a good look at him, as many had never seen him without his helmet on. Radnor finished his descent down the stairs and into the room. Once there, he felt unsure of what to do. The fear in the silence was palpable, and he was about to head back upstairs when he felt a hand on his shoulder. Radnor turned, and found himself facing not Elena or Rolf as he expected, but instead a young woman with her little daughter in tow. The daughter looked like she was no older than three, and was still munching on an apple she had been given. The woman looked worn, beaten down, and absolutely exhausted. The trek had been hard on her, the cold, the rain… the ghouls. In her hand, she held a piece of buttered bread. Trembling, she offered the bread to Radnor.

As he took it in his hands, she quietly said…
"Thank you."
Radnor bowed his head, and said…
"You're welcome."

Once this was done, conversation resumed across the group.

Radnor turned to see where Leif was, but found him engrossed in conversation with the innkeeper. Radnor wanted to discuss the day's events with the man. Leif's true feelings were known now, and Radnor needed to be sure they could still work together, as it looked like this was to be the case now. But there was another touch on his arm. He turned again, and this time it was Elena. She held a plate full of food for him. Roasted chicken, bread, and a variety of vegetables. Radnor thanked her for the plate, and turned to where Rolf was standing next to her, face full of chicken. The boy looked up at him and said...

"Don't look at me, I'm not feeding you."

Radnor laughed, and the three of them sat down at the nearest table. It was strange for Radnor at first, as others came and went from the conversational group. As time went on, the gathering became more raucous and celebratory. Musicians had been called up, and were now performing a jubilant dance tune for the crowd. News of the refugees' arrival had started to spread. Other citizens from the city were starting to arrive. Some were coming to check in on old friends from Neugeld. Others just wanted to see what the party was about. The evening passed quickly for Radnor, and eventually the group members began to find their rooms, and go to sleep.

After many hours, the torches outside began to go out, and moonlight became the only light in the city with its pale white glow.

"No, Radnor!" Elena exclaimed. "For the last time, I am taking watch tonight."

"No, Elena, you have already forced me to let my guard down long enough to take a bath."

"And wasn't it relaxing?" Elena remarked.

"Not the point. Besides, who says sleep will be relaxing?" Radnor quipped.

"I do," Elena quipped whimsically.

"You've never seen me sleep," Radnor said. He hesitated for a moment, and made an admission to Elena.

"I can't kill the monsters when I sleep."

Silence filled the room for a moment, as Elena thought about the implications of what Radnor had just said to her. In that moment, she just wanted to wrap her arms around him and hug him until he could sleep without nightmares. But, now was not the time, nor would he understand. So, Elena merely spoke as though nothing happened.

140

"Radnor, I don't care how much warrior training you have, and I also don't care about your immense strength. You, like all other living things, need sleep. Now go!"

Elena, stern look on her face, pointed into the doorway where his bed was.

"Rolf is already in his bed. Now, if the twelve year old knows when it is bedtime, I think the warrior should too!"

Radnor grudgingly stood up from the stool he had set up outside the room, and walked through the doorway.

"And don't get out of bed 'til morning!"

Elena closed the door behind him. Radnor tested its lock. Secure, but nothing that he couldn't break down if need be. Radnor sighed, and rolled himself onto the bed. Exhaustion overtook him and within moments, he was fast asleep.

Chapter 12

It was not until nearly midday that the sun's rays brought Radnor out from his deep slumber. Rubbing his eyes, he found himself feeling intense grogginess; another reason Radnor hated to sleep. Stumbling slightly, he awoke and found his sheets partially soaked with blood. His shoulder wound had been dripping slightly all through the night. Cursing under his breath, he made his way over to the wash basin, and cleaned his wound yet again. He desperately hoped the Hexverat would finish making their potion for him soon, as pain shot down his arm every time he moved his shoulder. Eventually, Radnor was as satisfied as he could be with his work, and he prepared to head downstairs.

Upon entering the tavern, Radnor noticed how many people were there. He stood, still somewhat groggy, and blinked at the noisy and crowded room. The jovial mob was very raucous, and people bustled this way and that as they went about ordering and eating their midday meals. Radnor was quickly accosted by Rolf and Elena, who were trying to find an open table in the busy tavern. Radnor joined them at their spot, and waited for a chance to sit down. Rolf was about to make a joke that Radnor should forcibly take a table from someone, when a strange man called to them from his own table.

"Stranger! You need a place to sit? I have three empty places at mine!"

Radnor turned to find the body paired with the voice. And quite a body it was. At a table with three empty chairs, there lounged a giant of a man. He was easily seven feet tall, and had a long mane of reddish-brown hair that looked as though it had not been combed in some time. He also had a long, scraggly beard that was in similar condition as the rest of his hair. He was dressed in a simple, brown tunic and pants and a long cloak that matched his height. This giant gave a friendly smile and motioned for the trio to sit down with him. Radnor nodded, and made his way to the table. The stranger stood, and politely pulled out a seat for Elena, who sat to the man's right. Rolf sat to his left, and Radnor sat directly across from him.

"What's your name stranger?" the man asked.

"I'm Radnor, this is Elena, and this is Rolf," Radnor answered.

"Well, I'm glad to finally see someone else who isn't local here. I've been here all day, and I've been so lost."

"What brings you here, kind gentle?" Radnor asked.

The man picked up a small ax from under his chair and handed it to Radnor.

"I'm here to return this to a friend of mine. He left it in my possession and I heard he was going to be here today."

"Good sir…" Elena started "surely, we must also hear the name of the man who has been so gracious as to allow us to sit at his table."

"Ah, but of course my lady, how rude of me to forget! My name is Halfdan, Halfdan Jugback."

"Jugback?" Rolf asked.

"Yes, it is quite an interesting…"

Halfdan trailed off, and looked at the door.

Radnor turned to look the door, and saw a man dressed in a dark blue cloak.

"Excuse me one moment my lord, the friend of whom I speak has arrived."

With that, Halfdan stood and approached the man at the door. When the man saw him, he gasped out loud. Halfdan spoke to the surprised man.

"Hello Kirri, might I have a word with you outside?"

Halfdan placed his hand firmly on the man's shoulder. Radnor wasn't sure, but it looked like the grip was strong enough to hurt. Kirri gulped, and found himself turning as Halfdan spun him around. Kirri moved mechanically as he was forcibly marched out of the inn. Once the two were outside, Radnor went to the window to watch what was happening. Halfdan was angrily shaking the ax at Kirri, and Kirri was literally shaking in his boots.

"Kirri Hanloffer, I charge that you attempted to murder me a year ago today with this very ax which I carry before you. Do you deny it?"

Kirri dumbly stared at Halfdan in the street, and continued to shake.

"Your silence is as good as a confession!" Halfdan yelled.

Radnor saw that a pool of yellow began to appear under Kirri's feet.

"And I sentence you to death!"

After delivering his verdict, Halfdan promptly buried the ax blade into Kirri's skull. The dead man slumped forward onto his knees, and fell into Halfdan's legs. Two of the town guards started towards Halfdan, but before they could continue, the giant man spoke to them.

"My name is Halfdan Jugback, a name I earned when this man tried to murder me by hitting me in the back with an ax. This jug, hidden under my cloak, saved me from death that day." Halfdan then removed said jug from underneath his cloak. There was a gaping hole in its side.

"On this day, I am merely returning his property to him."

Whether it was this explanation, or his imposing nature that made the guards decide not to arrest him, Radnor never did decide. Either way, the two men picked up Kirri's body and carried it to the guard house. Halfdan then returned to his seat with Radnor and the others. After he situated himself, he grinned at Radnor.

"I'm going to miss that ax: we have such a history together."

With that, he began laughing, and took a giant gulp from his drink.

"I'm staying in this inn, are you?"

"The same," Radnor replied.

Rolf sat still, staring out the window at the pool of blood left by the dead man. Halfdan took notice of this, and started to speak to him.

"How old are you young man?"

"Twelve," Rolf replied, still staring at red the stained dirt.

"Ah, a good age. When's your birthday, son?"

"In two months."

"Good, laddy. Where are you from?"

Rolf did not respond this time, and Halfdan gave him a strange look. He and Radnor met eyes, and then Halfdan made a gesture off to the side with his head. Radnor took the hint, and the two stood up.

"I'll be back in a little bit," Radnor said to Elena.

He then smiled at Rolf and went on his way. The two men walked outside. Halfdan led Radnor to the spot where Kirri's blood still soaked into the dirt road. Radnor took special care not to step in it, while Halfdan forcefully ground his boots into the blood soaked soil.

"What's happened to the boy?" Halfdan asked.

Radnor sighed.

"His village was wiped out. I was there when it happened."

A gleam of recognition lit in Halfdan's eye.

"You're with the group from Neugeld? Is it true what they say? That Southworlders came and ransacked the place?" asked Halfdan.

"Yes," Radnor lied, obeying Sigaberht's command.

Halfdan whistled in acknowledgment.

"Then this war is only going to escalate. They were on a sort of break, Sigaberht and Piarin. Not a formal truce or anything, just nobody had done anything for a bit. I guess that's changed now, and the destruction of a whole town like that..." Halfdan trailed off.

There was silence between them for a moment, and Halfdan returned to his more jovial self.

"Come, shall we not resume our seats and our merriment?"

Radnor nodded, and they both walked back into the tavern.

The group was able to pass the time eating their meal with great enjoyment in each other's company. Radnor and Halfdan got along particularly well, as both men had traveled the wilderness and had stories to share of close encounters with wild beasts, and of other travelers they had met on their journeys. Once the meals were finished, Radnor stood up to leave.

"Where are you headed off to?" Rolf asked.

"I need a new spear," Radnor replied.

"Won't Sigaberht give you one now that you're in his service?" Rolf pressed.

Radnor looked back to Rolf and shrugged.

"I prefer mine custom made. I also need to get Darestr shod. His shoes are worn out, and I don't want to make him suffer this old set any longer," he said.

As Radnor turned to leave, he heard Elena speak to Rolf.

"C'mon, we have a city to see. How many interesting shops do you think we can find?"

Rolf nodded, and joined her as she also prepared to leave.

"I'll just...stay here then!" Halfdan joked from his table.

Radnor collected Darestr from the stables and started walking. After a short while, Radnor found a blacksmith. Seeing the shop was open, Radnor lead Darestr inside. He found the blacksmith hammering on a piece of steel, and after not too long a time, the smith had it shaped into a horseshoe. Radnor coughed loudly, but that did not get the smith's attention. Then Darestr snorted loudly, and that did the trick. The blacksmith looked up at them, and proceeded to wipe his hands.

"What can I get for you my lord?" he inquired.

"I need my horse shod, and I would like it done immediately."

"Certainly sir, just let me see that you have money."

"Just let me know the price," Radnor replied.

The blacksmith smiled, and told him two pieces of silver for the horseshoes and the labor of putting them on. Radnor promptly paid him. As the man began his work, Radnor wandered around the shop and noticed a long steel bar over in a corner. Radnor walked over to examine it, and hefted it. It was about six feet long, and was about three quarters of an inch thick.

"Smith…" Radnor started. "How much would it cost me to use your forge and hammer for a brief time?"

"Another piece of silver, plus the cost of whatever you break. Why?"

"I think I can make use of this steel bar you have here."

The blacksmith looked up from his work, and looked at Radnor.

"That was ordered by a miller over at the edge of town. He never came to pick it up, and never paid for it. I assume he was able to fix whatever the problem was on his own."

"How much for the bar?" Radnor replied.

"Another piece of silver."

"Done."

The smith looked surprised, but showed Radnor to his tools, and Radnor again paid him. Darestr snorted his disapproval of the use of so much money, but Radnor ignored him. He was sure he could convince Sigaberht to reimburse him. The smith then took Radnor to a different room where a fire could be set and an anvil rested on a heavy oak table. Radnor smiled a little, and started his work. Despite the pain in his shoulder, he found satisfaction in making something with his own hands. Radnor heated the metal at the end of the rod, and when it was red hot, began to hammer. His strokes fell with the force of meteors striking the earth. Gradually, the metal began to take the shape of a spear point. Blow after blow he threw, and just as Radnor was fully absorbed in his task, he heard a familiar voice behind him.

"Enjoying your work?"

Radnor turned, hammer ready to strike at the form of Ashrahan standing behind him. The god smiled at Radnor's futile gesture and leaned back against the wall.

"Come now, if we are to work together, you must understand that I am going to drop in like this from time to time."

Radnor glared at the intruder, and wordlessly returned to his work. Radnor didn't see it, but Ashrahan rolled his eyes at the gesture. Then Ashrahan stepped directly into the anvil, blocking Radnor's view. Radnor stopped hammering, and glared directly into Ashrahan's eyes. The bemused god leaned into Radnor's gaze, his black eyes shining in the firelight, and smirked at him.

"The sooner you listen, the sooner you can get back to making your new poking stick."

Radnor pulled the half shaped spear point out of Ashrahan's form and looked it over, checking on its progress and making sure Ashrahan's distraction hadn't made him ruin the blade. Radnor then looked back to the grinning god.

"If you were here in person, could I kill you with this?"

Ashrahan burst out laughing, each laugh causing the fire to flicker as though it were terrified by his presence.

"No, only a weapon made by a god can kill me. A big iron bar hammered vaguely in the shape of a spear by a half-breed hardly counts."

146

Radnor hefted the rod in his hands for a moment, moving into a combat stance and pointing the tip at Ashrahan's heart.

"Someday, I would like to test that theory."

"I'm sure you would," Ashrahan said. "But I would advise you not to test it with Adramelach, he's liable not to give you a second chance."

Radnor put the spear down, and sighed.

"So that's what this is about? Your desire for Adramelach's death?"

"*Our* desire my friend," Ashrahan corrected. "As we established the other night, you want him dead too. I'm giving you another chance to join me in this endeavor."

"And if I refuse, just like last time?"

Ashrahan laughed again.

"Like I said then, I will keep giving you chances until you decide to help me. There is no way out of this."

Radnor sighed in annoyance.

"I have other obligations."

Ashrahan smiled at him.

"I did not say you had to run right out in a killing frenzy just this second. Though the thought certainly fills me with mirth."

Ashrahan became lost in thought for a moment. Radnor decided to make the best of this interruption, and started looking for information.

"While you're here, are you finally going to share with me why *you* want him dead?" Radnor asked.

Ashrahan sighed.

"Well, I will need to tell you sooner or later, so it might as well be sooner. You see, Adramelach is a fool. The kind of fool who would sooner hold himself and everyone around him in stagnation than take a single step forward."

"I'm not seeing your point," Radnor replied.

"Do you know the tale of Caelum? How he died?" Ashrahan asked.

"I know only *of* his demise, but I do not know the details."

Ashrahan smiled to himself for a moment in a way that made Radnor uneasy.

"Then allow me to show you," Ashrahan said.

The god beckoned for Radnor to approach a basin of water used for quenching hot metal. Radnor did as he was bidden and peered into the water. What he saw amazed and terrified him in a way he hadn't felt since he was a child. Fantastical colors and sounds played across the water. At first, these images were too abstract for his mortal mind to comprehend, but after a few moments they began to become more coherent, and soon

Radnor saw shapes and heard sounds with true understanding. What he saw then terrified him even more.

Fire streaked across the heavens as the creators waged war against each other, illuminating the night skies of a thousand worlds as mortal beings watched in terror from their paltry huts. Armies of gods and monsters battled across the stars, and nearly all of creation was burned to ash. Radnor shivered in terror at the destruction he saw play out before him. He had seen his homeland burned, but to see the homes of a million different races snuffed out in a fiery apocalypse was a horror Radnor would never forget.

He then felt the rushing of time in the vision, and his mind boggled at how many eons this war took to reach its bloody conclusion. The images became unfocused again, until finally, a scene became visible to him. Time stood still in the vision, giving Radnor a chance to take in what he was seeing.

Radnor saw a throne room unlike anything built by mortal hands. The room was massive, with vaulted ceilings that seemed to traverse to the sky itself. The walls were made of white stone bathed in what seemed to be golden sunlight, not from outside, but from within. Radnor could not identify the light source, and eventually, he gave up trying.

"What am I looking at?" Radnor asked.

"You are looking at the great hall of Caelum, one of the creators of all that has ever existed," Ashrahan replied.

Radnor stood in awe of what he saw, unsure of how to process what he was witnessing. Then, two figures began to take shape. Even though the images were vague at first, Radnor could see a sort of energy that surrounded each one. One figure had an aura made of pure, golden light. The other figure radiated an aura of shadow and fire.

"Who are these figures?" Radnor asked, resenting that he kept having to drag information out of Ashrahan.

"Those are the creators, Caelum, and Damiros. I'll let you figure out which is which."

Radnor continued to look harder at the vision, and finally their images came into focus.

The two creators faced each other, and prepared for their final duel. Radnor looked to the being who stood beside a gilded throne. This figure was a tall, but slight man with deep blue eyes. He wore armor that looked like bronze plates over gilded mail, and a bronze helm that left only a gap for his eyes. Given the aura of light that surrounded the man, Radnor assumed correctly that this was Caelum.

Radnor then turned his attention to the other figure frozen in the vision. The other man was as tall as Caelum, but was otherwise totally unalike the sun god. Where Caelum was made of a wiry strength, this figure appeared muscled beyond possibility. Where Caelum wore armor that reflected the light of his soul, this figure's armor was blackened by fire, a sign of the dark soul that drove him to clash with his brothers.

"I assume the dark figure is Damiros?" Radnor asked.

"Yes, he is my master and creator...brother to Caelum and Hymurr," Ashrahan replied.

"Hymurr is the god of my homeland," Radnor said. "I always thought him just a myth, to placate the fears of those who lived in terror of the Krigari."

"You are half right. Hymurr was the first of the three creators, but he has been absent since Damiros began his conquest."

Radnor took a moment to try to comprehend what he was hearing. His mind was swimming from Ashrahan's revelations. The demigod then gestured towards the form of Damiros.

"Why have I never heard of him?" Radnor asked.

"Just watch!" Ashrahan replied impatiently.

Time moved forward in the vision once more. Damiros smiled wickedly, knowing full well that Caelum's power had been diminished in their recent battles. The wicked god looked upon his foe, and noticed the look of defiance on his brother's face.

"You still have the gall to face me?" Damiros asked.

His question was answered when Caelum drew his sword, and the glittering blade cast starlight across the walls of the great hall. The sunlit god made his reply.

"So brother...why do you hesitate? Or do you still fear me even now?" Caelum goaded.

Damiros felt his blood boil at the accusation, and made a motion with his hand. A portal opened behind him, and several of his Krigari emerged. Without hesitation, the Krigari attacked Caelum as Damiros watched with glee. Their swords flashed with hellish flame as they launched themselves at the starlit god. In an instant, Caelum flashed from view, and stood behind the nearest Krigari. A blade of light cascaded across the room, and one of the Krigari lay dead, his body rent asunder by the energy in the blast.

The other two Krigari turned, snarled, and again launched themselves at their prey. Caelum deftly sidestepped a sword blow from one, and caught the other in the face with his hand. Caelum squeezed, and the Krigari's head dissolved into blood. The third Krigari launched a fireball that arced from his sword at the god of the sun and the stars.

Caelum cast a counter spell, sending a wave of starlight that cast the flame aside. As he did so, Caelum instantly closed the distance with the Krigari warrior and slashed his blade through his foe, cutting him in half.

Caelum looked up from the slaughter, and raised his hand to the ceiling. A beam of light shot from his hand, passing through the building and reaching high into the sky. After a few more moments, nothing happened, and Damiros laughed.

"There are no Malakon to save you this time. My Krigari will have made sure of that!"

Radnor looked away to ask Ashrahan yet another question.

"I assume the Malakon were warriors of Caelum?" Radnor asked. Ashrahan nodded.

"Were they equivalent to the Krigari?"

"Not really," Ashrahan said, pausing to grin at Radnor. "They lost."

There was a pause as Radnor considered Ashrahan's words. More questions filled Radnor's mind.

"Where were you when all this happened?" he asked

"I was part of the force that was fighting the Malakon while Damiros worked his way directly to Caelum."

"Then where did this vision come from?" Radnor asked.

"There was a witness who came to me not too long ago. It took a long time for this witness to find the courage...or the rage...to finally approach me. Before you ask, you will meet this person...and all my other conspirators at a later time. For now, you must simply watch."

Radnor turned his attention back to the vision in the water.

More Krigari and their demons poured into the fight, each one launching more and more powerful attacks at Caelum. Fire lashed across the hall, scorching the walls with their power. Caelum dodged and flowed around his foes, showing his true might as a creator of worlds. Blades of sunlight and starlight flew from his sword and cut down all that tried to face him. The god of starlight was hounded at all corners, but after a tidal wave of violence that made even Radnor's stomach turn, Caelum killed all that Damiros set before him. The vision then focused on the last Krigari left standing, who stood restlessly beside Damiros.

"Who is that?" Radnor asked.

"That...is the object of your desires."

"Adramelach!" Radnor exclaimed.

Now his enemy had a face.

Radnor took the time to pore over every feature of his foe. Adramelach was a bit shorter than Damiros and Caelum, and was nearly as muscled as his creator. He too wore blackened armor like Damiros, but was not wearing a helmet of any kind. His face bore several scars, showing his experience in battles against the Malakon. Radnor hoped those wounds hurt. Adramelach's eyes were the same black as Ashrahan's, and his short, close cut hair matched his eyes. In his hands he carried a spear made from the same black steel as his armor.

Damiros looked to Adramelach and drew his great ax. Caelum, panting and exhausted, prepared for one final battle. It took a great deal of energy to kill those Krigari, but he would still do his best to take Damiros with him. Damiros laughed at Caelum's stubbornness, and the blade of his ax became wreathed in black flame.

The two ran for each other, blades clashing as fire and light drove against each other. Damiros lashed out with his great ax, only for a beam of light to deflect it away. Adramelach joined the fray, thrusting for Caelum's head. Caelum slid away from the blow, and struck out with his own blade, nearly killing Adramelach on the spot. Before Caelum could finish Adramelach off, Damiros surged forward, his great fist smashing into Caelum's body. Caelum fell, skidding across the floor. After a moment, he stood and prepared to meet his foe again.

Starlight and fire danced in Caelum's hall that night. Their struggle seemed endless as each god fought bitterly to destroy the other. As they fought, the damage to the hall became so great it gradually crumbled around them. As the stones of the ceiling fell, the creators let out bursts of energy to shield themselves from the falling debris, destroying the building once and for all. Standing amongst the wreckage, and with no walls to block his view, Caelum looked upon the city of light. He wept as he saw the home he had built for himself and the beings he created burned around him. Caelum turned his gaze up to the sky, and looked longingly at the moon he had made for his world. A part of him hoped to find refuge from his sorrow in the embrace of its pale light. Knowing such thoughts were folly, Caelum turned and glared at Damiros, who now spoke to him.

"Your powers are still mighty, but these are all tricks taught to you by Hymurr… and I know them well, brother."

Caelum did not speak. Instead, as tears swept across his face, the heart-broken creator reached for the sky with both arms. Without breaking his gaze from his most hated enemy, Caelum threw his arms down, and brought the moon crashing down upon them with such speed and force none had time to respond.

Radnor nearly took a step back at the sight of the destruction. The entire city was leveled in an instant, and darkness overtook the vision before him. Fissures appeared in the ground, and lava flowed up through the cracks in the earth. Screams could be heard echoing across the land as

Caelum's world was brought to ruin by its own creator. As the debris settled, the evil light of Damiros's black flame appeared. Then, starlight lashed out against the fire, striking with all its might, but the black flame held. Eventually, the starlight subsided, and the two creators stood before each other.

"That trick may have killed many more of my Krigari, but you should know that such powers are useless against my own," Damiros said.

Adramelach emerged from behind Damiros's black flame shield, and readied his spear once more. Caelum simply nodded, and their fight began again, starlight and flame lashing out with such fury that nothing could survive a direct strike. The power of the spells the creators unleashed on each other were so great that holes were burned in the very fabric of the cosmos, leaving only sinister black pits that led outside of creation itself. Every time Caelum thought he might have an opening to wound Damiros, Adramelach was there to protect his creator. When Caelum would try to single out Adramelach, he had to turn his attention to defending against Damiros' renewed assault.

Finally, Caelum's strength gave out, and Damiros tore his weapon from his grasp. Gasping, Caelum was dashed to the ground. In that moment, Adramelach cast a spell which pinned Caelum where he lay. Unable to move, Caelum muttered his final words to himself.

"Daughter, why have you betrayed me?"

Damiros grinned wickedly as he swung his ax. The blow came swiftly, and Caelum, the starlit creator, was no more. Damiros barked an evil laugh as his victory was secured.

"Why are you showing me this?" Radnor asked.

"Shush! This is the most important part!" Ashrahan replied.

Radnor could not imagine how anything could be more important than what he had just witnessed, but he continued to watch and listen. He saw glee flash across Damiros' face as the reality of his victory became apparent.

"Victory is mine!" Damiros roared, clasping Adramelach on the shoulder.

The creator turned back to the body of his foe, and gloated over the remains of the now dead world. Damiros' heart filled with elation, but much to Radnor's surprise, there was a look of dread spreading across Adramelach's face. Before Radnor could ask Ashrahan about this, Adramelach did something even Damiros had not expected...he drove his spear deep into Damiros' back. Lightning burst forth from the blade and drove agony through Damiros' body. Not taking the time to verify if the

152

wound was mortal or not, Adramelach hastily dragged his creator to the nearest of those deep, black pits.

"Why?" Damiros demanded.

Adramelach looked down at his creator, and answered.

"You know as well as I that my kind have no place in the world you would create. We are expendable to you, and with your war won, you will wipe us away with a wave of your hand. You created me to be a survivor, and a leader to the other Krigari in battle. I will fulfill my purpose...but without you!"

Damiros roared in anger, and spat his reply as he struggled helplessly against Adramelach.

"You know as well as I that I can easily return! I was born from the abyss, and I can walk in it as well as either of my brothers could!"

Adramelach laughed, taking his own moment to gloat.

"I studied how Hymurr locked his world to us. After an eon of preparing for this moment, I understand how it was done. I shall lock you out the same way he has locked us out!"

Without another word, Adramelach threw Damiros' body into the pit before them, and watched as Damiros disappeared into the black void below. Quickly, Adramelach ran to Caelum's body and began absorbing energy from the dead creator. With this stolen power, Adramelach performed the spells needed to seal Damiros inside, preventing him from ever returning to the cosmos he had helped build. Once his work was done, Adramelach rose to his feet, and the vision faded to black.

Radnor looked back up at Ashrahan. The Krigari god then followed up the vision with his own statement.

"Adramelach told us that Damiros had gone in search of a way to Hymurr. For eons, we have sat idly by and waited for our creator's return, only to learn he had been destroyed and cast into the abyss by our very leader."

"You are angry at the betrayal?" Radnor asked.

"Not exactly. I would explain further, but my time here is running short. If I take too long in these talks, I risk discovery, and an agonizing death awaits me if that happens. You don't want that, do you?" Ashrahan jeered.

"Do you want an honest answer to that question?" Radnor replied.

"Perhaps you are more human than I thought. You see not in terms of what is best for all. Maybe, if you tell me what you want in exchange, I can help you get it."

Radnor glared at the grinning god before speaking again.

"There is something you could do for me."

"Yes?" Ashrahan said, as he leaned closer to Radnor with a hungry gleam in his eye.

"Drop dead."

Ashrahan took a step back, feigning insult.

"Sticks and stones my friend, sticks and stones. Well, you think on it for a time. I am in no rush. You don't commit deicide without a plan. But, if we know we have you on our side, then we can make such wonderful plans."

"We?" Radnor asked.

"I am not the only god who is unhappy with Adramelach's rule. There's you, me, the informant whose memory this is, and others. There are several of us working to put an end to him," Ashrahan replied.

Radnor picked up the spear again.

"Then you can all work together to kill your king on your own. I'm sure so many gods working together can come up with a way without relying on a half-breed with a poorly forged poking stick."

Ashrahan laughed again.

"I think you and I will make an excellent team. I will check on you later, and see if you change your mind."

Just as Ashrahan faded into the walls, the blacksmith opened the door and poked his head into the room.

"Are you talking to someone in there?" he asked.

"No," Radnor replied, eyes focused on the spear.

"Just thinking about how to proceed."

154

Chapter 13

Elena and Rolf were enjoying their wanderings around the city so much they barely noticed as their feet began to ache. Eventually, the adventurous pair decided to stop for a snack. As Elena was ordering some delicious smelling skewered meat from a boisterous street vendor, Rolf suddenly stopped and spun around.

"What's wrong?" Elena asked.

"I feel like I just saw something."

"Saw what?"

"I don't know. There was a man who looked like he was watching us, watching *you*," Rolf said nervously.

Elena looked at him, and then down the alley.

"I don't see anything. Tell me about him."

"He's gone now. He was tall, and he wasn't shaped right. It was like his arms and legs were too skinny for his body. He seemed to be breathing hard, almost out of breath, and his eyes...I didn't get a good look, but there was something wrong with them."

Elena continued to peer down the alley, and finally gave up.

"Well, whatever you say, he's gone now. Come on, Radnor will worry if we dilly dally."

Elena tugged on Rolf's tunic sleeve, and got him to follow her again.

As they continued their perusal of the market square, they ran into one of the Hexverat sisters, Bruna, who stopped and greeted them. She was headed to check on the refugees and make sure no one they had treated had relapsed, and remarked that she was glad to see that Rolf and Elena seemed to be doing well. Bruna then asked about Radnor.

"The warrior...the tall northerner you traveled with. What is his name?" she asked.

"Radnor. Why do you ask?" Elena replied.

Bruna smiled reassuringly.

"My sister and I will have the healing potion for his vampire bite ready after supper tonight. Will you be seeing him again today? If so, could you please let him know that we will expect him at our cottage when he is ready tonight?"

"I would be delighted to tell him," Elena said with a nod.

"Excellent!" exclaimed Bruna.

The healer abruptly excused herself and continued on her way.

A while later, an alarm sounded at the gates. Rolf turned to Elena, and the two of them decided to go see what it was about.

There was great commotion as the gate was slowly pulled open by the guards. A group of horsemen came through, leading a covered wagon loaded with goods acquired during their travels. The horsemen wore unadorned mail shirts with no tabards indicating to which lord their allegiance lay.

Rolf and Elena watched quizzically as the gate guards began giving the new arrivals water. One of the horsemen took his helmet off to take a drink, and when Rolf saw the man's face, he wept for joy. Before his very eyes stood his father, Leofric. Rolf ran forward into the group of horsemen, yelling and crying. Leofric looked up from his drink, and saw his only son running towards him. Shocked, he quickly dismounted from his horse and took Rolf into his arms in a tight embrace. He held his son there for a while, allowing Rolf's tears to flow freely, all while questions burned in his mind.

Why was Rolf here? Why was his son so upset? What had happened while he was gone?

Leofric looked up at Elena, whose face rapidly changed from joy to sadness. This change told Leofric something had happened to Neugeld. As Rolf began to calm down, Leofric broke the hug from his son, though still clasping Rolf's shoulders, and looked him in the eye.

"Rolf, I'm very happy to see you. But...why aren't you at home? Why are you and Elena here?"

Rolf was still choking down his tears enough to speak, when Elena spoke for him.

"Neugeld was...destroyed. The survivors are staying at Wecta's." Leofric's face went pale. He had been looking forward to returning home once his business with Sigaberht was done...but now there was no home to return to. Still burning with questions, Leofric restrained an outburst of his own, and looked into his son's eyes.

"Praise Caelum that you're safe...and here with me now."

Leofric then took Rolf into his arms again. Others in the party overheard the conversation, and they all turned to Elena for word of loved ones in Neugeld. For some, the news was good. For others...Elena had to tell them that their loved ones had died, either in Neugeld or on the road. Elena found herself comforting the broken hearts of multiple men from Leofric's group. Questions came at her faster and faster, questions that she did not know how to answer. The truth required her to break Sigaberht's edict that it was men from Drakomar that did this, and while normally she would have broken it to tell the truth, they were all surrounded by men loyal to Sigaberht above all else, so she stammered the story that she was instructed to tell. The men saw through the lie, and began to get angry with her.

One man shouted "Liar!" and took an angry step towards her. Leofric stepped between them, and the other man backed down.

"I am sure Elena has her reasons for telling the story as she does. If we want answers, we need to speak to our lord, and his truth will be the one we follow."

There were still angry glares from the group, but no one tried to argue. Leofric turned to Rolf.

"I am going to take the men to see his lordship. But I will be back, I promise."

Rolf nodded. Leofric then turned to Elena, and gave her a short bow.

"Thank you for looking out for him," Leofric said.

The angry party of men nearly stormed up the hill leading to Sigaberht's hall. A group of city guards had gradually formed around them, fearful of a riot. Once at the hall of Sigaberht, Leofric and his men were granted an audience with their lord, but not before being disarmed. When they entered, the men impatiently performed their proper bows before the royal family seated upon their thrones. Sigaberht watched, seeing the obvious tension in his people. This made him nervous, as these tradesmen were not what they seemed. These men were actually the finest warriors and spies in his army. Even more importantly, Duke Piarin believed these men were spies on his own behalf, making these men the owners of the most dangerous information to both parties. Sigaberht forced himself to appear undisturbed and waited until the men all reached the correct distance before he stood and greeted Leofric with a firm handshake.

"Leofric! What news from Drakomar?" he asked.

Leofric looked Sigaberht in the eye, and ignored Sigaberht's question.

"My lord, what happened to Neugeld? Why does my son rest at an inn here instead of in his own bed at home?"

Sigaberht blanched at Leofric's manner, and started to reprimand him for ignoring his initial question. Erelda saw her husband's anger and interrupted with gentle words before he could say something he regretted.

"Leofric, kind friend, we regret to inform you that Neugeld was destroyed by enemies of ours."

There was a murmur among the men that Leofric stifled with a wave of his hand. Sigaberht resumed his seat at his throne as Leofric addressed Erelda.

"Forgive me, my fair lady. That much we already knew. But that does not address the issue at hand. What actually happened there?"

There was a moment of silence as all three royals wondered what to tell them. Sigaberht looked at his son, and tried to see what was going through Ashveldt's eyes. Sigaberht saw genuine concern and compassion for these men in his son's eyes, and made a decision.

"Ashveldt, would you like to explain what happened to their homes?" Sigaberht asked.

Ashveldt nervously cleared his throat, and told the truth. He told them the story as best he could, from start to finish. Silence hung in the air as Ashveldt spoke, no man dared interrupt him. Once the tale was told, Ashveldt looked back to his father. Before anyone else could interject, Sigaberht spoke again.

"What we have told you now was told in complete confidence of your secrecy. Nothing can be done to change the past, but we can change how it affects our future. We are at a crucial moment of our war against Piarin, and we cannot have our people believe the destruction of Neugeld was done by anyone but him. If the world believes the lie, then perhaps we can prevent more deaths at his hands. Is that understood?"

There was grumbling in the room, as no one liked the idea of lying about something so important. Leofric silenced his men again, and spoke to Sigaberht.

"You know you have our obedience in this matter, but what of the others from Neugeld? Too many people know the truth to keep it hidden forever."

Sigaberht shook his head.

"You are right; I can't hide the truth completely, but if I can get enough people to go along with the lie, then that will become what the rulers of Wollendan and Ranrike believe. You've heard the truth...Veigarand, in the flesh? Demons? Krigari? No one will believe it is anything but unfounded rumor."

Sigaberht leaned back and took a drink from a goblet at his side, then continued.

"That is where you come in. When you return to spy on our enemy, I want you to spread rumors and lies in his court. I want you to report to Piarin that I accuse him of Neugeld's destruction. I also want you to present the truth as but a rumor that is being spread by miscreants. You should also report that there are rumors that Neugeld was not even attacked, and another rumor that I burned the town to the ground myself so I could accuse him. At some point, Ranrike and Wollendan will demand answers from him about my accusation. When that happens, we will let Piarin pick whichever rumor he wants to defend himself with. I hope Piarin accuses me of lying about him next time he speaks with Ranrike and Wollendan, and I want them to throw the ashes of Neugeld in his face. The only plausible story is that he attacked us, because what else is anyone to believe? Anyone who knows me knows I wouldn't attack my own town, and the truth is too fantastic to take seriously."

"And what of us? Where will we be when Piarin realizes we duped him?" Leofric asked.

"Hopefully, as soon as you give your report, Piarin will send you right back here to spy on me, and you will be safely behind my walls when all this happens."

"And if he doesn't send us away?" Leofric demanded.

"Then make an excuse to leave. Tell him you need to return to me to keep me from getting suspicious. Be creative."

Leofric considered what he was being ordered to do. It was quite a risk to himself and his men. This was the biggest lie he had ever had to tell, and keeping misinformation believable was difficult enough as it is. There was a high chance that Wollendan and Ranrike would smell something was wrong before Sigaberht could benefit from it. Leofric also knew that Sigaberht was desperate enough that he would consider this high risk, high reward venture his best option. Above all, Leofric knew he had no choice. His lord had given him and his men an order, and he must obey this order.

"Your will is done my lord. I must also ask, what is to happen to this wanderer? If he truly is Veigarand as you say, then perhaps it is better if you kill him."

Sigaberht laughed.

"Do not worry; he is paying his penance for what happened. He will be too useful in our coming battles to not keep in my service."

Sigaberht paused for a moment to allow the air to clear, and then continued.

"Now, with that business out of the way, what word do you have from Drakomar? What does Piarin plan to do?"

Leofric found himself growing angry. He had just learned the truth about Veigarand, a man whom his son had befriended, and Sigaberht dared force him to make a report now? Knowing better than to openly defy Sigaberht, Leofric resigned himself to giving his report.

"My lord, Piarin is making his winter preparations. He sent ambassadors to Ranrike to negotiate against us, but we doubt they will be received well."

"And why is that?" Sigaberht asked.

"Because they were set to bring a gift...a special potion that enhances the flavor of whatever food it touches. We replaced it with poison before their ambassador and his party could leave."

"Does this pose any risk of getting back to us? Will the poison do any harm in Ranrike?" Sigaberht asked.

"No," said Leofric. "The poison we used is one that will be easily detected by their court sorcerer. Additionally, we diluted it enough that if used with the same dosage as the flavor enhancer should use, it will cause extreme discomfort for a few days, but won't kill."

"And if the cook uses too much of the flavor enhancer?" Erelda asked.

"Then Drakomar will have just poisoned a member of the royal family of Ranrike, but with proper care from their doctors, the victim should survive the ordeal," said Leofric.

Sigaberht pondered for moment. Erelda had noticed the possible flaw in Leofric's plan faster than he did. It always disturbed Sigaberht when this happened. The responsibility of such decisions was supposed to be his alone, and he felt that he shouldn't have to trouble her with these tasks. But as always, he needed her as much as she needed him. Sigaberht liked to be independent, but he and his wife complemented each other too well for either of them to ignore the other's help.

"And what of the sorcerer? Will he not notice that the poison has been watered down?"

"We hope so," Leofric said. "I think Ranrike is more likely to believe that Drakomar meant only to send a message than actually kill one of their royals. Watered down poison makes that easier to believe."

"Good," Sigaberht said. "I appreciate that you have found a way to accomplish your goal in a way that shouldn't kill any of our allies. Where does Piarin believe you to be now?"

"He believes that I am here in Wulfgeld, spying on you for him. I will return to him in a few days to follow your instructions."

"Good," Sigaberht smiled. He stood and gestured to the door. "You have my thanks for your superior work in this venture. Now...go see your families, mourn your dead. Be sure to ask of me anything you need, and I will do my best to grant it."

Leofric and his men bowed before their lord, and exited the throne room. After they had left, Ashveldt spoke to his father.

"Why did you have me tell them the story?"

"If you are to rule here someday, you must be a voice that our people trust. To which I must ask you, why did you tell the truth when you know I wanted the true events to remain a secret?"

Ashveldt felt a lump rise in his throat. He had defied his father, but he had a good reason.

"It seems to me that these men have risked their lives for us. They regularly walk into the jaws of our enemies, all to protect us and Wulfgeld. If there is anything we can do for them, I think telling them the truth is the minimum."

Sigaberht nodded and smiled at his son.

"Your heart is noble. Always allow it to guide you. However, there is an even more important reason to have told these men the truth. Can you think of it?"

Ashveldt stopped to think, and realized what his father meant. He then gave his answer.

"Lying to your own spies is possibly the worst thing you can do as a ruler. Doing so would sow mistrust among your men, and make a quick enemy of a man who knows many of your plans."

"Very good," Sigaberht said.

"Telling them the truth is exactly what I had hoped you would do when I gave you the chance. Your first answer is good, but your second answer is better. When you are earl you will be responsible for too many people to let your sense of right and wrong be the only thing that affects your decision making."

"I am glad you trust me to do what is needed, father," Ashveldt replied.

"You are my son...If I cannot trust you to rule after me, then who can I trust?"

Sigaberht then turned to his wife.

"Just as I must always trust you to remind me of my place to these men. I get...above myself. Thank you for stopping me from saying something foolish. These last days have been trying for me. That and the deaths of Cynaric and his family...to a plague of all things...but you keep me grounded where I need to be, as always."

Erelda took her husband's hand in hers, and simply smiled, knowing that Sigaberht appreciated the gesture.

Chapter 14

The hours passed by relatively quickly. After Radnor had finished making his new spear he had taken some time to wander about the city and familiarize himself with its streets. Darestr seemed grateful for the chance to walk alone with his master for a time, especially with no stress or pursuit. After what seemed like ages, Radnor saw Rolf and Elena come back to the inn.

"Where have you two been? It's supper time already."

"I'm sorry Radnor, there were just so many shops…I've never seen so many people in one place before," Elena replied.

"Yeah, I tried to tell her we needed to get moving," Rolf said.

Elena chuckled before making her reply.

"When we were in the shop that sold little wooden birds, yes. But when we were in the place that sold the wooden *swords*, it nearly took a blow to the head to get you out of there."

Before Radnor could reply, Halfdan's voice came from behind them.

"You two certainly haven't gotten around much have you? Perhaps we should show them some more exciting places, like the Hall of Mirrors in Moravas, or the Snake Pits in Castellan!"

Radnor extended his arm and clasped hands with Halfdan.

"You would have them view such pathetic sites as those? Why, I would sooner take them to the great Spider Nests of Ranrike than either of those horrid places," Radnor replied, in an exaggerated tone.

There was a moment of silence as the two men stared each other down, then Halfdan belted a great laugh that turned several heads.

"The Spider Nests? Are you looking for relatives there?"

The group all gave a hearty laugh at Halfdan's retort. The burly man then gestured politely to the door.

"Shall we?" Halfdan asked.

The group entered the restaurant, found a table, and ordered their food in preparation for an evening of merriment and storytelling. As their food arrived, Leofric returned from his meeting with Sigaberht. Rolf leaped up and hugged his father. Leofric reciprocated his son's embrace and looked at the group sitting before him. Elena he knew, but he did not recognize Radnor or Halfdan. After a moment's thought, he began to introduce himself.

"Hello," he began. "My name is Leofric. I am Rolf's father. I have been told of what happened in Neugeld…" Leofric looked over his shoulder, and then in a low voice, he continued.

"I've been told the *truth* of what happened in Neugeld. So now I must ask, in addition to Elena, which one of you protected my son during the harsh journey here?"

"I did," Radnor said.

He looked Leofric over. Rolf was his spitting image. Leofric had the same sandy hair, and despite his age, he even still had a somewhat boyish face. He did not look like he was as strong as men like Leif or Ashveldt, but there was something in his eye that told Radnor he was no simple merchant like Rolf and the others believed. Leofric extended his hand to Radnor.

"I must offer you my thanks for protecting him. Given what I was told...you could have just as easily left them all to die in the wilderness. But you didn't."

Radnor took Leofric's hand, and understood that no matter what sin Radnor had committed in his involvement in destroying Neugeld, the act of protecting Rolf had been penance enough in Leofric's eyes.

"I am glad to see the boy's father still lives," Halfdan said, looking to stay in the conversation.

"Aye. For now at least. And who might you be?" Leofric asked.

"My name is Halfdan Jugback, and I am sorry to say...or happy to say depending on how you see it...that I never had the opportunity to protect your son. He is a fine young lad."

"Thank you," Leofric replied. "I would join my son at dinner tonight."

The others took this as a hint, and all stood to leave the man alone with Rolf, but Leofric waved them all back down.

"I did not mean you all needed to leave. I would love to speak with those my son considers his friends, both old and new."

Rolf found a chair for his father, and started to ask all sorts of questions about where he'd been. Leofric told fantastical stories about wandering the halls of Wollendan. It was not a burdensome task to lie as he did. Rolf did not need to know the truth about his work for Sigaberht. In fact, it was safer for Rolf if he didn't know. The stories Leofric told were from previous trips he had actually taken to Wollendan to help build the relationship with their royals. There was always a slight twinge of guilt when he lied to Rolf like this, but he reminded himself that in doing so he was protecting Rolf from the dangers of his work. Eventually Halfdan found himself asking questions, mostly about the beauty of the ladies of Wollendan. Radnor found himself content to watch and listen. After a short while he made his excuses, and left the inn. Radnor had an appointment to keep.

As the sun set, a chill wind blew through the streets of Wulfgeld. It was cold enough that even a northerner like Radnor felt it in his bones as he trudged to his destination. It took Radnor about twenty minutes to reach the cottage that had been set aside for the Hexverat to live in. As he prepared to knock on the door, it swung open to reveal Hilda standing in the entryway. She wore a long, flowing gown that hugged her figure in a suggestive manner that Radnor found surprising. For a healer about to engage in her work, the outfit seemed quite impractical. Radnor stood for a moment, unsure of what to do. Hilda saw his awkwardness, and quickly beckoned him inside.

"Come in, come in!" she said. "We can do you no good if you stand out in the cold!"

Radnor stepped inside, and found himself enveloped in warm air that felt like a comfortable blanket that had been thrown over his shoulders. He felt himself relax in this place in a way he had not felt for a long time. There was a homey sort of feeling that took him by surprise.

Hilda took him by the hand and led him to a room carpeted with furs. Before entering, the witch stopped to remove her shoes. Radnor took the hint and removed his mud-and blood-stained boots. As he did so, he studied the room further. It was dimly lit by candles, with enough light to see a cauldron in the center of the room, its contents bubbling gently. He saw Bruna sitting beside the cauldron, every so often stirring its contents. She wore her raven hair pulled back to keep it out of the way of her work. She wore a gown like her sister's, one which appeared ready to fall open at any moment. His eyes lingered on her chest for just a moment longer than his sense of nobility appreciated, and he quickly averted his gaze when he realized what he was doing. He jumped slightly when Hilda put her hand on his uninjured shoulder.

"Relax," she said. "No one here is going to hurt you, at least not on purpose."

The tension eased slightly, and Radnor felt more comfortable in his own skin again. He scanned the room for the third sister of the triumvirate, but he did not see her.

"Tell me, Hilda," Radnor asked. "Where is the third member of your group? In every tale I've ever heard about the Hexverat, there are always three of you."

Bruna looked up from her work, and answered his question in an oddly singsong voice.

"She is tending to a plague elsewhere. It is a small outbreak, one that requires only one of us to attend to. We first came to Wulfgeld for the aid of Sigaberht's family. Cynaric, the earl's brother, and his family grew deathly ill. Unfortunately, word of their grave illness reached us too late, and they had all perished before our arrival. We were able to stop the disease from spreading to the earl and anyone else, but that is all we could do. Since it is no longer an issue, we wait for our sister here."

While Bruna spoke, Hilda set up a padded bench for Radnor to sit on. As he sat, he realized the height of the bench placed his shoulder at a comfortable level for the witches to work on. Hilda went over to a wash basin at the far corner of the room, and began to soak her hands in an unknown potion. As she did, she spoke again.

"I doubt you remember, but we have met before, a long time ago."

Radnor found himself startled, and before he could ask, Hilda continued.

"Your father asked us to come visit you when you were a baby. He wanted to make sure you were as he intended you to be. We came and examined you, and found that you were...very unique. That pleased him greatly."

Radnor found himself burning with questions.

"How did you recognize me here...now?" he asked.

Bruna answered him.

"Everyone has their own unique aura, their own feeling from being near them. Yours was especially powerful, even as an infant. You carry this same aura with you now."

"I didn't believe it at first," Hilda added. "It wasn't until we got your name from Elena that we believed it was really you...after all these years."

"But, if you knew me all those years ago, how do you still look so..." Radnor started to ask.

"Young and beautiful?" Hilda asked. "We wouldn't be very good healers if we couldn't keep our bodies young, now would we?"

Radnor shrugged, unable to argue with her point. As he was getting ready to ask more questions, Hilda interrupted his thoughts.

"Are you ready, Bruna?"

"Yes. The potion is prepared."

"Good," Hilda said.

The blonde witch then came over to Radnor and gestured with an upwards motion towards him.

"Take your tunic off; we need to get at that shoulder of yours without hindrance."

Radnor felt his heart stop for a moment, and was surprised at his bashfulness. Somehow both eagerly and reluctantly, he pulled the tunic over his head. He felt himself jump a little again when Hilda began to massage the area around his wounded shoulder...and instead of pain, there was tingling warmth where her hands touched. Radnor looked at her quizzically. Hilda understood his confused look, and offered an explanation.

"I've been soaking my hands in an ointment that prevents pain. I wanted to get this on you before we started doing the nasty work of taking care of your wound. I hope you don't mind," she said, with a flirtatious smile.

"No, I don't mind," Radnor said, trying to keep himself from blushing.

After a few more seconds, Bruna came over and started slathering the potion from the cauldron on his wound. A strange sort of tension overtook his arm, but there was no pain. Radnor watched wide eyed as his arm began to spasm. There was still no pain, but he had no control over the arm's frenzied convulsions. Hilda vainly tried to hold the arm in place long enough for Bruna to pour more of the potion into the wound. Hilda found herself stumbling backwards from the force of Radnor's convulsions, and Radnor thought he saw faint traces of a smile on her face. He then saw her reach into a hidden pocket, and withdraw a gaulderen. She crushed the brittle object in her hand, and blew the resulting dust over his arm. The instant the dust settled on his muscles, his arm stopped moving...frozen in place. Radnor could feel the muscles continue to spasm, but the arm itself would not move. Bruna continued her work on his arm, while Hilda approached him. As she did, she gently placed his other arm around her waist, and stood extremely close to him.

"It's all right," she said as she watched her compatriot work. "Just an unexpected, but not unheard of side effect. The vampire that bit you must have been extremely powerful for that to happen. Do you feel any pain?"

Radnor shook his head. After several more minutes of being held in this position, he felt the strength of the spasms begin to lessen, and eventually disappear completely. Bruna asked Hilda for a mirror. Hilda obliged, and Bruna then used it to show Radnor his shoulder. Much to his amazement, there was now only a red mark where once there had been a deep wound."

"The red mark will fade in time," Bruna said, smiling.

"How do you feel?" Hilda asked, stroking his shoulder with her hand.

"I don't know...I still can't feel much on my arm."

"Oh, of course!" Hilda said.

With a wave of her hand, and a short incantation spoken in a language unknown to Radnor, he suddenly was able to move his arm again. Flexing the muscles in his shoulder, he found he could move freely without any pain at all. Without warning, Hilda took his hand and placed it firmly on her breast.

"Now how do you feel?" she asked coyly.

In shock, Radnor was slow to respond to what had just happened. He looked over to where Bruna had been standing to see that her robe had fallen open to reveal her voluptuous body. Bruna held a wicked grin on her face, and started to walk towards Radnor. Finally starting to mentally recover from what just happened, Radnor stammered out his question.

"What...what are you doing?" he asked.

"What's it look like we're doing?" Hilda said, as she began removing her robe too.

Radnor found himself unable to look away from the two beautiful women standing before him. He found himself enchanted by their beauty, and by what they were offering him. Hilda started to rub the inside of his thigh, and as Bruna began to undo the clasps on his pants, Radnor suddenly saw Elena's face flash in his mind. He abruptly stood up, nearly knocking both of the witches over, and went to retrieve his tunic.

Bruna placed a hand on his shoulder with firm pressure. Radnor turned to face her and saw a desperate look in her eye. He then looked past her at Hilda, whom had a look of crazed desire in hers.

"Do you not find us attractive?" Hilda asked, striking a provocative pose.

Radnor shook his head.

"It's not that. There's just, someone else whom I care for, and I don't want to hurt her."

Bruna took his hand in hers and looked into his eyes.

"Does she know how you feel?" she asked.

"I don't know," Radnor replied.

"Come to us, and find out how we feel about you," Hilda said, not giving up her pursuit.

Radnor felt himself getting angry...angry enough to fully break their hold over him.

"I've told you my answer. I am grateful for your healing my shoulder. However, I must decline your advances. If you wish to receive money in payment for your services, I am happy to oblige you."

Both Hilda and Bruna were angered by his remarks. Bruna slapped him, and Hilda began to shout.

"We have never been so insulted in our lives! We offer our services freely, and gladly! To think our advances on you were just to get payment out of you...that we would take advantage of someone like that...it's outrageous! Get out!"

Radnor finished putting his tunic on, and obliged them, snatching up his boots as he stomped out of the room. Anger swelled in his heart so much that he had to stop himself from going back inside and returning the slap.

Once outside, the cold air helped settle Radnor's temper as he walked back down to the inn where he was staying.

What in Hymurr's name was that about? He wondered.

Their seduction attempt was so sudden, so...unnatural that it took a moment to shake his discomfort over the whole thing. He decided that since he did not want to spend the whole evening angry, it was best not to dwell on the matter. Turning his thoughts to his route, Radnor found that he had made a wrong turn, and had to double back to the main street. While the crescent moon was not bright enough to light his way, the torches that lined the street provided the light he needed to find his way back to the inn. Once back inside, Radnor found his bed, and after much effort, was able to drift off to sleep.

Chapter 15

A fierce banging on the door woke Radnor with a start. The knocking continued, even louder than before. Radnor immediately dashed to the door and opened it, fist drawn back to strike the attacker.

"Radnor, it's me!" came a familiar voice.

"Halfdan?" Radnor said.

"Who the bloody hell do you think I am, the queen of the forest nymphs?" Halfdan replied.

"What are you doing here?" Radnor asked, ignoring Halfdan's quip.

"Radnor, they took your woman...Elena. They took her."

Radnor turned pale for a moment, and then something came alive inside him.

"Who?!" he demanded.

"I don't know. There were three of them. They came and took her."

"Why?" Radnor barked.

"How should I know? There were three men who moved swiftly. They were armed."

"How do you know she was taken?"

"Before I went to bed I saw her standing guard outside your room again. Just now when I left my room to fetch some water, I saw she wasn't there. I heard a noise outside the window, and when I looked, she was being dragged outside."

Radnor stared into Halfdan's eyes, searching for deception. He found none.

"Why was she guarding my room?" Radnor asked.

"How in Narakim should I know? You'd need to ask her," Halfdan replied.

"I will...I must go," Radnor said.

"I'm coming with you."

Radnor thought for a moment, and reluctantly agreed.

"Just give me a moment, I need my weapons."

Radnor closed the door and quickly rushed to his bag. He tossed on his mail shirt and helmet. Within seconds, he was fully armed. With his spear, sword, and shield, he stepped out into the hallway to see a surprised looking Halfdan. Halfdan shook off his momentary shock at Radnor's transformation, and spoke.

"If we are to find her, you must know that I overheard one of them speaking about taking her to an ogre's lair."

Radnor turned back to Halfdan.

"An ogre I can handle. I just need to find him. But first, we need to go to Sigaberht."

The two then hastily made their way down the creaking stairs.

After reaching the restaurant floor, the two men stopped moving. It was almost pitch black, with the only illumination coming from the moon. There was a soft, rhythmic dripping sound that made Radnor feel uneasy. Unsure of the source, he proceeded forward very slowly and carefully. Halfdan stepped out at an angle to try to watch Radnor's back as best he could. After a few steps, Radnor saw the illuminated outline of a man lying on the counter. Blood was slowly running down from his neck, and drops fell into an ever growing puddle on the floor. Radnor advanced, and saw that it was Wecta, the innkeeper. Radnor put down his spear and drew his sword. He heard the floor creak to his left, and he spun. The only thing Radnor could see at first was an ice colored pair of eyes reflected in the moonlight. There was something that looked like a man standing by a table that held a spear of its own.

Radnor started to advance on this man when his foe threw the spear at him. Radnor quickly dodged the throw and kept advancing. The moonlit opponent backed away into the shadows, and Radnor lost sight of him. The demigod looked around and backed off slightly. He listened for movement, and heard something to his left. Radnor turned again, and saw the man trying to sneak past him. Before the man could react, Radnor took two steps and was upon him. The only sound the man had time to make was a low growl as Radnor's blade came towards him. Radnor brought his sword down on him with such force his body was severed collarbone to hip before it had even begun to fall. As Radnor retrieved his spear, Halfdan stepped to be the first one to walk through the outer door to the inn. Radnor followed close behind. As he crossed the threshold, a new foe jumped from the awning above with a dagger aimed for Radnor's throat! As Radnor rolled to the side, Halfdan spun and slashed with his ax, taking the foe's head off as he fell. Radnor nodded his thanks, to which Halfdan replied with a small salute with his ax. As the duo made their way out onto the deserted streets, a scream echoed against the buildings. Halfdan looked at Radnor, and the two headed in that direction. However, Radnor saw that three men were closing in on them from behind.

"Halfdan, go on and see what that scream was. I'll handle them," he said.

Halfdan nodded, and took off in the direction of the scream. Radnor stood his ground against his new foes.

All of them were armed with swords and long, rectangular shields strapped to their arms. They wore armor made from leather plates tied together, and their helmets covered the tops of their heads, but not their faces, which were covered by black cloth.

"I assume you are the ones who took her," Radnor said.

He received no response. Radnor did not care, for he wished only to deal in death. The three men spread out in a half circle and started to close with him. Radnor stood his ground, but moved his grip on his spear closer to the back. As his enemies drew closer, Radnor raised his shield and moved into a fighting crouch. Once Radnor's enemies were close enough, the leader charged. Radnor took a step back and whipped the spear around in an arc, sending his opponent stumbling as it smashed its way across the man's shield. Radnor let his spear slam into his own shield to stop its momentum, and thrust to his left at the next opponent. The spear stabbed straight through the man's shield, and almost punctured the armor behind it. Radnor let go of the spear and stepped to the side as the third man came straight at him and swung his sword. Radnor stepped in a circle away from the incoming blow and drew his own sword. The man who swung at Radnor fell past him and pulled himself off balance trying to find Radnor. The northman turned to cut this man through his back, but instead had barely enough time to change the arc of his blow to parry a strike from a new opponent who came from behind him. Radnor snapped his head around and saw that three more foes had joined the fight. This made six in total, and Radnor was surrounded!

The first enemy had regained his balance, and let out an inhuman snarl as he leapt at Radnor. The demigod barely had time to slip the attack and regain his balance. The foe blew past him and rejoined its friends. There were six opponents, spaced out equidistantly from him in a circle. None of them made a move towards Radnor yet, which gave him time to observe them. Radnor finally noticed that none of them stood like men ready to fight, but rather, as animals ready to pounce. He realized that there was not a single pair of eyes which did not reflect the eerie light of the moon. Some eyes were not colored as the eyes of men but were instead yellow or an unearthly, icy blue. What had happened to these people?

One of the men to Radnor's left started an attack. As Radnor turned to face the threat, the man backed off and another came at Radnor from behind. As he adjusted his turn to face the new threat, this foe retreated and yet another one advanced. This pattern repeated itself again and again. They kept him moving and spinning, never letting him rest. Radnor could see where this was going. They were going to wear him out, and when he was too weak to defend himself, they would move in for the kill. Radnor knew that he needed to change the game if he was to survive.

When one of them tried to bait him again, Radnor charged. As he did, the man he charged leaped backwards, and the others converged on Radnor. Multiple swords swung at him at once. Radnor blocked two with his shield, while a third slammed against the back of his helmeted head. Radnor gritted his teeth against the pain, and focused on staying conscious. The pain awakened his training, and he found himself to be calm even as the blows continued to rain down on him. In this moment, he saw his opening. The final attacker in the group swung his sword in a wide arc, and Radnor stopped the attack by cutting off his foe's arm. There was a howl of pain as his opponent's severed limb dropped to the ground. Radnor's attackers backed up immediately in response to this new development. The wounded foe dropped to the ground, still yowling in pain. Radnor took a moment to breathe, and then lashed his sword through the skull of his crippled opponent. Radnor took stock of his enemies. One down, five to go.

The cycle began again. Five enemies surrounded him and resumed their taunting attacks, snarling as they went. After Radnor was sure they had settled back into their routine, he made a daring move. As the first man tried to bait Radnor's attention, Radnor moved like he was going to turn, and he waited for the other's charge. He waited just long enough to be sure the other was committed to his movement, and Radnor pounced. Before the second man could stop his frenzied charge, Radnor was on him. Blow after blow rained down on the savage predator as Radnor sought to overwhelm his defense in the time he had. The rest of the pack was closing on him, and Radnor only had a moment to reduce their numbers further. Finally, his opponent's shield splintered, and Radnor finished him with a blow which severed his head from his shoulders.

Confident his opponent was dead; Radnor instantly ducked, turned, and covered himself with his sword and shield as best he could. He felt one enemy sword graze him as he ducked, and others slammed into his guard. This time however, the barrage did not let up. Radnor had to duck deeper behind his shield to stay alive, blinding himself in the process. Radnor started to fall backwards, and he had to let his legs catch up to him as he ran. As he went, he tripped over a rock, and started to fall. Without thinking, he allowed his momentum to carry him into a spin as he righted his foot and prepared to plant it again. In this moment, Radnor had to counterbalance with his shield and sword to stay upright, so as he spun, he threw a wild slash with his sword to counter cut anything coming at him.

With great luck, Radnor felt his sword connect, and the gurgling howl and spray of blood told him it had connected with flesh. The other three enemies backed off as yet another of their number toppled to the ground in a heap, his gurgling throat gushing blood and gore across Radnor's shield and armor.

The three remaining men roared at him in anger, and rushed him. Radnor roared back, and charged. Just as they started to encircle him, he leapt to his right and smashed another foe to the ground. Without a moment's pause, Radnor turned to face the onrushing enemies. The first one to meet him had eyes which burned yellow with hate. Radnor threw a fast cut at the man's head. The man covered with his shield but it was cut apart by the force of Radnor's blow. The sword smashed into his enemy's helmet, stunning him for a moment. Then Radnor stepped to his left, rotated the sword in an arc to the opposite side, and brought it up and under the man's right arm, slicing into the body and into the collarbone. The enemy screamed in pain and dropped to his knees. Radnor stomp-kicked him in the chest to knock his body out of the way.

The next foe threw a fierce blow at Radnor from Radnor's shield side. The demigod cut into it with his own sword and knocked the blade out of his enemy's hand. He then swung a blow straight at the man's head. The man backed away and hunkered down under his shield. The blade bit deep into the shield edge, and bisected his shield hand. Radnor's foe collapsed to the ground, snarling and screaming in rage and pain.

Radnor's final enemy returned to his feet. He started to rush in, but thought better of his approach and stopped in his tracks. This one decided to be more cautious in how he advanced on Radnor. Now having the opportunity to be tactical again, Radnor looked at his foe and started to circle him. Radnor studied his opponent, and saw how he turned his torso to adjust, and then afterwards adjusted with his feet. Waiting for the right moment, Radnor kept circling until the man turned from the waist once more. Then...Radnor pounced. The foe had twisted his body enough that he could not get away in time. Radnor threw a flurry of blows. The man was able to deflect one with his shield, but Radnor brought the blade back around before the man could capitalize on it. Radnor's second blow caught him squarely in the head, cutting the helmet apart and gashing the man's skull. The third landed on the man's shoulder, breaking armor and cutting his arm off at the joint. Radnor's fourth blow hit the man at the base of the neck taking his head clean off. Before the body could start to fall, Radnor hit him with a fifth blow that severed the leg at the knee.

Radnor turned and found the one whose hand he had split. The man crawled, snarling and gnashing his teeth like a madman. Radnor stepped on his shield and kept him pinned. The man screamed as pressure was applied to his injured hand. Radnor looked at him, and asked this man a question.

"Where is she? The woman you took? What did you do with her?"

The man continued to snarl and tried to bite Radnor's foot. Seeing he wasn't going to get anything out of his mad foe, Radnor stabbed the man through the heart and stared into his soul until it resided in him no more. Finally, Radnor took some time to breathe...that is until he saw the change.

The body of the man he had just killed transformed before his eyes into the body of a wolf. Radnor looked around in surprise, and found that every one of the men he had killed were now all wolves. Fear ran through Radnor's heart at the sight. He had seen many strange creatures and powerful works of magic, but he had never seen anything that allowed wolves to walk as men before. This was not something even the oldest wolf chieftains could do without help from powerful forces. Radnor shuddered to think about not only whom would have the power, but also the desire to do such a thing. He was jerked to awareness again by rustling from behind him. Radnor saw someone lurking in the shadows, someone who had watched the whole fight.

"Identify yourself!" Radnor yelled.

The man did not oblige, but instead tried to run for the cover of darkness. Radnor drew a knife from his belt and readied it for a throw. As he did, the man threw an unusual looking rock into the shadows between two buildings. A bright light flashed for a moment, and a deafening crack of thunder filled the air. When Radnor refocused his eyes, the man was almost at a portal which had formed between the two buildings. The man had thrown a gaulderen! Space bent in the alleyway the man sprinted towards, and the buildings creaked and cracked as the world tried to fill the hole. Wind rushed towards the opening, its gale becoming more and more unbearable the longer the portal remained open. Radnor let his dagger fly, and the blade bit directly into the back of the man's leg. The blow was crippling, but it didn't stop the man from crawling. The buildings began to bow and snap, and the man continued trying to get to the portal. Halfdan dashed back up the street to find a shocking scene and hear what was now a deafening whirlwind of sound.

"Stop him!" Radnor yelled, barely audible over the roar.

Halfdan saw Radnor shout, and even though he couldn't make out the words, he could guess what he wanted. Halfdan sprinted for the fallen man, and scooped him up in his arms like a like a bag of grain. He carried the struggling man in his arms as he sprinted back away from the portal towards Radnor. There was a deafening crash as the two buildings finally collapsed under the strain, and the portal ceased to exist. Timber, stone, and dust all scattered about the streets. Screaming could be heard from inside the buildings as they came tumbling down, and people across the square poured from their homes into the streets below to learn what had happened.

Radnor tried as hard as he could to make sense of what had just happened. The screaming of the townsfolk made it hard to think. Each second he stood in thought, Radnor felt himself grow weaker. If only they would stop screaming! His head ached where he had been hit, and he felt like he wanted to throw up. His mind was no longer on what was in front of him, but instead on his desire to find Elena. Radnor looked up to the road, and decided that he had better not go alone. Fighting the pain in his head and muscles, Radnor tried to walk over to where Halfdan was holding the still struggling man. Radnor needed Halfdan's help, and as much as he hated to admit it, he also needed Sigaberht's help. As Radnor reached his friend, he leaned on his sword and started to stumble. Halfdan looked down at Radnor with concern as he choked the man in his arms unconscious.

"What the hell happened to you?" he asked.

Radnor looked up at Halfdan with glazing eyes.

"Wolves that walk as men. There were six of them. They really took it out of me. After that... I can't...kill an ogre by myself."

Radnor barely finished his sentence before nausea and dizziness overtook him. Radnor's vision narrowed, and all he heard was something that sounded like Halfdan's distant yell as he lost consciousness.

Chapter 16

Radnor awoke with a start. He sat bolt upright, and tried to stand up. He tried in vain to rise, and instantly felt very dizzy. Disorientation took him, and Radnor collapsed back into the bed. *That blow to the head I took must have been really bad,* Radnor thought.

He looked around his room and saw that he was in a cell of some kind. Simple, unadorned walls surrounded him. There was a heavy wooden door with a simple barred window. He was no longer in his armor, but was instead dressed in simple under-tunic and pants.

"My, my, we have gotten ourselves into a bit of a mess, now haven't we?" came a frustratingly familiar voice.

Radnor didn't try to turn this time. His head and stomach were already doing enough of that.

"What the hell do you want?" he demanded of the smirking god invading the room.

"I decided I wanted to look in on you, and when I did, I found that some very delightful events had occurred while I was away," Ashrahan replied.

Radnor slowly turned himself to face where Ashrahan was nonchalantly leaning against a corner of the room. He even appeared to be happily munching on an apple.

"You're not concerned that your weapon took a beating last night?"

"You should see the other guys," Ashrahan said between bites of his apple. There was no sound as he bit into it, and Radnor was unsure if it was his head injury, or something Ashrahan did on purpose.

Ashrahan started again, his mouth still full of the juicy fruit.

"Or should I say...the other *wolves*? Curious...is it not? How did so many wolves get into the town without anyone seeing them? Do you know?"

The longer Radnor sat upright, the better focused his eyesight became.

"They wore the faces of men when I killed them. It wasn't until after they lay dead that I saw them for what they were."

Ashrahan choked on his apple.

"Well, my, my, that is truly a delightful development indeed! I wish I could have seen the wonderful brawl *that* must have been. I see you still have all your bits, and that hateful stare you're giving me shows that your cudgel of a mind is intact. How are your companions?"

"Rolf is fine. More of the wolves took Elena somewhere. I don't know where though."

Ashrahan suddenly stopped chewing and tossed the apple aside. It went outside of Radnor's vision, and if it ever landed, it never made a sound. The eager god slid onto the bed to sit next to Radnor, and leaned in closer than Radnor would have liked.

"Do you remember our prior conversations? The one where you so rudely refused my generous offer? Is there anything you want now?"

Ashrahan grinned wickedly as he waited for Radnor to catch on. He did not need to wait long.

"No," Radnor replied.

The wounded man stood up defiantly. As he did so, the room spun even harder, and he had to sit down again.

"I have nothing I need from you."

Ashrahan frowned at the stubborn warrior.

"I will be around. I'm sure something will come up for me to bargain with."

The irritated god then faded from Radnor's world.

Radnor angrily watched as Ashrahan disappeared before his eyes. Radnor stood yet again, and found he could keep his balance this time. In the few minutes since he had awoken he felt a lot better, or at least well enough to tough out the rest. It was time to leave this stupid room.

Radnor stepped over to the door and found that it was locked from the outside. It didn't matter. His desire to find Elena turned to desperate rage, and he began to strike the heavy oak panels until one of them splintered under the force. There were panicked yells on the other side of the door, and the shouting continued as Radnor struck the door again and again. Piece by piece, he tore it apart, like he would do to anything that got in the way of finding Elena. As more holes appeared in the door, Radnor saw a gathering of armed men in the hallway outside. They were fully armored and carried spears and axes. A shield wall formed in front of him, with multiple spear points gleaming in the torchlight of the hallway. Radnor began calculating his odds of making it through them alive when a familiar pair of voices sounded.

"Radnor, calm down!" came Halfdan's voice.

Radnor slowed his pace a little, but it was going to take more than Halfdan to convince him to stop. Then Rolf spoke up.

"Radnor, we're fine. But Elena's still missing. Earl Sigaberht just wants to know what happened here, and you're the only one who can tell them. We need you to stop trying to tear the world apart and talk to us."

This finally stopped Radnor from doing anything foolish. He started slowing his breathing down, and eventually got enough of it back to speak.

"Thank Hymurr you're both all right. Where's Elena?"

"We don't know, Radnor," came Halfdan's reply.

"We were hoping you could tell us."

"I don't know," Radnor said. "What have you got from the man who opened the portal?"

A new voice sounded from the end of the hallway. It was gruff and full of authority.

"He hasn't said a word yet. We were hoping you could shed some light on the events of last night."

"Who the fuck are you?" Radnor demanded, his impatience removing all bounds of courtesy.

"I am Captain Talkos," replied the voice. "I am the leader of the men at arms who defend this town. And you are?"

"Really ready to get out of this room if you don't mind!" Radnor responded.

"Hold your positions men!" Talkos ordered.

The captain stepped out in front of his soldiers. Radnor recognized the features on the man that stood before him. This was the gate guard that Leif had spoken to when they first arrived in town. The mail armor he wore looked heavy as it draped around his stocky frame, and his face was pockmarked and chiseled by age and experience. His brown eyes were very sharp, and were evaluating Radnor much the same way Radnor was evaluating him. His high brow and smallish nose created a sense of bred nobility about him.

"I hope we can continue our conversation without you destroying the remainder of my door," Talkos said.

"Sorry about that," Radnor replied. "I didn't have a key."

Halfdan joined Talkos in front of the line, and smiled at Radnor. "Calm now?"

"Calm enough," Radnor replied. "Make my head stop spinning and I'll be even calmer."

"I may have something for that," added Talkos.

Radnor's manners finally returned to him as he calmed down.

"I would appreciate that greatly Captain. Please lead the way."

Talkos whistled, and the shield wall broke ranks and allowed the company to walk through.

As they walked, Talkos spoke to Radnor.

"I will take you to where your belongings are being stored. Perhaps you might like to explain things as we go?"

"Yes of course, but first...how long was I unconscious?" Radnor asked.

"Only for the night, the sun has barely risen on this day," Talkos replied.

Radnor sighed with relief. This would not be a repeat of what happened in Neugeld.

The captain led Radnor to a room which held all of his armor, and the weapons he had on him when he collapsed. Talkos picked up a cup that was sitting on a nearby shelf, and handed it to Radnor. The cup held a small amount of a mysterious green liquid. Radnor looked at the captain quizzically, hoping for an explanation.

"I knew you would want to get your things as soon as you woke up. I had the guards deliver this medicine given to us by the Hexverat. It will help the pain in your head."

Radnor thanked the man, and took a drink, and in a few moments he felt almost normal again. Radnor slowly put his armor back on, inspecting it as he went. He was annoyed at the dent he found in the back of his helmet. As Radnor finished putting on his armor, Sigaberht and Leif came into the room. Talkos stopped to bow. Halfdan did not. Sigaberht waved Talkos aside.

"Captain, I wanted to be here to listen to your questions for Veigarand. Veigarand, I expect you to tell the truth as best as you can. Do you understand?"

Radnor did understand. Sigaberht did not fully trust him yet, and was ordering him to tell the truth so that any lie would cause the black oath to do its awful work. Halfdan heard the name "Veigarand" and gave Radnor a confused look. The burly man looked Radnor up and down...reassessing the man he had partnered with the night before.

Talkos questioned Radnor intently about the events of the previous night, often asking Radnor to repeat the more fantastical elements several times. Though they never seemed satisfied, Talkos, Sigaberht, and Leif eventually accepted Radnor's words as truth. His tale matched some of the elements of Halfdan's account, and Talkos himself had seen the buildings fall. The collapse had claimed seven lives, and two other people were permanently maimed.

The topic then turned to that of the prisoner, and it was agreed that Radnor could interrogate him with the others in the room. When Radnor was back in full armor, he asked if he could be brought to the room right then.

"Dressed in that?" Talkos asked.

"When all they can see is my eyes, my foes' fear of me often makes them obedient."

Sigaberht nodded, seeing a change in Radnor's eyes that sent shivers down his spine. Radnor was led down the same hallway they had come, but the group stopped in front of a different, more intact door.

"The only thing I've been able to get the prisoner to tell me so far is his name. He tells me he goes by the name of 'Ferin'," Talkos said.

"Do not worry, my friend," Radnor said. "This 'Ferin' shall soon be providing an explanation of his actions and purpose."

"We have him tied to a chair to make sure he can't escape. We had to nail it to the floor to stop him from tipping the damn thing over."

"Nails, I can work with that," Radnor said. He saw that Sigaberht was the only one who did not cringe at the implication.

"Just be aware that I may have to perform some unsavory deeds against this man before the day is done."

Talkos swallowed nervously. He had seen combat, but torture was not something he could ever abide. He pulled his key ring from his belt, and found himself fumbling for the appropriate key. After a few moments of panicked searching, he unlocked the door. Talkos felt an ever growing aura around Radnor, one he was afraid would burst and burn all those around him to ash. Sigaberht felt it as well, but he gave no outward sign that he did.

"I think I will wait out here. I'm not sure I have the stomach for what may happen," Halfdan said.

Radnor nodded to his friend and then stepped forward to open the door. Inside, he found cold stone floors whose formerly grayish hues had long been stained by the blood of men whom had dared bring their malevolence to Wulfgeld. The prisoner was indeed tied to an uncomfortably small chair in the center of the room. He had obviously been beaten. There was a welt forming over his left eye, and he had a cut on his lip that was still dribbling blood. The prisoner looked up at Radnor with animal eyes. This was another wolf made into man. The abominable creature then spoke in a gravelly, inhuman voice that sounded unfit for the speech of men.

"Who are you?" he said, awkwardly forming the words with his unfamiliar human tongue.

Radnor stepped towards the prisoner, and stopped only when he was but a few feet directly in front of him. Radnor then leaned forward and whispered to the prisoner.

"You do not get to know my true name. But there are people who call me Veigarand. Do you know that name?"

The manner in which the prisoner held himself changed from one of empty defiance to one of absolute fright. No one in the room blamed the man for his fear.

Though this change gave Radnor his answer, he would not settle for anything less than a "yes" or a "no".

"I asked you a question…" said the stubborn warrior.

"Do you know that name?"

The prisoner nodded at Radnor, and his effort was rewarded with a sharp slap to the face that made his vision flash for a moment.

"I can't hear your head rattle!" Radnor barked.

"Do you know that name?"

"Yes!" gasped the terrified prisoner.

"Good, now we are getting somewhere," Radnor said.

Radnor came very close to the man again.

"What do you know of me?" he whispered.

Ferin shuddered before he whispered his reply.

"You can't be real. Veigarand is a ghost, the stuff of legends and songs meant to frighten children."

There was a wet thud as the back of Radnor's hand smashed across Ferin's face again.

"Do I feel like a ghost to you? I assure you, those stories came from somewhere. As it turns out, you stole someone from me, someone I care about. You've clearly heard the songs of my misdeeds. If you don't tell me everything you know about where she was taken, I will give these people here a new misdeed to sing about!"

Radnor had barely finished his sentence when Ferin began laughing uncontrollably. Radnor stood for a moment, confused by this sudden outburst. Ferin was only silenced when Radnor drove a fist into the man's stomach.

"What's so funny?" Radnor demanded.

Ferin looked up at him, directly into his eyes. He spoke slowly, stopping to find the words he wanted in the other worldly rhythm of his voice.

"You think if I tell…I will live…this amuses…me. Those who…command me hear and see all. They saw…much…and promises…were made. All we need is but a few more sacrifices…and your lives shall be but the playthings of the Hexverat!"

Radnor took a step back in shock. Even before he had a chance to process the terrible words spoken by the captive, far more horrific events unfolded before his eyes. An unholy smell pervaded the air around them. It was as though some twisted, demented thing which could only be a horrific imitation of death had entered to room. Ferin began to writhe in his chair, straining in his bonds. He began to scream in agony, and the reason soon became apparent. From within his body burst forth an array of twisting, bending, writhing black tendrils which strongly reminded Radnor of the roots of a tree. These things burst forth from all across Ferin's body. Thorns ripped their way through flesh, and blood poured out of Ferin's eyes as the tendrils enveloped his entire body...and devoured him.

When Ferin's screaming stopped, the world became eerily silent. A moment later, the silence was broken by the sound of Captain Talkos' retching. The sound broke Leif from his frozen shock, and the ealdorman suddenly grabbed Sigaberht by the shoulder and pulled him out of the room, shielding him from any further assault that may come from those dark tendrils. Radnor was nearly overwhelmed by terror as he stared at the silently twisting and writhing thorns before him.

"Caelum have mercy on us all," Talkos muttered, praying to the only god who might have intervened. He was praying to a god long dead.

Radnor turned to Talkos.

"Did this man have any markings on his body?"

Talkos stood upright again, wiped his mouth clean, and looked back at Radnor.

"We found a black brand burned into his flesh above his right shoulder blade. Why?"

"It's almost like this...creature swore a black oath to the Hexverat. But this is like no black oath I have ever seen."

"How so?" Talkos asked, still trying to collect himself.

Before Radnor could answer, Sigaberht and Leif re-entered the room with Halfdan close at hand. Sigaberht gave a stern look to the sheepish looking Leif, and placed his hand on his shoulder. The earl felt embarrassed that he had been dragged out of the room like that. Even though he knew it was irrational, he feared that Leif's dragging him from the room would be perceived as an act of cowardice on his part.

"I apologize," Sigaberht said. "Leif meant only to protect me from any further harm from those tendrils. Please, Radnor, continue with your explanation."

Radnor nodded, and continued.

"Normally, when someone breaks a black oath, he simply bursts into flames. But this...this was something altogether worse. He must have sworn not to speak of his masters and when he invoked their name he foolishly doomed himself. What troubles me more is that he claimed the Hexverat were his masters. Never have I heard of any crimes being committed by the Hexverat, let alone ones such as these. They believe in trying to be one with the world and at peace with those around them, not in bringing death and destruction."

"What will we do?" Talkos asked.

"The first thing we must do is summon the two sisters we have with us. It seems I am owed an explanation," Sigaberht said.

The earl turned to Talkos.

"Captain, I want the Hexverat sisters brought to my throne room at once. Arrest them if you have to. Leif, I want you to be there as well. Some of your people were taken last night, and it is only fair you are involved in how we get them back."

"Your grace, if I may..." Radnor started. "I would like to also attend that meeting. I have a feeling your people will need to be rescued by force, and I would be on that force if you would allow it."

Sigaberht nodded his approval.

"Be at my throne room in twenty minutes," he said.

Sigaberht left the room in a hurry, with Talkos and Leif close behind. Halfdan alone stood in the room with Radnor. He had been silent up to this point. Radnor addressed him.

"Halfdan, I must ask a favor of you. I need a moment to myself, to think something over."

Halfdan continued staring at the horror laid out before him.

"I can see why," he said. "If this is what is coming to this city...I do believe it is time for me to leave."

Radnor nodded.

"Thank you for your help last night. We are but newfound friends...and your aid in battle already has been more than any man could ask."

Halfdan nodded, somewhat ashamed of himself.

"If it were men...I could help you. But there's evil magic here. Shape changing wolves?"

Radnor nodded, perplexed that Halfdan didn't mention the obvious terror right in front of them. Radnor shook it off, and made his reply.

"I really do understand. There is no shame in knowing one's self."

With that, Radnor turned and left the room. Taking his first steps onto the paved street, he noticed as the sunlight suddenly dimmed. He looked up and saw the sun peeking out from behind its clouds, as a child peeking from under its blankets might do. When Radnor's gaze met the glowing embers of the sun's rays, the sun, still childlike, darted back behind its protective shield of cloud cover. Radnor walked around behind the building and made sure no one was within earshot of him.

"Ashrahan! Ashrahan, show yourself! I know you're watching this."

Radnor sighed in frustration, unsure of how to find the god.

"Probably laughing your fucking head off right about now," Radnor muttered to himself.

"I wish I could say I was," Ashrahan replied, appearing from the air behind Radnor.

"Were you in the room?" Radnor asked.

"Was I ever! It's been a very long time since I've seen anything like that," Ashrahan said.

"Wait…you know what that was?" Radnor asked.

"Yes, and I hate to say it, but this takes priority over all of our other plans. What you saw was chaos at work. And I don't mean the kind of chaos when people don't have their heads on right; I'm talking pure, elemental chaos. It seems in their efforts to understand the world of magic, those witches dug too deeply and found themselves at the edge of the ocean which we all float upon, but never see."

"You're not making any sense," Radnor said.

Ashrahan sighed in frustration, and resumed his speech.

"Before the world, there was chaos; nothing but an infinite, writhing mass of indescribable things… or… non-things which churned and spun and wove… in, around, and outside of themselves. At some point, either by chance or intent, the creators were born from this chaos. I believe you know them already, Hymurr, Caelum, and Damiros. Once they came into being, they learned how to mold and shape chaos to create whatever they desired. Shaping chaos like clay, they created the cosmos, and all of the worlds within it. The cosmos now floats atop the infinite, churning sea of chaos. The creators put up barriers to prevent chaos from simply sweeping in and devouring the world, like a dam prevents water from flooding city streets."

Ashrahan paused for a short moment to think. He ran his hands through his hair in a manner that betrayed his fear, and then continued.

"The only way those witches could give wolves the shape of men and forge a black oath so twisted like the one you saw today...they must be poking holes in the barriers to let chaos dribble in a little at a time. You've seen some of those holes in creation. Do you remember the vision I showed you? The pit that Adramelach cast Damiros into? The war left many holes like it across the cosmos, and each one has weakened the barrier. Now tell me Veigarand, what happens when you chip away at a dam, leaving small holes plugged only with patches?"

"The crashing water breaks through, and all in its way are killed," Radnor replied.

184

"Exactly," Ashrahan said. "You, me, everything in all of the worlds made by the creators will be destroyed unless we stop them. That being said, I must ask…do we have a deal now?"

Ashrahan grinned at Radnor again. Radnor frowned angrily, weighing his options, but it did not take long.

"I guess I have no choice. I cannot find Elena fast enough on my own. Is there a way you can do that?"

"What do you hope to gain by finding her? The focus must be on the witches," Ashrahan replied, disgusted at how easily Radnor was letting his human compassion interfere with their work.

Radnor chuckled at the shortsighted god.

"You think it a waste of time to go after my companion? She was taken prisoner by the witches. If we find her, we may be able to find them."

Ashrahan laughed at himself.

"So you can think beyond who you're going to kill next. Very well, you've convinced me. I can look, but I can't look everywhere at once. She must be near here somewhere, and if you have any clues, please feel free to let me know."

"Halfdan told me she was taken to an ogre. This beast must be in league with Hexverat," Radnor replied.

"That helps me narrow it down a lot actually," Ashrahan said. "I will be back shortly."

Before Radnor could reply, Ashrahan was off. Radnor found himself wondering why he had just been about to thank Ashrahan for his help.

The demigod did not have to wait long for Ashrahan's return. Radnor was just about to head to the throne room when the Krigari god materialized behind him again.

"Any luck?" Radnor asked.

"Hah!" Ashrahan scoffed. "Do you think I would be back if I hadn't had some? There is a watch tower of sorts just south of here. Follow the road that leads to the mountain, and once you reach the crossroads, turn to your right and head up the hill through the forest. There is no road to guide you, but keep walking in a straight line. The tower is at the top of the hill."

"How do you know the ogre is there?" Radnor asked.

"Because more of those vines that said 'hello' to your friend earlier dance upon the walls of the tower. I suggest you bring help with you. I couldn't look inside, which tells me that place is full of dangers like you've never seen before," Ashrahan replied.

"What good could mortal men be against the kind of defenses you fear would be there? Would I not just be leading these people to the slaughter?"

"If we don't stop the witches now, these men will be devoured by chaos anyway. At least this way they can die fighting for a chance to stop them. Besides, every time a man gets killed by some hideous trap, it tells you more about how to get past it. I'm also afraid I cannot help you for a while. If I keep disappearing from his sight to help you, Adramelach will grow suspicious, and I intend to stay alive long enough to help you bury a knife in his heart. Good luck, Radnor."

Ashrahan faded away once more, and Radnor found himself needing to talk Sigaberht into confronting horrors that make the songs of Veigarand sound like peaceful lullabies.

A grim mood lay upon Sigaberht's hall as they awaited the arrival of Bruna and Hilda. Sigaberht had dressed himself in his armor, a long, flowing shirt of mail split at the legs that reached almost to his ankles, with long sleeves reaching to his wrists. He wore a black tabard over it that bore a silver wolf's head crest upon it. His sword was at his belt, and he paced back and forth incessantly. Ashveldt and Erelda were also adorned in armor identical to that which Sigaberht wore. They were a family united in their preparedness for combat. Leif had not yet been issued a new set of armor, but Radnor saw that a new oath ring was tightly wrapped around his upper arm.

After a few moments, the great door to the hall cracked open, and the steward announced the Hexverat. Sigaberht resumed his seat on his throne, and motioned for them to be allowed in. Both Bruna and Hilda were marched in together with Talkos and half a dozen armed men behind them. Once they arrived at the proper distance for addressing the crown, the party stopped and awaited Sigaberht's acknowledgment. The angry ruler eyed the two sisters. They seemed nervous, but that was understandable given that they had just been marched into his court at the spear points of armed guards.

"I find myself at a loss for words," Sigaberht began. "I find that my city has been attacked...attacked by forces beyond my comprehension. Wolves that walk among us as men! My people attacked, abducted, and murdered. Two buildings were destroyed last night!"

"This is terrible news my lord!" Bruna started. "We will gladly help you in healing the wounded."

"Why have you not been helping already?" Ashveldt asked.

Sigaberht silenced his son with a small gesture.

"My son brings up an excellent point, but that is not why I brought you here," Sigaberht said. "I have brought you here because we took a prisoner, and that prisoner placed the blame for this atrocity at your feet. He claimed that the Hexverat are behind this attack on my people."

Radnor watched Bruna and Hilda's fearful expressions. They did know something. The two sisters looked at each other, and Bruna fell to her knees.

"Please my lord, I beg you! Allow us to explain; before you destroy any chance you might have of allowing us to heal again!"

Sigaberht glowered down on the witch.

"So you admit to being behind this attack?"

"No! No!" Hilda started. "We haven't been entirely honest about where our third sister is. Lenora...she is not tending to a plague as we told you. She has gone missing. We tracked her to this area, but we haven't been able to find her yet."

"Missing?" Erelda asked. "How is your sister missing? What happened?"

Bruna began to sob, and Hilda had to continue alone.

"We have traveled far and wide in our quest for knowledge. It has long been our goal to conquer every ailment mankind has ever known. In order for us to find true understanding, we needed to look upon that which all of creation rests upon. We traveled to the edge of the world and found a place where we could look upon the infinite gulf...and see that from all which things came. We looked upon an ocean of infinite void and chaos. We stared into its very heart...and it stared back."

Hilda started to lose composure herself, and started to weep. Bruna saw her sister needed her, and finally spoke again.

"It was a...traumatic experience. We still have dreams...nightmares...of terrors beyond mortal comprehension. I don't think any of us ever truly recovered from it, but Lenora... something...changed in her. She was never the same after that day. She became obsessed with it, wanted to understand more. When we tried to help her, she lashed out at us and ran. We have been trying to find her ever since."

"And you failed to tell me that your insane sister was here?" Sigaberht said coldly.

"We did not want to risk your attacking her," Bruna replied. "She needs help, we need to heal her. Your men would have killed her in her current condition."

Radnor saw truth in that thought, and understood their reluctance to give their sister up.

"Please help us find her," Hilda begged. "Find her, and let us heal her."

Radnor and Sigaberht locked eyes for a moment, and Sigaberht gave a gesture with his hand, indicating for Radnor to join the conversation. He did.

"Your sister has been tampering with a powerful magic. Chaos itself."

Bruna and Hilda both gasped.

"How can you be sure of this?"

"Because I witnessed the death of this prisoner with my own eyes. Almost everyone in this room saw it happen. There was an evil in that spell I have never seen before, and I say this having seen the malice in the very eyes of the Krigari. I do not know if she can be healed."

Radnor was unsure of how to proceed from there, so he gave Sigaberht a slight nod. The earl understood Radnor's meaning, and made his own decision.

"I can promise you that we will find her. But what I cannot promise is that we can take her alive. Not only because of what she did to my people, but because what she does poses a risk to us all. If there is an opportunity to heal her, I will let you have it. But if she forces us to, we will kill her. Do you understand?"

Bruna and Hilda both nodded their assent.

"Talkos, escort them back to their cottage. Make sure they stay there."

Talkos bowed to his lord, and led the witches out of the throne room.

Sigaberht then held his weary brow in his hands, while his wife placed a comforting hand on his shoulder.

"We must find this witch, and put an end to her mischief before she can destroy us. We cannot trust that her sisters will do anything but lead us astray. Radnor, do you have any idea as to where she could be?"

Radnor tensed. He did not want to reveal that he had been communing with Ashrahan, but he also could not lie to Sigaberht without dying a painful death.

"I think I may," Radnor said, choosing his words carefully. "I have heard there is an old watch tower in the deep woods to the south of here. If it's true, that is where I would start."

Sigaberht nodded.

"There is. And if my memory serves me, there has been word of strange sounds and lights coming from those woods as of late, and wolves have been sighted in that area with ever growing frequency. Very well. Leif...I would have you take Talkos, Radnor, and forty warriors to that

188

tower. I will risk no more of my defenses than that. You will find that witch, and you will find our people."

Leif bowed to Sigaberht, and motioned for Radnor to follow him as he left the throne room to carry out Sigaberht's orders. Radnor bowed as well, and followed Leif from the hall. He dared not allow himself to think on what foul things might lie ahead, for if he did, the thought would surely smother him in dread.

Part 3:
<u>A Howling Nightmare</u>

Chapter 17

After a whirlwind of activity, Radnor found himself riding down the southern road to the watchtower Ashrahan had pointed out to him. Talkos had confirmed the tower's location and told Radnor it had been abandoned for some time. It was a relic from the days before the fortress at Drakomar had been built, and had been the southerners' only defense against raiders from the north. As ordered, Talkos had assembled forty of his fighting men to accompany them. Sigaberht had his remaining soldiers on high alert, ready for any external assault. Every entrance to and from the city was locked and guarded until Lenora was found. No one was to be allowed in or out until the next morning.

The men were all silent as they rode. All of them had been told of what dangers might await them. Most had not believed it until Talkos showed them Ferin's remains. Once the men were assembled, they had taken a little time to say goodbye to their families before arming themselves. Radnor had seen Talkos speaking with his wife and embracing his young son before steeling himself to lead his men. Leif had not spoken since they left Wulfgeld. He sat atop his horse fortifying his grim resolve against what was to come.

It was now late afternoon, and the autumn sun was beginning to set over the horizon, casting unsettling shadows over the haunted forest the brave warriors needed to navigate. Once the party reached the crossroads, Talkos gave the order to dismount. The woods were too dense for horses, so they needed to proceed on foot. Darestr whinnied in concern as Radnor dismounted. Radnor stopped for a moment to give Darestr a reassuring pat as he joined the soldiers. Darestr gave him a very worried look and nudged him with his snout before accepting that he could not join his master in this battle.

Seeing the disarray of the broken terrain, with vines and branches littering their path, Talkos arranged the troops in a loose formation, organizing the men into groups of four. Onward they walked, eyes peeled for signs of trouble. As they approached the watchtower, signs of an evil corruption gradually appeared. At first the trees seemed to have a sickly color to them. Their bark was discolored by a shade of eerie, unnatural green that almost seemed to make the trees glow on that dim, cloudy day. As the men progressed deeper, the green on the leaves was overtaken by an eerie color no man had seen before, and could not describe. The pulsing, alien hue evoked fear and dread across the unit.

Suddenly, the men in the lead groups stopped dead in their tracks. Radnor and Talkos quickly joined them to see why they had stopped, only to discover the reason for themselves. It was as though a wave of death had run through the forest. There was an abrupt line that divided the forest in half, one in which life still limped on...and one that was totally dead. The once-proud woods had turned black with decay, and not a single autumn leaf remained on a branch. The trees stood in their own graves. What little grass was left was gray, brittle, and crunched underfoot. No one heard the chirp of a bird, nor the buzz of any insect. Death was all that remained in that part of the forest, and that was where they needed to go.

Radnor took the first few steps into the wasteland, and soon the others silently followed him. Onward they trudged, forcing themselves to take step after step in order to reach their goal. They found themselves ascending to the top of a tall hill, and the watchtower was partially visible at the very top through the gaps in the tree branches. The tower was visibly old, as wooden additions to the exterior had all but rotted away. From Radnor's view it appeared that the only thing keeping it standing were the writhing, pulsing, thorned vines which had wrapped themselves around the old keep.

With a creaking sound, there was a flash of movement Radnor barely glimpsed before a great tree limb hit him square across the chest and knocked him on his back. Radnor stood back up, feeling embarrassed that he had somehow walked into a simple branch. His embarrassment quickly faded when he heard the shouts of the others. He had not hit the branch...the branch had hit him.

Radnor leaped to his feet and surveyed what was happening. Several of the trees had lashed out at the soldiers, their fearsome limbs aiming for anything they could reach. Some of the branches had even begun to sprout massive thorns capable of goring a man. One brave man bent over to pick up his fallen comrade, but was gored by one of the thorns. He let out a cry of pain, and fell dead on top of his wounded friend. Radnor ducked another swipe by a tree limb, and slashed at it with his sword as it passed. The sword smashed through the brittle, dry wood, and the limb fell dead to the ground.

Talkos began rallying his panicked men as they were surrounded by the monstrous plants. They formed a circle, and covered themselves with their shields. Three men lay dead outside of the shield wall. Leif worked to set torches alight while the other warriors protected him. Radnor continued to dodge and parry the tree limbs that lanced towards him as he worked his way to Leif's position. The trees seemed to uproot themselves, and began slowly advancing upon the panicking group. The men in the circle were holding their own, as the limbs couldn't seem to penetrate the tight defenses and counter slashes from their weapons.

194

Finally, Leif got a torch lit, and began to rapidly light more using the first one.

Talkos made sure torches got distributed so that they could make their counter attack and set the trees ablaze. Radnor sheathed his sword and was about to take one of the torches when a piercing scream came from inside the circle of warriors. To Radnor's horror, he saw a man sinking into the earth on which he had just been standing. Blood flew up from the hole the man was slowly being pulled into, and the mud under him writhed in sickening motions which reminded Radnor of chewing. The men on either side of him instinctively leaped away from the danger, and then spun to try to help their friend. They tugged helplessly on his arms as he was pulled in deeper and deeper by that insane chewing. Other men panicked and broke from their formation! What had just been an organized fighting force became a panicked stampede of prey.

The malevolent trees took advantage of the chaos and lunged into the fray, goring and dismembering all who strayed within their grasp. Radnor was able to grab a fallen torch, and threw it at the nearest tree, setting it ablaze. There was an impossible, unearthly shriek as the tree swung its limbs wildly. Radnor barely ducked an errant limb and rolled to a safe distance. He checked to see what was happening, and saw that Leif also managed to set one of the trees ablaze. Talkos was slashing at an onslaught of tree limbs as two other men stuck a torch among its limbs. They caught fire easily, and soon the tree backed away from its attackers. Radnor then heard a deafening crash, and turned to see one of the burning trees had collided with one of the other attacking trees, and now they were both ablaze. The trees themselves were now in disarray, and their hollow, evil screams rang out against the cold evening air.

"Follow me! To me!" Talkos commanded. He ran through the most open path he could find between the attacking trees, and the other men began to follow.

Leif threw a torch to Radnor.

"Veigarand! Cover our retreat!" he yelled over the cacophony of agony.

Radnor caught the torch and used it to fend off a vicious assault from another tree limb. For every tree that was felled, another seemed to take its place immediately. Radnor forced himself to accept that there was no way to win this fight. Once the last man had left the area of the massacre, Radnor threw the torch into the nearest hostile tree, and joined the retreating force. He came upon the survivors a short while later, seeing them breathing heavily and clearly exhausted. Talkos had just finished a head count when Radnor arrived. Out of forty men they had to start with, only twenty two survived.

Leif moved to join Radnor, and handed him a flask of water. Radnor took it, and drank greedily before he remembered it belonged to Leif. He sheepishly handed the flask back to the ealdorman, who gruffly accepted it.

"It would be foolish of me to keep it from you. We all need your strength," Leif said.

Radnor nodded his thanks. He then gestured to where Talkos was taking care of his men.

"How are we doing?" Radnor asked.

Leif shook his head.

"Almost half our men are dead. The rest are terrified. Frankly…" Leif trailed off, and glanced around the group. "I'm terrified too. Those things…why does Caelum allow such abominations to walk the earth like this? What madness has befallen these lands?"

Radnor stood silent for a moment, until he found his response.

"It is exactly that. Madness has taken hold here. It is an evil, malignant sorcery that corrupts and destroys everything it touches."

Leif nodded.

"We won't even be able to bury them. Their bodies will lie there for scavengers to pick clean…the thought makes me sick. And how…how are we to advance Veigarand? When the trees lash out at us, and the very ground beneath our feet seeks to devour us?"

Radnor took a deep breath. Fear filled Leif's eyes, and rightfully so. Radnor was glad he didn't have to come up with a reassuring reply as Talkos began regathering his troops to move out again. Once everyone was back on their feet, Talkos began to give his orders.

"All right, we have no more time for rest. We must march to the place where our enemy holds our people, and we must free them."

Seeing that Talkos meant to continue with their mission, a few of the men started to run back to Wulfgeld. Leif moved to intercept them, but they were stopped by Talkos' suddenly booming voice.

"Any man who flees here today is a traitor to the family he runs back to. What you just saw is no reason to run. It is more reason to stand and fight. This is what that witch intends for not only us, but for all our wives and your children. We cannot turn back."

One of the men who had stood his ground added to Talkos' order.

"My daughter was taken last night while I was on duty patrolling the outer wall. My beloved wife, Ilora…was slain trying to protect her. I will *not* stop until my daughter is safely in my arms again. But I know that if I try without your help…I will surely die…and my little girl will too. I beg of you who would flee…help me…save my daughter! And if you do not, then I would place a curse upon you!" the man sat down again.

196

"Thank you, Valich," Talkos said.

When reminded of their families, the men whom had turned to flee rejoined the group. Radnor had to admire Talkos, with a few well spoken words; he had turned men ready to flee back into fighters. None of them heard Talkos praying to every god he knew of for help. Valich had been a huge help as well, his determination, or desperation, acted as a catalyst to bring forth the bravery of the men around him. Radnor fell into line as the warriors came into a close formation. Following Talkos' lead, they resumed their march up the hill.

Each step forward proved to be a tense endeavor. Fearful eyes watched the trees, the sky, and even the very dirt they trod upon. After slow, agonizing progress, they reached the crumbling outer walls of the tower. The ancient walls were so old and broken that they posed next to no obstacle to the men as they stepped over the ruined stonework. The courtyard was large, and the dirt beneath their feet was just as dead as what they had seen in the forest. They could see the tower up close now, and men grew sick as they watched the hideous tendrils writhe and slither around the walls. The tower seemed like it did not belong in this world, and instead was a denizen of some forgotten, ancient time and place of which no man should ever learn. As Radnor scanned for an entrance, he spotted a single large door blocked by a wall of the tendrils. The door was tall and wide, and it looked like it had been installed recently. Radnor noted that it looked like the door had been made to accommodate something much larger than a human. The ogre perhaps? Talkos positioned his men so they could watch for attack from all directions, and came over to where Radnor stood. Once they were in formation, Talkos spoke to Radnor.

"All right, we're here. Do you have any ideas as to how we're going to get in there? I've already lost too many to the corruption here. I do not wish to lose any more..." Talkos shook his head in sorrow. "...not like that."

Radnor stared at the vines, unsure of the best plan of attack.

He turned back to Talkos, and admitted to having no solid plan.

"I've never fought anything like this before. I think that a direct attack on the vines would end only in disaster. We should avoid touching them at all costs."

"Thank you for the morale boost," Leif said sarcastically.

"Do you think fire could burn them out?" Talkos asked, ignoring Leif's remark.

"Possibly," Radnor mused. "If we could light more torches...and hurl them at the vines...they may burn away so we can get in the tower."

"Assuming it doesn't collapse the instant the vines all burn away," Leif pointed out.

A shout from the men interrupted their thoughts. The vines in front of the gate had parted way, and a huge figure now stood in the door frame. The great monster stepped out into the dying sunlight and revealed itself to be the ogre for which they were looking. The humanoid beast easily stood twice as high as any man, and three times as broad. It wore no clothing, save for a wrapping which protected its loins from the elements. It carried a giant wooden club in its hand, and it smiled at the men arrayed before them the way a cat might smile at a mouse it's caught. Razor sharp fangs were revealed by its wide grin, and its pale eyes showed only amusement and malice.

"Who goes upon my land!" yelled the ogre.

Talkos spoke first.

"I am Captain Talkos. I have come here to retrieve people who have been wrongfully taken from us, and we hunt those responsible. We wish no quarrel with you, but we must have access to your tower in order to continue our search."

The ogre laughed menacingly.

"It is with great joy that I welcome you to my home! I shall take great pleasure in your company...as I crush you beneath my feet to make wine from your blood!"

The ogre took one massive step forward, and swung his club at the nearest group of men. They scattered as best they could, but one was not so lucky. Radnor thanked the gods that the man's death was quick as the club crushed him into the earth. A few arrows struck the ogre in the chest...and pinged harmlessly off his tough hide. The monster grinned again and started forward, brandishing his club as he came. Radnor used the distraction to come up from behind him, and struck a blow to the ogre's leg as hard as he could. Radnor almost fell over as his sword shook violently in his hand and sounded with an earsplitting clang. The ogre spun and tried to step on him. Radnor dove to the side, narrowly avoiding the massive heel as it drove into the earth with a crash. Scrambling to his feet, the northern warrior ran around the ogre's flank. He struck the ogre's other leg as he ran by, with the same effect as before.

As Radnor ran across the courtyard, he took a moment to glance behind him as the ogre chased him. The places where his sword had struck had now turned to stone, preventing his blade from biting into his foe. Panic ran through Radnor's mind as he sought to find a solution to the problem, but there was no more time to think! The ogre had caught up with him and swung its great club at him. Radnor marveled at how slowly the weapon seemed to soar through the air, knowing how fast it must really have been traveling to cover the long distance. Radnor guessed where the blow was aimed and rolled away. Radnor had not paid enough attention to his environment, and his roll placed him amidst the rubble of the wall. He tripped and fell so suddenly he dropped his sword. By the time Radnor realized what had just happened to him, the ogre had already adjusted its swing. Radnor could do nothing but watch as the club arced through the air to crush him.

But Radnor's luck suddenly changed! The ogre tripped over its own feet, and the blow went wide, smashing into the dirt a few feet from him. The ogre fell to one knee, and started leaning on its club to stay upright. Not taking the time to find the cause of this luck, Radnor retrieved his sword from the ground and began hacking at the giant arm holding the club. No blow could penetrate the skin, as each time it was struck; the spot would turn to stone. Radnor threw blows with lightning speed again and again, until he hit a spot already turned to stone, and the blade shattered into pieces. In his panic, Radnor kept striking with the broken blade, still hoping to have some effect on his foe. The ogre finally regained its balance and swiped at Radnor with its arm. Radnor took the full force of the blow and was sent flying down the hill!

He was able to maintain enough of his senses to roll when he hit the ground, and was relatively unscathed when he landed. He drew his dagger and staggered back up the hill towards the sound of men shouting and the ogre's roars. Once Radnor got back to the top, he saw the remains of three more men slain by the monster. Now able to observe the fight from outside, Radnor could see why the ogre had tripped. The places which had turned to stone when Radnor struck them never turned back to flesh. Parts of the ogre's limbs which should have been flexible were rigid and unmoving. Radnor noticed now how limited its arm movements were as there were several points where it had turned to stone. Radnor ran forward, picking up a fallen sword as he charged the ogre from behind again. As he did, he saw Talkos arranging his archers in a half-circle just behind the semi-intact portion of the wall as his spear men ineffectively threw their spears at the beast's massive bulk. Talkos, Leif, and a few others were harassing the beast as best they could, but one by one, men fell to the ogre. By the time Radnor got back, barely half the men were still standing. The ogre threw one man directly at the tower, and Radnor could only watch helplessly as his body was devoured by the nightmarish vines.

As Radnor approached, the ogre heard his footsteps and tried to turn quickly to meet him. Again, the ogre couldn't get its feet to move where he wanted them, and he stumbled. Radnor drove a hard blow into its massive foot, and kept on pounding blow after blow. Radnor was careful not to hit any spot already turned to stone, and kept circling the ogre to never let it get a good swing at him again. By the time the ogre could rise again, most of its lower legs had turned to stone, and it could barely stand upright. Radnor ran to avoid its swipe again, and took a second to observe the creature. Talkos saw an opportunity, and gave the order for the surviving archers to fire directly at the ogre's eyes. Most arrows pinged off harmlessly on its face without even enough force for the hard skin to turn to stone. But a few hit their marks, and soon the ogre's eyes had turned to stone. The great monster let out a roar of pain, and dropping the club, it brought its arms up to cover its face.

Radnor dove out of the way as the falling club nearly crushed him. More arrows struck around the monster's face. The men grew braver, and their glistening spear points probed the ogre's face, forcing it to keep its hands over its broken eyes. Radnor took this moment to step in again and strike blows at its legs until the creature fell to its knees. A few more strikes ensured that it would never be able to stand back up. Radnor then switched to striking the arms, and thought better of it. If he forced the arms to become stone while they still covered its head, he would never be able to deliver a finishing blow to its face.

Talkos' thinking was a step ahead of Radnor's, and the captain had moved to stand to the side of the ogre. With a herculean thrust, Talkos drove the point of his spear into the ogre's ear. The ogre jerked his hands way from his eyes, snapping the spear and taking hold of Talkos! The captain barely had time to scream before the ogre crushed him in its grip. Radnor stood in shock as Talkos' remains fell to the ground. The ogre took an arrow to the soft flesh of its open, screaming mouth. Suddenly, the whole mouth turned to stone and became locked in a wide scream. Radnor continued to hack and slash at his foe until the screaming stopped, and the ogre could move no more. Silence consumed the world for a moment, until Radnor became aware of his own haggard breathing, and the gasping breaths of the men with him.

Radnor ran over to where Leif stood. Leif took a moment to catch his breath, and walked to where Talkos' body lay. He spent a moment to mourn his lost friend, and looked up at Radnor.

"When I find Lenora, she will die, mark my words," Leif said.

Leif stood, and looked at the ogre's body.

"I had heard ogres were difficult to kill...but is this...normal? Or is his stone defense another form of this accursed power that holds this place?"

Radnor stared at the dead ogre in awe. Was it dead? Or just trapped within its own skin?

"I've never fought an ogre before, but this stone trick...I've never heard of it before. I believe you are right, it is something brought about by Lenora's dark sorcery."

More of the men began to regain their composure, and it became time for them to return to the task at hand.

The ealdorman, now acting captain, was staring intently at the dark tower that stood before them, its only door blocked by those devouring vines.

"I fear we have traded a battle for an unsolvable problem," Leif said.

"Those horrid growths will do to anything that touches them what they did to Ferin. I don't see a way past them, and if we try to burn them, chances are we'll set the whole tower ablaze and cook everyone inside."

Radnor stood and pondered the problem. He briefly considered hacking the vines down with his sword, but the image of a vine wrapping itself around his sword arm as he swung came to mind, and Radnor decided against that. Leif suddenly turned to face Radnor with a bright look in his eye.

"I think I have it!" he declared. "That ogre must have had a way inside the tower. Let's check his body and see if we can find anything of use."

The two then ran back to the vicious looking statue, now a permanent monument to its own agony. Leif ordered his men to search the body, and soon an amulet was discovered in a pocket in the monster's loincloth. One of the men handed it to Leif, whom clearly found it hard to look at. He was very eager to give it to Radnor when the demigod extended his hand to take it. The amulet was a solid black gem that did nothing to reflect the light of the dying sun. It instead seemed to emanate its own sinister aura. Around the gem was a metallic backing laced with a pattern that was inexplicably obscene to the human eye, as though the art was from an aesthetic wholly alien to anything Radnor had ever seen, be it god or monster. A loop with a simple chain on the back allowed a person to wear it as a necklace. Radnor looked up from the disturbing trinket and glared intently at the pulsating growths surrounding the tower. There was a moment's hesitation about entering, until Radnor thought of Elena in that hellish place. Radnor then threw the chain around his neck, and started for the door.

"Wait!" Leif yelled. "We don't know for sure if that thing is what we need!"

But Leif's wise words did not impinge on Radnor's will. He had made up his mind. Radnor didn't even slow his stride as he approached the deadly threshold and stepped through the hellish scene before him.

With a gasp from the men watching, Radnor realized he was through. Radnor was disturbed to find that he was somewhat surprised he was still alive, and surprised at what he saw. The door stood before him, like a normal door. This was the first time in what seemed like forever that the task before him was simple. All he had to do was open the door. Reaching for the handle, he cautiously grabbed...and turned it. Waiting for a deadly trap, Radnor found none as the door swung open with ease. Once Radnor was through, he found that the vines covered all of the walls inside the tower as well. They twisted and spun around themselves as they grew in and out of the stone blocks as though they had always been a part of the wall. Thankfully, the vines did not cover the floor, making whatever rescue he could manage at least a little easier.

Once past the entrance hall, Radnor found a spiral staircase which seemed to forever descend into the bowels of the earth. The horrid growth coated the walls of the stairway, and Radnor suspected that death would befall anyone who touched them without wearing the amulet. Radnor's heart sank at the thought of what might have happened to Elena if she had slipped inside this death trap. It seemed to get hotter as Radnor went down step by step. After a while longer, Radnor started to think he heard voices. After a little more time, Radnor realized it was Elena's voice. Without thinking, he called out to her.

"Elena!" he shouted.

"Radnor?" came her startled reply.

Radnor finally found the bottom of the stairs, and came face to face with a cell that had several people in it, Elena included. Radnor was grateful when he saw that the bars were made of simple steel and only held closed by a lock he could easily smash with his shield.

Radnor didn't notice, but Elena's face lit up a little when she saw his armored bulk finish descending the stairs.

"How did you get past the ogre?" she asked.

"I had help. We killed the thing, but many did not survive, including Talkos," Radnor replied.

Elena let out a sorrowful sigh.

"And the witch?" came the voice of a man whom had been sitting in the back of the cell.

Radnor leaned over to see past Elena's shoulder to look at a man hunched over in the corner of the cell.

"I haven't seen her. What do you know of her?" Radnor asked.

The man fearfully looked up at Radnor, and answered.

"She comes here sometimes. She has their servants kidnap people, and bring them here. Then the witch comes and takes the people who've been here the longest away. There were ten of us before, now it's just us three.

"Three?" Radnor asked, not seeing the third occupant.

Elena stepped aside and Radnor just caught sight of the skirts of a little girl whom couldn't have been older than four, whom had been hiding behind her.

"How exactly do you plan to get us out of here?" the man demanded.

Elena answered before Radnor could respond.

"You must have one of those necklaces, don't you? It's how they brought us in here. We were all wearing one when they marched us down here...but the necklaces were taken before they locked us in this cell."

Radnor checked the floor to be sure he wasn't standing on anything other than stone, and took his necklace off. With one solid blow with his shield, he smashed the lock off of the door, and quickly opened the cell. The man in the back stirred. At first Radnor thought he was just getting up to get in line, but then the man moved with alacrity that Radnor hadn't seen coming. The terrified man ran out the cell, making a grab for the amulet in Radnor's hands as he went by. Radnor quickly drew his hand away, and the man stumbled into the vines on the wall.

"Cover the girl's eyes!" Radnor shouted.

Just as Elena's hand flew over the girl's face, the man was ensnared by the growths on the wall. The things that were done to the man in those few seconds made would forever be burned into Radnor's and Elena's minds. A horrid smell soon filled the air that made even Radnor almost wretch. The sounds of the little girl's crying filled the room, echoing against the stone in that nightmarish place. Radnor turned again to see Elena comforting the girl. Radnor then gently tossed the necklace into the cell. Elena did not immediately pick up the necklace. She instead went to dry the girl's tears, and gave her one more hug. Elena then draped the necklace around the girl's neck, and gently nudged her to go through the door. But the girl wouldn't budge. The girl stopped dead, looked at the bloody remains of the man, and ran back to Elena, crying again.

Ice crashed through Radnor's heart when he saw how terrified she was. Sorrow gripped his heart. He understood that no matter what happened today, this was a trauma from which she would never recover. Leif was right. Lenora had to die. As these thoughts filled his mind, they momentarily distracted him from what Elena was doing. Elena was now carrying the little girl in her arms, and still had the necklace around the girl's neck. Elena had one arm wrapped around the girl, while the other hand tightly held the necklace down to make sure the girl wouldn't slip out of it. Before Radnor could object to this plan, Elena stepped over to the start of that treacherous spiral staircase. She nodded at Radnor, and she took the lead back up the stairs. With the necklace wrapped around the girl's neck, Elena had no protection if any mistakes were made. Radnor followed close behind, ready to catch Elena if she started to fall. Both were extremely careful not to touch any of the sinister vines that pulsed and throbbed on the cold, stone walls of the stair.

"Should you not also try to slip the necklace over you in some way?" Radnor asked.

"I don't want to risk weakening its protection," Elena replied. "How did you find us?"

Radnor told her about the fight in the town, leaving out the more grisly details to spare both her and the little girl some grief. Then Radnor told her of Ferin, and how he had let slip the name of the witches. Again, Radnor left out the gorier elements of his death. Not wanting to explain his conversations with Ashrahan just yet, he quickly added that what Ferin had told him gave him just enough information to guess where Lenora's captives were. After that, it had been a matter of time getting there. The little girl tried to shift in Elena's arms a little as they climbed. Elena only held her tighter. Up and up they climbed. The farther they went, the more panicky the little girl got. She tried to squirm more and more, and Elena did everything she could to calm her, but it was no use. The girl suddenly struggled, trying to break free of Elena's grip. Elena tripped, the girl tumbled out of her arms, and Elena landed directly against the vines that clung to the wall.

"No!" Radnor screamed, as he started to reach for Elena.

"Don't!" Elena yelled, waving him off. The little girl screamed as she lay on the stairs, having landed hard enough to hurt a great deal. Radnor found himself ignoring the little girl, and he stared at Elena in terror, helplessly waiting for her to be devoured by the tendrils. But...nothing happened. Then Elena noticed something. The tendrils not only did not attack her...they actively recoiled from her! Elena placed her hand firmly on the wall, and watched as the tendrils slunk away from where she reached. She looked in awe at what was happening. Radnor placed his hand on her shoulder, and she turned to look at him.

"I don't understand," he said.

"Neither do I. But we will have to figure it out later," Elena replied. She then got up, and picked up the little girl again.

They finally reached the top of the stairs, and Radnor sent them both through the sinister door of the tower. As Elena approached the door, the vines parted for her. Once she and the girl were both on the other side, Elena tossed the amulet through to Radnor. He quickly put it back on, the vines parted for him as well, and Radnor stepped back under the open sky.

Chapter 18

The sun had finished setting by the time Radnor left the tower. The cold crisp air blew through the rings in Radnor's armor and nipped at his eyes. After having been down in that pit, the frozen wind felt good. Snow drifted down from the sky and had already begun covering the earth in a light dusting. Radnor saw Leif's men rush over to give Elena and the little girl cloaks to help them stay warm. As they did this, Radnor did a quick headcount. Only nine of the original forty men remained. The little girl suddenly cried out. Radnor's hand flew to his sword, and he had it half drawn before he realized why she had yelled. She had just flown into the arms of Valich, her father. Radnor wasn't sure if it was the wind, or if the sight of the reunion that caused the tears that had begun forming in his eyes. Leif ran over to where Radnor stood, grimly assessing the situation.

"I see you found two. Were there any more?"

Radnor told Leif of the man who had died, and how he had tried to snatch the amulet. Leif shook his head in disgust.

"It's probably for the best that you never got his name. I'd rather not know if he had been a friend of mine. Come on, we need to get back to Wulfgeld. I fear we may be attacked again tonight."

Radnor shook his head.

"You go on. Defend your walls. Get the girl and Elena back to safety. Lenora will be here soon, and I will be waiting for her."

Leif shook his head back.

"Don't be stupid! That bitch will tear you to shreds the moment she sees you!"

Radnor smiled a smile that made Leif feel uneasy.

"I have a few surprises that might keep her from doing that."

Leif looked into Radnor's eyes and saw that the northman's mind would not be changed, for his eyes burned with the fire of an unstoppable killer.

Leif turned and gave everyone the order to head back to the town. Some objected to leaving Radnor there, but Leif insisted his orders be followed. Elena held them up for a moment by running to where Radnor stood.

"What madness is this, Radnor?" Elena demanded. She stared through the eye slots in his helmet and directly into his eyes. She matched the intensity of his gaze with her own. If she still held any of her former fear of him, Radnor couldn't see it. Radnor shook his head. This time without hesitation, he slipped his ring off of his finger and gently placed it in Elena's hand.

"Lenora is Hexverat. She's a healer by nature, not a murderer. I believe that she will hesitate when she sees me."

Elena saw there was no shaking Radnor from his conviction, and she gazed up at him with a different look. It took Radnor a moment to see it was compassion.

"Take care of yourself. I want to see you back in town with the rest of us tonight."

Elena took a moment to touch his shoulder, and turned to join the others.

Radnor stared after the party until they had completely disappeared behind the trees. He then started working to build himself a fire, but quickly decided against it as the possibility of the fire being used against him crossed his mind. In the end, Radnor decided it was best to avoid touching things in this hostile place. Instead, the steel titan settled himself beneath the head of the dead ogre, and watched the snowfall grow heavier and heavier as he waited.

The cold air whipped into Elena's face as she walked. The snowfall felt eerie and unnatural to her as she nervously looked over her surroundings. She was worried that Leif had insisted on keeping as many torches alight as possible while they walked. Given the threat they faced, she would have thought it better to move under the cover of darkness. She had kept her opinion to herself, as not to undermine Leif's leadership. They eventually came upon the smell of burnt wood, and a newly learned smell that filled Elena's very being with disgust. There was a massive clearing that was filled with the smoldering remains of trees, their limbs and roots scattered and twisted upon the ground. Ashes mixed with snow as the chill wind blew. At first it seemed to her that a brush fire must have happened here. Elena quickly dismissed the thought, as she noticed that even in the dim light of the torches she could see what looked like the outlines of human bodies partially covered by snow and ash. Leif held up his hand, and the group stopped behind him.

"We must go around. Only death awaits us this way."

Leif then led the group around this section of the woods in a wide arc, making sure to steer as clear of the smoldering remains of the dead trees as possible. Elena joined him at the front of the group, and asked.

"What happened here?"

Leif kept his eyes straight ahead on the path as he answered her.

"Things which mankind ought never to see, nor hear tell of."

Elena placed her hand on his shoulder, trying to find words to comfort him. He shrugged her off.

"Is your affection not reserved for Veigarand?" he asked bitterly.

206

Elena found herself taken aback by his remark.

"Can I not comfort a friend?" she asked.

Leif snorted. Despite fighting alongside Radnor time and time again, his anger was still strong. Elena shook her head.

"I know you still hate him. But after everything he's done to try to help us...don't you think—"

"Don't you think what!?" Leif scolded, wheeling on Elena as he did.

Leif didn't get to continue his thought, as one of the men shushed them both. Valich, still cradling his daughter in his arms, spoke next.

"Listen! There is something moving ahead of us!" he whispered.

Valich was right, there was a sound. It was like the crunching of footsteps on the new fallen snow, but there was something wrong with the rhythm. It was unlike any human way of walking. At first Elena thought it might be wolves in the darkness, but it didn't match any sound they would make either. Leif lifted his torch high, and started to walk forward, when a hand gently rested on his shoulder. He turned to see another one of the wounded men was standing beside him, one arm in a makeshift sling, and the other arm held a torch aloft.

"Let me go, lord ealdorman. For you see, I am badly wounded. The bleeding has not stopped, and if there is danger ahead, then I am not long for this world anyway," the man said.

Leif nodded and thanked the man for his courage.

The wounded man stepped forward into the darkness, bearing his torch to light the way for the others. As he was nearing the edge of the darkness, there was a flash of movement, and two fleshy, spined tentacles wrapped themselves around the man's legs. He screamed in terror as he was pulled to the ground and dragged into the darkness. There was a horrible, sickening sound, and his screams were no more.

No one moved a muscle. Everyone waited for a sign from Leif. The ealdorman did not have time to make a decision before a human like outline appeared at the edge of his torchlight. The outline then took a sickening step forward, and revealed itself to the survivors. It was a man, or had been a man at one point. Leif recognized the face as belonging to one of the men who had been devoured by the earth earlier that day. However, it was a sick, depraved imitation of a man that now stood before them. Its clothes were torn and bloody, its arms were broken and distorted so that they rested on its back like a pair scorpion stingers, with the bones sticking out of the wrists to make sharp points. Its legs were broken, and they wobbled with every step it took, somehow managing to stay upright through unseen means. There were holes in its skin that were roughly patched with pieces of charred wood and animal bone, as though something had attempted to piece the man back together with both human and inhuman remains. Two blood soaked tentacles extended from the man's abdomen. One still held some of the bloody remains of the brave man it had dragged into the darkness. The other reached out for Leif!

The ealdorman barely had time to deflect the blow with his shield. As he did, the second tentacle dropped its prize and lashed out at him! He moved to block with his shield, but the tendril stabbed one of its bony thorns through the face, and ripped the shield from his grasp. One of the other men leaped forward and hurled his spear into the creature's face. Blood gurgled from the wound, and a vile stench emanated from its damaged head. Before the man could retreat, the tendrils took hold of him, and dragged him towards the creature. No one had time to react, as the creatures belly opened to reveal rows of razor sharp teeth, and the tendrils forced the screaming man into its waiting maw. Blood gushed from the screaming man's body as the monster bit his head off. Satisfied its foe was dead, it let the soldier's body drop to the ground, and lashed out at Leif again. He swung at the first tendril with his sword, but it deflected off one of the bony thorns. The second tendril made its way towards his head, and Leif knew this was how he would die. Suddenly, a hand shot into his view, and grasped the tendril before it could reach him!

"Veigarand?" he yelled aloud, turning to find not Radnor, but Elena holding the tendril tightly in her grasp. She paid him no heed, as she miraculously was able to keep her grip on the struggling tentacle. The monster let out a piercing shriek, and tried to withdraw the tendril from her hand. Elena did not let go, and felt an energy begin to course through her body as she held on. Golden light emanated from her hand, and Elena stood in amazement at what she was doing. As her focus came off of her foe, the light faded, and her strength waned. The creature tore its tendril from her grasp, and tried to attack her! Leif struck a savage counter cut at the tendril as it whipped at Elena's head, and drove the monstrous lash into the snow. Elena wasted no time and took hold of the tentacle again. As she did, she focused all of her attention on keeping her grip. It felt as though her hand fused with the creature. She became a part of it somehow, and could feel the evil energy that drove it. The feeling disgusted and terrified her, but that fear quickly turned to anger as it tried to pull away from their connection. She then focused her thoughts on its destruction, and she again felt energy begin to flow out of her. The light returned, and golden flame began to work its way up the tentacle and into the abomination before them. The creature itself burst into flames with a shriek, and rapidly disintegrated into ash.

Silence then fell across the group as everyone tried to return to some semblance of calmness. Leif looked at Elena, awestruck. Before he could ask her any questions, she spoke.

"I don't know how I did that. When we were in the tower...I fell on those horrible vines...and they recoiled away from me. That's all I know."

Leif nodded.

"It seems there is more afoot than even the witch knows. Come on, we still need to get back to Wulfgeld."

As the group began to move again, Elena contemplated her place in the world, just who and *what* she was. Leif found himself worrying more and more as they walked.

Seven left! He thought bitterly. Of the forty men they had left with, there were now only seven. Leif silently prayed to Caelum that Veigarand would kill Lenora, and end this once and for all.

Chapter 19

Radnor felt like he had been waiting for an eternity. The cold air whipped through his mail armor, and he grew ever more anxious that he had made the wrong decision. Finally, there was a change in the air. Radnor almost thought he heard a faint rustle in the grass. His suspicions were confirmed when the wind took on an unnatural energy he couldn't quite explain. Lenora was near, though she could not yet be seen. After a moment's thought, Radnor decided he needed to show himself to move things along. He stood up, and stepped away from the dead monster. A female voice electrified the air as she exclaimed at the sight of him.

"Ah! I see we have a visitor tonight!" the voice said. It was excited, devoid of fear or malice, and it filled the space around them in a way that revealed great power.

Radnor turned to face the direction from which the words had come, and saw a beautiful woman standing illuminated in the moonlight. Her red hair tumbled and flowed along her back, and she walked with a litheness Radnor had rarely seen in anyone. While she was dressed only in a thin, unadorned black gown, she did not seem cold. Her eyes were dark brown, the kind in which a man could get lost. Radnor blinked to himself, and resolved to avoid looking her in the eye like that again. He really almost had gotten lost in her gaze! The woman laughed to herself, as though she had just heard the punch line to a joke only she could hear.

"Oh my!" she said. "Isn't this a surprise, the little boy I saw in Amaranthar so long ago, here in the flesh! I thought for sure you had died with all the others!"

"My name is Veigarand," Radnor said. "I am sure you know that name."

The witch laughed to herself again.

"Yes, yes, yes, I know that name. It was silly of me to never realize that the name Veigarand would be tied to little Radnor, the living weapon."

Radnor tensed at her disdainful reference to his nature, but returned his attention to his current purpose.

"Your sisters are worried about you. They want me to bring you to them. I hope you'll let me bring you back alive."

"Am I to assume that you were the one who killed our pet?" she asked, ignoring Radnor's statement.

"You know what I am. How could you assume anything else?" he said, icily. His hand fell to the hilt of his sword as he spoke.

"Quite right, quite right," she said. "Now comes the real question, are you here to replace him? Or are you here to kill my sisters and me?"

Radnor's blood ran cold. The way Lenora was talking...it was like she believed Bruna and Hilda were a part of this too. He had to find out for sure.

"You and your sisters have stood as a symbol of kindness, compassion, and grace. Every time men began to fear those who wield magic, the Hexverat reminded them that there is good in that world, and gave them hope. Now here you are, murdering innocent people, making insane deals with mad wolves, and experimenting with powers so dangerous you would allow the whole world to be devoured. You are undoing all of the work your sisters still try to do. Why?"

The look on the witch's face changed when Radnor made his speech. A whole range of emotions played across her beautiful features. First anger, then sorrow, then madness.

"You haven't seen what we have seen. My sisters and I...we traveled the world seeking out disease, and ending it. We healed wounds, rid the land of plagues, and ventured to many faraway places. We even traveled to the far north to Amaranthar once, to check upon the development of the king's new weapon. As we traveled, we reveled in the joy of overcoming new diseases; discovering how to use magic to heal all but death itself! We could even regrow long lost limbs if given enough time. Our thirst for knowledge became unquenchable. So, we journeyed to the very edge of the world. We wished to see that which our world rests upon, and perhaps learn more about how to twist the fibers of creation into what we needed. Perhaps even weave some of our own. We found the very edge of the world, and stood upon the shores of hell. We saw shapes when we gazed into its maw. By the creators, I think they were eyes! There is something inside the chaos...something has merged with it... become a part of it! It is an evil, malevolent force unlike any of the puny gods you think you were created to slay. If given the chance, whatever it is would use chaos to devour this world in an instant."

"Then why do you poke holes in the barriers to let it in? Why do you play with it as though it were a toy?" Radnor demanded.

The witch then cackled with a laugh that truly revealed her madness.

"When we left that place we hoped to forget what we saw...but it did not forget us. Our dreams...it came to us in our dreams! We saw its monstrous desires, heard its terrible call! It wanted us to help it devour the world! If we are to destroy this chaos, we must first learn how to use it, to shape it. We must learn what makes it work! Only a weapon forged from chaos can kill chaos. There is another, an evil one who walks this earth who would unleash horrors upon this world beyond your imagination. Only with a weapon made from chaos can we defeat him!"

"If that's true, come back to your sisters! Perhaps together, we can find a way to stop him without leading to more bloodshed. Your sisters want to save you from this madness!"

Lenora cackled even more wildly. Growing impatient with this, Radnor tried to learn more of their plan.

"Making this weapon...that would take more power than even the three of you together could muster," Radnor said.

"Which is why we need a sacrifice. But not any sacrifice will do. The sacrificed souls of an entire city would be needed for us to attempt such a feat."

Radnor almost shrank back in horror when he finished putting all of the pieces together.

"That's why you need the wolves. They will slaughter the people of Wulfgeld for you, and you collect their souls as they do it. But, why would the wolves help you?"

"We promised them a great deal. Imagine, if you can, a world where wolves look like men! They can walk like men, even talk like men! They would be able to feast like they never have before! We sacrificed the souls of people the wolves already captured, and used those souls to cast spells which make wolves walk as men."

Radnor shook his head in disgust.

"Your sisters told me you were mad, but this is evil beyond madness."

The dreaded witch let out a cold, hateful laugh.

"If I am mad, then let me be so! I know the truth of the world... and so do my sisters."

The implications of what she had just said were not lost on him, as Radnor realized he had been played for a fool. Lenora hadn't gone rogue; the triumvirate stood together in this! And that meant while he was chasing one mad sorceress out in the snow, two more were inside the walls of the city, ready to loose a legion of fanged horrors upon its populace.

She began walking a circle around Radnor, lithely placing each bare foot into the fallen snow as though it were a soft, warm blanket. She spoke again.

"Tonight, every man, woman, and child in Wulfgeld will die. And you could have prevented it had you not interfered! But instead, you had to rescue the girl, and now you've left us no choice but to slaughter them all!"

"Girl, which girl?" Radnor said, in a panic he couldn't quite understand.

She blinked in surprise, a gesture which caught Radnor off guard.

"You do not know? How curious. The pale beauty with the black hair; she came in with the refugees. She is filled with power, more power than any of us have ever seen! More than the three of us combined! When my sisters saw her, we knew we could save so many lives. The only sacrifice we need…is her."

Radnor stood; stunned by what Lenora was telling him. His blood boiled at the thought of the mad witches using Elena as a sacrifice to power their twisted magic. Lenora continued.

"And to think, we had hoped we could use you to bring her to us."

Radnor scoffed at the notion, to which Lenora responded in a mocking tone.

"Did you think my sisters' sexual advances on you were because of actual lust? No, there are spells of the mind which require…certain contact to be fully effective on one with *your* parentage."

The witch's mind seemed to wander elsewhere as she thought out loud, almost forgetting Radnor was there.

"And then you came running to save her. My sisters did say you traveled with them, and here you are now, protecting her again."

Her eyes widened in sudden realization.

"The threads of creation are woven strangely indeed," she muttered to herself.

Her eyes returned to focus on Radnor.

"Fate continues to be cruel to you."

Radnor had had enough.

"I cannot believe what I'm hearing right now. You leave me no choice."

Radnor drew his sword, and started towards the witch. She took one step back, without an ounce of fear showing on her face. There was the snap of a twig to Radnor's right, and he whirled to face the threat. Halfdan stood at the edge of the tree line, looking blankly at Radnor, as though he was unsure of how he had gotten there.

"Halfdan, what are you doing…" Radnor started.

The witch cackled again, the laugh sending chills down Radnor's spine.

"We had a plan in case the town put up more resistance than we expected. You see, Kirri had good reason to put a blade in your friend's back. Maybe when your friend is done ripping your throat out, he will tell you about it."

The witch then drew a sinister looking gaulderen from her dress. She crushed it in her hand, letting the pieces fall into the gathering snow. The gaulderen emitted a strange light which blinded Radnor as Lenora faded into the trees. Before Radnor could begin to give chase, Halfdan started to scream.

"Run, Radnor, run! I can't control it! I'm..."

Halfdan began to convulse uncontrollably, and collapsed onto the ground. His body twisted and bent as bones and muscle reformed themselves into new shapes. Hair grew all across Halfdan's huge body. It was only then that Radnor looked up and saw that the witch had used the gaulderen to change the moon. It was now full. Halfdan's arms elongated and razor sharp claws sprouted from his fingers. His face transformed into a long snout, and fangs began to appear, ready to tear flesh. Fear gripped Radnor as he watched his friend transform into a monster he had only heard of in legends...a werewolf!

By the time Radnor had come to grips with himself, Halfdan's transformation was almost complete. Radnor's mind was racing to remember the weakness of such a monster...he needed a weapon made of silver...and there were none nearby. Knowing he had no weapon that could harm the monster, he did the only thing he could do. Radnor turned, and ran. Into the trees he tore, his thundering footsteps crunched against fallen leaves and branches and left indelible marks in the carpeted snow. He knew he had to evade Halfdan as long as possible, hopefully even lose him altogether. But for now, Radnor just needed to get distance between them.

A long howl made Radnor look back for a moment. The transformation was complete, and the predator was coming for his prey. Radnor continued to flee. His legs burned with each step, and his heart pounded harder and harder. As his seemingly endless flight dragged on, he found himself slowing down. Once Radnor realized this he intentionally stopped to gather his breath. He was soaking wet, as a mixture of sweat and melted snow coated all of the clothing under his armor.

Moonlight reflected off of the snow that continued to fall in the dark, twisted forest. Which way had he run? Radnor did not know, and stopped for a moment to figure out where he was. He found that even though he was Halfdan's prey, he couldn't help but think only of how best to make sure Halfdan stayed away from Elena.

His thoughts were interrupted by the thud of heavy footsteps against the snow. They were rapidly closing in on him. Just as Radnor turned to face the sounds, from out of the darkness Halfdan leaped upon him. Radnor turned Halfdan's fangs aside with his shield, and reflexively swung his sword into the werewolf's neck. The force of the blow sent

Halfdan tumbling to the ground, but the werewolf was otherwise unharmed. Radnor swung again, hoping to stun his foe. The werewolf caught the blade in its grip, and twisted the sword out of Radnor's hand. With its other claw, Halfdan slashed at Radnor's face.

The desperate warrior drove the sharpened edge of his shield into the giant hand, and the edge chipped and bent under the force of the werewolf's attack. Radnor took a step backwards, while circling around behind Halfdan's shoulder. The maddened beast spun and tried to slash him with its claws again. Radnor ducked and drove the shield into Halfdan's abdomen. The werewolf snarled in rage, and grabbed hold of his shield, its sharpened edge useless against the impervious flesh of the werewolf. The great beast lifted the shield, taking Radnor with it as he did not loosen his grip on the handle. Radnor kicked up into the monster's throat as hard as he could, feeling his boot connect with soft flesh. The monster reeled back, still holding onto his shield. It seemed all Radnor had done was make it angrier. It whipped its arms rapidly, forcing Radnor to let go of the shield or be flung into a nearby tree. Radnor dropped to the ground, and broke into a run; heading in what he hoped was the opposite direction from where Leif and Elena would be headed. Radnor was lucky, as Halfdan took the time to tear the iron shield asunder before continuing to hunt him. This gave Radnor just enough of a head start to find a pace he could maintain. This chase had transformed from a sprint to a marathon.

Elena did not think it was possible to feel more grateful to find horses than she was at that moment. Leif had successfully led them out of the cursed forest and brought them to the crossroads where their horses stood. Elena quickly found Darestr, and patted him on the shoulder.

"Do not worry friend," she said. "I don't plan to leave Radnor here."

Leif took her by the wrist.

"Too many of my men have died to save you for you to throw it all away over him. The command from the earl is to take you back to Wulfgeld, and I intend to do that!"

Elena pulled her hand away from Leif's grip.

"Is that all you ever think about? Your mission? Your duty to Sigaberht?"

Leif nearly struck her.

"That's not fair!" he spat. "I just risked my life to come out here to save you, and this is how you thank me? I could have been the one to have my body twisted into some...horrid abomination! Veigarand wasn't the only one who came to your rescue. We all took that same risk, and you spit on their sacrifice by acting this way."

"The only reason you weren't killed by that thing was because *I* saved you!" she said.

"Making it even more important we get you back to the city!" Leif shouted. "You did something even Veigarand can't do. That makes you more important than all of us, even him. I *have* to get you to Wulfgeld. You are too important now to squander trying to save him. You need to come back with us. You know he would want you to."

Darestr came up behind Elena, and nuzzled her in the back. Elena realized Leif was right, and she bowed her head in shame.

"I'm sorry Leif; I shouldn't have said what I did."

Leif closed his eyes, and calmed himself again.

"It's all right. You care about him, and were just acting on your feelings. Just know that I would have come to rescue you even if Sigaberht had not given the order. You're one of my people, and I will fight for every one of you until the end."

Elena nodded, and clasped his shoulder.

"I really am sorry," she said.

I just wish you could start to see Radnor as one of your people too, she thought to herself.

Elena mounted Darestr, and saw that the others were waiting for her and Leif to finish arguing. A sudden, unearthly wind whipped up a flurry of snow into their faces. When the gust ended and the snow settled, there was a gasp from the entire group. The crescent moon had just become full. There was a howl in the darkness, and the group knew that wolves were upon them. They rode their horses at a full gallop, desperately trying to get ahead of the dreaded pack. Onward they rode as the snow whipped into their faces. Fear gripped the horses, and they did not care how hard they ran. They knew only that they must escape. The walls of Wulfgeld eventually came into view, and as the harried group rode toward the gate, they found a tree had been felled and was now lying across the road. There were men using the tree for cover.

Elena saw one of their eyes reflect the pale moonlight, and realized it was a trap. She barely had time to yell before several men with spears leaped from the shadows, and gored two of the onrushing horses. Both horses and riders toppled to the ground, and the wolfmen descended upon them, slashing with their crude weapons and murdering the warriors of Wulfgeld. Leif leaped from his horse, slashing with his sword. He cut down one of the wolfmen as it attacked one of the downed riders, and beheaded another as it turned to face him. The other warriors dismounted and joined the battle. Elena was just about to dismount and join the fray when Darestr kicked one of the wolfmen in the face, and started galloping down the path, leaving Leif and the others behind to fight the monsters alone. Leif paused for a moment to see Darestr run with Elena on his back, and smiled. The ealdorman let out a fearsome battle cry, and resumed his bloody work. Another one of his men fell, torn down by several foes at once. The wolfmen were not individually skilled fighters, but their animal ferocity and superior numbers made them dangerous foes. An errant swing from a club caught Leif on the shoulder. Leif hit the ground hard, and yet again found himself ready for a killing blow to end his life. Instead, a spear thrust from Valich ended the monster's life. Leif looked up at the man.

"What are you doing here? Run! Save your daughter!" Leif yelled.

Without a word, Valich turned and ran back to his horse where his daughter was still perched. One of the wolfmen noticed this, and ran for Valich like a wild animal. Leif did not have time to warn him, and the monster tackled him to the ground. The vicious monster sank its teeth into Valich's flesh and tore skin from bone. Valich screamed, and using his unpinned hand, drew his dagger and stabbed the beast in the throat. The wolfman toppled to the ground, twitching as it died. Leif rushed to where Valich lay, and hoisted the man up.

"Go! Go!" Leif yelled.

The ealdorman helped the father up onto his horse.

"Do you think you can make it?" Leif asked.

"For her I will. But I will not go to Wulfgeld. We must flee this place completely if my daughter is to have any chance of safety. The walls are no longer safe," Valich said.

Before Leif could object, he took off down the road, and turned away from Wulfgeld. The wolfmen did not give Leif a chance to see which way Valich went before he had to defend himself yet again. After several more grisly moments, the fight was over. The bodies of both men and wolves were strewn across the road, telling the tale of what had transpired there. Leif and two others were all that remained of the original forty. After catching their breath yet again, the group mounted their horses, and completed their flight to Wulfgeld. They raced madly to make it to the gates that were opened for them. The gate slammed shut as soon as they entered. They were safe inside the walls. Elena was still at the gatehouse, waiting for them. Leif dismounted, and prepared to make his report to Sigaberht.

Radnor felt his strength begin to ebb. He was running out of the energy he needed to run from the werewolf's endless pursuit. The creature seemed to have no limit to its endurance, and he knew it was intentionally just keeping pace with him, running him down until he was too tired to fight back. But onward the demigod ran. As irrational as it was, he was still doing everything he could to keep that monster away from Elena. Just as he was considering standing his ground and trying to fight again, he smelled a horrid, foul odor. Radnor then realized he had made a terrible mistake. He had run in so many different directions trying to lose Halfdan; he had managed to run on the path Elena would have taken to get back to the horses. Radnor cursed himself, and decided now was the time to stand his ground against Halfdan. He would do it here, and not let the monster get any further than this.

Radnor tried to still his mind, and listened for the sound of the werewolf's approach. Instead of the patter of feet, he heard a faint creaking. Turning, Radnor saw one of the trees slowly start to move in his direction. Weaponless, Radnor knew he must flee from this foe. Just as he turned to flee again, a thought occurred to him. He did not run, and instead positioned himself in the open. A few moments later, the manic werewolf came into view, its mouth drooling in anticipation at having finally caught its prey. Radnor waited for the right moment, and darted towards the hostile tree. He narrowly avoided a tree limb that was swung at his head, and leaped over a root that tried to ensnare his ankle. He made it through!

Radnor then heard an angry snarl from the werewolf. He looked back as he ran, and saw the monster was now engaged in combat with the tree. Another one of the foul plants came up behind Halfdan, and ensnared the werewolf's paws with its roots. Radnor stopped and watched for a moment as he saw the werewolf use its mighty jaws to break one of the roots holding its claws. Once freed, the werewolf began to tear at the tree, ripping chunks of wood even as more limbs moved to strike at the wild beast.

Satisfied he had a proper opportunity for escape, Radnor continued to run for where the horses had been kept. He was not sure if either side could win that fight, but as long as neither one could pursue him, he was content for now. Radnor then turned his attention to getting back to Wulfgeld. Sigaberht needed to be warned of the impending attack before it was too late.

Chapter 20

Sigaberht furrowed his troubled brow, his thoughts turning over grim tidings. He had just listened to the tale Leif and Elena had told, and his mind raced with fear. This was one of the few times in his life he simply did not know how to proceed. Several ideas ran through his mind, but none of them seemed possible. Leif and Elena stood before him in the dimly lit throne room, awaiting his command. Sigaberht had also summoned Leofric to this meeting, as he was one of his most trusted advisors and spies. The earl's family sat beside him. Ashveldt was looking at him with childlike fear. Under different circumstances Sigaberht might have been annoyed at his son for being so sheepish, but given the horrors that had just been described, he could not blame him. Erelda was the first to speak, breaking Sigaberht from his internal torment.

"I think the first question is this...what do we do with the two Hexverat sisters we have? Do we employ them to the defense of the city? Or do we kill them now, as a measure to make sure they don't betray us for Lenora?"

Sigaberht nodded, understanding their predicament. He spoke first to his wife, then to Leif.

"You're right, my love. Leif, I would have you bring men to the witches' cottage…"

Sigaberht trailed off. He looked at his son, and thought of what he needed to do to keep him safe. Having now made his decision, Sigaberht turned back to Leif.

"The sisters seem to have underestimated Lenora. I want them brought before me under heavy guard. I shall tell them of what has happened, and I will wring the truth from them. Leofric, I have a special task for you. Arm your men. You shall have one responsibility...protect Elena. If what you say is true, then she is our best chance at destroying this evil that rests upon our doorstep. Lenora would surely wish to kill Elena to prevent that."

Leofric and Leif bowed and started to carry out their orders. Elena spoke.

"And what of Radnor, my lord?"

Sigaberht shook his head.

"I cannot risk men to go look for him. Great horrors lie outside these walls, and the gates must remain shut. If Veigarand is going to find his way back to us, he will have to do so alone."

Erelda was the next to speak, faintly smiling in an attempt to ease Elena's nerves.

"Take heart. If there was any man who could make his way back alive, it would be him."

Elena started to speak up again, but Leofric gently took her by the shoulder. Seeing further argument was pointless, she went with him. Leif gave Elena a polite nod as he went by with a group of Sigaberht's soldiers to collect the Hexverat. Elena turned to Leofric.

"I'm going out to find Radnor," Elena said.

Leofric sighed in exasperation before making his reply.

"No, you're not. My orders are to protect you, and that is exactly what I am going to do," Leofric said.

"Well, I am going. If you want to protect me, then you are just going to have to come with me."

Leofric wheeled to face her, and looked her directly in the eye.

"I know you care for him. But we cannot go out there. Nobody knows what other horrors await us outside and nobody knows if you'll be able to stop them the way you did before. There are other people in this world besides Radnor. The men you would force to go with you have families. I still have a family. I love my son, and I will not abandon him in this crisis. This will not be another Neugeld! Now come on, I must gather Rolf and my men, and then we must head for the keep. That's where you will be safest from attack."

Elena understood Leofric's point. Radnor wasn't the only one in danger. Everyone in Wulfgeld was under threat, and everyone had to protect the people they loved.

It was only a few minutes before Leif and his men arrived at the witches' cottage. The layer of snow continued to grow deeper, covering the city in an icy blanket of fear. As soon as the armed warriors reached the door, Leif knew something was wrong. Checking around the corners of the cottage, and finding nothing, his alarm grew even greater.

"Where are the other guards?" he asked.

None of Leif's men had any idea where the cottage guards could have gone. Drawing his sword, Leif set himself to open the door to the cottage. His soldiers followed suit, and prepared for a fight. Leif decided haste mattered more than stealth, and he threw the door open. Out poured a frightful stench that caused several men to start retching almost immediately. Leif gagged, but was able to hold firm. His blood ran cold. The ealdorman had only recently learned of this stench, but already he knew what it meant.

Inside, he found what remained of the lifeless corpses of the guards whom had been standing outside the cottage. Pieces of human viscera were scattered throughout the interior. What had once seemed a

220

calm and inviting place was now filled with terror and dread. Leif continued to advance and found that the sitting room that had been a place of healing was now an altar of death. Rugs were torn to shreds and tossed all around the room. Pots lay scattered and broken about the room as well. The few pots that still stood upright were filled with what appeared to be human blood. There were strange symbols drawn on the wall and the floors that emitted an eerie, unearthly glow. Upon closer inspection, Leif realized these had been painted using the blood of the dead guards. For a moment Leif considered the possibility that wolfmen sent by Lenora had gotten inside already and attacked the witches. Leif took another hard look at the unearthly symbols on the walls, and decided this was not the case. Spells had clearly been cast here, and that pointed to the witches. Leif's blood ran cold with fear. His gut told him this place needed to be destroyed as quickly as possible. The ealdorman spun angrily and addressed his men.

"They're gone. We need to tell the earl at once. Burn this shack to the ground."

With that, Leif led his men out of the cabin. Two men worked to light the cottage ablaze. Leif stayed only long enough to make sure the cottage did catch fire, and then he and his men hurried back to Sigaberht's hall atop the hill, hoping they could reach him before something terrible happened.

"The least you could do is give me a sword," Elena said angrily.

Elena was starting to feel scared. There was a foul feeling in the air that told her something evil was going to transpire in Wulfgeld that night. She could tell others felt the same way. The entire group had been uneasy as Leofric gathered his men. He had also retrieved Rolf so that he could keep an eye on his son. Leofric was not taking any risks.

"There's no time to go get one. Besides, you have never had any training," Leofric said.

"Pointy end goes in the enemy," Elena retorted.

"There's more to it than that," Leofric replied.

The group was hurrying through the snow covered streets. They were headed to the keep near Sigaberht's hall at the top of the hill. It was the best defended position in the city, and Leofric insisted that they head there for protection. Rolf walked quickly; brandishing the war ax his father had given him in an aggressive manner, hoping it would hide his fear. There were twelve men in Leofric's group, and they were all fully armed. These men were well trained and battle hardened, having acted as warriors, spies, and saboteurs alongside Leofric for many seasons. Their eyes scanned warily across the throngs of people that were milling about the city. Some of the population could feel there was something wrong, and there was a furtiveness to the way the crowds moved. The people all felt a general desire to return to the seeming safety of their homes and hearths.

As the party arrived at an intersection, there was another group of armed men bearing the wolf's head sigil of Sigaberht. Leofric bowed his head to their commander, and gave them the right of way. Their commander wordlessly returned the bow before leading his men down the street. As they passed, Elena thought she caught a glimpse of something in their eyes…like reflected moonlight. As the last soldier was passing her, she peered more closely, and saw that this man's eyes were yellow. Elena stifled a gasp, and moved her eyes away as quickly as possible. Elena tugged on Leofric's sleeve to get his attention. The man turned to face her quizzically.

"Those men...they're wolves!" she exclaimed.

"Are you sure?" Leofric asked.

His adrenaline raced, fearful that the monsters were already inside the city.

"I'm positive. Their eyes were wrong," Elena replied.

Leofric felt duty bound to intercept the armed band. If Elena was right, he could not allow them to continue their ghastly mission. Leofric turned to Rolf, and saw the look on his son's face change from fear to determination. Leofric felt proud as he saw his son was ready for the fight. He then turned to face the armed group, and made his move.

"Halt!" Leofric shouted.

All of his men turned and drew their weapons, prepared to fight alongside their leader. The wolfmen made no response, and continued walking on their path.

"I command you to halt!" Leofric yelled.

People in the streets took notice, and began ducking out of the way as Leofric and his men advanced to follow the wolfmen. The warriors picked up their pace until they were close enough that there was no way the wolfmen could not respond if they wanted to keep their cover.

"Halt!" Leofric yelled again. This time, the wolfmen stopped in their tracks, and turned to face him.

Their leader gave Leofric a wide eyed grin, and mockingly bowed once more. There were fifteen wolfmen in the pack arrayed before Leofric. Before anyone could react, the leader of the pack let out a savage, inhuman roar and the wolfmen rushed Leofric's men. Several bystanders frozen in terror were cut down by brutal slashes from the wolfmen's blades. Bodies fell, and blood ran through the streets. Citizens panicked as the onrushing horde swarmed down the street, seeking to unleash their bloody wrath. Leofric's people were well trained, and they immediately formed a shield wall with Rolf and Elena behind it. The monsters collided with the wall head on, kicking and slashing with all of their animal ferocity. The human warriors had to brace themselves with all their might against the assault, finding themselves unable to properly fight back against the wolves' animal strength.

One of the wolfmen dove for a man's shins, and was able to sink his teeth into an ankle. The warrior toppled to the ground as his leg buckled. Seeing this opening, the wolfmen pressed their attack, but the first wolf who tried to punch through the hole was met with the blade of Rolf's ax as it smashed into its skull. The wolfmen continued to press through, totally indifferent to their own casualties. More wolfmen pushed the soldiers in the shield wall aside as they broke the line, forcing the wall to disperse. Two of the wolfmen launched themselves at Rolf. Leofric turned and caught one of them in the back with his sword, sending the monster sprawling to the ground and gurgling on its own blood. Leofric only had time to see Rolf engage the second wolf in combat before he had to turn his attention back to the foes in front of him. The line had fully collapsed and his men found themselves fighting for their lives in a chaotic melee. The clash of steel, battle cries, and yells of agony filled the city streets with their awful cacophony.

Leofric parried a fierce blow from one wolfman with his sword, and deflected a blow from a second foe with his shield. He stepped to the side, trying to place his enemies in a line so that they had to come at him one at a time. The lead monster leaped forward so aggressively it caught Leofric before he was set. He barely had time to block the ferocious attack as he moved. The second monster engaged him again, and Leofric swung wildly with his sword, his only goal to keep them at a distance. The wolfmen hesitated for just a moment, and then moved in again. One swung its sword at Leofric in a wide, untrained arc. Leofric brought his sword around in a much tighter arc and threw a brutal counter cut into the arm of his lead foe. The monster howled in pain, and dropped to the ground to clutch at the dangling remains of its arm. The second wolfman stepped forward and threw a powerful blow at Leofric's head. Leofric was able to turn the blow aside with his shield, and stepped in for a precise thrust to the beast's heart. Leofric's point found its mark, and the beast collapsed in a heap on the ground. He tried to remove his sword from the beast's body, and found the blade was stuck!

As he struggled to free the bound blade, another wolfman approached him from behind. The sounds of battle and the screaming of the citizens drowned out its predatory snarl. Leofric only learned it was behind him when the biting edge of its blade struck against his armor with such force that he was sent toppling to the ground. Leofric rolled onto his back in time to see the monster standing over him with an ax, ready to deliver a killing blow. Leofric tried to crawl away, but slid on the snow covered street. The monster grinned wickedly at him, but before it could deliver the final blow, Rolf leaped up behind it and swung his ax into the monster's unarmored leg, severing it through the knee. The creature dropped its sword as it collapsed in a heap. Rolf was much faster at delivering a killing blow than the wolfman had been, as his ax crashed down upon its skull with devastating and bloody effect. Leofric quickly rolled to his feet, retrieving his weapons as he did.

"Where's Elena?" he hurriedly asked.

Rolf spun. In the chaos of the fighting, he had lost track of her. Many of the wolfmen now lay dead in the blood soaked streets. To Leofric's disappointment, several of his men also lay scattered across the road. The clatter of combat still rung in the air, and Leofric and Rolf ran to help. After teaming up to kill two more wolfmen from behind, they saw Elena. She had picked up a fallen sword from the ground, and was hurriedly parrying the wild swings from one of the wolfmen. Leofric and Rolf both rushed to her aid. They had almost arrived when the frustrated predator over committed to a heavy strike while Elena was just outside of range. Seeing the monster was off balance, Elena drove the point of her sword into the creature's throat. It collapsed in a bloody heap, twitched for a moment, then died. Leofric and Rolf stopped in front of Elena. Her dress and face were covered in blood. Elena looked at Leofric.

"Pointy end goes in the enemy," she said.

Leofric gave her a friendly nod, and they turned back to the fighting at hand. By the time they had crossed the distance over which the violence had spread, they found that only a scant two of the original fifteen wolfmen still stood. Given how severely outnumbered they were, the remaining monsters were dispatched with relative ease. Leofric gathered his men, and found they had lost five of the original twelve. Leofric found himself thanking Caelum that his son was unharmed in the brawl. He turned to Rolf, and was about to praise his son for his bravery in battle when there came a tremendous alarm from the north gate. They all turned to face the sound, and were surprised to hear the alarm begin to sound from the east and west gates as well. Fires became visible over the rooftops, and everyone in the group knew that hell had come to Wulfgeld.

Chapter 21

Leif had just finished making his report to Sigaberht when the alarm was heard in the great hall. The earl was still weighing his options with regards to the witches, but none of that seemed to matter now as the bells rang out against the cold air of the night. Leif stood in the great hall and looked to his lord for guidance.

"What shall you have me do?" Leif asked.

"You and I are going to go out, and meet the host that has come to die on our doorstep," Sigaberht said.

He then turned to his son.

"Ashveldt, you are my only surviving child. You are to head to the keep and protect your mother."

Ashveldt rose to object, but his father placed a firm hand on his shoulder.

"You must defend your keep, do you understand? As earl I must go out and meet the enemy head on, but my heir must remain here and defend his mother. We are beset by an enemy unlike any we have ever faced, and I need all of your strength now more than ever. I command you as your lord to do this."

Ashveldt clasped his father's shoulder, and nodded. He turned to face his mother, who smiled reassuringly at him. Sigaberht then came to Erelda, and gently took her hand to lead her aside in the hall. He held her in his arms, and spoke in the manner of his vows to her.

"My darling wife, thou whom hast carried our children, and hast held me in thy close embrace...please know that no matter what fate Caelum has in store for me...I fight for thee."

Erelda leaned forward and kissed her husband. Once their lips parted, Erelda spoke.

"Do not worry, my dear husband. Today will be a day of victory for thee. Thou foes will be slain, and thou will return to my arms this very night."

Erelda paused for a moment, and shifted back to her normal speech.

"I love you."

"I love you too," Sigaberht replied.

He then turned, holding back his fear as he did. He told himself that this was just another battle, like all of the others he had fought. But his heart knew this was not so. His servants had returned with his armaments, and Sigaberht came to them, arming himself for the coming battle. Once fully armed, he turned to Ashveldt again, who was just tightening the strap on his own helmet.

"Ashveldt, the rest of the guards will remain here under your command. Leif, I will accompany you and your men. We need to rally as many of the soldiers as possible into a single fighting unit."

Ashveldt and Leif both nodded. Sigaberht marched to the end of the hall and took charge of the soldiers that had been waiting just outside the door to the throne room. They left the room and headed to the outer door to the great hall. As they reached the exit, one of the guards grasped the handle and started to open the large door. As soon as it had partially creaked open, the soldier met his death. A raging, snarling wolf leaped through the gap and tore the man's throat out before he could react. Wolves poured through the open door, and the men inside found themselves fighting for their lives. These were not wolfmen, but ferocious animals bent on the destruction of every human that stood before them. Teeth tore flesh and blood flowed freely as the fighting grew to a fever pitch. The wolves were as agile and cunning as they were ferocious. They deftly avoided sword strokes, and returned to assault the wielders with intensity and strength. Sigaberht and Leif found themselves split up, and each fighting for control of a different half of the great double-door gate. The carnage inside the entryway would send most men into a panic, but these men held their ground.

A wolf leapt directly at Sigaberht's face, fangs bared to tear at his face and throat. The earl stepped aside with the alacrity of an experienced warrior, and cut the feral beast down as it flew. A second wolf rushed low and tried to drive its fangs into his leg. Sigaberht brought his shield down on its skull and drove the beast into the ground. The wolf quickly stood again and leaped backwards, snarling at Sigaberht as it did. Sigaberht's sword lashed out to strike the wolf's face, but it turned its head aside and let the blade go by. The beast pounced, trying to catch the earl off balance, but the earl was too skilled a swordsman for that. Sigaberht deftly stepped aside and brought his blade around in an arc that decapitated the monster.

With no foes actively attacking him, Sigaberht ran to the door, and tried to force it closed. Seeing what he was doing, two of the soldiers ran to help close the door against the onrushing horde. Wolves descended upon the trio, and one man was dragged down by the tearing fangs. Leif then leaped to defend his lord, swinging his sword and killing one of the wolves attacking the earl. The other wolves turned to face their new threat, which gave Sigaberht time to finish closing the door. After several more brutal moments, the door was sealed again. Sigaberht and his men were now able to turn their attention back to the remaining wolves in the entryway. Ashveldt came rushing into the room with more men, and the

226

wolves that remained were quickly dispatched by the expert sword work of their human foes. Once their work was done, Sigaberht sat down to catch his breath. He looked up at his son, who was now staring out a nearby window.

"What do you see?" the earl asked.

"Wolves, everywhere," Ashveldt replied.

Ashveldt turned away from the window, and cringed as he did.

"The men outside the hall are dead...torn to pieces. The wolves are encircling the hall. There are men with them...or...things that look like men."

Leif shook his head to himself.

"Caelum!" he exclaimed, praying to a god who would never answer. "To what purpose does your malice hold? Why must I live to see the fall of yet another home?"

Sigaberht understood Leif's pain, but he needed the ealdorman to hold himself together.

"Leif!" he yelled. "I know you have seen much, but your people need you! You need to be the man I made ealdorman! I need your strength!"

Leif looked up at his lord, and stood at full attention.

"I apologize, my lord...it was but a moment of weakness," he said.

Sigaberht waved the idea aside.

"There is no need to apologize. This is one more link in a chain of horrible events that have befallen you this past month. But, you have managed to elude death thus far, and I believe you will do so again."

Ashveldt spoke up next.

"Should I tell mother it looks like we will be staying here for the time being?" Ashveldt asked.

Sigaberht smiled grimly at his son.

"I might as well tell her myself," he said, and he then started off back into the main hall.

Cold gripped Radnor as he hurried the rest of the way back to Wulfgeld. He had needed to stop and rest several times already; trying to regain every bit of strength he could for the fight that awaited him back at the city. His rest had proved less helpful than he would have liked, but it was enough that he could still fight. As he began climbing a hill, he could see the lights of fires burning in the sky. Fear gripped at his heart as he worked his way up to the hill's precipice and the city itself came into view. He gasped at what he saw. There were indeed fires inside the city, and Radnor could hear panicked screaming as the ravenous wolves killed as they pleased. Despair tore at him as he saw that the gates were flung open, giving the monsters easy access to those who dwelt within. He found himself praying to Hymurr for some sort of help against this evil. Soon though, his warrior mind came back into focus. The shock started to wear off, and he began to think like himself again.

Thankfully, the wolves had left the paths outside the city wall unguarded; as they all had entered Wulfgeld to gorge themselves on the innocent. Still weaponless, Radnor made his way through the gates. Upon arriving, he found there were still a few wolves there to prevent anyone who tried to flee from leaving. Radnor spied the torn remains of many guards. A fierce fight had occurred there, as the bodies of many wolves and wolfmen were among the dead. Most of the wolves at the gate were too preoccupied with devouring the bodies of their victims to notice Radnor as he snuck upon them. Picking up a fallen sword from a dead guard, Radnor announced his presence with a vicious slash into the belly of one of the wolves.

The ferocious beast howled in agony and fell to the ground. The others turned to find out what had caused their pack mate to die so loudly, and saw the fearsome Veigarand, armor glistening in the light of the burning buildings. The wolves howled in unison, and ran to attack this new threat. Radnor picked up a second sword from the ground as they ran and danced among the beasts, turning and slashing. Death surrounded him as the wolves fell one by one to his deadly blades. For the first time that night, fear gripped the beasts as they watched their comrades fall to the fearsome warrior. Some of the wolves cowered in fear as their brethren fell. Radnor gave no mercy, and soon even the terrified wolves threw themselves into the fray, knowing that killing him was their only chance of survival, but their efforts were futile. By the time it was done, ten wolves joined the bodies in the snow, butchered by the ghost of the north. Radnor looked up from his bloody work and sought out the hill upon which the great hall stood. Figuring that Elena was most likely there, Radnor began following the road to his goal.

Leofric and his men waited quietly for the wolves to pass. They had taken refuge inside a darkened store front, hoping to stay hidden from the rampaging fiends. The wolves had already killed the store's original occupants, and the beasts were being so systematic about their hunt for humans that they hadn't come back for some time. However, Leofric knew it was only a matter of time before a scouting wolf investigated, and they would be found. He was hoping he could find a way to escape with Rolf before that happened.

Elena sat on the floor next to him. She was exasperated with Leofric's actions. She knew he was just trying to protect Rolf, but hiding would do no good in the long run. The only thing they could do was to find those witches and stop whatever they were doing before it was too late. She had tried to bring this to his attention before, but he wouldn't hear of it. Now that the wolves seemed to have moved on, she was about to bring it up again when Rolf spoke.

"Father," he said. "We need to do something. We need to stop them from killing everyone!"

Leofric looked at his son.

"I'm proud of your bravery, but this is no time for heroics. I wasn't there to keep you safe when Neugeld was destroyed. I will not allow any harm to come to you here."

Rolf grew angry with his father.

"You're right; you weren't there to keep me safe. So you can't understand that I will not go through this again. Wulfgeld should be my new home now...but I'll never get to let it be my home if we let it be destroyed like Neugeld. I will not lose another home to monsters."

With that, Rolf stood up and made his way for the door. Elena jumped up to take him by the shoulder, but Leofric had already stood.

"Wait!" he said.

Rolf turned and looked at his father.

"Very well son," he turned to his other men. "Is there anyone here who wishes to try to make their escape, and not hunt the witches? There is no shame in turning back. I know you all have families to find."

None stood or raised any objections. They all knew that the best way to save their families now was to face the enemy that lay before them.

"Then let us go forth," Leofric said.

He joined Rolf at the door. He placed his hand on his son's shoulder, proud of Rolf's bravery. Then Leofric stepped outside into the cold night wind. The snowfall had intensified, and visibility was poorer than before. Leofric took off in the only direction that made sense to him....the market square at the city center. He had a feeling the witches would be coordinating the wolves from there. The group stealthily exited the shop and headed down the streets now bathed in firelight from burning houses. There were a couple of close calls during which they were almost detected by wolf packs that also seemed to be heading for the city center. The wolves seemed in a hurry, almost panicked. Elena hoped that meant good news, but also dreaded that they may need to fight more wolves at their destination. After many twists and turns to avoid wolf packs, the group eventually arrived at the great market square.

The various carts and booths had been thrown aside as though by some great, unstoppable wind. There were wolves and wolfmen all across the square, pacing angrily as if they waited for something. Elena then spied the Hexverat at the very center of the market square. They stood in a circle, all facing inward towards some sort of altar. An eerie blood-red glow emanated from the surface of the altar. The light twisted and formed a sphere around the witches, forming a barrier that meant death to any who tried to approach it.

Even from where she was, Elena could hear the witches arguing.

"The werewolf was supposed to be here to protect us, not be sent after the weapon. You knew that," Bruna argued.

"What choice did I have?" Lenora sniped. "If he had been allowed to live, he could have jeopardized everything! And if your seduction had worked...he'd be the one doing the carnage!"

"I fear it may not matter," Hilda said. "The humans are winning too quickly. We need more carnage! Without the souls of dead humans, we simply do not have enough energy to build the weapon."

"There *must* be a way!" Lenora replied.

"Recall the werewolf!" exclaimed Hilda.

"I've already tried. I don't know why he isn't here yet...there was no way for Veigarand to kill him out there," Lenora said.

Elena's focus on their argument was shattered as wolves came out into the open. More wolf packs gradually gathered in the square and took up positions to guard the witches. They were afraid. Something was going wrong. Elena looked at Leofric, and saw that he was carefully studying the situation. There were close to thirty wolves and wolfmen in the square, with hundreds more fighting throughout the city that could be called back. But...the witches were in plain view...in the open...and Leofric saw an opportunity to end this once and for all, but there were just too many wolves. Leofric decided they needed to find more men if they wanted to assault the witches and have a hope of winning. Despite Rolf's protestations, the men withdrew from their positions near the square, and began hunting for signs of other soldiers that could help. They did not have to search long, as they quickly came upon a street littered with dead wolves, many whom had been pierced by arrows. One of the wolves lay twitching on the ground until Rolf ended its life with a stroke from his ax.

"Where did they go?" Rolf asked, pulling an arrow from the recently dead wolf, and holding it up into the light.

"Here!" came a cry from one of the buildings. A bowman stepped out of one of the darkened buildings, followed by a group of civilian men, women and soldiers.

The lead soldier shook hands with Leofric.

"It looks like you're in charge here, but I don't recognize you as one of the guards. Who are you?"

Leofric shook his head.

"My name is Leofric, and I am a father fighting to protect his son."

The soldier looked past Leofric at the band of elite men who stood with him.

"Uh-huh," the man replied.

"How many in your group?" Leofric asked.

"Close to thirty," the man said. "Not all of us are soldiers, but we are willing to fight, and die to defend Wulfgeld if need be."

Leofric looked up and down the group. Almost all of the civilians carried hunting bows or wood axes. The soldiers were all armed with swords, spears, axes, or shields. There were only a few soldiers among the group, but Leofric hoped they would be enough. Leofric then looked at the men in front of him.

"We believe we know how to put a stop to this, but we need your help. The witches who are behind this are all in the town square. They are guarded by many wolves. With your help, we may be able to end this insanity."

The leader of the improvised fighting force nodded in agreement.

"We will go with you!" he said enthusiastically.

Leofric smiled and was glad he had the men he needed to make a difference.

Sigaberht watched as his son paced impatiently up and down the throne room. Clearly Ashveldt was extremely tense about their current predicament. They were locked inside the hall with no way out that didn't involve getting torn to shreds by the hungry wolves outside the doors. Leif was out walking the halls, checking to make sure no wolves had made it inside the palace. They had not yet done so. Sigaberht stood next to his wife, and the two held hands as they weathered the attack. Erelda finally stopped her son.

"Son, sit with us awhile? There is nothing more we can do for now."

Ashveldt stopped in his tracks, and looked at his mother with an intense expression that reflected the fear she felt in her own heart. Sigaberht came over and clasped his son's shoulder.

"Save your strength my boy. There are monsters to slay, and we will slay them soon enough."

Ashveldt silently nodded, and took a seat with his mother. Sigaberht was about to join them, when the smell of smoke wafted into the throne room. The earl leaped to his feet, and even as he ran to confirm his fears, guards rushed through the doorway.

"*Fire!*" they yelled.

Sigaberht found himself staring at the doors into his palace, now burning. The fire was spreading into the wooden interior. Panicked soldiers scrambled to put out the flames, but it was no use. Sigaberht knew that fast action was needed, but there was something he needed to say first. He turned to his wife, and held her in a tight embrace.

"It seems you are to join me in battle, my love. Please, remember what I taught you, and stay out of the main fight as much as you can. I cannot have your life on my conscience."

Erelda looked up and smiled at her husband.

"Your concern is appreciated, but have more faith in your teaching. I have learned a great deal since we met."

Sigaberht chuckled slightly.

"Yes, you have. But this is different. These are not men we face tonight. Please, if anything were to happen to you, then my soul would surely perish."

Erelda kissed Sigaberht, then donned her helmet.

"I will stay in the back with a spear, but if you think for a moment that I won't hurl myself into the fray to protect you or Ashveldt...then you are sorely mistaken."

Sigaberht embraced his wife once more, and the two only parted once Leif and his patrol returned to the throne room.

"Is everyone here?" Sigaberht yelled.

Leif nodded, and looked to the burning door.

"What are we to do, sire?" Leif asked.

The ealdorman found himself in a very similar position to the one he was in when he left the temple of Caelum in Neugeld. There he had escaped the burning building through a back window. He was now unsure of how best to make their escape, since the hall was fully surrounded.

"If we stay here, they shall surely burn us out," Sigaberht said. "So instead, we must go out and meet them. We must see if we can punch through them, and perhaps find more soldiers to help us in the city."

Leif nodded. Sigaberht continued.

"Prepare the men. We will exit through our own burning door."

Sigaberht turned to face the door, weapon drawn. More and more of his soldiers lined up in formation to face the enemy that would flood inside to kill them as soon as it opened. Several of the soldiers were armed with bows, ready to fling death into the faces of their enemies. The company did not have to wait long, as the wooden beams holding the gate shut had been weakened by the flames.

Almost as though sensing that the fight was near, the wolfmen began to smash a ram into the door, its crashing sound echoing in the great hall. Sigaberht stood, sword drawn, firelight glittering off his armor.

Ashveldt stood by his side, spear ready to unleash death upon his foes. Sigaberht suddenly found that Erelda stood next to him, carrying another spear with which to fight. The earl smiled to himself. Thus was his wife's love for their family.

There was a final splintering crack, and the door burst open. Several wolfmen were the first to enter, followed by a swarm of slavering wolves. Arrows flew into the faces of the wolfmen, leaving several dead upon the threshold. The wolves ran under the hail of arrows, and sought to bite exposed legs under the shield wall. Axes, swords, and spears hacked at their foes as the men were driven back. More wolfmen entered the hall, lashing at the defender's faces with the points of their sharpened blades as they poured inside. Within moments, the shield wall was broken, and the fight was forced into yet another brutal melee. Sigaberht did everything he could to protect his son and his wife, while they brought death to their foes with well aimed spear thrusts. Sigaberht did not have time to check on Leif, who was expertly dueling two wolfmen at the same time. The earl was barely able to see Leif thrust his sword through the neck of the first wolfman before a blow aimed for his head was deftly turned aside by Ashveldt's spear. Sigaberht ducked deeper under his son's spear, and saw his wife's spear point thrust into the belly of one of the wolfmen. Sigaberht then finished the monster with a devastating blow from his sword.

"They seek to keep us inside!" Sigaberht yelled. "We must push them harder! Drive them back!"

Leif gave a few sharp commands. In a few moments the human warriors had reformed their lines, and were now driving a wedge into the torrent of wolves trying to hold them inside the burning building. The wolves fell back, seeing that the humans now had the upper hand. The monsters arranged their formation into a half circle in front of the exit, forming a kill pocket through which the humans would have to fight. Wolfmen with spears lined the entire formation, and Sigaberht knew they would have to break through this wall of death if they were to survive. His men advanced forcefully through the doorway, and out into the open ground. Leif noticed the spearmen were not well armored, nor were they supported by many wolfmen with shields. He turned to the commander of the archers, but it seemed the archers were already thinking the same thing. They began firing arrows from behind the shoulders of their comrades...and into the spearman's faces at point blank range. Several of the wolfmen fell immediately, and several more instinctively tried to find cover from the arrows that lashed out from behind Sigaberht's formation. Seeing their spears begin to fall under the arrows, a horde of wolves descended upon the band of men, ripping and tearing at anything they could reach.

The sheer weight of the mob pushed the shield wall apart again, and soon the humans found themselves once again locked in a chaotic brawl with the fearsome animals. Ashveldt and Leif fought back to back as the monsters closed in on them. They were gradually driven away from the others, and neither one could see how to get the attention of anyone else. Everyone was locked in deadly combat with the slavering beasts.

A fierce blow from Ashveldt's flank forced him to move away from the protection of Leif's shield, and Ashveldt soon found himself fighting two wolfmen at close range with just his spear to defend himself. He did what he could to protect himself against their axes, but several blows got through, pounding against his armor as he sought to gain leverage with his spear. Just as he had a line to strike back, a wolf joined the fray and tried to bite him on the leg. Ashveldt expertly turned his spear's motion into a thrust that killed the wolf instantly, but the deviation caused him to move his spear to where it was no longer protecting his head, and a monstrous blow struck his helmet. Dazed, but not dead, Ashveldt tried to maintain his balance. Before he could find his footing again he was struck with a second blow. The prince fell to the ground, the world spinning. His foes stood over him...ready for the kill. Ashveldt groped for his dagger, hoping to die fighting.

Suddenly, a spear blade slashed through the head of one of his assailants from behind! Ashveldt blinked, and saw his mother locked in combat with his second attacker. He tried to sit up...to help her...but every muscle seemed to hold him down. Erelda was holding her own with the wolfman. She had been training for the day she would have to defend her son from Piarin's men...and there seemed little difference to her when fighting these monsters. The foe before her was very strong...but she was well trained in neutralizing an enemy's strength when fighting with blades. She danced in the firelight as her foe desperately sought to destroy her. Seeing an opening, Erelda swung at her foe's leg, and her blade bit deep into the muscle. Her foe crumpled to the ground with an agonizing scream. Before Erelda could finish off the monster, two wolves jumped on her from behind, knocking her into the cold snow. More wolves joined the fray, and Ashveldt could only scream as he saw them find the openings in her armor and begin to tear at her legs and throat.

Through rage and sheer force of will, Ashveldt suddenly leapt upon the wolves with a fallen ax. Two wolves fell before the others noticed him...but the rage of Erelda's son was too much for them, and all of them were dead in mere moments. Ashveldt then looked upon his mother...and wept. Her screams had ceased, and her eyes were lifeless.

Ashveldt felt a stillness inside himself, as though time itself had stopped. The sound of battle seemed distant in his mind as he looked upon his mother's body. He heard Leif call his name, and Ashveldt came back to reality. He picked up a fallen shield from the ground, and turned to face the horde. A berserk rage gripped Ashveldt, and he leaped into the torrent of flesh and fangs, hacking and swinging wildly with his ax and shield. The wolves did not know what to make of this, and panicked as this mad man exceeded their ferocity with his own. Sigaberht saw Ashveldt's furious attack and leaped to join him in the fray, protecting his son from those that still assaulted him. Their foes began to retreat and regather further back down the hill. Sigaberht and Leif had to physically hold Ashveldt back from following them...his cries of rage echoing against the cold air of the night.

Once the last wolf had been killed, Sigaberht then saw what had become of his wife. Grief stricken, he threw down his weapons and sprinted to her body. The anguished husband took her into his arms and cradled her tightly, begging Caelum for help. He received no answer. There was no beacon of light to descend upon them, no deliverance from this evil. She was just...dead. Soldiers tried to gather to see what had happened, but Leif held them back to allow their lord the space he needed. Sigaberht knew they were watching, and kept his tears silent as he wept for his dead soul mate. Everything seemed to be still for Sigaberht, even as snow whipped into his eyes. After a few moments, time seemed to move again for him as he remembered that the battle was not yet over. He finally rose to his feet and came to his son, whose tears left streaks across his dirt covered face. Sigaberht embraced him, and the two felt their sorrow become one.

"I'm sorry...I'm sorry…" Ashveldt started.

Sigaberht squeezed his son tighter, holding him closer than he had even when Ashveldt was a baby.

"I love you, my son," Sigaberht said.

There was a moment's pause as the two embraced.

"My lord," Leif interrupted. "The wolves are advancing for another attack."

Sigaberht nodded. Father and son loosened their embrace, and the two men separated. Sigaberht then choked down his final tears and called his men to him.

"The lady Erelda...has…" he stammered, trying to find the words. After a moment more, he found the rage he needed to push forward. "She has been slain. By the foul beasts that lay before us. Now is not the time for tears! Our enemies will swarm and devour all if we do not destroy them now! Oh, no, now is not the time for tears! Now is the time for vengeance!"

There was a cry from the soldiers as Sigaberht finished speaking. Leif began to drum upon his shield with the flat of his sword, and soon the other men joined him. Fear filled the hearts of the wolves as they saw the wrath of the men that stood before them. These were not the simple peasants the wolves had been feasting upon in the houses below. These were the fighting men of Wulfgeld. They would fight to the last man, and take as many wolves as they could with them. Despite their fear, the wolves climbed the hill, set in their grim purpose to destroy every man, woman, and child arrayed before them in the carnage of the city. Unbeknownst to the wolves, there were close to a hundred fighting men making their way up the hill behind them, coming to the aid of their lord. Soon, their battle would begin anew, and the wolves would learn of the wrath of men.

Chapter 22

Wasting no time, Radnor pushed deeper into the city. Bodies lay strewn in the streets, torn to pieces. Only the wolves' insatiable desire to kill kept them from devouring the prey they had already slain. He moved through the streets, searching for Elena. He hoped beyond hope that Elena would not be among the bodies he found. He happened upon a pair of wolves who were pacing around the bodies of other wolves in the streets. It seemed they were mourning their dead. Radnor took no pity upon them as he slaughtered them before they knew he was there. Up the hill he walked, the sounds of battle ringing in his ears as he went. Evidently, Sigaberht's warriors had moved up the hill from behind the wolves and unleashed a deadly assault. Spent arrows lay scattered throughout the battlefield, as archers had unleashed fire upon packs of wolves climbing the winding, ramping streets. The archers themselves were gone, probably having advanced up the hill. Radnor continued climbing as the sounds of battle grew closer and more intense.

He eventually found a great battle being fought just outside Sigaberht's hall. He spotted Leif just outside the door, and Sigaberht himself was caught up in the fray, fighting with as much ferocity as the wolves themselves. Radnor smiled to himself, feeling glad Sigaberht put his money where his mouth was on the battlefield. There were now close to a hundred warriors with Sigaberht.

Finally, the ghost of the north finished climbing the hill, cutting down wolves as he went. None of the canine carnivores expected yet another enemy to join the fray, and Radnor killed four of them before the others noticed him. The wolves turned to face him, but he did not care. His assault was relentless as he struck with both swords, killing more than one at a time. The wolfmen in the group abandoned their assault on Leif and Sigaberht to face Radnor. A spear point leaped towards Radnor's face, but he cast it aside with one sword, and gutted the spearman with the other. A wolf leaped at him from the right, but Radnor deftly stepped aside, allowing it to sail past him. As the beast landed and turned, Radnor was already upon it, cutting its head off in a single stroke. Two more wolves leapt at him, and he was able to kill the one, but the other landed clear on his shoulder. Radnor was thankful for his armor, as the beast could not get a hold of him with its fangs. Radnor shook the beast off quickly. He delivered a rib crushing stomp into the wolf's body as it fell, killing it almost instantly. More and more of them began to face him, and Radnor soon realized he was severely outnumbered. A few seconds later, he found himself running backwards to avoid swords, axes, and biting fangs as they pressed him. Just as it seemed that the wolves might overwhelm him, Sigaberht, Leif, and their soldiers smashed against the wolves from behind. The wolves and wolfmen quickly found themselves surrounded, and their strength withered before the fury of man. Axes, spears, and swords pierced them from all directions, and one by one, the monsters were slaughtered. When all of the wolves attacking the burning hall were slain, Leif came over to a breathless Radnor, and forgetting his hatred in the heat of the moment, clasped him on the shoulder.

"Veigarand!" he shouted. "I thought you might not make it! What happened out there?"

Radnor held up his hand for Leif to wait a moment. He was out of breath, and what energy he had regained before entering the city was close to being gone. Exhaustion was beginning to take him, and he needed to stop and breathe for a moment. Leif took the message, and decided to give Radnor the time he needed. The ealdorman waved his arm towards his men for water, and once he was handed a canteen, Leif handed it to Radnor, who took it gladly, and quickly gulped it down. When he was done, he finally answered Leif's question.

"Lenora expected me. All three of them are in on this," Radnor said.

"We found that out," Leif replied. "The other two killed their guards and escaped...we're still not sure how."

Radnor swore a curse that Leif hoped his men didn't hear.

"Do you know how they got in the walls?" Radnor asked.

"As near as we can guess, the wolfmen were sent in before we locked the city down. Shortly after sundown, they ambushed the gate guards in a coordinated attack and opened the gates. After that, this terrible horde rushed in. It's been hell, Veigarand. These things are relentless in their assault, and utterly ruthless. We hadn't been able to make it past this point until you showed up. The only reason we survived is because of the reinforcements that came from the city center. How is it down there?"

Radnor shook his head.

"It's bad. But not all hope is lost. Is Elena here? I must find her!"

Leif shook his head.

"No. She is with Leofric. He was supposed to find a safe place for her, but I haven't seen them since they left the hall to regroup with the rest of his men."

"His men?" Radnor asked.

Leif sighed.

"Now is not the time. Let's just say he is more than a trader."

Radnor stood up. Every muscle in his body ached in protest, but he did not care.

"We need to find Elena," Radnor said, expecting argument from Leif.

Instead, Leif nodded.

"I agree. She may be the key to ending all of this."

Radnor gave the ealdorman a confused look. Leif motioned for Radnor to follow him.

"Now is not the time; I believe we will move out soon," he said.

"Where is the earl?" Radnor asked.

"He is...grieving," Leif said.

Before Leif could continue, there was a shout among the men. Ashveldt stepped forward with the other soldiers. The grieving prince gave Radnor a nod, and Radnor's heart fell as he saw that the young prince carried Erelda's body. Every warrior present stopped what they were doing and held a mournful vigil as Ashveldt joined his father. Together, they placed her body in the burning hall, turning Erelda's home into her funeral pyre. Father and son then exited the hall, and stared into the blaze, grief consuming them both. After a moment more, the pair wiped away their tears, and prepared for the battle that was to come.

Sigaberht gave the order for the men to move out. Radnor moved up to the front of the group, and began to lead them through the carnage. Progress was slow. The group had to tread carefully over the piles of corpses that carpeted the streets. Sigaberht shook his head as they came to the bottom of the hill. Sadness took him as he saw the torn up remains of his citizens, guards, and the wolves that had attacked them.

"Veigarand...where do you think those whores will be right now?" Sigaberht asked.

Radnor stopped to think for a moment.

"Probably in the center of the city. Their goal is to collect as much energy from the carnage as possible...they are trying to harness chaos to make a weapon to fight what they believe is an even greater evil than what they have wrought here."

"An even greater evil?" Ashveldt said. "I can hardly imagine it."

Radnor nearly agreed with him.

"I think they're telling the truth," Radnor said.

Leif scoffed at him.

"What in Caelum's name makes you think that?" Leif asked.

Radnor thought to the vision Ashrahan had shown him, the horrible black scars in creation that led to chaos...and the dread god that had been cast into one of those pits. He then chose his words carefully, still not wanting to reveal the source of his information.

"I know from my journeys that places and enemies like what Lenora described to me do exist," Radnor said.

Ashveldt was next to weigh in.

"Or, it's possible that the witches believe they are telling the truth, in their madness."

"Well spoken, my son," Sigaberht said.

Before anyone could press Radnor for more details, a horde of wolfmen leaped from the nearby buildings, surrounding the company of men! Anger surged in Radnor's heart. These beasts were yet another obstacle to him finding Elena. Time stood still as both sides sized each other up. No one was willing to make the first move, not even the wolves. No one that is, except Radnor. He saw that one of the wolfmen was carrying a large, two handed ax. It looked crudely made, but Radnor decided he wanted it. Without hesitation, Radnor launched himself at the wolfman, and cut his foe down before the others could react. Taking Radnor's cue, Leif followed him and prevented any of the other wolfmen from hitting Radnor in the back as he moved. Radnor quickly grabbed the ax and unleashed a torrent of powerful blows that sent the wolfmen scattering. One of his foes did not move away in time, and was cut in half by the force of Radnor's fury. Leif found himself having to back away from the northman as Radnor's swings swept around in wide arcs, scattering all who stood too close. Leif decided it was best to leave Radnor to his side of the fight alone, and went to help Sigaberht. At the other side of the street, Sigaberht and his men were locked in a violent brawl against the wolfmen. The ferocity of the fighting was unparalleled, as man and beast fought tooth and nail to kill each other. The humans were outnumbered, but the wolves were untrained and unprepared for the sheer force of violence the humans had mustered. Fully half of the wolfmen tried to blow past Sigaberht's men and aid their fellows fighting Radnor, but were unable to advance as Sigaberht's soldiers gave them no quarter.

Two wolfmen tried to jump on Radnor simultaneously, swinging their swords wildly. Radnor threw a blow that sent both enemy blades clanging to the ground, before turning the great-axe along a tight arc that allowed him to cut the head of the lead wolfman clean off. The second wolfman tried to grab the weapon in Radnor's hands, but the northern warrior sent a hard kick against the creature's knee that sent it sprawling to the ground. The monster had no time to save its own life before Radnor's blade split its head open. Radnor looked up from his fight to see that other wolfmen had begun to back away from him in fear. Radnor grinned to himself, finding a savage satisfaction in his work. The demigod

240

danced among the devils, slashing and striking them down wherever they stood. Wherever a wolfman tried to attack him, the foe was met with either the blade or the haft of the great-ax Radnor wielded. In response, several of the wolfmen formed a shield wall, forcing Radnor to back away.

Leif turned from having just killed another beast, and saw that Radnor needed help. The strong ealdorman got the attention of Ashveldt, and the two men joined Radnor on his side of the fight. Ashveldt had only his spear, but he could make good use of it in a fight like this. As the wolfmen tried to attack them, Leif was able to protect the group with his shield, twisting and turning to deflect the enemy attacks. Ashveldt probed at openings with his spear, and Radnor took advantage of any hesitation by the wolves to bring the great-ax down on the enemy shields with all his might. The wolves' wooden shields splintered and broke under the force of Radnor's blows, and Ashveldt's spear was always ready to thrust into a newly formed opening. Within a matter of moments, all of the wolfmen that had formed the shield wall lay dead in the street. On the other side, Sigaberht and his men were locked in a fierce battle, fighting chest to chest against their foes. Sigaberht and two other men were working together as a kill squad. They looked to help any men they could, attacking wolfmen from behind wherever possible. The fighting felt like it dragged on forever, but it was actually over in a few short, bloody minutes. By the time the enemy had all been killed, seven more of Sigaberht's men lay dead. The earl shook his head in sadness.

Ashveldt quickly broke him from his melancholy.

"Father...we must go. We must end the witches before it is too late."

"Your words are sound, but I would speak before we continue," Sigaberht said.

The earl choked down several tears, and turned to face his men.

"We stand here...on the precipice of destruction. Never before have we faced an enemy so cruel, so relentless, so filled with reckless hate as the one we face now. But they do not know us! They think they are strong! These monsters from the darkness think they have beaten us! *They have not!*" Sigaberht shouted.

The warriors of Wulfgeld found themselves whipped into a frenzy and ready for blood as Sigaberht continued his speech.

"Tonight, these monsters will see why their kind cowers in fear before us! Our fury shall be told of in song unlike any other told by men!"

The earl took a moment to breathe, and looked at Radnor.

"We have with us a very powerful ally..." Sigaberht gestured to Radnor.

"Veigarand...the ghost of the north fights by our side!"

There were several murmurs from Sigaberht's men, as they had no idea who Radnor was until now.

"These monsters attack us with all of the hate they can muster...but you all know the tales of Veigarand...and the fire of his wrath shall burn our enemies to cinders before us!"

Radnor raised his ax in solidarity with the grieving earl. As the warriors regrouped to continue their march, Radnor spoke to Sigaberht.

"Your grace. I have a strange request to make of you. There is a werewolf among the enemy, and I fear it may be at the square when we arrive."

Sigaberht's eyes widened in fear.

"How do you know this?" he asked.

"We fought in the woods. I had no weapons that could damage him, and was forced to lose him in the forest."

"It's a miracle you're alive at all! What would you ask of me?" Sigaberht said.

"I need a weapon made of silver to defeat the beast. I still do not possess any such weapon. But...you do," Radnor said, looking at Sigaberht's arm.

Sigaberht blanched at first, shocked at what Radnor was suggesting. Then the necessity of what Radnor required became apparent to him, and he relented.

"Just don't break it," Sigaberht said.

After a few short moments, the warriors were on their way again. Their goal was the most likely place the witches would be performing their dreaded, unholy ritual...the city center.

Chapter 23

Leofric and his men took up positions in the streets and alleys surrounding the city square, their grim purpose in the forefront of their minds. There were close to fifty men in the group now, working in squads of five or six to create a wide front on one side for their fight with the wolves. The men were still outnumbered two to one, but Leofric felt that they were running out of time. He believed that they had to attack now or risk losing everything. He hoped their numbers would be enough to allow his plan to succeed. He had discussed the matter with Elena and his other soldiers, and they had all agreed it was the best course of action.

He and the men would launch a direct assault on the wolves guarding the witches. They would drive into the enemy with great force from one side. The goal was to draw wolves away from the far side of the square and leave that side exposed enough for Elena and a few bodyguards to make their way to the witches. He hoped that Elena could get close enough to use whatever power she had to break the shield protecting the witches while they performed their ghastly ritual. Leofric knew his plan was a long shot, with too many unknowns to be sure it would work, but time was running out. The red light emanating from the altar had grown stronger, and more otherworldly hues were beginning to show. Greens, magentas, and colors never before seen by a human eye pulsated across the snow covered buildings.

Leofric looked to his son, and held him in a close embrace. Rolf returned the embrace, and readied his short ax for battle. Leofric realized Rolf didn't have a shield. With no shields to spare, Leofric gave his own shield to his son, speaking as he did.

"Now remember, you have no armor. You must take caution and stay behind me. I need you to watch my back, understand? No heroics."

Rolf nodded to his father, ready to fight and die for him if he must. Leofric knew this of his son, and wished he didn't have to put Rolf in this position. The elder warrior stopped his thoughts for a moment. He didn't put Rolf in this position...the witches did. The false healers were to blame for this.

Leofric brandished his sword, and let out a great cry, signaling the start of the attack. The wolves and wolfmen standing guard were caught by surprise as a mob of humans charged headlong at them. The wolves eagerly met their challenge, and a brutal brawl started. Man clashed against beast, and blood ran heavy across the snow covered streets. Leofric fought with great ferocity, severing the head of a wolf at every sword stroke. Rolf was able to kill a few wolves that tried to get behind them. Arrows hissed through the air from windows and found their marks on the unarmored faces of the wolfmen trying to form an organized line. More of the wolves from the opposite side of the square rushed to join the fray. Leofric's plan was working!

Elena stood and watched from the shadows as the assault began. She could see the witches look up from their work with panic, but couldn't make out what they were saying to each other. More and more wolves from Elena's side of the square made their way over to join the fight. After only a minute or two, her entire side of the courtyard was deserted...or so she thought. Just as she and her bodyguard were about to make their way onto the battlefield, another pack of wolves came from one of the nearby buildings. Then another came...and another...and then a band of wolfmen soldiers...and then another pack. More and more arrived on the scene, and it seemed that every one of the monsters that assaulted the city was now here in the square. Finally, a single, massive wolf came into view. It was unlike anything Elena had ever seen. It was larger and stronger than anything else on the battlefield. It looked like it could tear men in half like paper. What Elena did not know was that this abomination was Halfdan. He had escaped from his foes in the forest, and now arrived to slay as many people as his monstrous mind pleased. There was nothing Elena or anyone else could do but watch as the monsters poured into the square.

Rolf heard panicked shouts from the men as he fought. It was only then that he noticed the torrential onslaught of wolves that was now descending upon him. Where there had been only fifty wolves remaining, there were now several hundred in the square. Men fled in terror as the great werewolf descended upon them. Arrows bounced harmlessly off his invulnerable exterior, and he tore through all men who stood before him with ease. The force of the wolves' assault became overwhelming, and Rolf was now struggling to defend himself. There were so many wolves around them that he had been driven away from his father. Rolf had cried out as he was forced back, but his father could not come to his aid. Rolf was on his own.

Back and back he stepped as two wolves harassed and assaulted his guard. He found himself backed up against the house from where the archers were firing. He was able to keep the wolves back, but he wasn't able to mount a proper offense with which to kill them. On and on their assaults went, wearing him down more and more. He tried to remember Radnor's training, but there just hadn't been enough time to learn it properly. He knew he needed to move, but move where? Every route he had was blocked by glistening fangs.

Suddenly, a dagger came from a window above, and struck one of the wolves directly in the back. It yowled in pain, and its partner hesitated for a moment. This gave Rolf the opening he needed, and he lashed out with the ax at the uninjured wolf's face. His blade connected, and the beast lay dead on the ground. Rolf struggled to get the ax free as the wounded wolf prepared to pounce on him. Just then, one of the archers leaped from the window and landed directly on the wolf. Without missing a beat, the man yanked out the dagger from its back, and plunged the blade into the wolf's breast. The wolf snapped its head around, and bit deeply into the man's throat. The man continued to fight, and again and again he struck until the wolf was dead. Rolf ran forward to try to help his rescuer, but it was no use...the man was dead. A second archer jumped down to check on them.

"Are you all right?" the man asked.

He received no reply, for when Rolf looked up onto the battle before him; his worst nightmare was coming true right before his eyes. He saw his father locked in combat with three wolves. One had grabbed his arm in its fangs and tried to drag him down. Leofric stood his ground, and killed another wolf that had just bitten onto his leg. Spinning suddenly, Leofric whipped his arm around and the wolf flew off, taking chunks of flesh with it. His left hand useless, Leofric let it hang at his side as he continued to fight the third wolf. Blood was rushing from his wounds, and Leofric quickly found that he was having trouble standing upright. The third wolf leaped for his throat, and steel flashed as Leofric's blade arced towards the monster. He lost his balance as he swung, causing the blade to miss his foe. The wolf fell upon him, tearing at his throat. Leofric's thoughts turned to his son in his final moments. Rolf screamed and started to run for his father. The sturdy hands of the archer were the only thing that held him back from running to his death. Rolf screamed and screamed, but it was no use. The battle was lost.

Arrows suddenly whistled through the air, piercing wolves from their flanks. They came from the wrong side for them to have been shot by Leofric's archers. Rolf turned to see where this help was coming from, and saw a great band of men advancing into the square from the palace road. At the front he saw Sigaberht, sword and shield in hand. Rolf saw Ashveldt, wielding a blood soaked spear. Leif was there as well, covering Ashveldt with his mighty shield as the wolves turned to face their new foes. Rolf also saw Radnor...wielding a great-ax, ready to deal arcing death to all that opposed him.

The wolves hurled themselves at this new threat, and were slaughtered. The tides of the battle turned once again, and the wolves found themselves on the back foot. They had under estimated the fury of the men they had come to gorge themselves upon. There were cheers as Radnor tore his way through the sea of battle, often killing two wolves at once as he danced among them as an icon of death.

Halfdan then joined the fight, picking up a man in his claws and tearing him in half before meeting Radnor on the field once again. Radnor saw the great werewolf and prepared for his ferocious foe. The monster leaped directly at him, but Radnor was able to deftly step aside and evade its reaching claws. Halfdan landed heavily, and turned to find Radnor now standing almost within range to bite...but then Radnor did something the werewolf did not expect. Silver flashed in Radnor's hand, and he struck the werewolf with great force. The weapon was Sigaberht's silver oath ring! The force of the blow was so great it sent the werewolf reeling to the ground. Halfdan yowled in unexpected pain from the blow. A second blow came upon its head, and a third crashed into him. The werewolf backed away from Radnor as fast as it could. As it did, it saw the source of Radnor's ability to inflict harm. That was what Halfdan needed to defeat. But there was no time, Radnor resumed his assault, and pummeled the werewolf again and again. Every time the witches' champion tried to fight back, he was met with another shocking blow from the demigod. Other wolves tried to join the fray, but Leif and other men did all they could to give Radnor the space he needed to finish his work.

The witches looked on in terror. Their army of wolves was dissolving before their eyes, and even the werewolf was now being beaten to death by Veigarand. They did not know what to do.

"No...no..." Hilda cried out.

"It's not done! We need more death!" Bruna answered.

"Sisters, we cannot fail. We have sacrificed too much to turn back now!" Hilda said.

"It does not matter. The wolves...they needed to kill more if we were to make this work. But Sigaberht's army—" Bruna started to answer.

"And Veigarand," Hilda interjected. "Veigarand has caused this failure. He has doomed us all."

Silence fell between the panicked witches for a moment, before Lenora spoke with a fearsome resolve.

"No he hasn't," Lenora said.

The other witches looked to their sister to continue.

"The werewolf...release him from his bondage tonight. He cannot help us anymore," Lenora ordered.

"But..." stammered Hilda.

"Just do it!" Lenora shouted.

Hilda reached into one of her pockets for a gaulderen. This one looked to be made of thin bone, which Hilda snapped in her hand. A green light emanated from where the bone snapped, and the moon returned to its natural, crescent setting in the sky.

"Is it done?" Lenora asked.

"Yes," Hilda said.

"Good," Lenora said. She then drew a dagger from deep inside her cloak.

"We have only one more opportunity to complete our work. Bruna, take everything from me, you will need it."

Sensing their sister's purpose too late, Hilda and Bruna could only watch as Lenora slashed her own throat with the dagger, and collapsed upon the altar.

"No!" Hilda cried out as she watched her sister die.

Bruna worked to fulfill her sister' dying wish, and began to gather all of the energy released by her suicide. Once the energy was gathered, the two surviving witches used it to finally finish their dreaded incantation. The altar upon which they worked exploded in a beam of red light. Space seemed to tear and warp around it, and Lenora's body shrank and withered as flesh and blood were sucked into the void. There was a deafening roar as if some unearthly and unholy presence had become enraged. The fighting in the courtyard ceased. Even the wolves stopped to look upon the witches in wonder and fear. Arrows pinged off of the witches' barrier in a vain attempt to break through, but they were unable to do so. Gradually the light and daemonic roar gradually faded away, and the witches could be seen weeping over the loss of their sister. The surviving wolves fled in panicked terror as men returned to the slaughter. Radnor stood over a now human and delirious Halfdan, whose only memory of the night's events was that the change had happened...again.

The enraged soldiers started to march on the witches, surrounding their barrier. The surviving Hexverat scrambled to their feet, and Hilda drew a gaulderen from her dress. Bruna looked defiantly at the sea of men before her, and lifted the result of their creation...a sword. Its black blade glowed faintly with an unholy light few men could stand to look at directly...except Radnor, who forced himself to lock his eyes on the new threat. Studying the weapon before him, the edge looked to be like any other sword. However, there seemed to be a familiar, vine like shape twisting along the blade's fuller. Radnor blinked again as he watched the sword. The twisting seemed to stop for a moment, but then resumed its awful motion. It was like some trick of the eye that never ended. Radnor did not know what the sword was capable of, but he knew it could not be good.

A stalemate emerged in that corpse filled courtyard. The humans wished nothing more than to destroy the witches that stood before them, but the barrier was quite impenetrable to them, even Radnor. Many were also afraid of the sword...that sword born from chaos. However, one person overcame their fear of the witches and the dreaded blade. Elena stepped through the crowd of men with stalwart resolve. Several of Sigaberht's soldiers tried to block her path, thinking she was a traumatized civilian, but Sigaberht waved them off. Elena slowly approached the witches' barrier, and Radnor saw what she meant to do. Before he could raise any objections to her touching the shield, Hilda raised her gaulderen high above her head.

"If she takes one step closer, we will leave your city in ashes!" she cried out, gesturing with the gaulderen.

Elena stopped in her tracks, unsure of what to do. Radnor was also unsure, not fully aware of Elena's ability to defend against chaos.

Sigaberht laughed. He bellowed his laughter in a way that told all of the people of Wulfgeld of his grief, and they were afraid.

"If you could do such a thing, you would have destroyed us already. And would you really destroy yourselves so soon after achieving your prize? I think not."

Bruna and Hilda looked to each other, as now they were unsure of what to do. Radnor felt like this was not part of their plan, and that the witches themselves really were at a loss for how to continue.

After a moment's hesitation, Bruna answered Sigaberht's reply.

"You are correct, Earl...if our goal had been to utterly destroy you, we would have. It was not, and is still not. Our terrible purpose is this...we have a great enemy to destroy. This enemy threatens not only your city, but the entirety of creation. He seeks to unleash chaos upon this world..."

"Which you already have done!" Sigaberht interrupted.

Bruna winced at the truth in Sigaberht's accusation.

"You are correct. My sisters and I thought on our actions tonight at great length. We tried to destroy the enemy when we first encountered him, but he was impervious to every attack we could muster. We were forced to flee, and we knew that the only weapon we could find that can harm the being we must destroy is a weapon made of chaos. We had to learn...we had to learn what needed to be done. When we did...we did a little evil...to serve a greater good."

"A *little* evil?" Sigaberht shouted.

248

"Hundreds of my citizens have been slain! Children...whole families." Sigaberht stopped for a moment to choke down his rage, and then spoke again.

"My wife is dead! You killed her! There can be no forgiveness for the horrors you have unleashed upon us!"

Bruna and Hilda stood and watched Sigaberht, and could not help but feel sorrow for his loss. Their only consolation was that they believed this sword was worth the cost. Silence again fell over the crowd as both sides considered their options. The snowfall finally ceased, and even the wind seemed to still itself. Hilda spoke again.

"I know you have no reason to trust us, but you must let us leave. We must accomplish our mission, or else all is lost."

Sigaberht laughed again.

"Do you think I would let you leave with that sword in your possession? How much of a fool do you think I am?"

The witches consulted for a moment, then Hilda answered Sigaberht.

"The sword will not be in our possession. We would give it to one who is worthy of wielding its power. We would give it to Veigarand, who stands before you now on the field of battle. He will wield the sword for us against this dreaded foe."

All eyes turned to Radnor. Some held looks of shock, and others were filled with suspicion. Could it be that this had all been a ploy? Could Radnor have been in on it the whole time? These were the thoughts that ran through the minds of many of the men standing there. They went briefly through Sigaberht's mind, but he quickly rejected them. Leif also quickly rejected those thoughts. However he felt about Radnor, he knew this wasn't a path Radnor would choose. Rolf felt the same way Leif did, and the idea never even crossed Elena's mind.

Radnor looked to Sigaberht, also now unsure of what to do. Bruna spoke again.

"If you do not let us do this, then we will all die here together. It does not matter to us, for if you do not let us go, the whole world will be destroyed anyway. I know you must think we aim to deceive you, but this is not so. Do you think our sister would have slit her own throat to finish the sword if we were doing this just for power?"

The humans all looked upon the withered corpse of Lenora, and saw that Bruna was speaking the truth. Sigaberht weighed his options in his mind. It was a gamble whether or not Elena could break the barrier. If she did, Sigaberht could only hope that his people could kill the witches before they unleashed the threatened power of that gaulderen upon them. However, if they failed...it could mean that the insane witches would kill

249

everyone there. And what if the Hexverat were telling the truth? What if there was some evil greater than them they needed to destroy? Sigaberht was having trouble making up his mind, when Ashveldt spoke to him.

"Father, we cannot risk attacking. These men died defending their families. Mother died protecting me. We can't throw away her sacrifice on such a risk."

Sigaberht nodded.

"I thank you my son. You have given me the wisdom I needed."

Sigaberht then addressed the witches.

"You shall leave Wulfgeld unharmed."

Shocked protests erupted from the soldiers and townspeople. Sigaberht roughly raised his hand to quiet the crowd, and once silence was achieved, he continued.

"But only to complete your mission. Veigarand will go with you, alongside twenty volunteers from my army to assure that you return here to face judgment for what you have done tonight."

The witches looked to each other, and then back to Sigaberht.

"We have one more demand," Hilda said.

The witch then turned and pointed to Elena.

"This one comes with us as well."

"No!" Radnor bellowed. "I will not allow it!"

Hilda looked to Radnor, and addressed him directly.

"Her power is strong, greater than any of ours. If we are to prevail, I believe the woman's presence will greatly contribute."

Elena came over to where Radnor stood. Only her presence was able to draw Radnor's glare away from his enemy. Elena took him gently by the arm, feeling the cold steel rings of his armor against her palm.

"It's okay. I will go with you. Do you remember what happened in the tower, with the vines?" Elena asked.

Radnor nodded.

"After we left, we were attacked by some...thing. I destroyed it just by touching the thing and thinking on its destruction. I have, some sort of power...I don't understand it. I can do things...I don't know. But if I am ever to have a hope of understanding myself, then I need to go with them."

Radnor found himself filled with questions. *Was this possible? How had she attained this power?* He had seen the first incident with his own eyes and he trusted her word about the second, but Radnor was still having trouble believing that such a power to destroy chaos existed. After a few moments, Radnor nodded to Elena, and looked to the witches.

"Give me the sword," he said.

Bruna nodded to Hilda. Hilda withdrew a new gaulderen from her robe, and used it to lower the shield. There was a tense moment as Bruna strode towards Radnor. Everyone waited, ready to strike if a betrayal should arise. There was none, a low murmur swept the courtyard as Radnor took the sword from Bruna's hands. The hilt felt like any other sword hilt. After a moment though, he felt that it fit his hand perfectly. In fact, it seemed too perfect. Had it changed to better suit him?

Radnor turned and nodded to Sigaberht. The earl turned to face his men, and bellowed his question to the crowd.

"Who would go with them? What brave soul shall ensure that these witches are brought to jus—" Before Sigaberht could finish, he was interrupted.

"I will!" Rolf shouted, lifting his ax into the air. "I will fight alongside my friends, and I will be sure that these monsters return here for judgment."

Radnor sighed to himself. He recognized the look in Rolf's eye. Radnor had seen that look many times before...in a mirror. Rage and grief streaked across the boy's face. Revenge was what now drove Rolf's whole being.

Sigaberht looked at Rolf carefully.

"Normally, I would say no to such a request. But I recognize you. You are the son of my man Leofric. Where is he now?"

Rolf turned towards his father's body, still lying in the snow. He pointed with his ax, and then turned back to Sigaberht. The earl sighed, and spoke again.

"You wish to fight in his stead. It seems you already have done so. I accept. This boy is the first volunteer to face the evil ahead. Who else will go with him?"

Ashveldt stepped forward next.

"My mother was slain on this night. In my own way, I share in the grief of the son of Leofric. I will go with him, and share in his danger as well."

Before Sigaberht could respond, Leif stepped forward without hesitation.

"The heir cannot risk himself to such a mission. I will go to lead in his place."

Ashveldt started to object, Sigaberht overrode him.

"I am glad of you, my ealdorman. You will command this force in my name," Sigaberht said.

Other warriors of Wulfgeld quickly volunteered until the roster was full.

At the witches' prompting, they began gathering near the altar. Sigaberht motioned for Radnor to come join him where he was for a moment.

"Your mission is to discover if there is any legitimacy to what the witches claim. If there is, find it and destroy it. No matter what, once the job is done, you will bring them back here to me to stand trial."

Radnor nodded.

"If I cannot bring them back?" Radnor asked.

"Then they had better be dead already, if not by the hand of the enemy, then by yours. You must return to me when the task is done. Your word will be proof enough, for if you defy my order, you will die. Remember this."

Radnor nodded, knowing full well the power the black oath held over him. Not that it made much difference in this case. Radnor fully planned on killing the witches himself if the opportunity presented itself. Before Sigaberht could continue, Halfdan interrupted the conversation.

"My lord...I must beg a boon of you. I am not one of your soldiers, but I wish to join in the fight."

Sigaberht looked Halfdan up and down, and then recognized him.

"You are the werewolf whom Radnor defeated."

Halfdan nodded.

"Please know my lord that I was forced to take that form against my will. I never intended harm to you or any of your people. I would like a chance to redeem myself, by serving you."

Sigaberht looked back to Radnor.

"It seems you are not the only one here who seeks redemption. If Veigarand will have you, I will grant your request."

Radnor looked at Halfdan, and after a moment of hesitation, he shook Halfdan's hand.

"You owe me a new shield," Radnor said.

Halfdan smiled, and the two joined the others near the altar.

"How do you plan to get us to our objective?" Radnor asked.

"We have a portal ready in a gaulderen. We need only use it, and we will be within a short walk of our destination," Bruna said.

Elena came over to Radnor, and handed him his ring back.

"I believe this is yours," she said.

Radnor nodded, taking it back from her once again. Before he could say anything, Bruna spoke again.

"Is everyone prepared?" Bruna asked.

There was a grudging acknowledgment from the force assembled there. Elena took Radnor's hand in hers. There was a flash of light and the force was transported away.

Chapter 24

Darkness reigned supreme. It took Radnor a few moments to realize they had re-materialized, and that they were someplace very dark. A cool breeze grazed Radnor's face, contrasted by the warmth he felt in his hand...Elena's hand. Radnor started for his sword, but felt an arm gently press against his.

"Radnor!" whispered Elena.

"Look up!"

Radnor did as he was told, and found himself looking up at a sea of stars. The group was far from any human settlement...far enough that no firelight or chimney smoke rose to block the heavens. Radnor was too busy pondering the threat they faced to notice the beauty in that night sky the way Elena did. Some might say she was distracted, but that was not so. She was very aware of the danger they faced, but unlike others who saw only gloom in dark times, Elena tried to find the good. She shuddered as she gazed upon the stars, feeling tension leave her body as she took just a moment to admire something beautiful before she faced whatever hideous things lay ahead.

There was a murmur as more and more people collected themselves and realized they were in the middle of nowhere. A light appeared among the group. It was a small flame held aloft by Bruna. Hilda soon produced one of her own. Leif came over to them and demanded to know where they were.

"We are in the woods at the edge of the world," Hilda said.

"They have no name, for no mortal man has ever ventured here," Bruna added.

"You said 'no mortal man' has been here. Have other beings been here before?" Elena asked.

"Yes," Hilda said. "There was a race of beings that lived here, long before mankind walked this earth. We have also been here, and the being that we come to destroy is here."

"You still haven't told us exactly where it is we are going," Elena said.

"Or how far it is...or how it is defended," Leif interjected.

Hilda looked to Leif, and answered him.

"It is far enough away that we will be undetected as we sleep tonight. As for defenses, we cannot say, for we do not know. There is one foe we know we need to face...and he will be hard to kill. But there may be more evils inside."

"Inside what?" Elena pressed.

"We are going to a place...an ancient city. One that was inhabited by the first race placed upon this world to rule."

"First race to rule?" asked one of the men.

"Yes, we were not the first that the creators placed here. There were others...majestic beings that counted the creators as their friends."

"Are there walls we will have to mount?" Leif asked, focusing on the task at hand.

"There are not. The city was built an age before war was introduced to this world."

"And what happened to its inhabitants?" Elena asked.

"The inhabitants did not survive long *after* war was introduced to this world," Hilda answered.

Silence took the party for a moment as the implications of her words set in. After a few moments, Leif broke it.

"Shall we not advance to our objective?" Leif asked.

Bruna and Hilda both shook their heads.

"Not tonight. Your men are tired, and our enemy grows stronger at night. We must make our assault during the day. We are only a few miles from the city, and another mile from the old palace where we must go."

"About our enemy..." Radnor interjected. "What can you actually tell us about him?"

Everyone gathered around, as they all wished to know more of the threat they would face in the morning.

Bruna and Hilda looked at each other, unsure of how best to answer. Finally, Bruna spoke up.

"We do not know exactly who or what it is. Our best guess is that it's a Krigari or other being left behind after the wars of the old ones destroyed this place. Whatever the case, this being has been twisted by proximity to chaos, and now seeks to help it destroy the cosmos. As we have mentioned, our enemy is extremely powerful, and we will need to take every precaution when we face it. He uses chaos as a weapon in ways we do not fully understand, nor can predict."

Elena spoke next.

"You said he was corrupted by *proximity to chaos*. How is there proximity to chaos here?"

It was Hilda's turn to answer.

"The city where we must go is the site of a terrible wound in the world. The creators fought there with great vigor, and the world was damaged. There is a pit...or hole in the world where with but a little help, chaos would be allowed to pour through. That is all we know."

"What stops it from pouring through now?" Leif asked.

"We are unsure. We just hope that we can stop our enemy from breaking whatever holds chaos back."

There was a moment's pause as the group considered their problem. Leif finally spoke again.

"You say we will be safe here tonight?"

Hilda nodded. Leif turned to face his men. He paused as a realization struck him. Yet again, he was working with someone that had brought death and destruction upon his people. His blood started to boil with rage, but he reminded himself that as before, he needed to put his mission ahead of revenge. Taking a deep breath, he finally gave his orders.

"The witches say we will be safe here, so we will make camp here for the night."

Leif turned to his men and gave orders for them to find comfortable places to sleep. Leif divided the men into shifts for the watch. Upon Elena's insistence that Radnor be sure to get some sleep, he took the second watch. It did not take long for the sleepers to begin their slumber, as the men were exhausted after the long day of fighting. Leif patrolled the area as a part of the first watch. He found that the night was eerily silent when compared to the screams of battle he had heard mere hours before. He felt a strange sense of shock in the sudden contrast. This was not the first time he had felt this way after a battle, but it had never been this strong before. Leif did his rounds swiftly, checking on each of the men.

Halfdan approached him, and Leif spun as though threatened, leading Halfdan to raise his hands in submission.

"It is I...Leif. I wish to speak with you."

Leif looked at the giant man, sizing him up. There were many questions he had for the werewolf, and so he gestured for Halfdan to approach.

"What is it you wish to speak with me about?" Leif asked.

Halfdan took in a deep breath, setting himself up to speak.

"Radnor...is he...is he really who they say he is?"

"Veigarand?" Leif asked. "Absolutely."

"And the stories?"

"As true as the one we are a part of right now."

Halfdan shuddered.

"Then I should consider myself lucky to be alive," he said.

"Yes, you should," Leif said.

Halfdan blinked, taken slightly aback by what Leif's tone. The ealdorman drew his shoulders back, and spoke again.

"He was uncharacteristically merciful with you. I've seen him nearly twist a man's head off for less. I hope you are feeling better after your ordeal?"

Halfdan felt a pang of guilt strike his heart. He had to tell the truth.

"I...I do not think I will ever 'feel better', as you put it," Halfdan said.

"I think I know what you mean," Leif said, sighing before continuing. "My world changed after I met him. So much death...it just seems to follow him around. Trying to escape it seems...like trying to escape from a vicious undertow. Every time you think you're near the surface, it just pulls you right back under."

"That's not...that's not what I mean," Halfdan said, also pausing before continuing. "I've been caught in that undertow for far too long already."

"What do you mean?"

"Do you think my being in wolf form was just some curse the witches placed upon me tonight?"

Leif turned away for a moment and sighed.

"No, but I was hoping."

"Hope is a dangerous thing," Halfdan said.

Leif gave Halfdan a curious look, which Halfdan took as an invitation to elaborate.

"It drives you mad, making you travel across oceans and continents, searching for a cure. And after enough time, you stop hoping for a cure, and start merely hoping you won't kill anyone the next full moon. At least that hope is achievable...sometimes."

Leif grew angrier with Halfdan, but he kept it choked down for the moment.

"How long has it been for you?" Leif asked.

"Since I became a werewolf? I've forgotten the count of the years. I do still remember my village...my home. I remember my wife, Algretta."

Tears welled up in Halfdan's eyes as the image of his wife came to his mind.

"Did Radn...I mean Veigarand, tell you my full name?" Halfdan asked.

Leif shook his head.

"I go by Halfdan Jugback. People called me that after a man tried to kill me from behind with an ax, but the blade got stuck in the jug I had slung under my cloak. I found him in Wulfgeld...and I killed him in the street."

"When he tried to kill you, was this when you were...?" Leif asked.

"Yes. But only just after I had turned."

"Is that why he tried to kill you?"

"He and I loved the same woman, but she married me. Kirri was willing to abide by it, or so I thought. A wolf attacked our sheep. It attacked alone, but it was strong. I fended it off, but I was bitten. I did not yet know the curse had been laid upon me...until the next full moon, when I..."

Halfdan trailed off for a moment, and struggled to get himself to speak again. After choking down his tears, he finally managed it.

"I turned and killed my dear Algretta. After that, I was driven from my village, and Kirri tried to kill me as his parting gift."

"He was enraged that you killed the woman he loved," Leif said.

"No!" Halfdan said. "It was he who summoned the wolf! He brought this curse upon me!"

"How do you know this?"

"There could be no other!" Halfdan shouted.

Leif glared at Halfdan, seeing how desperate he was to blame everything on Kirri. The ealdorman became angry that Halfdan had come to Wulfgeld and put so many other people in danger to satisfy his need for what was probably an unjustified revenge.

"You should be more thankful to Veigarand than you know, Halfdan. For if it were I, you would have died in that courtyard," Leif spat.

Bruna heard the growing commotion and came over to them.

"Is everything all right?" she asked.

"Yes," Leif said, softening his tone. His eyes never left Halfdan. "We were having a heart to heart."

Bruna nodded, and turned to Halfdan, whom had fallen silent at Leif's rebuttal.

"You should sleep, Halfdan," she said.

"Stay away from me!" Halfdan shouted.

Bruna ignored Halfdan's statement, and turned to Leif.

"You should too, when your shift is over."

"Assuming I can trust that you won't slit my throat in my sleep," Leif said.

Bruna smiled to hide the sting of his words.

"Do not worry, Veigarand will keep you safe from us," she said.

The witch turned back to Halfdan.

"And you need sleep now. Your strength will be needed when the day breaks."

"I said, stay awa—"

Halfdan suddenly slumped to the side, losing his balance. Leif reflexively tried to catch him, but Halfdan's bulk was too much, and all Leif could do was help him fall without getting hurt. Leif glared up at Bruna.

"I suppose you think you're so clever, with your tricks. You're nothing but a selfish bitch!"

Bruna shrugged at the angry ealdorman, and wordlessly walked away.

Several hours passed, and then the guard changed. The witches joined the others in sleep. Leif and Radnor met to pass off leadership of the guard. During their meeting, Leif decided to tell Radnor Halfdan's tale of woe. Radnor took the information in thoughtfully. Halfdan had given up hope of lifting his curse, and had achieved his revenge on Kirri. Now he was a man without a purpose. Such a man could be extremely dangerous, werewolf or not. As Leif started to find a spot to lie down, he left Radnor with one final statement.

"Be sure you keep silver on you, Veigarand, I would hate for you two monsters to slay each other before your usefulness had ended."

Radnor continued with the patrol that Leif had established. Everything seemed normal, until a shrouded shape came into view. Radnor squinted at it at first, peering into the man shaped shadow. It took a step towards him, and Radnor drew his sword, the black blade writhing in the fire light.

"Nice to see you too," Hilda said.

Radnor looked at the witch. Her eyes gleamed with a voracious hunger. He did not sheathe his sword.

"Do you think that I would come to fight you, alone?" Hilda asked.

"Are you alone?" Radnor replied, his hand ready to slash at any moment.

"Yes. Even Bruna doesn't know I'm here," she said.

"Why are you here?" Radnor asked, still not sheathing his sword.

"I come here to make a final request. I am sure you must know that our seduction was...less than genuine. To control a mind such as yours takes certain spells which require intimate contact. That being said, while I cannot speak for Bruna, I was not just trying to manipulate you when I tried to seduce you. I wanted you to know that, and I wanted to see if, on the eve of battle, you would indulge my fantasy."

258

Without another word, her robe fell open, revealing her naked body.

"We are more similar to each other than to those mortals, you know," she said.

The witch took a single step towards Radnor, but he pointed his blade at her heart.

"You truly are mad," Radnor replied.

Hilda smiled again.

"Would you prefer it if we involved Bruna? I'm sure I could convince her to…"

Radnor now placed the point of his sword against her heart.

"What would happen to you if I gave just one more push?" Radnor asked.

Hilda's eyes widened slightly.

"Surely, you do not find me attractive?"

"My heart belongs to another," Radnor replied.

"I know it does," Hilda said, replacing her robes across her body.

"Then why do this?" Radnor asked, finally sheathing his sword.

Hilda scoffed at him.

"Why does anyone try for the impossible? Their yearning overcomes their senses," Hilda replied.

"Indeed."

"So tell me, Veigarand. What do you yearn for?"

"Revenge," he spat bitterly.

Hilda was taken slightly aback by his response, but adjusted her question.

"Let me rephrase. Whom do you yearn for?"

"You know who," Radnor replied.

"Say it," Hilda pressed.

There was a pause as Radnor was unable to admit the truth out loud. Finally, after what seemed like an eternity to him, he admitted it to himself. He did not know why he was admitting this to the mad witch, but it felt right to do so in this moment.

"Elena."

"Why do you not go to her then, on this night before battle?" Hilda asked, quizzically.

"Because she should not return my feelings," Radnor replied.

"And why not?"

"Why should she? We have known each other for so little a time…"

"What should that matter?" Hilda demanded.

Radnor stammered for a moment before answering her question.

"It is unnatural. I am drawn to her...like a moth to flame."

"And her to you, Veigarand."

Radnor turned his gaze away from the witch. He did not know why he was telling her any of this, but, here he was. A valve had been opened, and he did not have the energy to close it. After regaining himself slightly, Radnor faced Hilda again.

"Do not give me hope. I have naught to live for but vengeance."

"On whom, the Krigari? Your parents? Yourself?" Hilda pressed.

"I am a monster," Radnor replied, very matter-of-factly.

"And she may be also!" Hilda snapped back.

Radnor gave Hilda a puzzled look.

"I assume love has not blinded you so much you do not see her power?"

Radnor shrugged.

"Perhaps you cannot see it the way my sisters and I do. I have trouble remembering that others cannot see the ebb and flow of energy in the world and its inhabitants. Elena has a power unlike anything I have seen before. You have strength, but yours is a very mortal power. Elena has something like mine, or my sister's, but far more complex...and terrifying."

Radnor looked directly at Hilda before making his reply.

"Lenora spoke of this power. She told me that you would have sacrificed her instead of all of those people to make the sword."

Hilda nodded.

"One life would have been taken so we would not need the lives of all of the others, yes. But thankfully, you stopped us."

"Thankfully?" Radnor asked.

"I fear the world will need her strength not just today, but again and again. Protect her Veigarand. Help her understand her power. She needs you...and you definitely need her."

Hilda turned to rejoin her sister at the camp.

"It is now time for me to sleep, and prepare for the battle on the morrow."

Radnor nodded, and shook his head to himself. As he walked, he wondered why he didn't go to Elena that night. He quickly shook the thought from his mind. Regardless of her feelings, now was not the time or place for love. It also occurred to him that maybe he should be more skeptical of advice from a mad witch.

The darkness continued to press upon the company. Sunrise was merely a few short hours away, and no one in the group stirred in their silent, deep sleep...except for one person: Rolf. The boy opened his eyes, set his mind on his task, and rose to carry it out. Dagger in hand, he silently stalked across the campsite, inching his way closer to his target...the witches whom had killed his father. No matter what, their blood would be spilled tonight, and he would be the one to do it. Hatred filled his eyes as he advanced on the pair of foul sorceresses sleeping next to each other. He was just considering which throat he should slit first when he felt a warm, familiar hand placed firmly on his shoulder. Rolf sighed in frustration and turned to face Elena.

"I have to do this!" Rolf whispered, his rage seething through every word.

"No, you don't," Elena replied.

"I must have my revenge," Rolf said defiantly.

Elena shook her head.

"Not like this. We have a mission to complete."

"The mission is a lie! They mean to escape and leave us in this place! Better to kill them now to prevent it!"

"Rolf, I say this with love...you are reaching, grasping at reasons to kill them this instant when there are none. If nothing else, we need them alive to get home. Unless you know how to walk back to Wulfgeld from here."

Rolf shook his head.

"Now Rolf, give me the dagger," Elena said.

Rolf was reluctant at first, but finally handed Elena the blade.

"Thank you," she said. She then took him by the hand, and led him back to where they had been sleeping.

"How did you know?" Rolf asked her.

"I saw the look in your eye before we left Wulfgeld. The crazed, angry look I've seen in *his* eyes. Since then, I've just been waiting for you to make your move. In a strange way I'm proud of you. You never used to be this patient."

Rolf looked up at Elena, and his would-be sister tried to smile down at him. Rolf soon replied.

"I had to be sure they were asleep, lest they bewitch me and stop me."

Silence fell between them for a moment.

"What do you think he would do if he were me?" Rolf asked.

Elena shrugged.

"You are not him. You do not need to be him. His life is full of rage, and pain. His single minded purpose blinds him to everything else around him."

"And yet you care for him?" Rolf asked.

Elena hesitated for a moment, hoping it was not that obvious.

"Yes, I suppose I do," she said.

"Do you love him?" Rolf asked.

There it was, the moment of truth, for herself if no one else.

"Yes. I do," Elena said.

"What will you do?" Rolf asked.

"I don't know. We shall have to see. But we have more pressing matters to attend to. Tomorrow we shall battle an evil no man has ever faced before. Let us focus on that, shall we?"

Rolf nodded, and rolled back over to sleep.

"Thank you, for caring about me," Rolf said.

Elena kissed her would-be brother on the cheek.

"You're welcome," she replied, before she too fell back asleep.

Chapter 25

An eerie light played through the thin fog that had settled on the company over night. Dawn had come to this foreign land, and soon the company of warriors arose to prepare themselves for the battle ahead. Men were carefully checking over their equipment, looking for any imperfection in the fit of their armor, or in the sharpness of their blades. At the insistence of the witches, each man also carried a tree limb or other wood usable as a torch for when they were inside their dreaded destination. Satisfied with their work, Leif had them fall into two lines of ten men each. He stood at the head of the line, keeping the witches with him to help navigate. Radnor and Halfdan acted as a rear guard, with Elena sheltered in the middle of the formation.

Once everyone was prepared, the company marched onward to what many believed would be their doom. The light played and danced through the trees, but it did nothing to lift the mood of the armed travelers. They had a mission to complete. It did not take long before the ruins of great, stone buildings became visible through the trees. Soon after the company exited the woods they were greeted by an awe inspiring sight. The remains of tall, cyclopean buildings were strewn about wide, angled streets as if some great being had just swept them all down with a wave of its hand. Shattered and whole bricks carpeted the entire area, making a rough road for the companions as they attempted to navigate it. There were signs that at one time these stones had been painted in bright colors, but all that was left were random streaks.

Upon entering the city, they were beset by a terrifying sight. Almost every building that had once grazed the sky was now cast down to ruin. After a moment's observation, their destination became clear. At the top of a hill near the city center, above a trail of destroyed stairs, a lone building remained. This monolith was windowless, and had one giant double door marking its only clear entrance. The entire structure and the remains of the stairs leading up to it appeared to be made of a black, basalt rock. The front was supported by a series of arches, but something seemed off about the angles...they were all wrong, yet the building still stood. When studying the building, Elena felt like it must have been erected *after* the city was destroyed. But how? And by whom?

As the party continued their crossing, one man lost his footing and yelled as his leg fell in a hole. After a moment spent helping him, the man screamed again. He had just removed his foot from where it had fallen, and the bones of some hideous thing were now visible at the bottom of the hole. No one knew what it was. Not even the witches had seen its kind before. Some of the bones were recognizable as being human, or at least belonged to something vaguely humanoid. But the shape of the skull was unlike anything human or animal that anyone in the party had ever seen before.

After an arduous trek, the group finally made their way to the base of the hill, and found that the ruined stair they saw from a distance was actually intact. While others thought they had just been mistaken about the stairs, Hilda and Bruna exchanged worried glances with each other. This intact stair had indeed been a ruined tumble of rock just a few minutes before, and no one had seen it reassembled. It just...was intact again. Nervously, Bruna stepped onto the first stair, and waited for some ill thing to happen. Nothing did. Satisfied, she began to climb the stairs. In its own way, this made Radnor even more nervous. Had the thing they came to destroy repaired the stair? Was it leading them inside? In the end, it didn't matter. Radnor knew there was no choice but to ascend the stairs.

Seeing that no trap was sprung, Hilda joined Bruna, and the others swiftly followed suit. Up and up they climbed. The remains of more skeletons were visible in the patches of dirt that ran alongside the stairs. Nothing grew there. Radnor thought he recognized the skeletons of ravens along the path as well, but said nothing so as not to unduly alarm anyone. This place was cursed, but everyone had known that when they'd first volunteered to plunge into the darkness.

Once at the top of the stairs, the company was able to get a closer look at the pair of great double doors. They stood three men high, and ten men wide. The walls were flat black, with no markings or decorations of any kind upon them. There were black, ring shaped handles mounted on the doors, clearly the only handles usable to get inside. Leif grabbed hold of one of the handles, and to his surprise, found that the door moved easily. Men unsheathed their weapons as the door swung open. No light seemed to penetrate into the darkness that lay inside. Bruna and Hilda cast their spells of fire, and lit the men's torches. Bruna then cast her fire inside, where it came to rest upon the floor. Much to the relief of those in the party, this light did penetrate. The light revealed a dark, suspiciously empty room. No one wanted to enter at first.

After a moment's hesitation, Radnor was the first to step through, brandishing the chaos sword as he did. Hilda was close behind, giving him the light he needed to see. Soon, the entire company hurried through the door. The rectangular entry room was massive, and their company did not fill even half the space. Torchlight flickered off of the black walls inside, casting shadows and specters across the floor. There were two open doors at the end of the hall, each one large and imposing. Bruna walked forward, her eyes focused in terror on something no one else but her sister could see.

"Do you see it Hilda?" she asked.

"Yes," Hilda said, rooted to the spot in fear.

Sensing the horror in the room, Radnor stepped forward to face whatever threat loomed in this place.

"What is it?" he and Leif demanded almost simultaneously.

Before either of the witches could answer, the outer door slammed shut behind them. Panic struck the crowd of men as they tried to smash their way back through the door, but it would not budge. Fear strangled the men as they slowly realized that the door no longer existed, and was now a solid wall.

Bruna looked sorrowfully at Radnor.

"We should never have come here!"

Without warning, something took hold of Bruna's legs and dragged her to the floor. There were shouts of surprise as the men inside watched her scramble, clawing her way to her sister. Hilda ran to grab her arms, but it was too late. The invisible force took Bruna's legs and dragged her screaming through one of the doors. The door slammed shut with a terrible sound that echoed off the blank, black walls of the entryway. Panic struck the men as Hilda's screams resounded across the chamber. Men again ran back to where the outer door had been, striking the wall in the vain hope of breaking it open. They would not listen when Leif tried to calm them. Radnor tried to approach the other door, but it too slammed shut. There was no way out of the room. After much commotion, it was Halfdan who was able to force the men to calm themselves enough to think again.

"All right!" Halfdan yelled. "We have an enemy to slay, and if we are to survive, we must not let him drive us mad! Do you hear me?"

There was a murmur from the crowd as his bellowing voice overpowered their will to flee.

Leif chimed in next.

"Do you hear him?" he shouted.

"Yes, sir!" the men shouted in unison. Order had been restored to the warriors of Wulfgeld.

Leif nodded his thanks to Halfdan, then turned to Hilda.

"Do you have any ideas of how to get out of here, witch?" Leif demanded.

But Hilda would not speak. She simply sat upon the floor and sobbed. Radnor came over to her.

"What can we do? We must do something!" he shouted, shaking Hilda by the shoulder as he spoke. All she could say was...

"It's too strong. It's too strong now. All hope is lost."

Radnor stood, giving up on trying to bring Hilda to her senses.

"The witch is useless. We must find our own way out of here," he said.

"But which way should we go?" Elena asked.

"Might I suggest we not try the door Bruna was just dragged through?" Halfdan suggested.

Radnor spoke again.

"That only leaves the left door. Leif, do we have anything that can break it down?" Radnor asked.

Before Leif could respond, an evil laugh permeated the air around them. It was cold, sinister, and full of malice. Fear gripped the room, and even Radnor found his resolve start to break. Suddenly, Elena stepped out from the crowd, and approached the door.

"I think I should try it," she said, answering Radnor's question.

"What are you doing?" Radnor asked.

"I don't know," Elena replied.

She then placed her hands on the door. There was a moment's pause, and then inky black vines wrapped themselves around Elena's arms. Radnor ran to her, terrified of what was to come next. Before he could reach her, the vines burst into flames as Elena touched them, and soon the entire door was alight. Elena stepped away, and within a few seconds, the door fell into ashes on the floor. Radnor stopped, shocked at what he had seen. Elena turned to face him, and shrugged.

"Don't ask. I don't understand it myself."

Radnor nodded. Other soldiers began to cautiously join them at the door. Seeing Elena's ability to destroy the evil brought courage back into their hearts. Everyone approached the doorway, but someone needed to go inside. Halfdan was preparing to throw Hilda through by the hair when she finally returned to her senses, and stood up to join the others.

"Who should go through the door first?" Rolf asked.

Radnor started to take the first step, but Leif stopped him.

"I will go, Veigarand. I should have done it at the outer door. Neither you nor Elena can be the first ones into the room. If either of you die, then we are all doomed."

Just as Leif started to pass through the door frame, Hilda stepped beside him. Leif started to protest, but saw the look of determination on her face, and decided better of it. With Leif's torch held aloft, and Hilda

266

with her handheld fire, the two stepped into the black room. Thankfully, their light penetrated back into the hall. Leif called back that nothing had attacked them yet, and so the others filed into the room. They again found themselves in a massive, empty room. This one was circular, and had a ceiling so high that no one could see it. There was a single door visible on the other side of the room that was shut against their advance. Obviously, the goal was to reach the door on the other side of the room. Leif felt it was too obvious.

"Spread out! Keep each other covered!" he ordered.

It was cynical, but he wanted any ambush to only kill one or two of them before they could respond. The group continued their slow advance, almost inching their way across the black, stone floor. Just as Leif was nearing the far door, there was a sudden scream. Leif turned just in time to see one of his men pulled up into the shadowed ceiling, screaming as he went. The other warriors were wildly swinging their weapons at invisible arms that might take them away.

"Order! Order!" Leif yelled.

Silence reigned for a few moments.

"Who saw what happened?" he asked.

There was no need for a response, as Leif saw a pair of slimy, fleshy, blood soaked tentacles descend from the ceiling. At the end of them, there appeared to be what Leif swore were human hands. They grabbed for the shoulders of the nearest soldier. This man was more prepared, and so turned aside before those monstrous hands could snatch him away. Uttering a battle cry, the man swung his sword, slashing at the tentacles. The blade bit into the slithering tendril and black blood gushed from the wound. There was a hideous shriek, and the tentacles retreated back to the shadows. Before the man could regain his guard, four more of the tendrils reached for him. In the blink of an eye, the warrior was snatched into the clutches of the monster that lay in wait on the ceiling.

Everyone was deathly silent, waiting for the monster to strike again. Hilda reached into her dress, and withdrew a gaulderen.

"What is that?" Elena asked.

"It's something Lenora saved for something like this. I think it's time we used it. Everyone stand back, and keep your heads down."

Hilda then clutched the gaulderen in her fire wreathed hand. After waiting a moment, she threw it with all her might at the ceiling. The burning gaulderen struck something, and a great ball of flame erupted across the top of the room, engulfing them all in a bright light. There was an infernal shriek, and then something dropped down from the ceiling, nearly crushing several of the men. Now that it stood among them, the humans could now see what they faced.

It was a beast that could only be described as an enormous spider, or something that had been a spider once. Now it was a malignant, festering monster, totally corrupted by chaos. It stood on eight great legs. Some were hairy, some were covered in scales like a dragon, and others were fleshy, pulpy masses of gore. Its abdomen and head had partially merged into one bulbous mass, with hair, bone, and rock jutting out of its bleeding, pustulous flesh at odd, unnatural angles. Its head was barely a lump on the front of its abdomen, bearing more than a dozen eyes of various shapes, sizes, and colors. Its mandibles were similar to that of the household spider they had all seen, but led to a gaping mouth filled with needle like teeth.

After landing, the creature rose to its full height, standing tall above all the men beneath it. The long tentacles could now be seen snaking and writhing from its underbelly. They did indeed end in human hands.

Its presence fully revealed, it assaulted the humans anew. Tendrils snaked and snatched at men's ankles, ripping them from their feet and pulling them toward its horrific mouth. Warriors leaped towards the monster, striking blows at its legs where they could reach. Their weapons bounced harmlessly off of the hardened exoskeleton. Even its mandibles were impervious to the dying blows of the men engulfed in its maw. Leif made a move for its soft looking underbelly, but a swift kick from the creature was the last thing he saw before he was dashed against a wall, and everything went black.

Elena tried to grab one of the tendrils, seeing if she could burn it like she had the monster in the woods. Instead, the tendril smashed into her, knocking her down onto the floor. She grabbed onto it, and felt energy start to surge through her body. Fire seemed to work its way onto the tendril, but Elena's actions were cut short. A barbed leg tried to stomp her, but Elena barely rolled out of the way in time. The barbs grazed her as she moved, cutting her arm. She could damage the monster, but it could kill her too. She then turned and saw Hilda trying and failing to cast a spell. Elena ran to her to find out how she could help.

Rolf made a run for its rear. Just as he was about to strike, the face of one of the men that had been devoured appeared before him and screamed. Rolf fell back in terror. The face seemed to extend towards him, its mouth opening wide. A long, snake like tongue came from where the face had appeared, splitting the nose as it drew forward. Petrified, Rolf could only watch as it came for him. Just as all hope seemed lost, a black blade slashed across where the face had appeared, severing the deadly tongue. Rolf came back to his senses, and dove out of the way as Radnor slashed at the beast again.

The blade cut through the abdomen with ease, and the creature turned to face the demigod. It tried to kick Radnor with a barbed leg in the same way it had with Leif, but Radnor's counter-cut with the chaos blade proved effective as the blade effortlessly slashed through the creature's leg. The creature screamed as the severed limb crashed to the floor. The monster was not deterred, and it lashed out at him with its mandibles. Without a shield to parry the rapid attacks, Radnor had to throw himself out of the way. The creature had turned faster than he had expected.

Quickly regaining his footing, he threw a counter cut at the onrushing mandible, and severed it from the monster's face. Black blood sprayed across Radnor's armor. He was about to press his attack when one of the tendrils caught him by the ankle, and tossed him to the ground. Radnor lashed out with his sword as he fell, and the blade connected with the monster's face. The monster screamed, ignoring the feeling of other weapons bouncing harmlessly off its exoskeleton. More tendrils reached for Radnor. He slashed and rolled away, barely keeping himself alive as the assault came again and again. He did not yield, and soon had severed more of the tendrils. But they just kept coming. It was as though the creature was regrowing them as quickly as he destroyed them. Then one fearsome tendril came for his face. Radnor ducked aside just in time to see that this one had reshaped the human hand into a deadly, bony spear point. The assault was proving to be overwhelming for Radnor. His muscles ached after days of fighting, and there were too many tendrils for him to track.

Suddenly, there was a blinding flash of light. A bolt of lightning burst through the air, striking the creature in the side. It roared in agony, and a horrible, foul smell erupted into the room as organs spilled out of the creature's body. Radnor took his opportunity, and began slashing at the creature's face, over and over again. Eventually, the creature slumped to the ground, and more of the men were now able to reach its underbelly, piercing and slashing the monster to ribbons, until nothing was left but blood and ichor.

Silence reigned supreme again. After their work was done, Radnor turned to see Hilda, her hand burned from the power of her spell. Elena was holding her other hand, looking somewhat weary. Halfdan was with them, his ax bloodied, as several of the tendrils lay by their feet. Hilda looked up at Radnor, and gestured to Elena.

"I'm not very practiced with offensive spells like that...but Elena, she...somehow lent me the power I needed to force one through."

Radnor looked to Elena, and she shrugged in reply. Again, Elena did not seem to understand how she did it.

"Halfdan kept us covered while we got the spell figured out, though your sword was the only one that could really hurt it, it seems."

"Yeah, it *hated* you," Halfdan added.

The men began to mill about, unsure of what to do next.

"Where's Leif?" Halfdan asked.

"Here!" Rolf shouted.

The others rushed to where Leif had fallen. He was out of sorts, but otherwise unharmed. After a few moments and some water, Leif was back on his feet.

"All right. The beast is dead. Roll call! Who do we have left?"

After the roll call, Leif learned that only half of the twenty volunteers still breathed. Rolf stood aside from the others, ashamed of himself for what happened. Radnor came over to him. Rolf tried to turn away.

"Why do you not face me?" Radnor asked.

"Because I am a coward," Rolf replied angrily.

Radnor merely shook his head at Rolf's silliness.

"You are no coward. You stood before the beast, same as any one of these men. We all did our part to destroy it."

Rolf shook his head.

"I froze! It grew that face...and I froze!"

Others gathered to hear the conversation. Radnor shook his head at them, and then whispered into Rolf's ear so that none of the others could hear his confession.

"Now you listen to me. We are facing things no man has ever faced. When it first came down from the ceiling, I froze too. It was for but a moment, but I did freeze. *Everyone* in the room did. All that matters is that we are alive now. Learn from it, and move on. All right?"

Rolf nodded, and retrieved his ax from the floor. Radnor took a look at the men around him. Morale was low, but they had to press on. Radnor and Leif were the first to move towards the door again.

"Elena? Do you have the strength to destroy this one too?" Leif said, gesturing towards the ominous door.

"I believe so," Elena replied. "Is everyone ready?"

The soldiers gathered themselves up and prepared for another assault. Elena stepped forward and reached for the door handle. This time, the door swung open without incident. Rolf was the first one to step through this time, cutting Leif off in the process. Again, there was no immediate threat. It did not take long for everyone to surge through the door. They were in another large, circular room. This one was lit by a dim, eerie light with no obvious source. A thin fog rolled about their feet. No one noticed the fog; however, as their eyes were all drawn to the great, black pit at the center of the room.

"Everyone keep back!" Leif ordered, though no one needed to be told.

A dark figure rose from the ground in front of their eyes, bending the floor into his shape as he did. He appeared as a shadow, black as night, save only for a pair of glowing red eyes that burned into the souls of everyone there.

"It's him!" Hilda exclaimed.

Radnor readied his sword, prepared for the battle ahead. The evil laugh echoed across the chamber again, only this time, it was different. It was now feminine, and familiar. The men all exchanged wary glances with each other. A second dark shape began rising from the pit, and the laugh grew louder and icier. As the shape moved from the pit, it began to take on a more familiar form, and as it stepped into the light, there was no denying what this new foe was.

"Bruna?" Hilda questioned.

Bruna was now here, in the flesh, with an evil, inhuman look in her eye. Bruna opened her mouth wide, revealing row after row of teeth. A voice emanated from her without her actually speaking.

"You never should have interrupted my work. Now you will all perish," she said.

A dozen tendrils burst from Bruna's back, and her hands erupted in flame. The men raised their shields against her incoming attack. Some threw their torches at her to no effect. Fire leaped from Bruna's dead hands, but was blocked by a barrier thrown up by Hilda. Absorbing the energy from Bruna's attack, Hilda cast the fire back at her dead sister, who took the full force of the spell. The flames burned and charred Bruna's skin, but when it was over, she still stood, dripping blood and flesh.

More tendrils burst from Bruna's body, and she stepped forward to launch a fearsome onslaught. Men moved to intercept her, as tendrils snapped towards Hilda and Elena. Swords slashed and flew as they tried to stop the monster, but for every tendril they severed, a new one grew in its place.

Radnor moved to attack Bruna, but Hilda yelled to him.

"No! Destroy him! Your sword is the only thing that can end this!"

Radnor looked past Bruna, and saw the black, humanoid shape on the other side of the pit. Radnor leaped forward, and started off at a run around the edge of the black maw. As he got closer to his foe, bones began to rise from under the basalt floor. These were the bones of those that had dwelt in the city before, and now they rose under the will of the nameless foe. They collected and gathered into an army of misshapen, illogical things that no longer resembled the creatures from which they had been born. The monsters lashed out at him, whipping themselves towards him with sharp points and edges. Radnor stepped aside and cut them down, almost dancing as he moved. His powerful sword cut through them effortlessly, but more and more appeared. Soon, the entire room was filled with the monsters.

Leif was leading the men doing battle with Bruna. Two men had fallen in a matter of moments, leaving only eight more to finish their task. Hilda had tried every spell and gaulderen she could to destroy Bruna, but none of it had any effect. The power that controlled Bruna's body was too strong. It seemed the only way to destroy it was for Radnor to destroy the shadowy figure.

Just as Leif was about to order his men to retreat, he saw skeletal monstrosities heading right for him. Soon Leif and his men found themselves in a battle on two fronts. A thorny mass of bone tried to spear him, but Leif deftly stepped aside and smashed it to pieces with his sword. But as he turned to fight Bruna again, the thing reformed itself, and was on him again. Onward, the skeletal monsters pressed, driving the men into Bruna's tendrils of death. Leif turned to see if Elena could help, but she was nowhere to be seen. He saw Hilda pick up a fallen sword, all her offensive sorcery spent. It was all they could do to stay alive as the horrific monsters closed in on them.

There was a blur in the corner of Leif's eye. He tried to dive out of the way, but there was no need. The movement was not coming for him. It was Halfdan, running with all of his might at Bruna. Catching her by surprise with his aggression, he was able to summon the strength needed to drive her to the ground. Her hands burst into black flame, and she grabbed Halfdan's leg. Searing pain ran through his body, but he did not care. Summoning the strength needed from his other form, Halfdan took hold of the tentacles erupting from her back at the base, and tore them from her body. The creature struggled against him, but he would not be deterred. Once his work was done, Halfdan slumped to the floor. Bruna stood, her tendrils removed, and no flesh remained from which they could spring.

Bruna's blood soaked skeleton continued to swipe and strike at the others, but with her tendrils gone, she was much less dangerous. Rolf dove for Halfdan, and tried to drag him from the melee. Hilda rushed to assist him, and together they were able to get him away from the fight. Using a gaulderen, the exhausted witch cast a healing spell which began working on Halfdan's leg. Had he been an ordinary human, the flames would have consumed him, but his power as a werewolf had held the black flame at bay long enough for him to tear the tendrils apart. It was not long before Hilda and Rolf were attacked by more of the skeletal monsters, with Rolf swinging his ax wildly to keep them at bay while Hilda finished her spell.

Radnor continued to cut his way through the skeletal monsters before him. He just couldn't kill them fast enough. The power of his sword prevented them from reviving, but it seemed that the bones of everything that had ever lived in the city were set against him. He was not sure what to do, as yet again; he felt his strength starting to wane. His years of training with the sword were useless against these foes. All that mattered now was raw power, agility, and the will to survive.

A flash of golden light came from his left, and cast a bony monster into ashes. Radnor looked to see where it had come from, and he saw Elena in her full aspect, fire outlining her body as she wielded a sword made of gilded flame. She slashed again and again, casting waves of golden flame across her foes, felling entire groups of the creatures at a time. Radnor looked on her in awe, and felt himself reminded of the power he had seen wielded by Caelum against Damiros. However, there was no time for Radnor to contemplate this. More of the monsters attacked, but Radnor and Elena danced together among them, slashing and burning their foes asunder. More of the skeletal monstrosities came from the other side of the room, desperately summoned away from fighting Leif and his men to stop the godlike pair. But it made no difference. The two fought their way closer and closer to their evil foe.

Finally, they came face to face with their enemy. Red flame flew from the monster's hands, arcing towards Radnor. Elena simply reached out and golden light cascaded from her hand, destroying the fire in the air. Radnor took this opportunity to rush his opponent down, and slashed through the shadowy form before it could escape. His blade met resistance, but he drove it straight through from shoulder to hip. The black blade glowed, and Radnor thrust for his enemy's shining red eyes. He buried the tip of the blade into the face of his foe, the glow in its eyes disappeared, and soon his foe dissolved into nothing.

The sudden sound of clattering echoed across the room, and Radnor looked to see that the skeletal monstrosities had collapsed into heaps on the floor. Bruna too had collapsed, her bones becoming mixed with all the others. There were four survivors of the original twenty volunteers, if anyone could call them survivors. Rolf was now sitting, looking at a bad cut that ran across his arm. One survivor sat at the edge of the pit, gibbering mad. Leif tried to pull him away from the edge, but it was too late. As soon as he saw Leif reach for him, the madman hurled himself into the pit of chaos. The silence in the room was deafening as everyone tried to comprehend the horrors they had just witnessed. Finally, Elena broke the silence.

"Radnor?" she called.

Radnor turned to face her. She was stumbling towards him, returned to her normal state. Radnor took a step forward to catch her, and she collapsed into his arms, not unconscious, but truly more exhausted than she had ever been in her life. He reflexively stroked her hair as he held her, and after a few moments, Elena pulled herself upright again. She reached up to stroke Radnor's face. Time stopped for both of them.

The pair was disappointed when the moment was broken by Leif's interruption.

"Are you all right?" Leif asked.

"I don't know," Radnor said.

"I wasn't asking you, Veigarand," Leif replied, turning to Elena.

Elena took a deep breath.

"I think so. I feel weak, but otherwise I'm all right."

Ignoring Leif's return to his usual resentment, Radnor looked past the ealdorman, and saw Hilda standing alone. Radnor and Leif then locked eyes for a moment, knowing full well what needed to happen next. Radnor looked to see if Elena was all right, and then scooped up his sword from the hard floor. Elena saw the look in Radnor's eyes, and knew his terrible purpose. She almost made a move to stop him, but she knew it had to be done. Radnor stepped past Elena and Leif, towards Hilda. Hilda saw him approach, and laughed a little. She turned to see that everyone had noticed Radnor's hostile approach, and were now watching to see what Radnor would do. Rolf stepped forward, ax drawn. He intercepted Radnor.

"I need to do this," Rolf said.

"No, you don't," Radnor replied. "Do not become me."

Hilda spoke next, sorrow resonating in her voice.

"There is no need for either of you to do this."

Radnor and Rolf looked to her.

"If you think begging for your life will save you, you are mistaken!" Rolf spat.

Hilda smiled a sad smile.

"Do you think we ever had any intention of leaving this place alive? I know what I did, and I am sorry for it."

"You killed my father!" Rolf yelled.

"I know," Hilda said. "I killed yours, and many other fathers. I killed mothers, and I killed sisters and brothers. I know this. I know where I must go. But before I do…"

Hilda paused, and withdrew a final gaulderen from her pocket.

"Take this. Bruna and I made it last night. Throw it to the floor, and it will create a portal back to Wulfgeld. Make haste once you use it. It will not last longer than a few moments."

Hilda tossed the gaulderen to Rolf. She smiled one final time.

"Perhaps I will find my sisters below," she said.

With her final words, she threw herself into the abyss.

Elena came to Rolf, who now stood with tears in his eyes. She took the gaulderen from his hand and tried to embrace him. Rolf turned away, not yet ready to face his pain. Leif gathered the few survivors, and helped a finally conscious Halfdan to his feet.

"Is everyone ready?" Elena asked.

Leif nodded, and Elena threw the gaulderen to the floor. A purple, shimmering wall opened in front of them. In order to limit hesitation, Radnor jumped through the portal first. His leap had the desired effect, as everyone made their way through before it abruptly shut behind them.

__Epilogue__

The party found themselves back at the city center. It was nighttime, with torchlight and moonlight illuminating the great square. Snow still blanketed the city, and there was almost a strange sense of peace in the way the moonlight reflected off of it. Guards swarmed around them in alarm as the party suddenly appeared before their eyes. Leif gave orders to the guards that word be sent to Sigaberht of their return. Others went to Halfdan, and quickly loaded him onto a stretcher to be taken to join the other wounded being treated at the keep.

Rolf stepped away from the group, and went towards one of the damaged buildings. Elena recognized where he was headed, and followed him. Rolf knelt in the snow where his father died. Tears streamed down his face, and Elena took him in her arms. This time Rolf did not turn away, and Elena comforted him in the cold, snow draped city. Radnor soon joined them. He placed his hand on Rolf's shoulder, but struggled to find anything to say. Rolf's sobs continued, as all of his grief came pouring out all at once. As his tears slowly subsided, Rolf resolved that they would be his last. Finally, Rolf separated from Elena. Radnor was struck by the hard, focused look on Rolf's face. He knew then that Rolf would never be the same.

"We should get out of the snow," Rolf said.

"Agreed," Radnor replied.

The trio started to rejoin the others, but Rolf pulled away.

"I'm going to go on ahead to the keep and check on Halfdan," he said, giving Elena a knowing look before making his way on his own.

Radnor almost started to follow Rolf, wishing to find words to help him through his grief, but Elena took Radnor by the arm.

"Let him go," she said. "I think he just needs time to grieve by himself."

Radnor cast a final look in Rolf's direction, then turned to face Elena. There was silence between them for a moment. Neither one spoke, neither one moved. Finally, the two embraced.

"Are you all right?" Elena asked.

"I don't know," Radnor replied. "Are you?"

Elena paused for a moment, and gave her answer.

"I am...when I'm with you."

Radnor was taken aback.

"Are you sure?" he asked.

"Yes."

"How long have you felt it?"

"Since we met. You?"

"The same."

Both of them stared dumbly for a moment longer.

"What do we do?" Radnor asked.

Elena reached up and stroked Radnor's face.

"I think we should do what our hearts tell us."

Radnor almost pulled away, but couldn't bear to do so.

"But...we are drawn to each other so strongly...doesn't it feel like it's...forced?"

"Or perhaps it's meant to be," Elena said, pausing only a moment before continuing. "I don't know how or why, but I have a power unlike anything the world has ever seen...and it seems connected to you somehow. I don't understand myself yet...and I need to. But when I do...I want you standing beside me."

Radnor nodded, finally giving in to his heart. He bent down, and kissed her. She returned the kiss, and the passion of her response warmed Radnor's heart in a way he had never felt before.

Once their lips finally parted, there was a new understanding between them.

Sigaberht's men finally came to bring the exhausted party to the earl. There would be many questions to be answered, and plans to be laid. But these thoughts were not on Radnor's mind as he kissed Elena once more. After finally breaking the kiss, Radnor and Elena went with the guards, hand in hand. Whatever challenges lay ahead, this was how they would face them...together.

Made in the USA
Coppell, TX
04 October 2023